W9-ABS-158

WITHDRAWN

# REBEL, BRAVE AND BRUTAL

# REBEL BRAVE AND BRUTAL

## SHANNON DITTEMORE

AMULET BOOKS · NEW YORK

Cataloging-in-Publication Data has been applied for and may be obtained from the Library of Congress.

ISBN 978-1-4197-5770-9

Text © 2023 Shannon Dittemore
Jacket illustration by Ruben Ireland
Map illustration by Yvonne Gilbert
Book design by Chelsea Hunter

Printed and bound in USA
10 9 8 7 6 5 4 3 2 1

Amulet Books are available at special discounts when purchased in quantity for premiums and promotions as well as fundraising or educational use. Special editions can also be created to specification. For details, contact specialsales@abramsbooks.com or the address below.

Amulet Books® is a registered trademark of Harry N. Abrams, Inc.

**ABRAMS** The Art of Books
195 Broadway, New York, NY 10007
abramsbooks.com

For every rebel breaking under the
weight of their own heart.

You were never meant to travel this road alone.

Find your crew.

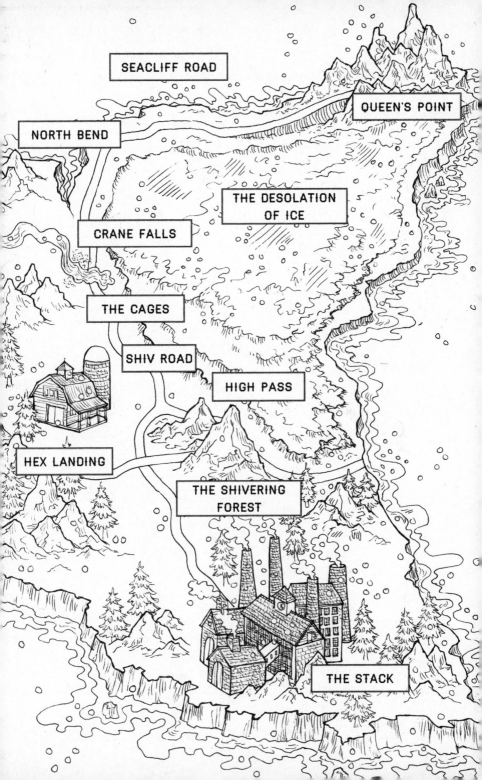

# CHAPTER 1

WINTER BITES.

Her teeth are jagged, and she's not shy about using them. Not when she's being ordered about. Hours of practice commanding Winter, and frostbite crusts my lips. My throat is raw from shouting into the wind, and my legs ache from negotiating the ever-tilting deck of this wretched ship.

"You've stopped listening, Miss Quine." Mars stands next to me at the railing of the *Maree Vale*, same as he did yesterday. Ordering me about as I order Winter.

"But you haven't stopped talking," I say. "One of us is going to have to adapt."

"My thoughts precisely." He crosses his arms, nods at the storm I set swirling just far enough off our port side that Winter's rains can't touch us. "You've done well to establish yourself as Winter's superior, but you're still wrestling with the nature of your commands. You're giving her creative license, letting her choose when and how to comply."

I stifle a yawn. "And that's wrong?"

"Revelation number four, Miss Quine. You must be specific. She has to obey your commands, but she's not obliged to assume your intentions. If you leave your orders open to her interpretation, you may cause damage you didn't intend."

"Right. You said that."

"I did. And you need to keep it in mind. Your next task is to compel Winter to act against her own interests. Not just to obey when she'd rather not, but to follow your orders even when it diminishes her."

"Diminish— What? How?"

"However you can."

"I have no idea how to make her do that."

"Think on the wolves, Miss Quine. At High Pass."

High Pass. When Mars forced her to attack the Frost Whites, her favorites.

"There are no wolves at sea," I muse, "but I suppose I could—"

He holds up his hand. "You need not be specific with me, but you must be with her. Do you understand?"

"I understand."

But right now, I'd trade all the magic in my blood for some shut-eye.

The *Maree Vale* has a lively crew. They're a lot like the riggers I know, except there's no relaxing out here on the Kol Sea, and to stay alert, they make bawdy jokes and sing songs that ring out over the deck of this three-hundred-year-old vessel day and night.

And then there's the bell at the helm, ringing loud and long at the top of every hour, reminding all those on board, save Mars and me, to swap their twyl chewing gum for a fresh piece. A necessary inconvenience to keep the kol madness at bay, since the black mineral is thick in both the water and the air, but that bell is impossible to sleep through. After just two days at sea, I'm already scraped hollow.

And still our pace is glacial. We cut slowly through the waves on Mars's order. He wants to make sure I have time to practice commanding Winter before we leave her behind for the duration of the journey.

It won't be long before we sail clear of her waters. Even now, silhouetted against the horizon, I see Winter's Gate, a crescent-shaped islet jutting into the sky. Mars says it marks the eastern border of the Kol Sea, the farthest Winter is able to reach. She cannot cross beyond it, and though I'm ready for the quiet of blue waters ahead—the bell will stop, surely, and the lessons with Mars, of course—I've never been in a place where Winter isn't.

"If you stand there debating any longer, Miss Quine, we'll reach Paradyia before you choose your command." Mars has scaled the ratlines and reclines in the ropes overhead, lazily flipping a coin.

I whisper an order and Winter freezes the coin solid. Mars lets it fall twenty feet to the rotting boards beneath him, purses his lips.

"Clever. But you're stalling. Playing with Winter. Remember, she's not your friend."

"Want me to shut him up?" Kyn asks, stepping closer, placing his hand on my back. "I could cut the rope that's holding him aloft? Might buy you a few minutes of peace." My insides unwind at his touch, and I breathe him in, catching notes of the twyl gum tucked into his cheek and something spiced, a fragrance that's his and his alone. A craving stirs in my chest, and I tamp it down, my eyes on the black sea.

"It's just . . . Mars can fly."

"Forgot about that."

I smile and a blister ruptures on my bottom lip.

Kyn tenses at my pain. "Flux, you're bleeding. Where's that rag Leni stitched you?"

She's stitched me dozens, to be honest, but I've lost them all. I press the sleeve of my coat against my mouth instead, hating that the bond Kyn and I share means he can feel my hurts now. There's no denying it. The connection between us is growing. And not up and out like a tree's trunks and branches, but deeper, into parts of me I'd rather keep hidden.

"I'm fine. Really."

"Any day now, Miss Quine." The frozen coin hits me in the back and then clatters to the deck once again.

Kyn scoops it up and chucks it hard at Mars. But Mars is quick: He slows it with a word and catches it cleanly. Another word and the coin is fully thawed. He flashes a grin and holds it aloft so we can see.

"Swift, decisive commands, Miss Quine. It's your turn now. Stop stalling."

I offer Kyn a shrug and turn back to the task at hand: compelling Winter to act against her own interests.

Black waves slosh against the ship now, peppering my chest and face. The sea spray sets the open wounds on my mouth ablaze, but I shut it out—I shut everything out—and with my fingernails digging into the ancient railing of the *Maree Vale*, I sort through every Kerce word I know.

Finally, I land on the perfect combination and despite the bite I know is coming, I lean out over the water and shout into the storm, making yet another demand of Winter.

*"Chyka Abaki!"*

She bucks and screams, a shrill protest that lifts the hair on my arms and has Kyn cursing.

"What's she doing, snowflake?" he asks.

"Watch."

Winter doesn't love her Abaki as she loves her wolves. They're nothing but cobbled together arms and legs torn from seafarers who once had the misfortune of crossing into the Kol Sea. Soggy limbs in a variety of combinations, bloated heads on occasion—their bodies held together by Winter's magic and the kol. And though they fill these waters in abundance, the monsters do belong to her, and she'd rather not waste them. Especially not on my order.

**THEY'RE NOT YOURS TO DESTROY!** she cries. **THEY'RE MINE. MINE!**

Her resistance tugs at my bones, but she has no choice and she knows it. My command left no room for interpretation, and though her energy is wearing thin, she has enough left for this.

Still, she's slow to act, and I'm forced to repeat myself. I receive another frosty bite, but there's a tug in the air as she gathers her energy, turning her focus to the gray rock rising from the waves.

It's not much larger than the ship we stand on, but there are nearly a hundred Abaki crammed atop it. We're far beyond their reach, but the warmth of our flesh calls out to them, and they reach greedily for our ship. It's instinct that drives the Abaki—instinct and Winter, ever dissatisfied with her abominations, ever wishing they were living, breathing souls. Demanding of them what they cannot give.

But not for lack of trying. Her monsters climb in and out of the black sea, searching for arms and legs, for their souls, long ago stolen by death.

Since I found a command that forced Winter to keep her monsters off our ship—at least temporarily—that gray rock is the closest they could get to us.

And now, on my order, Winter crashes down upon it, a deluge of cloud and rain that turns the Abaki into nothing but scattered limbs and washes them into the sea.

Kyn pulls me in for a hug and I melt into his arms. "Good job, snowflake."

I'm exhausted—I bet I could sleep through any number of bells just now—but I lift my face to Mars, expectant. I wasn't sure I could even do what he'd asked, and I did.

"Well?"

He cocks an eyebrow and peers down at me through the gaps in the ratline. "I've aged twelve years since I set you that task, Miss Quine. A feat I didn't know was possible considering my cursed youthful state."

"But I did it. I forced Winter to act against her own interests."

He flips me his coin again. "And I'm sure Winter is grateful it cost her so little."

# CHAPTER 2

"**S**YLVI! YOU DID IT! YOU DID IT!"

"Huzzah!"

I turn to see Hyla's daughters standing next to Lenore, one on either side, their tiny hands clapping, droplets of sea spray caught in their golden curls, wads of twyl gum in their cheeks. They've spent the past two days running up and down the deck of this ship, getting under the feet of the sailors, but no one's dared to complain.

Kree is the quiet one, the older sister, offering fewer tears and fewer grins. Six-year-old Katsy though, she does both in a big way. The laughing and the grieving.

They've every right, of course. It's been less than two months since they learned their mother died at the hands of Winter's monsters. Hyla Reyclan—Paradyian warrior, wife to Dakk, mother to Kree and Katsy, and the kindest, strongest person I've ever met—left her family and her home to help the rebels on Layce. And with all my power, I couldn't keep her safe.

It's my fault these girls won't have their mother as they grow. So when they weep, I don't let myself look away. Instead I watch as Dakk pulls them onto his lap, crying when they cry, and then tickling their ribs until they laugh; I watch as he answers questions they need answered and then staggers away alone, his chest heaving as he fights to steady himself. He's grieving too and it's not just his partner he's missing. It's half his soul. Hyla taught me that. That over time, two can become one.

In her absence, her family has taught me something else. Something I didn't realize before.

That grief doesn't look any one way.

It was a comfort, really. That lesson.

I've felt plenty of shame over the past few years thinking I never really mourned Old Man Drypp. He'd given me a home, raised me alongside his granddaughter. In those early days, my grief felt inadequate—it was so different from Lenore's—and I figured I must be broken inside.

So I picked up a job, and another one after that. We needed the money, so I climbed into the Sylver Dragon and got on with it.

I didn't have anyone like Dakk to guide me then, but now I think there isn't really a right way to grieve death. There's just surviving it. Surviving a reality that is different and more unfair than you thought to expect.

In that way, I think we're all grieving Hyla. Kyn and Mars and Leni and me. She was our friend, and she came to the cold dark of a cursed isle to fight for our freedom, a freedom she herself already had in Paradyia. If we can honor that, we should.

"That was good, Syl." Leni digs a handkerchief from the wide pockets of her skirt and presses it into my hand. "So much power! And to do it all without taking us down too. Amazing. Truly."

Her eyes are a little too wide and her affirmations a little too sure for someone who was quick to remind me just yesterday that I'd be further along in my training if I'd paid closer attention to our tutor, Mystra Dyfan, when we were children.

"Don't flatter her, Miss Trestman." Mars swings down from his perch. "She's still taking too long to find the words."

"I got it done, didn't I?"

"But you're far too considerate of Winter. We must break you of that."

"Stop being a brute," Leni says. "She's trying."

"What's a brute?" Katsy asks, her brow puckered.

"A monster," Kree answers.

"That's right," Kyn says, a sideways grin creeping up his face. "Mars Dresden is a monster."

"No, look! Look!" Kree points a trembling finger at something beyond me. She stumbles backward, grabbing Leni's hand as she goes. Her sister sees it next.

"Monster!" Katsy cries.

I whirl around to see an Abaki climbing over the railing, gray fingers clawing for purchase, a skull devoid of flesh coming into view. Kyn reaches for his gun as Kerce words gather on my tongue, but before even Mars can get a command off, there's a flash of light and the Abaki's skull splinters into a thousand pieces, an invisible force carrying the rest of his magicked body into the sea.

I tip my face to the sky. Dakk's on watch and the gauntlet he wears is the only weapon I've ever seen that collects light and shoots it like that.

"It's gone, little ones. Gone." Dakk leans over the rail of the crow's nest so his girls can see him. "Don't cry, Kats. I'm coming down."

Leni's whole body is trembling, but she drops to a knee, wrapping one arm around Katsy and the other around Kree. And then Dakk is there; I smell the burn of the rope on his gloved gauntlet. Its leather and bronze construction is exquisite and unfathomable to me, though he did try to explain. It collects sunlight and compresses it into a shimmering projectile, he said, even on Layce where there's very little sunlight to be had.

*"There is always light, Sylver Quine. Sola, the High Queen of Creation, is light. Even when we cannot feel her touch, we can be certain she is near."*

*"But how?"*

*"Because without her light, we would see nothing at all. Not even the darkness."*

If I'd said that, it would sound like nonsense, but the Paradyians are certain by nature, convincing in their speech. And it's hard to argue with them when the things they make lend credence to their words.

Dakk's boots clatter onto the deck, and seven feet above, his sandy hair blows on the wind. His close-cut beard is a little unkempt these days, and his chapped face verges on wild. He scoops his girls up, settling one on each forearm. "We won't fear them, will we? Kree? Kats? No, we will not. Winter's monsters cannot hurt you. Do you know why?"

Their golden curls shake left and right.

"Because Sylver Quine will keep them off this ship with her magic. Yes?"

His girls are nodding, but his gaze is on me. It's almost an order, the look in his eyes, a reminder that his girls shouldn't be confronted with the creatures that killed their mother.

Of course they shouldn't. The very idea drains the blood from my face and I'm light-headed as I nod.

"Good. Come girls, come. Let's talk of better days ahead." He passes gaping sailors as he moves toward the ship's prow.

My eyes mist as I watch him go. I can't believe I forgot to remind Winter to keep her Abaki at bay after my initial command. She's a forgetful tyrant and commands like that must be repeated again and again. I know that. I do.

Kyn slips his fingers into mine. "You OK?"

I nod, my throat tight.

"You were distracted," Mars says, his black eyes unforgiving. "You can't ever be distracted."

"I know."

The bell rings and both Leni and Kyn move to the rail, spit their twyl gum overboard, and dig a new stick from their pockets.

"Come, Miss Quine." Mars pushes away from the mast. "We must plan our next lesson."

"I think it might be time for a break," Kyn says. "Sylvi's face—"

"Will heal," Mars says. "I don't need her blood in my veins to know she's hurting, Kyn. I'm not unsympathetic, but these lessons cannot wait. When we return from Paradyia, we'll have an army. We'll have a war. And the time for practice will be over." He turns on his heel and climbs the short set of stairs leading up to the ship's wheel. "Additionally, her irises are still sylver. They're always sylver. Have you noticed that, Kyn?"

"I have, yeah."

"That tells me she has plenty left to give."

"Stop talking around me." I release Kyn's hand and follow Mars up the stairs. "What do you mean by that? 'Plenty left to give'?"

He stops, turns so fast I nearly run into him. I step down a stair, but he leans in, close, bats his lashes at me.

"My eyes cannot get any blacker, can they? They're full up. In fact, when I use too much magic, the kol fades, my power depleted. But you, the amount of kol in your blood . . . ?"

His pause invites a guess. "The amount of kol in my blood is . . . still growing? Is that what you're trying to say?"

"That's not at all what I'm saying." He turns and strides to the ship's wheel, relieving the sailor there with a slap on the back. "I assume you have the same amount of kol in your veins that you've always had. The same amount I do, I would think. Or thereabouts. Everything I've learned about the kol in our blood indicates that of all the Kerce survivors, unsurprisingly, Maree Vale—our mother, not the ship—received the largest quantity of kol when she made her covenant with Winter. The others were never as powerful as she was. Never as powerful as I was, even. Over the years, I've observed that the kol in our veins, and the authority over Winter it affords our people, diminishes with each generation. But not once have I seen it increase. So no, I wouldn't think the amount of kol in your blood is growing, but I do wonder if some of it remains dormant in your veins. I wonder if, after so many years of playing nice with Winter, parts of you remain frozen."

Winter chuckles in the distance, a wide-open sound that sends a chill right through me.

But surely it's not possible? I *command* Winter. I compel her to follow my orders.

"Her heart? Is that what you're saying?" Kyn climbs the final stair, his voice unsettled, the emotions in his gut even more so. "That Winter has hold of her heart?"

"*Her* heart? I'm right here."

They ignore me.

Mars leans across the wheel, points a thumb in my direction. "You'd know more about her heart than anyone, Kyn. What do you think?"

Kyn turns toward me. He can't quite meet my gaze, but there's no stopping the anxiety that spills from his gut into mine. Because Mars is right: Kyn does know better than anyone. He *feels* Winter sneaking around inside me. He's told me as much.

But just because her voice snakes inside my head at times—just because I don't always hate it—that doesn't mean she has hold of my heart, does it?

No. It can't.

I have the control. That's what matters.

Kyn's next to me now, close. I feel the brush of his stone knuckle against my hand. "If parts of Sylvi *are* still frozen, if her power never reaches full capacity—"

"If Winter maintains a hold on her heart?" Mars stands taller.

My jaw clenches at the idea. "Stop talking about me like I'm not here."

Mars turns his entire body toward me now, his gaze grabbing hold of mine, tight, squeezing. "If you let Winter keep hold of your heart, Miss Quine, you'll never be strong enough to send her away from Shiv Island."

Frustration washes over me, mine or Kyn's, I don't know. Our feelings are too tangled to parse and I haven't the energy.

"I thought it wouldn't matter if Winter held a small part of her—of you," Kyn says. "I thought she'd leave your heart when you sent her from Layce."

My spine stiffens, chin lifts. "Maybe she will. Maybe Mars is wrong, and I'm strong enough."

"Maybe," Mars says. "But maybe is an insufficient bartering chip when we're asking the Paradyian king for an army, Miss Quine."

The ship's wheel is positioned between Mars and me now, and I curl my hand around one of the spokes, his face framed between two wooden handles. I need him to hear me. "I'll keep practicing. Even when we leave these waters behind, all right? I don't have to be in Winter's domain to work on my Kerce; Leni will help me. I'll do the work. You just have to trust me."

There's a beauty about Mars, especially out here on the sea—his black hair blowing on the wind, the cutting angles of his face, his generally pale cheeks smoldering pink with wind chap and exertion, thick lashes and brows framing eyes that look like chips of a cloudless night sky. Did his looks come from our Paradyian mother or the father we never talk about? My bet's on our father. Every Paradyian I know shimmers gold and bright. Mars's look is darker than that.

He wraps his hand around mine. His face isn't unkind, but his voice is as sharp as the tip of a pickaxe. "How can I trust you, when you don't even trust yourself?"

"Don't trust—?" I rip my hand out from beneath his. "I have the utmost confidence in my abilities."

"You trust what you can do with Winter's help. But your heart is not safe in her keeping."

My teeth grind. "I know that."

"I'm not convinced, Miss Quine. If you continue to believe she's anything but a liar, she'll maintain residence in your heart. It's not just a metaphor. It's a lesson I do not know how to teach you."

So much emotion in his voice. So much angst. I take a deep shuddery breath to rid myself of it.

"You've taught me plenty, Mars, and I'm grateful." I mean it too. I've always been a miserable student, and yet my command of the Kerce language has grown rapidly under his tutelage. My power over Winter is much more controlled, more strategic, than I ever believed possible. "Really, I am. I've never pretended to be perfect."

"I'm not asking you to be perfect. I'm asking you to grow."

"I have. If you can't see that—"

"We all see it, Miss Quine. But you can't stop now. That's what I'm telling you. You can't be content with the progress you've made. You won't be strong enough."

"'Whatever you say, however you say it, she has to obey.' You told me that once. What's changed?"

"The task. The stakes. We're not just crossing an ice road; we're attempting to send Winter away. It's a job I could not accomplish on my own. We'll need all the power we can summon, and that requires the kol to run quick and unimpeded through your veins. There is no room inside you for her."

"It's not a conscious decision I'm making here, Mars! Tell me how to do it and I will."

He shakes his head and turns his attention to Winter's Gate, now looming large in the distance. When he speaks, he's spent, his voice tired. "I don't know. I never let Winter get close. It's not a battle I've had to fight, and no one but our mother was ever powerful enough for Winter to exert the effort. Which did not end well. For her or her people."

"Or the Shiv buried beneath the ice," Kyn says.

"Precisely. Mere days with Maree Vale and Winter gained a foothold in her heart." His gaze falls softly on me now. "She's had years with you. How do we fight that?"

My shrug is a big heavy thing. I imagine Winter shaking off her Ryme coat.

"Like we've fought everything else, I guess. With words and whatever we can lay our hands on. I don't know what that will look like, but I'm all you've got, Mars. I'm going to have to be enough."

He swallows, nods. "Here's hoping your *enough* is stronger than mine. If it's not, your heart isn't the only thing we stand to lose. As tragic as that would be, there are others depending on you. Nations and kingdoms across the Wethyrd Seas need you to get this right."

My eyes meet Kyn's, the first and most intimate of those depending upon me.

"I couldn't forget that if I tried."

# CHAPTER 3

I STAND ALONE ON THE BOW OF THE SHIP waiting for day.

The wind tears at my hair and I lift away a strand that's caught the frostbite on my lip. The blisters Winter leaves behind don't heal as quickly as my other wounds, but they do heal. Even now, I feel them crusting over.

It takes far more work to manage my hair than it does to manage the frostbite. After that first day at sea, fighting it, rebraiding it constantly, losing my stocking cap, I gave up. And now with my white hair blowing wild, I wonder why I ever bothered.

It's our third day on board the *Maree Vale,* and the morning dawns a shade lighter than yesterday. The clouds are still thick overhead, but Winter's holding back the rain, and her fierce winds are driving us toward Winter's Gate. She's not fighting to keep us here, that's for certain.

The islet is now near enough I can see the veins of kol running through the white rock. It's tall and we're so close it scrapes the sky and the horizon on both our port and starboard sides.

"That keyhole looks awfully small, yeah?" Kyn sidles up next to me, then leans on the rail.

"Have you passed through it before?"

"Nah. I've only made the trip to Paradyia once, and we sailed south first."

"To Crantz?"

His smile spreads, teeth gleaming. "The beaches there are nothing like what we have on Layce. The sand is rich and almost orange. And they grow the best coffee I've ever tasted."

The nostalgia in his voice is hypnotic. I can almost see it. "I've never had coffee. Too expensive for a rigger from Whistletop. We stick to boiled chocolate."

"I bet Mars has a tin somewhere. I'm certain he does. That's probably coffee he's drinking right now."

I cast my eyes toward the helm where Mars stands with a steaming mug in his hands, bending the ear of his navigator and glowering at the sea. "Leave him alone. He seems grumpy."

"He is, yeah." Kyn stands tall, stretches himself awake. "When all this is over, we'll go. You and me. To Crantz. You can lie in the sun, burn that white skin of yours to a crisp, and I'll try my hand at spearfishing."

The idea of running away with Kyn warms me in a way my jacket can't. "Mars doesn't visit Crantz for the coffee though. Or the spearfishing. I heard him talking the other day."

Kyn's smile fades. "The Majority has gotten vicious over there, withholding food until the coffee farms meet their quotas. It's not just Layce who's struggling in their grasp. If you stay to the coastal towns, you might not see it. But the farther inland you get, it's all starving kids and angry overseers."

"Mars was saying something about black market food shipments?"

"Yeah. Hyla and Dakk were able to secure these supplement packets from the Paradyian army. It's what their soldiers use when they're out in the field. Taste like feet, but they'll keep a kid from starving. Mars delivers them to Crantz when he can, brings back intelligence."

"And coffee."

"Well. He is a smuggler."

The board beneath my hands is starting to splinter. I pick at it. "What if he's right, Kyn? What if I'm not strong enough? Once we cross beyond the gate—"

Kyn hooks his finger gently under my chin and tips my face so he can take in the blisters on my lips, the kol in my eyes. "Once we cross through the gate, she won't be able to do *this* anymore, ice witch. That's cause for celebration, isn't it?"

His deep brown eyes are warm as he examines the damage to my face, his smile gentle, but I'm not the only one hurting. He hides it better than I do, but he's in a lot of pain.

I'm starting to believe he feels my injuries more deeply than I do. It's hard to separate which pain started where, but this much is true: There's simply more pain flooding his body than mine. I don't know if it's because my body heals itself or if it's some other effect of being born in the Pool of Begynd, but it's unfair. The orders I give Winter are mine, and the consequences should be mine alone.

"It's hard to blame Winter when Mars insists on provoking her."

His hand falls from my face. "It's hard for *you* to blame Winter. Period."

"Kyn—"

"We're here because of what she did. That's all I'm saying. Mars isn't picking a fight with Winter. *She* started this. You keep forgetting that."

He's right. Of course he is. But there's more to Winter than her faults. If my sins were constantly counted against me—

"But we're almost free of her," Kyn says, stepping closer, running his thumb across my knuckles, stilling my fidgeting hand. "At least for a few weeks, yeah?"

"Except for that part of me she's taken captive, right? The part that's frozen."

"Paradyia's not Crantz," Kyn says, his eyes sparkling, "but there's no shortage of sunshine there. Maybe you'll thaw."

"So many maybes," I say, leaning against his stone bicep, cushioned only by a thin coat. He lifts his arm and I slide beneath it, laying my head against his chest. We stand like that for a long while, his warmth washing over me, our hearts slowing, like soldiers falling into step. We watch as Winter's Gate grows closer, its rough features coming into focus.

The opening through which we'll sail does, in fact, look like a keyhole. It's a small breach in the islet—Kyn's right—but it's large enough for the ship to navigate. Here and there though, rocks jut from the surface of the water, scraggly plant life flapping in the wind.

The bell rings and Kyn presses his lips to my temple. "I'm out of gum," he says. "I need to check on the cargo too. Back in a few, yeah?"

I nod, but my eyes are on the waves below. "Are we shallowing?"

"Don't worry, snowflake. Mars has been navigating that keyhole for a couple hundred years. He's not some hack."

The sound of his boots fades as he makes his way toward the main deck and the hatch that leads to the cargo hold. It's become an obsession of his, checking that the hull is watertight, the cargo secure. I get it: The *Maree Vale* is a three-hundred-year-old sailing vessel, and our haul can't handle much water.

To ensure the Paradyian army is able to make the crossing unscathed by kol madness, we're carrying as much twyl as we could gather. No small feat considering the rebel's entire stock was set ablaze just weeks before by Bristol Mapes. A man who has since been summarily convicted of several crimes, the least of which is sabotage.

The whole crew is awake now, their rough voices singing in the morning. Mars drifts past and climbs up on the prow, his hand wrapping around the bowsprit.

"The Ten Revelations, Miss Quine. Let's hear them."

"Are we shallowing?"

"We are, yes."

"And your helmsman there? Is he up to the task?"

"Once again, you underestimate the quality of people I employ."

I turn toward the wheel, to the sailor steering us onward. I've met this one; Mars calls him Squints. There's a serious set to his jaw, but he's young, his gaze startled as he takes in the rocks, his hands jerky on the wheel.

"How many times has he . . ."

"This will be his first. Oh, stop worrying, Miss Quine. I won't leave him to figure out the keyhole by himself. We've a few minutes before it gets dangerous. Now stop stalling. The Revelations. All ten."

I'm tempted to argue. But I promised I'd practice. I said he could trust me. I wet my cracking lips and begin. "Revelation number one: Winter is not your friend."

"And why is that important?"

Winter snarls, a rumble that rolls over us in gusty blasts. I have to raise my voice to be heard. "She cannot be trusted and will use any means necessary to ensure her rule on Layce. Engaging her as your equal is unwise and a waste of magic."

"Good. Two?"

"Winter's natural state is to rage. Demanding anything else of her requires effort and energy on her part. Three: Winter is first a tool and then a weapon. To preserve her power, wield her in that order. Four: Be specific. Tell Winter what to do and how to do it. She will take advantage of ambiguity. Five: Emotion has no place in Kerce commands. Soundness of mind will keep the kol moving quickly through your veins so that Winter cannot linger in your heart." I stop, stretch my neck. Pretend that one's not a problem for me. "Six: Winter is powerful but not all-powerful. There is a limit to how much she can accomplish at one time."

Razor-sharp ice cuts through the wind now, and Mars whispers a command reminding Winter to keep her fingers off him. "Pardon the intrusion, Miss Quine. Seven?"

"Um. Seven," I say, fighting to find my rhythm again. Recitation doesn't come easy to me. "Winter has a short memory. She requires reminding. Eight: Winter is not omnipresent. She can spread herself wide, but not unreasonably so. Don't presume she is accomplishing a task if you can't see her do it, but always assume she's doing things you can't see. Nine: Winter must obey the children of Maree Vale, but she is not obligated to assist anyone outside the commands she is given. If she does, do not presume to know her reasons."

"And ten?"

I remember the day Mars took me out on the ice to teach me these hard-learned lessons. I should be grateful, I should. Unlike me, he'd had no teacher, no one to explain why certain commands were a bad idea. For Mars, there was only experience. And while I appreciate that he's willing to share what he's learned, he's had three hundred years to perfect it. I've had six weeks. I'm going to make mistakes.

"Miss Quine—"

"Ten: Winter lies."

He nods. "Which brings us back to one: Winter is *not* your friend. If you remember anything at all, let it be that."

"Captain!" A shout from above. "There's a ship closing in on us fast."

Mars and I turn, peering through the ropes and the pulleys, the two masts and their taut sails, the sailors leaping into action, back to the stern of the ship and beyond.

A Majority vessel. No sails. Nothing so slow or romantic, nothing that would speak of adventure. Just a heavy-duty steel contraption with an engine the *Maree Vale* couldn't match. She puffs white smoke into the air as she screams toward us.

"I thought you said the Majority doesn't use this shipping lane."

"They don't," Mars says, leaping off the railing, then offering me a hand. "Their ships are too heavy, can't make it through the shallows, definitely can't make it through the keyhole."

I jump down. "Then what are they doing here?"

"The Majority who has a price on your head? What are *they* doing here?"

"But how could they possibly know we'd be sailing for Paradyia?"

"That's a good question, but one we'll have to answer later. Now go. Sink that ship."

Kyn rises from the cargo hold on the main deck, joins us as we run. "Where did *they* come from?"

"Later," Mars says. "Stay together. Winter's up to something, I can feel it."

I feel it too. A spiky trill that runs through the air, sets my head itching.

"What are you going to do, Mars?" Kyn asks.

"I've got to get us through that keyhole before we shatter on the rocks."

"And before Squints gives himself a nosebleed." I nod toward the man at the helm, who is squinting hard into the storm, his knuckles white as he grips the wheel.

"Indeed."

Winter's pushing hard now. Mars whispers a word and Winter flies him up the stairs and onto the quarterdeck.

"I could make her stop," I say, my boots slowing at the realization. We don't have to let her push us around.

"Not this time, Miss Quine." Mars reaches down and tugs me up the stairs. Kyn follows behind. "We need the wind; the

Majority ship doesn't. Just drop that beast to the bottom of the sea, you hear me? Nothing fancy. Kyn, you have your gun?"

"Always." Attached to the leather strap over his shoulder is a shotgun he scavenged from the weapons stock at Queen's Point. He swings it into view.

"Good." Mars sprints to the helm and pushes Squints aside.

Kyn and I continue to the stern as Mars shouts orders at his crew, orders I couldn't begin to understand. From here, we have a terrifyingly clear view of the Majority ship.

"Holy Begynd, it's fast," Kyn says. "Look at those guns."

The Majority ship is armed to the teeth, but they're still too far to fire. Sick at what I'm about to do, but sure it's the right move, I give the command and receive a gleeful nip on my lip. It's never a good thing when Winter approves of the order you give her.

But there's no time to reconsider. Rain crashes down, on the sea, on the deck of the *Maree Vale*, on the Majority ship across the way. I give Winter another order, as detailed as I can make it. She bites me hard this time but does what I ask.

With an inhale that splits the sky, she sucks up a vast quantity of water and sends it over the sidewalls of the Majority vessel. The ship pitches sharply forward into the vacuum Winter created. Sailors tumble over the side, screaming and paddling hard to clear the area before the vessel upends on top of them.

But you can't swim hard enough to escape the dangers of the Kol Sea. Dead arms and legs reach up from the depths, dragging the Majority sailors under.

A cheer goes up on board the *Maree Vale*.

Guns fire, and at first, I think that's celebratory too. But then a fear-laced cry whips me around and I see a headless Abaki scrabbling aboard, laying hold of Squints. Sailors fire and miss, fire and miss. Kyn moves to get a clear shot, but Mars, still steering, still sneering, snaps off a command to Winter and the monster flings itself into the sea.

"I'm trying to work here, Miss Quine."

"Well I'm not playing pick-up sticks!" Still, Winter needs reminding and that's something I can't afford to forget. *"Eloy Abaki leonti ley,"* I shout into the wind. *Keep your abominations off our ship.*

The *Maree Vale* quiets. Winter too. Her rains fall contentedly as cries from the flailing, drowning sailors slice through the sky.

"You OK?" Kyn asks.

I can't tear my eyes from the sea, from the dead and still dying. "Remember when you told me to look, Kyn? Out at the Desolation and all those trapped beneath it. You said it was the respectful thing to do. You remember that?"

"I do, yeah."

"Look," I tell him. "This is war. This is what you wanted."

"Mars wanted war, snowflake."

But Kyn's having a hard time hiding things from me as well— this connection of ours works two ways.

"No, Kyn. You. You and Mars and every rebel that conspired to get me here. Every one of you wanted war."

"And what did you want?"

"Peace! The quiet of the open road—"

"Fair enough," he says, his hands raised in surrender. "You wanted peace. Back when you thought peace was the same as freedom. But it's not. Freedom requires some fight, and, ultimately, you chose a side." He points to the metal keel bobbing in the distance. "You did that."

"Winter did that."

"No, no way. You destroyed that ship because the goal here is a free Layce. You killed *them* because they would have killed *you*. And if *you* die, so does the rebellion."

The truth doesn't make it any more palatable. "It's still horrible."

He turns me toward him, stooping so we're eye level. "Yeah, it is. But you don't have to lie to yourself about it. You're not just an ice witch anymore, playing games with Winter. And you're not just a girl tricked into trucking a fake haul by a cocky snake-eyed smuggler."

"No?"

"No, Sylvi. You're a rebel, by your own choice. You're fighting for the future of Layce using Winter as your weapon. That's nothing to be ashamed of."

He's so sure. So solid. And again, he's not wrong.

"And so we make peace with it? With the death of those who are only following orders?" I jerk my head toward the floundering ship. "Most of the Majority's fighters are forced into service. They're not so different than you and me."

"Are you *still* trying to convince yourself that war is our best option?"

"Why aren't you?"

The rain's stopped, and a slice of sunlight cuts through the clouds. It shimmers on Kyn's stone cheekbone. The smile on his lips is a sad one. "Because it's our *only* option, snowflake. We've tried everything else. Desy and the others? They're not warmongers. They've tried diplomacy, but the Majority bastards are greedy. They won't leave Layce. The kol here is too valuable. Either we let them use us to mine it and truck it—to their benefit and our demise—or we fight back."

I lay my hand over his, and something inside my chest unwinds at this physical connection. At the touch of his skin. I understand him better this way. When we're close. When flesh and blood give context to the storm raging between us.

"I just wish there was another way," I say.

"If there was, we'd have found it already, yeah?"

"Yeah."

Kyn's always up for a fight, but he doesn't crave bloodshed—a subtle but important distinction. His own violent encounter with death lingers in his skin—I've felt the nightmares that shake him awake, memories of the Frost White opening its jaws and clamping down on his throat, his fingers moving over the scars—and when the cries of the Majority sailors reach us on the wind, I feel the shudder that runs through his body. Together, we turn away and let Winter do our dirty work.

"Well done, Miss Quine." Mars turns the wheel deftly, guiding us through the shallows and toward the keyhole dead ahead. "You remembered revelation number four! You were *specific*. Specific!"

I swipe my drenched hair away from my face. "If I have to hear that word one more time—"

"No, yeah, he's insufferable," Kyn says. "Tell Winter to throw *him* overboard. You think she would? Could she use your orders to attack him?"

A fair question really. Mars and I are both children of Maree Vale. The covenant she made with Winter keeps the icy spirit subservient to us both. The only real difference is that I was born in the Pool of Begynd and he was not.

My lips twitch. "I have to believe Winter would choose me over him. Right?"

"Oh, yeah."

"It's an experiment worth trying anyway."

He grins and rubs his hand down my arm. "There's still some ice witch in there. Be back in a sec." He squeezes my hand and turns away, dropping down the stairs into the hull of the ship, off to check the cargo once again.

I glance around the deck; the captain's cabin catches my eye. I should check on Leni and the girls—I haven't seen them this morning—but Winter's voice stops me cold.

YOUR MOTHER WASN'T NEARLY SO RELUCTANT A KILLER AS YOU, she coos, her winds settling around me, chill and damp, slapping my cheeks. BUT YOU'RE LIKE HER IN OTHER WAYS. YOU HATE THE MAJORITY JUST AS SHE DID.

I should ignore her. Revelation number one: Winter is not my friend.

But she knows things I don't, and it's not friendship I'm seeking here. She's a brilliant strategist, and I need information.

"Tell me, is there another way to defeat the Majority?"

She snorts, lifting my hair, sea spray dampening my face.

"Can there be a free Layce without so much killing?" I press. "Kyn says it's not possible."

Winter growls. THE STONE MAN SAYS A LOT OF THINGS I DO NOT AGREE WITH. HE SAYS THE PAST IS

IMPORTANT. AND YET HE SEEKS TO ERASE ME FROM YOUR HEART. AM I NOT ALSO YOUR PAST?

"You befriended me so that I wouldn't send you from the isle." I cock my head, daring her to contradict me. "You saw benefit to our friendship, that's all."

DID YOU NOT SAVE THE STONE MAN FOR YOURSELF? YOU'VE SAID AS MUCH. AND STILL, HE BENEFITED FROM THE RELATIONSHIP, JUST AS YOU'VE BENEFITED FROM OURS.

I immediately think of Bristol, terror stricken as Winter swooped down the chimney and tore him off my five-year-old body. Then I remember the dice falling just so after a gust of wind ensured the Sylver Dragon would be mine. And then little Crysel tiptoeing to safety after Winter stopped the rig in its tracks before it could barrel over her. I see the melting ice road across the Serpentine refreezing at my word.

"I've benefited from our relationship, yes. But I've also suffered. My friends have suffered. My family . . . Did you forget that your Abaki nearly tore Drypp's arm off? Or that my mother is still buried beneath the Desolation, that you used her to carry out your own revenge on the Shiv and their creator?"

IT WAS YOUR MOTHER WHO WANTED REVENGE—YOU WOULD DO WELL TO REMEMBER THAT. THE KERCE QUEEN DISCOVERED WHAT I'VE ALWAYS KNOWN: THAT THE SHIV LOVE BEGYND, NOT BECAUSE HE CARVED THEM FROM THE ROCK AND BREATHED LIFE INTO THEM, BUT BECAUSE HE INDULGED THEM. HE GAVE THEM EVERYTHING THEY WANTED. OF COURSE THEY WORSHIPPED IN HIS WATERS.

"But you've taken that away, have you not? His pool frozen,

he gives them nothing now. And still they await his return. Their devotion runs deeper than gifts, I think."

THEY'RE A FOOLISH PEOPLE. BEGYND IS DEAD. I SAW TO THAT. SEND ME AWAY IF YOU WILL, BUT NEITHER BEGYND NOR THOSE BURIED BENEATH THE ICE WILL EVER LIVE AGAIN. IT IS I WHO MEETS YOUR NEEDS. I WHO TOOK DOWN THE MAJORITY SHIP.

"On my orders."

BUT IT IS I WHO SEES WHAT YOU CANNOT. WHO CAN PROVIDE CLEAR WATERS BEFORE YOU, MAKING YOUR PATHS STRAIGHT. AND STILL YOU SEEK TO GIVE MY HOME UP TO WAR.

There's little I can say to that. All of it bears some truth; it's bent and broken like everything she breathes upon, but it's hard to argue the particulars. "I simply want to see the people of Layce free of the Majority."

AND OF ME.

Harder still to argue that. "The kol has addled your mind, I think. Turned you into something you never ought to have been." It's a sad thought really, considering all the time we've spent together. All our adventures. "I've always liked your storms," I say, my throat tight with the idea that one day soon she just might be gone, and that my word would be the cause. "But everything you have was stolen from others, taken by force. You have that in common with the Majority. So yes, it might be time for you to go."

A mighty cry shakes all that I can see: the water and the ship, the clouds hovering just above. The air around me vanishes and I can't catch my breath, can't find—

GO THEN! she cries. BRING MY DOOM!

She bellows and air is everywhere again, violent in its sudden arrival, throwing me through the sky, stopping only when I collide with the mast on the main deck. I drop hard, my back pressed to the wood beam as the *Maree Vale* skids forward across the surface of the sea.

A black wave rises high, and the ship plummets down its slope. There's a keening sound as the keel scrapes over the rocks, Winter's wrath shoving us toward the towering white islet that separates the kol-stained waters from the vast blue of the Wethyrd Seas.

I can hear Mars but can't see him, my head still reeling. Boots pound the deck and gear grates across it. Rusting cannons slide over the splintered boards, the crew stumbling after. High above, a fiery-haired rebel dangles from his bootstrap.

"Another ship!" he cries, flailing as he tries to point out to sea. "Beyond Winter's Gate, there's another ship!"

"Fluxing Blys," I murmur, scrabbling to my feet.

"What's going on?" Kyn cries, suddenly there, a gash across his forehead.

"Look! Look!" The white wall grows ever larger in the distance. Every wave pushing us closer. And then my gut clenches because I know what she's done. *"Est stíyee! Est stíyee!"*

*"Stíyee! Eya a tsee,"* Mars yells from somewhere behind me, his voice scratching with desperation.

Winter groans and settles, quieting enough for us to hear one another. But the damage has been done. There's no stopping the *Maree Vale* now. We're moving too quickly, heading one of two places: into the string of black rock that surrounds the shallows here, or through the keyhole, but only if we're positioned perfectly.

Mars knows it as certainly as I do, and I see the moment when he turns his attention from Winter to the sea, shouting commands and spinning the wheel until we're pointed directly toward that keyhole-shaped slice of open water.

This has been our heading all along, but certainly not at this speed. And not with an enemy vessel waiting on the other side. Through the opening, I see it: a Majority ship twice as fierce as the first.

"Call down your Winter," Dakk yells, holding tight to the foremast. "Call her down and destroy them."

"We can't," I cry, my heart thudding with the truth of it.

Dakk's weapon sags. "What's that you say, Sylver Quine?"

But my mouth is dry and I'm having trouble seeing through the tears. I did this. I let her distract me. I gave Winter an opening.

In the end it's Mars who answers. But not until Kyn, Dakk, and I have tripped and stumbled our way close enough to hear, grasping one another and anything we can find for balance, feeling our way toward the ship's wheel.

"Winter's Gate marks the very edge of her domain." His pale face and neck are splotchy with rage, his lips covered in frostbite. "She cannot venture beyond it. Once we clear the keyhole, we leave the Kol Sea behind. Other spirits rule these waters. Spirits who have no allegiance to the Kerce."

Dakk's forehead creases. "Can you not order *them* to destroy the Majority ship?"

"No, friend. I cannot. Nor can Miss Quine. We do not speak their tongue, and even if we did, they have not wronged us as Winter has. They owe us nothing."

"What does that mean?" Dakk demands.

Mars's gaze lands on me, disappointment in the tightness of his mouth, in the stiffness of his spine. "It means we're on our own."

# CHAPTER 4

W E HAVE NO ANSWER FOR AN ENEMY LIKE this. Their guns will be in range long before ours. We must have help.

I turn my back on our certain death, gripping the ratlines in front of me. They swing as I climb. I hate that everything on this ship sways. I hate the rise and fall of the tide. The raw kol blackening everything it touches, threatening the crew with madness. The salt burning my frostbitten lips.

The shift of a melting ice road is far preferable to this.

"It's not going to work, snowflake!" Kyn calls.

But I lean away from the ship anyway and shout into the dying wind. Again and again I call, but Winter's only a cackle in the distance now, a jeer riding the waves. She knows we're not long for this world and that pleases her. Of course it does. With Mars and me—the two people who can keep her power in check—destroyed, the isle of Layce would be in her grip forever.

Angry tears blur my eyes because I know better. She's nothing but bitterness and deception. And still I let her in, still I let her speak to me like an old friend.

When I think of what an eternally frozen isle means for the rebels, for the Shiv who cannot be reunited with their maker until the island thaws, shame slices through me.

I take a deep breath and call once more for Winter.

But a shadow passes over me and I feel the impotence of my words. We're passing through the keyhole, passing beyond Winter's Gate. Abaki shuffle on the stone ledges overhead, their waterlogged limbs reaching out for us as we slip through, but we're there and then gone.

The sun strikes my face, so warm a shiver races across my scalp. The gray clouds fall away and a sky bluer than anything I've ever seen stretches vast and wide before us. We've passed outside Winter's province. She couldn't help us now even if she wanted to.

And she's *never* wanted to. A truth Mars reminds me of daily.

He and I can bark Kerce commands all we want out here, but we've left Winter behind. And with her, our power.

"At least there will be no more monsters," Dakk calls.

I drop to the deck. "There's still the Majority."

"What's the plan, Captain?" Kyn asks Mars.

"The plan, Kyndel, was not to let Winter blindside us. A task Miss Quine assured me she had under control."

My pride tastes of blood and kol, of salt. I swallow it down. "I'm sorry. I just thought—"

"Yes, you did. But we're done with that."

"With what?"

"You. Thinking. You've lost that right. Now, you're taking orders."

"Excuse me?"

"Take the wheel." He doesn't wait for me to comply; he simply releases it and I scramble to take hold before I have to bear responsibility for yet another disaster.

Mars hops up onto the half wall of the quarterdeck, and leaps for a rope dangling nearby. He scales it, climbing as high as he can before hooking his boot around the rope, pulling a spyglass from his waistband, and pressing it to his eye.

His curse is loud and long. "That ship is captained by Farraday Wrex. It seems the Majority have commissioned their very best Kol Master to track us down."

"He's Kerce then."

"Indeed."

Because we're more resistant to the kol, only the Kerce can hold such a post within the Majority ranks. There aren't many on the isle with kol left in their blood and a select few have both the resistance and the knowledge to act as Kol Masters, guiding the most valuable of the Majority ships through kol-saturated waters to and from the isle of Layce.

A cannon fires in the distance. I turn toward the sound, but I can't see the projectile, just the rippling-hot trail it cuts as it flies toward us—straight for a long stretch and then arcing into the water with a splash that peppers our deck with sea spray.

"Testing their range." Mars drops next to me and takes the wheel. He turns it, hand over hand, increasing our distance from their guns.

"We should turn back," Kyn says. "Get them to follow us into the Kol Sea where Winter can help."

Mars tears off his leather coat and flings it aside. Then he places his hands on the wheel, speeding up, making it spin faster. "There's no getting back through the keyhole. The currents make it a one-way trip. Wrex knows that. We have to engage."

I sputter. "With what? This ship is over three hundred years old!"

"*I* am over three hundred years old."

"*You* were frozen in time. The *Maree Vale* was not. I hate to tell you this, Mars, but she's aged some. She'd still win a beauty contest, but *that* ship was built this century and it was built for destruction. You could have at least upgraded your cannons."

"Accurate assessments all around, Miss Quine. But I didn't criticize your rig and I'd beg you to please not criticize mine."

"What's Dakk doing up there?" Kyn asks, craning his face to the sky.

Mars smirks and it's almost likeable. "Reyclan! You ready?"

"Nearly there!" Dakk cries. "Nearly there!"

Dakk's straw-colored hair blows on the wind. He stands in the crow's nest, his feet spread wide and holding what looks like a massive pipe on his shoulder. The lookout crouches next to him, hands over his ears.

"I am ready!" Dakk calls.

"Then fire away!"

Mars turns toward the Majority vessel, but I can't take my eyes off Dakk. I'm too far away to see him pull any kind of trigger or press any kind of button, but I know the moment he fires the weapon. With a whoosh that sends a ripple through his clothing and hair, light launches out the front of it, a cloud of smoke out the back. Twice more he fires, and twice more light screams toward the Majority ship.

Kyn shakes his head. "Paradyians, man. The things they come up with."

"How's it look, Reyclan?" Mars calls.

"Direct hits, all of them!"

Mars leans forward, squinting at the Majority vessel. After a moment, he shrugs. "Very good then."

"Should we cover our ears?" Kyn asks.

"Perhaps so, Kyndel. That would not be a bad idea." Dakk crows and leaps from his perch, his long body straightening into a perfect dive and slicing sharply into the sea.

Tentatively, I lift my hands to my ears, but there's only the sound of the sea and the gulls screaming overhead. Mars leans forward, all of us watching, expecting something to explode.

Kyn tugs my hand from my ear, leans closer. "Did he miss?"

Slowly, a strange feeling creeps over me and I realize it's embarrassment. I'm embarrassed for Dakk. Clearly something went wrong with his fancy weapon.

"Maybe?"

Together we move toward the bow, hoping for some sign that the enemy ship has taken damage.

And then the cursing begins. Loud and raucous, echoing across the waves. Lights flash and tendrils of smoke curl from the hull of the Majority ship.

Dakk's done it! We didn't need Winter after all!

And yet pandemonium has broken out on board the *Maree Vale* as well.

"Drop sail!" Mars calls, panic in his voice. "Quickly!"

The crew moves with speed, and I watch as the sails flutter and then snap flat against both masts.

"Move it, Reyclan!" Mars pushes between Kyn and me, craning to see over the edge of the ship. "Come on."

"What is it?" Kyn asks.

But I know exactly what has Mars concerned. The wind. It's picked up, sudden and unnaturally strong at our back, the current shoving us closer and closer to the Majority vessel.

"Winter," I say, turning, staring at the subtle crease in the sky where her storm-gray clouds give way to the clear blue overhead.

Kyn grabs the spyglass from Mars and peers through it. "We're beyond her reach here, yeah?"

"You would think!" Mars barks, running back to the ship's wheel. "But she's a clingy, needy, vindictive . . ." The wind swallows his rant.

"We're beyond her direct reach here," I say, my stomach sick at the thought. "But the rules of nature still apply. She drops a stone in her waters, and we feel the ripple."

"She's pushing us into their firing range." Kyn swings the spyglass around, peering at the Majority's ship, still smoking but also still floating.

"Their guns will be in range within moments," Mars warns.

"And ours?" I ask.

"It'll be more than moments for ours, I'm afraid. Kyn, keep an eye out for Reyclan and pull him aboard as soon as you can.

Miss Quine, if you could see that Miss Trestman understands the severity of the situation, I'd greatly appreciate it. Everyone else, take cover and brace for impact."

I dash to the captain's cabin, calling Lenore's name before I even get there. I yank open the door and Kree lets out a squeal, jabbing an oar in my direction. It's just a reflex. She's too far away to do any damage, curled up with Katsy and Lenore in the corner of Mars's bed, which is lavishly covered with furs dyed shades of deep red and black.

A book lies open on the bed before them, ancient and full of Kerce history. I could tell Mars was anxious when the girls had unearthed it, but their tiny fingers were gentle. They're about halfway through it now, Lenore reading the words quietly so they have to lean close to hear.

"What is it?" she says, looking up, her face strained. I wouldn't trade all the violence of Winter for the job this must be—keeping these grieving children safe and calm—and here I am to ruin all her efforts.

"There's a Majority ship. We . . . need to be prepared."

"What does that mean?" Kree asks, her features wide, her chin trembling.

"A Majority ship here?" Leni asks. "That could hardly be a coincidence."

"Mars said the same."

Lenore's eyes close briefly, and she squeezes the girls a little tighter. Dakk tried to send them back to Paradyia on his own ship with Hyla's body, but they were inconsolable at the thought of leaving him, and who could blame them. The last time they said goodbye to their mother was the last time they saw her alive. He conceded, but instead of returning home with them, he insisted on seeing Hyla's mission through. On seeing to it himself that I sailed across the Wethyrd Seas to meet their king. It seems foolish now, keeping the girls with us, but no one anticipated the Majority finding us here.

Kree rises up onto her knees, the oar pulled tight to her chest. "Are the monsters back?"

"There are no more monsters, Kree. Thank you, Sylvi. The girls and I will have a talk."

I swallow and back out of the room, closing the heavy door behind me.

Dakk stands at the railing now, dripping water all over the deck, towering over Kyn's six-foot-tall frame. I'm crossing their way when a voice high above me cries, "Incoming!"

There isn't time to hit the deck before the first shell slices through the hull of the ship. A dull thud reverberates through the air, and I hear the wooden planks splinter.

Mars curses. "Majority bastards."

"What can I do?" I ask, deviating course and climbing the stairs to the helm. "Tell me how to help. Can I bail water or—"

"The crew will do that, Miss Quine. As well as they're able at least."

"We need to take out their guns," I say.

"An exceptional idea, but we're still too far out to use our cannons and the closer we get, the easier it'll be for them to attack strategically. Reyclan, tell me you hit something that matters!"

"Oh yes, Mars Dresden. Fear not. They'll go down."

Another shot rings out, flies over the deck, taking a chunk of the mainmast with it. Everyone ducks, curses.

Kyn rises slowly. "Before they blow us out of the water, yeah?"

"Paradyians do not promise the future, Kyndel, you know that."

"I should have let Hyla upgrade our guns," Mars says. "That's what I should have done."

"Or we could have taken Dakk's ship," I say again. "He did offer."

Mars turns the wheel, adjusting course to avoid the thrust of Winter's current. "I'm not the captain of Dakk's ship, Miss Quine. I'm the captain of the *Maree Vale*."

"Right," I say, clenching my jaw.

"But it wouldn't hurt to have their guns about now, you're right. Kyn, let's load up the—"

"Incoming!" the lookout calls. "This one's low!"

"Brace yourselves!" Mars shouts.

But when the hit comes, it's worse than expected. The ship's wheel shudders and Mars yanks his hands away, cursing as it spins loosely on its pedestal. "Damnable, wretched . . . They've taken out the rudder."

"So, we can't steer?" I ask.

"Not with this we can't." Mars flicks his wrist and the wheel spins uselessly. "We're going to have to use the sails."

"But I thought—"

"You're not *thinking* anymore, Miss Quine. Remember? Just . . . just climb." He points to the footholds along the mainmast. "Their projectile took out the line there. We'll have to unfurl the sails manually. I'll call out instructions. You deal with that one and I'll take care of these."

I want to protest, but he's already moving swiftly up a nearby rope. Clumsily and as fast as I can, I scale the mast, but I'm not yet in position when the call comes again.

"Incoming! This one's high!"

"Get off that rung, Sylvi!" Kyn calls, but it's too late, and somewhere below me the mast takes a direct hit. My bones shake with the impact, and I bite my tongue trying to avoid a beam swinging down from somewhere high above. And then the mast is cracking and pitching sideways and I'm falling.

"Sylvi!"

I feel the fear tightening Kyn's stomach as he tries to reach for me, the terror as he realizes I'm too far away. The mast goes over, slamming into the railing. I tighten my grip on it, but the momentum is too much, and my arms scrape against the wood as I'm thrown into the sea.

# CHAPTER 5

MY FACE HITS THE WATER AND PAIN explodes through my body, extinguishing light and sound.

The water is frigid, and I gasp. My nose and mouth fill with seawater, and though I've no great experience swimming, my survival instincts are strong. I kick for the surface.

My legs are caught, tangled in the sail, and I can't flail hard enough to get free of it. Above me the blue is lighter, the sun overhead pushing through the surface. There's a shape there, something solid to hold on to. I stretch for it, but my fingers find only water.

With my lungs burning, I bend in half and reach for the sail wrapping my feet. The knot is complicated and I'm so tired. I fumble with the thick canvas, my fingers numb and aching. My eyes close and when I try to open them again, they refuse.

I see Shyne then, hovering over me, disappointment in his eyes—*why's everyone always so disappointed in me?*—a stone pressed to my chest.

A bubble of air escapes from my lips and then another, and I wonder if this is right. A righteous repayment for all the pain my mother caused the Shiv. I wonder if Shyne would approve of such an end for the daughter of the woman who saw his kin encased in ice.

Pressure circles my chest, and my body convulses. Against my better judgment, I gasp again and to my surprise, this time I find air. It burns and it soothes all in one great gulp and I'm coughing. Kyn is there, treading water and holding my waist.

"Breathe, snowflake. That's it. Just breathe."

But all I can do is cough and spit, an undignified effort to stay alive. When at last the fit ends, I take a deep breath and my body shudders as I let it out.

"Good, good," Kyn says. "Flux, you scared me. I thought we agreed you'd run all potentially fatal decisions through me first?"

"Just following orders," I say.

"Fluxing Mars." And then we're laughing and kicking and holding tight to each other as we fight to stay above the waves.

He brushes the sopping hair away from my face. "Hold on to this barrel. Both hands. Yeah, good. I'm going to cut you free."

It's a moment before I realize my arms are draped over something hollow and wooden and Kyn's gone. I feel his hands on my boots, first one and then the other, and then the weight of the sail disappears. I blink the salt water from my eyes and look around. The *Maree Vale* rises up before me, the splintered mast hanging out over the water, sprouting a mess of ropes and pulleys and gear I couldn't name if I tried. All of it swings wildly, the current throwing the ship back and forth.

She's taking on water. The hull bears three fractures that I can see, none of them massive but all of them sufficient for her destruction given enough time.

Kyn resurfaces, shaking the water from his hair and dragging a hand down his face.

"She's going under," I say. "We need to tell Mars."

"He knows. He's just too stubborn to admit it."

"So much for taking down the Majority," I say. "We can't even survive one fight."

"We're not dead yet, little ice witch."

"Anyone else go in the water?" I ask.

"Dakk and Mars were still on deck when I jumped, but I don't know about Lenore and the kids."

"The ship is on fire. If they're still on board . . ."

He tips his face to the ship, taking in the creaking, flaming vessel. I hope the Majority ship is hurting just as bad, but I can see nothing of it from here; the *Maree Vale* fills our entire field of view.

"Come on," Kyn says, grabbing my hand and kicking closer to the ship. He guides us toward a gaping hole blasted in the side. The edges are splintered, and a plank of wood juts out into the sea. Kyn pulls himself up, belly first and then swivels to offer me a hand. I take it, my toes finding purchase on something below. I push myself into the teetering hole, loud with creaking wood and sloshing water.

A blackened, bloodied body floats past. I reach out, but Kyn stops me. "Don't. He's gone."

I swallow down the sick in my throat, but another glance and I know he's right.

We're in the cargo hold, I realize. We shift, trying to find our footing and I watch the store of twyl jostle back and forth, the stacked boxes swaying and sliding along with everything else. Water teems around the sodden, tilting goods. The lower boxes have already turned to mush, exposing the blocks of twyl chewing gum in their Majority sealed paper wrappings. The uppermost boxes sizzle and smoke in the damp flames.

There will be no salvaging them now. I expect some outburst from Kyn, but he only pauses briefly as he catches sight of the boxes, curses under his breath, then pushes toward the fractured stairwell. We make our way up the stairs, moving faster when we reach the uppermost steps.

The ship lists to its port side, and it's hard to keep our feet moving in the direction our toes are pointed. But I catch a flash of color amid the smoke and ash, a woolen skirt in bright Paradyian colors, a gift from Hyla to Lenore.

"They're OK," I say, my heart rejoicing. "Look."

Leni stands at the bow, shoulders back, an arm wrapping around the bowsprit. Hyla's girls cling to her skirt.

Mars stands atop the railing to her right, his spyglass in one hand, a rope in the other as he leans out over the water and scans the sea. Dakk paces the port side deck, peering into the waves. I can see their mouths moving, likely calling out, but the wind is so loud, I can't tell what anyone is saying.

Katsy is the first to catch sight of us. She squeals as she tears away from Leni, her feet much steadier than mine. She collides with my hip and wraps her arms around my waist.

"You're alive!" Her body shakes with tears and her sister hits next, wrapping Kyn's legs tight, laughing and crying all at once, the oar still in her hands and dangerously close to Kyn's face.

They all turn, Mars and Dakk and the sailors searching the waters alongside them.

Kyn lifts Kree into his arms, though she still refuses to release the oar. I take Katsy's hand in mine and we make our way to the bow of the ship, navigating splintered and protruding planks, holes blown into the deck itself.

It's the captain's cabin and the immediate area surrounding that's billowing with flame and smoke. It looks like something beneath it exploded, which would explain the massive hole Kyn and I climbed through.

"How did you survive that?" I ask Leni.

"We'd just come out onto the deck when it was hit. We saw you go over." Leni squeezes me tight. "I would have never forgiven you if you'd died."

"Miss Trestman's wrath would have been nothing to mine." Mars's hands are bloodied, and his white shirt is torn from shoulder to hip. It billows open in the wind, ash and soot smeared across his face.

"I know very little about ships, but I don't imagine she can stay afloat like this." I pass Katsy to her father and climb up onto the rail next to Mars.

"Not for too much longer, no."

Both masts are broken, rendering the sails useless. We can't steer and we can't generate any momentum on our own. We're at the mercy of the sea.

"I'm sorry, Mars. Your mother's ship."

He raises a brow, but he doesn't correct me, doesn't remind me that she was my mother too. "Winter's raised it from the waters before at my command. If the currents are friendly, perhaps it will drift into the Kol Sea once again. History is only lost if we give her up."

He's tired and pale, the kol in his eyes diminished enough that the sunlight touches the green behind, illuminates it. "I'd mind it less if we'd managed to take down the Majority ship as well."

I watch the Majority vessel smoke, but Mars is right. She's not going down. The crew has settled and whatever damage Dakk caused—it wasn't enough.

His eyes move over the ship in the distance, calculating. Usually he curses Winter, gives her an order after such a moment, but with that option unavailable, he stands utterly still. "It won't be long now, and they'll be patched up enough to fire again."

"There are lifeboats," I say, catching sight of them dangling next to the railing. "The Majority ship can't make it through the keyhole, right? They'll have to go all the way around Winter's Gate. We could paddle back to the safety of the Kol Sea, be there long before they arrived."

Mars laughs. "*The safety of the Kol Sea.* No one in the history of the world has ever said that."

"But we're cursed, you and me." My voice is more desperate than I intend. "We've magic that keeps us safe, turns us into the dangerous ones. And we could really use that magic about now."

"We'd hardly need to use our magic, Miss Quine. The Majority ship wouldn't think of pursuing us there."

"The other one did."

"They were intentionally sacrificed, I think. The goal was to drive us out into open waters where a larger, meaner vessel waited. See that man there?" Mars nods at the Majority ship, its broadside toward us so that we can see its imperious steel shape, cannons gleaming despite the smoke.

She's all steel teeth and hammer fists. And there, pacing back and forth on a raised platform, is the shape of a man, his long coat billowing in the wind. His features are impossible to make out from this distance, but there's something about his stride. Something one would remember.

"Is that Farraday Wrex then?" I ask.

"It is."

Leni shields her eyes from the sun. "How can you recognize him from such a distance?"

"His gait," I say, the light shifting, the currents bumping our ships closer to each other. "He leans heavily on his left leg."

"Indeed," Mars says. "I've yet to meet a Kol Master who's evaded the Abaki entirely, and Wrex there is no exception."

"What happened to him?"

"An Abaki got the drop on him, attacked from behind, tried to pull his leg from his body. As luck would have it, Wrex had a flare gun in his hand and he fired, setting the Abaki ablaze. And even with his hip dislocated, he managed to steer the ship to safety, arriving in port two days ahead of schedule."

"Or so he says." Kyn snatches up the spyglass, presses it to his eye.

"Fair point. Like most of the Kerce, he rather likes telling stories. But it bears noting, his limp is not the disadvantage many assume. He is *very* good at his job. He has a knack for knowing how the kol rides the currents." There's a barb in his voice, sharp, venomous.

"You know him well?"

"There aren't many Kerce left. And Wrex here was in my employ for a short time."

Kyn scoops up a splintered plank and wings it out into the sea. "He's an egotistical jagoff."

"Wrex also bested Kyn at arm wrestling," Mars says.

"I was twelve years old, you snake-eyed bastard! Wrex was a grown man, already navigating ships through the Kol Sea. And it was just the one time."

Mars holds up two fingers, and Kyn punches him in the shoulder.

"I could take him now."

"Has he been to the camp?" I ask.

Mars rubs at his shoulder. "No, we were still meeting north of Dris Mora back then, but Wrex was a very good student and knows the history of Queen's Point. Having met us here, he will have made assumptions that could put the rebel camp in danger."

"Anything else we need to know about him?"

"His Kerce is excellent."

"He *talks* to Winter?" The idea is uncomfortable enough that I wonder if it's jealousy I'm feeling.

"Not so she'll acknowledge it, so far as I can tell," Mars says. "He came to me initially because he wanted to learn to command her. I knew right away he hadn't enough kol in his blood for that, but he has other skills."

"What kind of skills?"

"He's a very good listener. He listens to Winter, reads the wind and her rage, decodes her whispers. He's been doing it long enough that he knows her tendencies. It irritates her, it seems. But it's his birthright, same as it's ours, and he has a gift for it, a gift that caught the attention of the Majority. He's been their best Kol Master for years now."

"If it's his birthright, why can't he command her?" Leni asks. "If he's Kerce, I mean. Mystra Dyfan said—"

"Mystra Dyfan said a lot of things, Leni. But she was Kerce too, and she never commanded Winter. If she'd had that power, she could have kept me out of trouble."

"That's debatable," Mars says, "but neither Mystra Dyfan nor Farraday Wrex have enough kol in their blood to compel Winter to do much at all. It's the kol that keeps her accountable, remember?" His chest rises and falls several times before he speaks again. "I think you're right, Miss Quine. The lifeboats are our best option. A blister or two, and we'll be back on shore. Weeks lost, of course. And our twyl stores gone for the second time in as many months." He sighs and turns his eyes to the lifeboats. "We'll need at least two, I think."

Across the way, voices on the Majority ship rise. And it's more than chatter. We stop what we're doing and watch as shadows dash to and fro across the deck. Bellows echo across the water, shouted commands. Panic breaking over them like a wave.

Wrex jumps off the railing and onto the deck of his ship.

Their guns fire.

We all flinch, but they don't seem to be firing at us. White puffs of smoke tell me they're aiming into the distance, at something beyond them.

Mars reaches out a hand. "The spyglass. Quickly."

Kyn tosses him the instrument and Mars peers through it, a smile catching him off guard, pure joy—a rare occurrence indeed on the face of Mars Dresden. He murmurs something in Kerce.

"Who's an impatient scoundrel?" I ask, translating on the fly.

"Hawken Valthor," Mars answers. "You might want to cover your ears, Miss Quine."

"You sure? 'Cause I covered my ears last time and . . . nothing."

Dakk and Kyn stand on the deck of the ship to my left, while Lenore and the girls are pressed to the railing on Mars's right, all of us staring at the shadow rising tall beyond the Majority ship.

"Ah, flux." Kyn throws his hands up. "Seriously everyone, cover your ears."

"What is it?" Leni asks, she and the girls obeying reluctantly.

And then a flash of light so bright I stagger backward. The sound of an explosion rattles my bones, and the Majority ship is nothing but flames. My ears ring and I totter on the railing. Mars reaches out a hand to steady me as a massive ship emerges from the cloud and mist, from the black smoke of their own guns.

"Huzzah!" Dakk cries, his arms high in a V. "The king has arrived!"

The Paradyian ship is three times as tall as the Majority vessel, and much wider, its sails full and seemingly big enough to cover an entire mountain village. At first, they appear white, but the sun catches them, and I see there's a gold sheen to the cloth, a metallic-orange sun blazing in the center of each.

The ship has an old-world feel, a royal sailing vessel, much like the *Maree Vale*, but even from here I can see how modern it is, how technologically advanced. Their guns swivel on well-oiled mechanisms, parking themselves even as their heat ripples on the air.

The concussion of their blast was well factored and well timed. Though it sends powerful ripples of water our way, the waves do not swamp us, and the Paradyian vessel sails directly through the smoking rubble of the Majority ship.

Dakk lifts the girls in his arms in one swift movement and all three of them are cheering and dancing. Leni collapses to the deck, weeping silently, her face in her hands.

I pull Kyn up next to me on the railing, and he wraps his arms around my waist, speaking across me to Mars. For a guy who smiles easily, the look on his face is concerned, and the sick in his gut even more so. "I'm happy they're here, yeah? Don't get me wrong, I'm pleased down to my boots, but why? We said we'd come to them, let the king meet Sylvi before they brought their armies all this way."

Mars doesn't answer, but that calculating look has returned to his face.

And then from behind, shouts and cries. "Be aware!" comes the call. We're all turning, then we're all gasping as a wave rises up behind us. I can taste Winter's breath on the wind, and I know this current began in her domain. We're too far away to hear her voice, and that spot in my chest that always warms when she speaks to me? It's cold and empty.

But this is her. I'm sure of it.

She's determined that we should not return, and as the wave crashes over Winter's Gate, I can't believe I ever thought I was safe with her. The very moment she's unconstrained by the covenant, she strikes.

And it won't just be the captain who goes down with the ship.

# CHAPTER 6

KYN HAS MANAGED TO MAKE IT ON BOARD the Paradyian ship with one of his boots still in place, but I'm barefoot and we're both dripping puddles onto the polished wooden deck. We stare gape-mouthed at the artistry around us. At the carved railings and the detailed finishes.

There's so little art on Layce, so little beauty outside of Winter's. And hers leaves behind dry rot and rust. Here, there is no splintered or rotting wood. No tarnished bearings or gears to replace. No corroded, weatherworn surfaces to tread upon carefully. Everything is clean and bright. Well-crafted and interesting.

Nothing like the utilitarian ships used by the Majority, and quite a step up from Mars's smuggling vessel fashioned of wood and held together with nostalgia.

There are two ships off our port side and one off to starboard, each of them big enough to house the entire village of Whistle-top. The Paradyians have indeed brought an army.

My eyes catch on the glass-covered control panel built into the sidewall of the ship and I have a sudden desire to take it apart just to see how it works. But my body is trembling with the cold and my fingers are numb. I couldn't zip up my own coat like this, which hardly matters considering that was lost as well.

Sailors bustle around the deck in white trousers and blue shirts, pulling at ropes and snapping latches into place. They call and acknowledge orders in a singsong cadence that feels practiced and polished to my muffled ears, their movements like a dance.

A few of these sailors buzz around Kyn and me, but I'm only vaguely aware of them. They lay soft hands on my shoulders and towel my hair dry. It's possible they've asked questions that have gone unanswered, but the ocean cold is like a poison that's settled deep in my bones. Everything is muffled and aching and so, so hard.

Blankets are wrapped around us, and we're shuffled to another part of the ship. We're climbing a twisting staircase when my ears finally clear and I realize Kyn's talking.

"We'll see Mars there?" He's addressing a red-caped, gun-wielding official escorting us across the ship. "Average height, pale skin? Black stuff in his eyes, scabby lips. You know him?"

"We know Mars Dresden." The man's voice is so deep it startles me.

"He's here then?" Kyn asks. "You pulled him up, yeah? He's on the ship? 'Cause those waves, I could have sworn—"

"This way." The man gestures toward another short set of stairs. "After you."

But Kyn is slow to move, his need for answers outweighing anything else.

We caught sight of the others when we were pulled from the sea. Of Lenore and Dakk, Katsy and Kree, many of the other rebel sailors under Mars's command—all of them were lifted by crane-like apparatuses, cranked aboard by Paradyian sailors. We watched as they climbed into the baskets lowered for them, counted everyone, but we didn't see Mars.

My last glimpse of him came as the sea swallowed his ship. The two of us standing side by side on the prow, his fingers wrapping around my wrist—instinct I think, a futile attempt to keep us from getting separated.

He knew we were going under, but there was no resignation on his face. It was all fight. All fury.

And truly, it's hard to believe there's a wave strong enough to keep him under.

But the sea is powerful, and we were tugged apart. My wrist bears proof of it: four thin scrapes sting the top side, while one marks the bottom. I cover them with my other hand to hide them from the salty sea air.

I follow the official, nudging Kyn's arm and pulling him after me. "I don't think he knows where Mars is. We'll find someone who does, OK?"

Kyn nods, but he keeps talking, and the official walks faster, outpacing Kyn's questions. After several winding staircases and a long stretch through a glass hallway that showcases the sea all around us, we reach the very front of the ship. The space is crowded with towering Paradyians. Arching walls and brightly colored curtains divide the area in mysterious ways. Viciously green plants in jeweled pots and sparkling gold statues sitting on pedestals frame a walkway of sorts, and still the ocean air breezes through. It starts a shiver at my spine that I can't quell.

Kyn shrugs off his blanket and wraps it over the one already draped around my shoulders. He takes my hands in his, first one and then the other, blowing warmth back into my fingers as he speaks. He can't stop talking, can't stop moving.

"Hey," I say, and then more firmly. "Hey. Look at me." I place one of my frozen hands on his cheek. "It's Mars, Kyn. Mars. He was raised on the sea, remember? I'm sure he's fine."

Kyn stills and I can feel him searching my feelings to see if I truly believe what I've said. But I've never been more certain of anything.

"Really, Kyn. I'm sure."

It's a moment before he nods, and when he does, his entire spine seems to unwind and suddenly he's three inches taller. He rubs the back of his neck and releases a pent-up chuckle. "Yeah? Yeah."

And then I hear the unmistakable ring of Mars's steel-toed boots. As if we'd summoned him, he drifts in from beyond a marble pillar. How he managed to keep his boots is beyond me, but his coat is gone now, sunk with the *Maree Vale*, no doubt. Like Kyn and me, he could use a change of clothes—his torn shirt is streaked with smoke stains and ocean grunge—but he seems unbothered as he leans in to hear the quiet words of a barrel-chested man wearing linen trousers and a floor-length red cape trimmed in gold. The man's hair is thick and white, settling in soft curls on his shoulders, and a thin gold circlet rests on his head.

"Hawken Valthor," Kyn says, awe in his voice.

"The king of Paradyia. You've met him?"

"No, but I've heard plenty."

"What have you heard?"

He rises on his toes, peering around a Paradyian woman whose flaxen braids add several inches to her already tall frame. "He's a genius, they say. Has a mind for governing. Can you even see? Here, stand on my boot."

"I'm fine, Kyn. He has a mind for governing, you said, but . . ."

He swallows and drops back on his heels. "I've never met him, Sylvi. I shouldn't say."

"I won't tell anyone you're a gossip. I just need to know what we're dealing with here."

The woman in front of us has moved and we're given an unobscured view.

Kyn watches the king closely. "He looks happy, yeah? But that's not what Dakk tells me. He says the queen's illness is all he can think of these days. That it colors every decision he makes. That his sadness was one of the reasons Hyla was so intent to find a cure for his wife."

"That's good for us, right? He needs what we have to offer."

"It's good for anyone who can convince him they have a remedy. Good for anyone who's brave enough to offer healing."

"Oh."

"He's been focused solely on her for such a long time, Dakk says there's a growing concern that corruption has leaked into the court."

"Traitors," I say, remembering the letters the rebels once had in their possession. Letters that proved someone in Paradyia's high court was trading secrets to a Majority councillor. "You think there's more than one?"

"Dakk does."

As Mars speaks to the king, his fingers flash. He grins and leans against the pillar, painting a picture in the air with his hands. I let my eyes wash over the king as he listens, and suddenly it's Hyla I see. The color of his cape is the precise red of her jacket, and how many times had I seen her and Mars have a similar moment?

A stab of regret slices through me, so sharp and fast, I press a hand to my gut to still the ache inside. My gaze wanders the deck and I wonder, *Did these people know her? Have they been told she's gone?*

"Where's Dakk?" I ask. "And Lenore? The girls?"

Kyn leans sideways, peering around those in front of us. "They'll be here somewhere, yeah?"

I catch glimpses of the sea and sky between the frames of official-looking persons, all of them as tall as trees, their skin burnished and warm. A people pulled from the pages of Mystra Dyfan's fairy stories. It's not at all difficult to imagine Sola, Queen of Creation, crafting each one of them from rays of sunlight. Most of them wear their hair long, while beards are trimmed short. Some have their tresses styled soft and curling with sunbeam combs holding them in place, and others display elaborate braids woven with shimmering thread and delicate beads.

Their cloaks and wraps, tunics and capes are all constructed of materials in creamy oranges and yellows, sunshine colors secured with belts of leather and intricately woven chains. Many of the women wear necklaces and earrings set with jeweled stones. Here and there I see diamonds.

I bite back a snort. I can't think of a single rig driver or kol miner on Layce who wouldn't get a good chuckle out of seeing Paradyians dressed up in waste rock.

A melodic sound rings out, like the plucking of a fiddle string but deep and low. The space empties, Paradyians casting curious glances in our direction as they disappear behind curtains or down staircases. At last only the king, Mars, Kyn, and I remain.

"Please," the king says, speaking in the common tongue and gesturing to couches spaced around a brazier. "Sit. Be warm."

I don't sit, but I do move to the fire, reaching out, hoping it will thaw the numbness in my fingers, in my bones.

"I wouldn't have thought the cold would affect you like this," the king says. "I assumed you'd be quite impervious, my dear."

His words are clear and unbroken, and there's a brightness to his voice. I imagine he's an excellent storyteller.

Mars encourages me with a gentle nod. He's found another pillar to lean against and there's something on his face I'm not used to. Hope maybe? Curiosity? He wants the king and me to get along.

I'm willing. Despite my hesitancy to go to war, Hyla thought well of this man, so I'm predisposed to like him.

I splay my fingers, purple and wrinkled, letting the heat slide between them. "This feels different than Winter's chill. Different than anything I've felt on Layce. I don't think I've ever been this cold."

"You haven't," Mars says. "Most certainly. The magic in your blood cannot numb you to the chill brought on by other places, other spirits."

That explains why this wind feels so unfamiliar, so thoroughly disinterested. Winter's hatred is a form of flattery I've grown far too accustomed to.

"If your magic has failed you, we must find another way to warm you through. A drink, yes? One that never fails to send a chill on its way." The king turns to one of his officials nearly hidden by a bright green fern. "Rombee cider, Lieutenant. We'll all have a glass."

The lieutenant touches his forehead with the tips of his fingers—a salute—and disappears through an archway.

"The rombee tree is native to our Paradyian shores," the king tells me. "The fruit is round, its skin brown and tough as leather, but once that's cut away, there's a red, jellied center. Delectable, I tell you. Its seeds must be carefully strained, but it's juicy, so juicy! The trees themselves are quite a sight too, tall and thin." He stretches his hands up into the sky. "We had two on our estate when I was a boy. The trunks would lean and sway when I scaled them, my mother crying from the window for me to *get down, get down!*" He chuckles, shrugs. "I have always been at the mercy of the things I love."

He paints a beautiful picture. "We don't have much fruit on Layce. What we get is very expensive."

He nods, strokes his beard. "I have tried, you know. Offered the Majority terms for opening trade between their islands and ours, but not without proof that they treat their workers fairly. I will not purchase or resell goods that have been harvested, *or mined,*" he says with a knowing look, "by means of forced labor."

The lieutenant returns with a tray of steaming goblets. He offers one to each of us and then disappears into a fern once again. The metal cup warms my hands instantly, and I have to force myself to drink slowly so as not to scorch my throat. A low noise radiates from Kyn's chest, his eyes closed as he drinks. The king was right; the rombee cider is good. I gulp down one final mouthful and then press the warm goblet against my breastbone, letting it warm my skin.

"Delicious, isn't it?" the king asks.

"I've never had anything like it," I say.

"It's my wife's favorite too. You would have liked her, I think." My stomach flips.

Kyn opens his eyes, his cup forgotten. "Is she—"

"I misspoke, didn't I? Fyeeri's alive, though so much of her has withered—her light dim—but if she's well enough, she'll join us for dinner."

"Hawken." Mars's voice is careful. He moves to the couch gingerly, the same way Leni always moved when she was tending to Drypp. "Tell them why you've come. Miss Quine needs to understand why you could not wait for us to come to you." He takes a seat next to Kyn and lifts his eyes to mine, encouraging me with a little nod.

"I have reservations," I say.

"Reservations?" the king asks.

"Sending Winter from Layce, unleashing war on an island already so ravaged . . . I need to know that it's not only best for you and your wife but for the people of Layce."

"It is good that you do not make this decision lightly." Hawken's wide brow creases and he leans toward me. "Let me ask you this, Sylver Quine. If the queen could be restored by other means and this bargain of ours was not so easily struck, would you go on bickering with a petulant winter spirit, giving her free rein instead of doing the difficult thing and severing your ties to her? Would you continue to allow the Majority to impose their will on those who cannot fight for themselves simply because you fear the alternative?"

Within my chest, shame and rage rise in equal measure. "It's not that I don't—"

Mars holds up a hand to silence me. "Hawk, just tell her."

The king exhales and shrinks by half. "Fyeeri's time is nearly gone. The doctors cannot tell us what it is that inflicts her so violently, but there is almost nothing left of her to fight it off. The medicine has ceased to provide relief, and she is in pain continually. She'd rather die than go on suffering. When news of Hyla's death arrived, it was all I could do to stay her hand. She was Fyeeri's favorite, you know? Hyla. Acted as the queen's personal guard whenever she and Dakk were stationed in the city. I don't think Fyeeri would have let her come to Layce if she'd understood the danger."

"Hyla came because I asked her to," Mars says. "I told her about the pool, about what was possible for Fyeeri if we could free the isle of Winter's hold. I knew the risk, but I valued her company, her wisdom. Her death is on me, Hawk."

"Hyla's death belongs to no one but herself. She's lost enough; we should not deny her the dignity of choosing to die for those she loved." His voice is strong, but tears leak down his face, disappearing into his beard. Together we take a deep shuddering breath.

"Now though, we must honor her by finishing what she started. Do you not agree, Sylver Quine?"

"Just—just Sylvi," I say stupidly.

"Sylvi then." He stands and crosses to my side at the brazier. "I would do anything to see my wife well. Anything at all. Even bring war to a people who have grown comfortable in their oppression. What would you do to honor Hyla's sacrifice?"

I've been trying to figure that out for weeks now.

"Sir, I don't know if you remember me—" Thank Begynd for Kyn, kindly giving me a moment to pull myself together.

"Of course I remember you. Kyndel, yes? Descended from the very people that Begynd himself cut from the rock. You were not much of a believer when last we met."

"I wasn't, no. But I've seen things now, and I understand . . . well, very little if I'm honest. Journeys are like that, yeah? They answer some questions and dredge up a bunch more. There's just something you should know about this great pool. Before you decide this is your best option." He glances at Mars, and something passes between them. A warning maybe? "I don't know if you've been told, but if your wife finds her healing there, in the Pool of Begynd, she won't be able to leave Layce. Ever. You do know that, yeah?"

Sometimes truth is a dagger, straight to the heart. This one slides in all the way to the hilt. Of all of us, Kyn knows best that restoring the queen's health is not a gift she can accept freely. There is a cost. The king's face does not change, and I'm not sure he understands.

Mars stands, slides his hands into his pockets. "Fyeeri's healing will be tied to the pool, Hawk. It will be dependent upon her proximity to it."

The lines on the king's brow deepen. "If she leaves, her sickness will return?"

Mars nods. "And if you stay with her on Layce . . ."

"My throne will be forfeit." His ruddy cheeks have gone white.

"I would think so."

The king clears his throat, but when he speaks, I can hear the emotion trapped there. He is decided but not unfeeling about the choices he's made. "Good. I am unfit to rule such a people. Unwilling as I am to put them first. Willing even that they should go to war that my wife may live. I understand it is a selfish thing I do. If the pool hadn't demanded I stay behind on your cursed isle, my court might have."

"You've made your peace with it, then?" Mars asks.

"What peace? We have a responsibility, do we not? To do right by our people. To uphold our family name." Hawken's crystal blue gaze is back in the present now and focused on mine. "You are a Kerce princess, Sylver Quine. On Paradyia, we would call you Sessa."

It's what Hyla always called me, but I thought the title translated to *my lady* in the common tongue. "*Sessa* means—?"

"Princess," the king says. "Daughter of the sovereign. Have you not heard this word before?"

"I've heard it," I say, my gaze darting to Mars. "You could have told me."

He shakes his head. "It wasn't the right time. Far too early on our journey." He turns to the king. "Apologies, Hawk. Please continue."

It's a tiny thing, that I never understood Hyla's name for

me. But images of her death surface again, and I see her there, sprawled on the Seacliff Road.

There's curiosity on the king's face, but before he can ask, I shake the memory away. "Yes, sorry. You were saying?"

"I was telling you of your family. The great books of history say your father held the Kerce throne for as long as he could, fighting to the very last, until the Majority overwhelmed them. You and Mars represent the last royal line of your people. You have a duty to replicate your father's courage and to undo the wrongs of your mother."

The words are light on the king's tongue, but I nearly buckle under their weight. *My father's courage. My mother's wrongs.* Two more responsibilities to carry. Small maybe, but snowflakes are small. Weightless on their own. Only, they never come alone, do they? They fall in droves. I've seen a mountain pine break under the weight of snow.

"I want to do the right thing," I say. "For everyone."

"And you're trying to figure out what that is, are you? How long will it take, I wonder? Will Fyeeri still be alive when you decide?"

"Take it easy, Hawk. You said yourself it's good to think these choices through."

"Do not reprimand me, Dresden! Not now!" His face is red, but it's from fear, not rage. "We are in impossible times, yes? Impossible! But if the stories are true, you have magic at your disposal. Both of you. Magic that will reveal Begynd's powers to the world once again."

"It's not that simple—" I start.

"I do not think anything about this is simple. I know what it is to make life or death decisions—or have you forgotten who I am?" He strides to a nearby railing, his cape billowing around him. "But the books say it's possible, and Mars Dresden has assured me it is." A long moment passes and then he turns toward us, his face like marble, the setting sun turning him into just another golden statue lining the deck. "For the very *possibility* of success, I offer the children of Maree Vale my army. I offer you the ability to fight your oppressors, and I ask, Sylvi of both Paradyia and Kerce, will you do this for me? Will you give up the life you thought you were entitled to? Will you do everything you can to overthrow the Majority and free Layce from the stranglehold of a corrupted spirit?"

"So that your wife can live." My lip trembles as I fight to keep my emotions in check. The storm raging in my chest could put Winter to shame. There is much to respect in what Hawken Valthor says, and much to hate. I cannot find it in me to simply pretend his motives are purer than my mother's.

"Yes," he says. "So that my wife can live."

# CHAPTER 7

"I UNDERSTAND THIS IS COMPLICATED, MISS Quine." Mars watches me pace the deck from his seat on the couch. We're alone now—Kyn, Mars, and I—the king and his officials having left us in a hurry.

"He's too emotional," I say.

"Snowflake, we're all emotional about this."

"I don't trust him to make sound decisions."

"I'm certain he feels the same about you. Sit, Miss Quine. I can't discuss this with you if you're always on the move."

But I can't sit. I'm still thinking about the queen's maidservant who, just moments ago, bustled in with tears racing down her cheeks and pleading for the king to come quickly. He took his leave then, sprinting down the stairs, all decorum gone. He could have been anyone then. Any frightened husband. And it's that, his humanity, that terrifies me the most.

Instead of sitting, I cross to the railing and imagine the murky outline of Layce growing closer in the distance. We're still too far away, but it's there, somewhere beyond the blue. The sun is high in the sky, but we're pointed straight toward the Kol Sea, and though we'll have to approach Queen's Point from the south to avoid Winter's Gate, there's no avoiding her rage.

I wonder if she knows we're coming back so soon. If she's aware we've turned around. I don't know how her sight works, the mechanism of her mind. It seems her awareness extends beyond her borders, but how far?

The king's ship is called the *Heraldic*, Mars tells me. At least that's how it's translated into the common tongue. I don't know the names of the ships flanking us, but I can see they're heavily armed. Unlike the *Heraldic*, which also carries members of the king's court, the sister ships are loaded with troops and weapons for war.

And though I don't see a Majority vessel on the horizon, there's no way these ships will go unnoticed by them for long. They're too big, too bright, too worthy of attention.

How small of me to think I could prevent war by simply withholding my gift. The Paradyians intend to cross into Layce's waters with an army. War is coming. The only thing left to decide is whether to fight or stand in the way.

It's a paralyzing feeling, and I'm reminded of the stag I ran down in the Sylver Dragon. There was no hope I'd get the rig stopped in time, but with two strides, the stupid deer could have been out of danger. I laid on the horn, fought to slow, but some unnatural instinct kept the creature rigid, its unblinking eyes wide in the light of the headlamps.

I blink the memory away. It wasn't the first animal crushed beneath the Dragon's tread, and I doubt it will be the last. I've spent enough time at the wheel to know exactly what happens when a machine at full steam is bearing down on you.

War is coming and I can fight it or be crushed. With Winter on our side, perhaps I can ensure a little less bloodshed.

I turn and stride to the couch, taking my place between them. Kyn and Mars stare at me, waiting. One of them anxious, the other annoyed.

Mars scowls. "What's that expression on your face, Miss Quine?"

"Why do you continue to call me Miss Quine?"

His brows lift. "You prefer ice witch? Snowflake?"

Kyn punches him in the arm.

"How about Sylvi?" I say. "Or if you insist on formality, Sylver. But this Miss Quine business feels intentionally distant. Like you refuse to acknowledge that I am, in fact, your sister. And truth be told, Quine was never really my name, was it? Certainly not my given name. Mistress Quine was born three hundred years after I was. So please. Stop patronizing me. We're equals."

Amusement settles on Mars's lips. "You're wrong, sister. We are *not* equals. *You* are my superior in every way. It is deference, I offer. Not distance."

"Deference?" I have no idea what to make of the idea. "You're heir to the Kerce throne, not me."

"The Kerce throne no longer exists," Mars clarifies.

"Deference is not necessary. But I will have your respect."

"And referring to you as Miss Quine robs you of that?"

"Yes." In truth I've lost track of the argument, but I'd rather he not take this as a win.

"Fair enough." He leans back against the overstuffed cushions. "I shall *respectfully* give your new moniker some thought."

Kyn's eye roll is so intentional I can feel it in every nerve of my body. "Are you two done yet?"

"Sorry, Kyn. He just . . . Never mind. Here's the thing. We can't send Winter away just to appease the king."

Mars and Kyn speak at the same time, both of them protesting.

I ignore Mars and turn to Kyn. "Remember what happened in the Shiv cave? What happened when their Great Father drank from the Pool of Begynd?"

"He grew young again, and then . . ."

"And then he froze solid, and his arm shattered into a million pieces when you struck him with Shyne's walking stick."

"It did, yeah. Hard to forget."

"Your point, Miss Vale?"

I snap straight and jab my finger at Mars's face. "*No.* No." Maree Vale was my mother; I've come to terms with that. But she's the reason we're in this mess. I've no desire to take her name.

He shrugs. "Your point, nameless wonder?"

I cock my head at him in warning and he grins. "My point is that even if the Pool of Begynd once offered healing, there's no knowing what it offers now."

"What it . . . offers?" Kyn asks.

"It could kill her as easily as heal her," I say.

Mars leans back against the couch, crosses a boot over his knee. "Sending Winter away does more than just thaw the pool . . . Sylvi?"

Kyn's face sours. "No. Not Sylvi. Not from you."

"Agreed," Mars says, tipping his head back against the cushions. "Sending Winter away means she takes her curse with her."

"You'd be hard-pressed to prove that, but let's say you're right. When Winter leaves, she takes her curse with her. But what about the kol?"

"What about it?" Mars asks, closing his eyes.

"Ohhhh," Kyn says. "I see what you mean."

But Mars hadn't been there. He hadn't seen what happened to the Shiv man. He needs to understand.

"When the Great Father froze, his eyes turned black and then sylver," I say. "Winter used Maree Vale to introduce kol into Begynd's waters, and though Winter's magic may accompany her when she's sent away, she cannot simply lift away the kol. The kol that remains will still affect those who bathe in the pool."

"Wrong." Mars's eyes remain closed, his posture relaxed. He's so certain, so smug. "Winter used kol to bind her curse together, but it's wrong to say she *introduced* kol into the pool. This isle has always had veins of kol running through it. It's at the very heart of Shiv Island. Begynd created the kol. It was not new to him. Nor can he be corrupted by it."

"And yet the kol made Winter's magic more than it was. *Winter's magic* became *more*, Mars. Begynd was cowed beneath it. Frozen solid."

Mars snorts. "We cannot possibly guess what did or did not happen to Begynd when Maree Vale—"

"Your mother," Kyn interjects.

"—plunged the cursed medallion into the fount."

"That's exactly my point. At the very least, even if we're certain that Winter's curse breaks when she leaves, we cannot predict how it will have changed the great pool."

Mars sighs and his eyes open. "What are you saying, sister?"

"I'm saying we cannot guarantee the queen's healing."

Mars rolls his face toward me. "That's why they're here, remember? They came for *the pool*. It's our one bargaining chip."

"Then the king has to make good on his word before we make good on ours," Kyn says, a thread of stony determination in his voice.

I reach out and put a hand on his knee. "Yes, exactly. That's how this has to go. The king and his Paradyian army help us defeat the Majority. Then, and only then, do we send Winter away. Because if that pool doesn't do what the king expects it to—"

"It's not just the king," Kyn says. "The Shiv too. They're expecting miracles to live beneath the surface of that thing. If there's only death there . . ."

I shiver at the thought. "Right. If Begynd's power has been corrupted, we lose our bargaining chip. Best hold on to it until we have what we need."

"And how do you suggest we do that? The queen will not live long enough to survive a war."

*Can we use that to our advantage?* I wonder. *Can we make good on our end of the deal without a slaughter?*

"So maybe war isn't our best option."

# CHAPTER 8

DINNER IS SERVED ON THE DECK OF THE SHIP, in a corner strung with lanterns that look like tiny suns. We sit at long oak tables under a sky slowly fading from blue to pink. From pink to orange. And back to blue again, a darker blue this time, black edged with stars winking down at us.

I've never seen a sky like this. So free of storm. So full of color.

New boots have been found for me, brown leather ones that lace to my knees. They aren't waterproof and they're so pliable they feel like socks, but they're warm. I wear them with woolen leggings and a cream-colored tunic shot through with gold stitching. It's lighter than I'm used to, but it keeps the wind off my arms, and the material is so soft I can't stop touching it. I've rebraided my hair as well and, despite all that lies ahead, I feel almost relaxed.

Kyn too has changed: a long-sleeve orange tunic with beaded trim paired with linen pants and gold sandals. Impractical for

Winter's domain, but here where it's windy and not nearly so cold, he looks comfortable. Sola's colors suit him well.

He enters the seating area with several of Mars's sailors, all of them clean and changed into Paradyian garments. But there's a weariness to them, a heaviness that weighs their shoulders low as they walk, and I'm reminded that they've lost some of their own today. My friends have survived, but many of theirs have not.

Kyn sees me and excuses himself, then slides into the seat across from mine. "You can't see it from this side of the ship, but the Paradyians are pulling our dead from the water now. I had to drag the crew away. We still have two men unaccounted for."

And suddenly the fragrant food turns sour on the air. I had wondered why we weren't moving.

"And the Majority ship?"

"They're pulling the Majority dead up as well."

Of course they are. I remember Hyla's insistence that we give Jymy Leff a proper burial. The Paradyians consider it the height of dishonor to leave anyone behind.

Mars hasn't returned from wherever they shuffled him off to, but Lenore slides in next to me. She's wearing an outfit similar to mine, though the colors are bolder and brighter, and her auburn hair has been let down, a simple golden band keeping it away from her face. It's been a long while since I've seen her without braids. She looks very grown-up.

"Have you seen the queen?" she asks in a low whisper.

"No, you?"

She shakes her head. "Dakk is taking the girls to her now. They've been asking to see her since the moment we stepped aboard."

"She's out of danger then?"

"Seems to be. She's not well enough to come to dinner, the king said, but she'd like to pay her respects to the girls. Apparently, they're all very close. Did you know Hyla was the queen's personal guard?"

"Not until the king mentioned it today."

"We'll have to stab Mars for keeping that from us." She tears the corner off a loaf of seeded bread, dipping it in a bowl of pink oil before sliding it into her mouth. "Begynd-bright-and-holy, have you tried this?"

Before I can answer, Mars is at my elbow. "Can I steal you for a moment?"

His voice is calm but there's tension there.

I flash Kyn a questioning look, but he shoves a slice of bright blue fruit into his mouth and shrugs. "Want me to come?"

"No, it's OK." I slide off the bench and follow Mars through a narrow doorway and down a flight of stairs that takes us deep into the bowels of the ship. "Where are we going?"

"Down," he says, our footsteps echoing around us. "Someone has asked to meet you."

He revels in the opaque, Mars does. He wants me to ask him about this *someone*, so I don't. "Why haven't you changed?"

"I got sidetracked."

"And you're not chafing? Salt water is no joke, brother."

"I'm not chafing." He steps off the bottom stair and onto a landing. A soft yellow glow fills the space, flickering gently like firelight, though there's no fire to be seen. The light seems to be coming from vents cut high into the walls. "We're here."

"Where exactly is *here*?"

"The brig."

I was expecting the queen, I think, so everything about those two words surprises me. I step closer to the doorway on the opposite wall. It looks like an open archway, but there's glass here. Thick and clean.

That's my first thought, actually: how remarkably clean it is for a prison, all-white walls with a built-in wraparound bench. Twelve or thirteen Majority sailors are scattered about the cell. All of them have been given white linen pants, not so different from the ones Kyn now wears, and matching white shirts.

Two Paradyian guards stand watch, one on either side of the arching door. As we approach, they nod at Mars and step a respectful distance away. Inside the cell, the prisoners shift, and Farraday Wrex comes into view. He's sitting against the far wall, the only man inside who refused clean, dry clothing.

"Someone else is chafing," I whisper into Mars's ear.

Wrex stands, his brown duster hovering just above the toes of his boots. From this distance, I can see it's been tailored to fit, hemmed so deftly you can tell it was made for him and him alone. He looks strong in this coat, and I understand why the simple white linens, though dry and clean, would not appeal to him.

He crosses to the glass, his right leg dragging slightly, his gaze groping and curious as it passes over me. I suddenly realize how exposed I am. How bare I must look. These clothes show off the shape of my body in ways I'm not used to, and for the first time I can remember, I've no weapon to speak of, not even Winter.

I'm tempted to step back—to put more distance between this man and me—but a glance at Mars, leaning a shoulder against the glass, eyes shrewd, almost bored, and I remember who I am. I'm the daughter of the Kerce queen, and though there is no longer a throne, this man is a wayward subject who's given his loyalty to our oppressors.

I step closer. "You wanted to meet me."

"I did." Wrex's voice is softer than I anticipated. Uncomfortably so. No one this big and broad should sound like a child. His size is not something you can understand when you're staring across a great expanse of water. But here, framed by the walls of his cell, he's a force. He has a head of shaggy brown hair and, for a villain, he's not unpleasant to look at. His pink lips are full, his hazel eyes bright and lively with slashes of kol striking both from corner to corner. "I'm Farraday Wrex."

Something in the way he says it—the growl of his last name maybe?—catches me off guard it's so familiar. I wonder why I didn't recognize it before.

"Wrex. As in Tiberius Wrex?"

"You know your history," Wrex says.

"Not well, no. But the name . . ." My mind spins, fighting, trying to land on a single fact to tie to this person, any fact at all. I riffle through what I remember of Mystra Dyfan's stories, attempt to conjure up her sketches, but there's nothing. Only the name.

"Tiberius Wrex," Mars offers, "was the original captain of the *Maree Vale*."

"Oh." Never in a million years would I have landed there.

"The good captain's story is fraught, I'm afraid; his reputation marred by negligence at the wheel. But our mother cared for him deeply, covered up his addictions to her own detriment. And here is his descendant, *Farraday* Wrex, come to kill us."

"Is that true?" I ask. "Your ancestor knew my mother?"

A single shoulder shrug. "So they say."

"Don't be coy," Mars says. "There was a time we couldn't shut you up for the bragging."

"Youth should be forgiven their boasting, don't you think? You too were once full of your own bluster."

"That wasn't youth. That was power. I haven't been young in a great while. But you know that. You know more about our history than most. You've simply chosen to side with those who'd like to erase who we are and where we came from."

"I'd like to build a future for myself, Dresden. For my kin. The Majority offers me the greatest opportunity to do that. Despite what my ancestor may or may not have done hundreds of years ago, there is no Kerce kingdom to swear allegiance to now. No *king* to pay me for my services."

"Do you see me wearing a crown?" Mars asks.

"Never," Wrex says, and there's a world of meaning there I couldn't begin to decipher.

"So you follow the coin then?" I ask.

Wrex turns to me, tilts his head. "Like you, I imagine."

"It's not the same." A hot chill climbs my back and suddenly the soft Paradyian clothing on my body itches. "I've never taken coin to hunt down and kill another human."

"I'm not simply hunting down another human, am I? You're a threat to the Majority, rig driver. You and Dresden both. Your very existence threatens the government that ensures my way of life."

"By theft and corruption and oppression. By mining and shipping and trucking a volatile mineral carved from the isle by those who cannot protect themselves from its dangers."

"They could submit to Majority rule, work hard, show loyalty, and lift themselves out of the muck of menial tasks. I am living proof that the council rewards loyalty."

"Or we could rid the isle of them altogether," Mars says. "Throw a party in their council rooms."

"Oh yes," Wrex croons. "Your little rebellion. I've heard of your plans."

"From who?" I ask.

He laughs then, a small sound, like wind chimes three streets over. "You two are very much alike, aren't you? So worried you might have a traitor in your midst."

"Very few people knew about our crossing," I say.

"But you both want a name. Dresden here thinks your traitor is Paradyian. What about you, rig driver? Do you doubt the intentions of the golden isle?"

"I couldn't say." My eyes slide to the guards who are studiously pretending they can't hear us. "We know they have at least one traitor. Someone has been trading secrets for kol. We've seen the letters."

"It's against Majority law to trade with Paradyia," Wrex says.

"It's against *Paradyian* law to trade secrets, but we *know* that's happening." Mars turns to the glass, his torn shirt and mussed hair framing him as reckless, but I know he's anything but. Mars is as calculated as it gets. "And while you're hiding behind Majority law, it occurs to me that perhaps you've received permission from the council for this little undertaking. Orders even, to keep this Paradyian traitor happy. You're popular with Councilman Sworn, I recall."

"Ask your question, Dresden."

"With Councilman Sworn's approval, have you been meeting covertly with a Paradyian official? On a neutral island perhaps, somewhere easy to access as you carry out your duties as Kol Master?"

Wrex doesn't flinch.

Mars continues. "What does it look like, this transaction? I've some idea, you know. We *have* seen the letters."

Nothing from Wrex.

"I'd wager it looks something like this. You select a busy marketplace on a neutral island. Leeds maybe, or Zaphyn. It's a dead drop, I assume. Or a handoff? Yes, a handoff. No shared meal. Nothing like that. You simply bump into this Paradyian traitor as you pass, very haphazard, very casual. Apologies are made—he's a member of the royal court after all—but as he walks away, he slips a hand into his pocket and finds a carefully sealed package of processed kol. In exchange, of course, he's dropped into your pocket a tidy little envelope full of gossip he's collected while listening at doors up and down the palace halls."

Wrex smiles. "You've quite the imagination, Dresden. But, as always, you're asking the wrong questions."

"Correct me then."

"You shouldn't be asking for a *name*. You should be asking why anyone in Hawken Valthor's court would be willing to make such trades. The very fact that there *is* a traitor should tell you all that you need to know."

"And what's that?" I ask.

He stares down at me now, his nostrils flaring. "This king is not nearly as popular as you've been led to believe, rig driver. This war you're coercing the Paradyians into is not widely supported.

They are a proud people who do not appreciate having their priorities dictated to them by outsiders. When it comes time to fight, you may not have the army you've been promised."

"But I'll have Winter," I say. "So army or no army, I like our odds."

His chin tips up and the shadows cast gruesome lines across his face.

"Chafing?" I ask.

Mars laughs, loud, hunched over, his hands on his knees.

"Are we done here?" I ask him, grabbing the collar of his thrashed shirt, hauling him up. "I'm starving."

"That's it?" Wrex sputters. "After all the stories I've heard about an ice witch so fierce she flies a steel dragon through the mountains, you simply look at me and walk away. I expected more."

I shrug. "You aren't the first man I've disappointed. You won't be the first to make me care. You wanted to meet. We've met. Something that would not have happened if you'd succeeded in destroying the *Maree Vale*."

"I beg to differ." Wrex offers a smile that stiffens my spine. "I did destroy the *Maree Vale* and yet here we are." He spreads his hands in victory.

I rap a knuckle against the glass. "It's hard to credit you for that one. Hard to believe you had anything at all to do with Winter's treachery. I've heard she's no fan of yours."

His smile falters. "We can't all be her favorite."

"I suppose that's true."

"Done now?" Mars offers me his arm.

"They say you're siblings," Wrex says, his effort to keep us there startling and effective. How could he possibly *know* that? *I've* known for only a handful of weeks. And though it is beginning to spread among the rebels, it isn't widely known.

"Who says that?" I ask, slipping my hand into the crook of Mars's elbow, fighting for nonchalance.

A shrug. A smile. "I'm a very good listener."

I want a name so badly I can taste it, but asking is pointless. I change tacks. "I've heard that about you. That you've a gift for decoding Winter's whispers, her winds. It's a pity you chose to use the kol in your blood to help the Majority and not your own people."

His eyes flash for the first time and I know I've struck something tender beneath his breastbone. He presses a hand to the glass. "The kol in my blood helps me do my job, rig driver, just as it helps you do yours. I'm grateful for that gift, but I was born on Layce under a Majority Council who rewards loyalty. The kingdoms of old continued their nepotism long after they knew better. After the Majority showed them the great value of burning the pages of yesterday in pursuit of a brighter tomorrow. Their refusal to see that better way will be the end of the great Paradyians, just as it ended the Kerce. I will not swear allegiance to a throne that no longer exists."

"It would be foolish to expect you to," Mars says lightly.

"What's foolish is inviting the Paradyians to Layce. They have designs on this island, surely you know that. When the Majority is gone, who do you think will take their place here?"

"Good to know we have your confidence," I say.

"Once, you may have had a chance to root out the Majority, but not now. Now that I've seen these ships. When I tell the council what I know, your little war will be over, and the Majority will repay me handsomely, will they not?"

"They certainly should." I rap my knuckles against the glass. "Though you're ill-positioned to share anything with them just now."

"That's true," Wrex says. "I'll have to give that some thought."

"We'll leave you to it then," I say, then let Mars lead me up the stairs and away from a villain I thank Begynd we were able to secure.

Farraday Wrex is dangerous.

No good can come from letting this man wander free.

## CHAPTER 9

THE PARADYIANS OFFER US ACCOMMODA-
tions, and while Kyn and Mars stumble off to warm beds,
I drag Leni across the deck, to the very couch the king sat
on just hours before when he told me I should bring war to Layce
so his wife could live.

A light blanket is draped over the seat back. We kick off our
shoes and snuggle beneath it, staring up at a sky full of stars.

"If the only thing Winter took from us was this sky," Leni says,
"I'd still hate her."

The brazier is smoldering, just warm enough to heat our
toes, and I don't feel the need to answer. Words often become a
weapon on my tongue more than anything else. I want to savor
this moment, not destroy it.

Leni prattles for a bit: her concern for Hyla's girls, how badly
she misses her father, her worries for Mystra Dyfan. It seems our
childhood tutor has had trouble finding work in recent years. If

something doesn't materialize soon, she'll have no choice but to return to the ships where she began.

I've no great attachment to Mystra, but it is sad. She'll never survive the ships—she's too old, too set in her ways to obey a Majority overseer.

"You think Mars could find her a place?" Leni asks.

"If anyone can, it's him. But his mind is occupied with war just now."

"If we destroy the Majority, everything will be different anyway. For Mystra. For my da. For all of us."

She's right, of course. A whole world of opportunities would open to Mystra if the Majority were gone. I drift off wondering what a different Layce would look like. I can't conjure it though, and the canvas of my mind stays vast and white and empty. I wake to the flickering of sunlight on my lashes and the smell of rombee cider in my nose. A light layer of dew has settled across our blanket. Leni's already climbed out from beneath it. She sits upright, her legs crossed one over the other, and stares out at the rising sun. The goblet of cider in her hands steams into the morning air.

"Seven hours," she says, glancing down at me. "That's the longest you've slept in days."

"No bells," I say, pushing myself upright. "It's amazing what happens when there are no bells."

She lifts another goblet off a nearby table and passes it to me. I sip the cider slowly, my mind waking, my body warming. The sun dances across the water, changing colors as it lifts slowly from the sea.

"You know, only a fool would leave this sea for ours," she says.

"You've been trying to run away to Paradyia for years though. What if it isn't the fairy story you think it is?"

"I don't need a fairy story. Just sunshine. A garden. Somewhere my father can rest. No kol to addle his mind. No overseers taking advantage." The sun is lovely on her face, turning her auburn freckles to gold flakes.

"Sounds like a fairy story to me."

"Maybe," she says, laying her head on my shoulder. "I'd run away to Paradyia in a heartbeat. But if we don't go back, the Majority wins by default, Winter ravages the isle, and everyone we love suffers. What about you?"

"What about me?"

She sits up. "After all this, after everything, would you ever leave Layce behind? If we do this right and Winter leaves, why stay? Drypp's gone, so's the tavern, the garage. We could have a view like this every day, Syl."

The mountains are my home. I could say that, but it won't make any sense to her. She's never understood my love for the road, the peace I feel in the driver's seat of the Sylver Dragon.

"I can't think that far ahead right now," I say instead. "But I have to go back. Even if no one else does. I'm not done with Layce, Leni. I'm not done with the Shiv buried beneath the ice. Shyne and Crysel and the rest in High Pass. There are things to be said."

"And Winter?"

"I'm not done with her either."

The Reyclan girls find us first, and they come bearing gifts: breakfast rolls layered with sugared spices and glazed pecans. Kree sits delicately between us, balancing the tray, while Katsy leaps at me with a fierce grin. They're so trusting, these girls. It slices me wide open. Leni wraps the blanket around their legs, and all four of us stuff ourselves sick with the sticky rolls.

Mars and Kyn follow, sobering the festivities with news that we'll be at the border of the Kol Sea within the hour.

"Thank you," Kyn says to me, dropping onto the arm of the couch. He opens his mouth so Katsy can shove a roll between his teeth.

"For?"

"You slept," he says, his mouth full. He's tracked down another shotgun. This one Paradyian; it hangs from his shoulder on a braided leather strap.

"I did." I hadn't thought about how restless my lack of sleep might make him; it's easy to get caught up in my own exhaustion. Even now I can feel an ache threading through me, and I can't tell if it started in his body or mine. "You are very welcome."

Dakk appears before too long, his hair washed, his beard trimmed. He's wearing a Paradyian naval uniform, much like the officials buzzing around the king yesterday. It suits him.

"The king is asking for you, Mars Dresden." He plucks a pecan from Kree's chin. "You too, Sylver Quine."

I lift Katsy off my lap and stand. "I'd like Kyn to come as well."

Dakk slaps Kyn on the back. "Come. Winter is close. Girls, back inside now. The queen is better today, and she would like a longer visit."

"I'll take them," Leni says. "I'd much rather be indoors if we're heading into a storm."

Dakk leads us to the navigation deck, the wind picking up as we go, feeling familiar, the sky darkening at its edges. Off to our starboard side, I see Winter's Gate and her shallows. They're small in the distance, far enough away to offer no threat.

One final staircase and I see it: the Kol Sea, dead ahead. I can't hear Winter yet, but she's making a fuss, her storm nearly as black as the waves.

"Hawken, you're going to have to drop anchor here," Mars says.

"Don't be foolish," the king says. "We cannot fight a war from this distance."

"The dock at Queen's Point is still being expanded. It's far too small for more than one of these vessels," Mars explains. "If the fleet comes any closer, three of your ships would have to drop anchor in the Kol Sea. Anyone coming ashore will need to be shuttled across the expanse in small boats, which means either Miss Quine or I would have to stay with the ships to keep Winter's Abaki off you."

We can't be bothered with such tasks, not now.

An official standing next to the king steps forward. I recognize him as the man who led Kyn and me to the front of the ship yesterday. "Every sailor here is also a soldier, Dresden. We can fight off her monsters."

"But not the black sea," I say. "Our twyl stores went down with the *Maree Vale*. We can offer you no protection from the kol and the madness it brings."

"We brought the twyl you delivered on your last visit. Rations have been dispensed to those on board. Will that not be enough?"

"Not for a long-term stay, no. But it will get *this* ship to Queen's Point. Your other ships can stay here, and we'll send instructions."

"Send? How?"

"We fly," I say, relishing the surprise on the king's face.

"Show-off," Kyn says.

"One ship, Hawken," Mars says. "That's all we can handle right now."

The king's brow creases, and he scratches his beard as he turns the idea over in his mind. After a moment, he calls out to the commander of his fleet, and they step away to make arrangements. It seems to take forever, but eventually, a series of flags are raised as they communicate with their other ships. Finally, three anchors are dropped and the *Heraldic* pushes forward, sailing straight into Winter's storm.

The navigation deck looks down on much of the ship. By my count, at least fifty sailors man their stations. Sailors who are also soldiers, but there are nearly that many passengers on board, members of the king's court whose reason for making the crossing are thoroughly unknown to me. Women in gowns and men in suits. Why bring them if they're not going to fight? Why bring them if they're simply going to drain resources? This isn't a pleasure trip.

A thought slices through me then: Perhaps Wrex was right.

"Snowflake?" Kyn asks. "You good?"

I lean in, so only he and Mars can hear my concern. "Why do you think the king brought so many members of his court? Doesn't it seem like—"

"Stop thinking about things we can handle later." Mars turns to the king. "Can we have a little space to work here, Hawk?"

The king's face is all surprise. "Are you sending me away, Mars? I've never *been* sent away."

"Not *away*, just over there." Mars points to the ship's wheel, currently manned by a helmsman in a sharp blue uniform pretending to be above whatever we're discussing over here by the rail.

The king laughs, a single chuckle that puffs his mouth and lifts his shoulders. "No, no. I rather like being given instruction. It removes all the guessing. I shall be *over here* if you need me. Let us know when you're done discussing our fate."

"Will do," Mars says.

"You're going to pay for that at some point," I say.

"Most certainly." Mars steps up next to me and his fingers drum a quick *rat-a-tat-tat* on the railing. "Forget about the king. Focus on the task at hand. You've got to get this ship to Queen's Point, yes? Which, very generally speaking, is in *that* direction. Using Winter as a tool, how will you do that?"

Kyn cracks open his shotgun, checks it, snaps it shut. "I thought we were done with lessons, yeah?"

"It's fine, Kyn. I said I'd practice." I tug my braids from my collar, desperately wanting to get this right, and finding it easier to think without Winter chattering in my ear. "The island is fragile right now, so I want to be careful not to strain Winter's magic."

"Right. Her power is not unlimited. If you ask too much here, her hold could slip elsewhere and suddenly a mountain village is covered in snow."

"Her natural state is to rage," I say, remembering.

"Correct. If you demand she stop entirely for the amount of

time it would take us to cross the expanse, it will require too much energy on her behalf. So what should you ask of her?"

I'm very aware that I'm being watched. That, in a way, I'm auditioning for the king of the most powerful kingdom in the Wethyrd Seas.

"I'll ask her to cut us a trail through the storm," I say. "She cuts a path through the snow for you all the time, right? I've noticed how little power it takes her to do that."

Mars leans forward. "Hardly any effort at all. Very good . . . Princess?"

My nose wrinkles. "In the short time I've known you, have I done or said anything *at all* that makes you think I want a title?"

He winks at Kyn. "I'm running out of ideas here."

"Stop thinking about things we can handle later," Kyn says.

"Good advice all around. You ready, sister?"

Winter's domain is so close now, the churned-up sea spray freckles my face and arms. I hear words on the wind, but they're strange, garbled.

"Something's got her riled up," I say. "There's something unnatural—"

"Unnatural is her natural state," Mars says, taking a step back, leaving me at the rail to stare down a storm that's strengthening by the moment. "Let's show Paradyia what real power looks like, yes?"

I nod.

"We're ready, Hawk," Mars calls. "Take us forward."

Behind me orders are given in Paradyian, and those whose presence is unnecessary begin to race for stairwells. Hatches are closed and a quiet readiness takes over the deck.

The great golden sails unfurl and the *Heraldic* lurches forward. Here we trade blue waters for black, and a disinterested ocean spirit for Winter. Winter who is guilty of many things, but never, ever indifference.

Rain lashes my face, pounds the deck, hard and cold and so familiar it feels like coming home. But there's something else on the wind, something...

"Now, Miss Quine. Before we lose a sailor."

I tamp down my irritation, stuff away my concerns about what else is going on out here, and I call for Winter.

She bucks and groans, and that empty spot in my chest burns cold as she shifts her attention to us, to Mars and me here on the *Heraldic*. The sky shakes and I have to grab hold of the railing to keep my feet. Hail drops like bullets onto the deck. Planks are damaged, sailors cry out.

I whisper a string of Kerce words into Winter's winds and though she whines at the order, a rumble splits the sky. She has to obey.

Overhead, the clouds part like a veil, taking their rains with them and leaving a carpet of glassy black ocean before us. As the sun explores this new pathway, rainbows of light shoot like arrows across the sky. Winter's granted us passage, but it's narrow and causing problems for the helmsman.

"The ship's fighting me!" he calls. "I can't keep her straight."

I doubt it's an enemy so innocuous as a ship. It's Winter who's fighting him and she has no right.

I call into the wind, blisters springing up on my lips as, inch by inch, Winter expands our passageway. She makes me pay for every word, every specific command. By the time our path is three times as wide as the *Heraldic*, my face stings and I can hardly move my mouth.

**I WILL MAKE YOU HATE ME**, she says. **FOR BRINGING THAT GOLDEN SHIP INTO MY WATERS, I WILL TEAR YOUR TONGUE TO SHREDS.**

Mostly she reserves such nasty threats for Mars. But she's angry the Paradyians have come. Not curious. Not mischievous. Not remotely interested in these new people. I feel her disdain, her outright disgust as she moans and spits.

**AND FOR WAKING THOSE DAMNABLE SHIV**, she continues, **I WILL MAKE YOU BLEED.**

*For waking who?*

"Mars Dresden!" the helmsman calls. "Your Winter is steering us into the storm! Get her off us."

The ship continues to move forward, but it's pushing right.

Winter laughs.

Mars leans forward, his words for me alone. "Have you an order, Miss Quine?"

"Stop calling me that." I look up, taking in the sails. Is she controlling our direction with her winds? It doesn't seem so. Is it the rudder? I have so little knowledge of ships and their many parts.

Kyn lays his hand over mine, shouts my name, but I have no answer. I don't know what she's doing.

"*Stiyee*," I say. "*Stiyee, stiyee, stiyee.*"

Winter howls in delight. She likes it when I'm lost for words.

"It's the Abaki," Mars says, disappointment dripping from his blistered lips. He might be hoping I'd take the lead, but he hasn't let me fight alone and the weight of his frustration is that much heavier. "They've got hold of the rudder."

"Mars, I don't know how . . . I don't have the words. How do I—"

"I'll do it. You keep that pathway open. Constant, specific commands. She'll forget if you let her." And with that, he swings over the railing, screaming into the wind, his torn shirt flapping. Against her will, Winter catches him with a kol-flecked gust, and he disappears toward the stern of the ship. The king gapes.

I'm turning back toward the prow when I see them—two Abaki, no three, climbing up over the starboard rail.

"Heads up," I call.

Sailors leap into motion. Some in red and some in blue, weapons strapped to their arms and legs. They shoot and swipe and take down the Abaki as they climb aboard.

Kyn fires and an Abaki spills backward into the sea. "How did you do it before, Sylvi? How did you keep them off the *Maree Vale*?" Panic fills his chest and there's something of Mars's disappointment there too.

There was a command, I think. But Winter's loud in my head, and there's something strange on the wind. Something that doesn't sound at all like her.

"Do you hear that?" I ask. "It's . . . it's like . . ."

But Kyn curses and fires his shotgun again. My ears ring with the sound and I realize Winter's taking advantage of my divided attention again. The path she's carved for us is beginning to shrink, to fold in on itself. The king's hand comes down on my shoulder and I jump.

"Don't worry about her monsters, Sessa. The soldiers will take care of that. You get us to shore."

I nod and get to work, reminding Winter of what I've

commanded her to do. I tell her to make the way clear, to keep our sails full, to keep the Abaki beneath the waves—yes, that's it! That's the command! I repeat it again and again, and I throw in an order or two about shutting her yap so I can think, but it's a lot to manage and suddenly I swoon, the pain making me ill. My energy wanes and my eyelids flicker like a candle.

My legs fold and I crack my knee against a metal post before Kyn grabs me and pulls me upright. He's hurting too, I feel my nausea in his gut, an ache in his chest as he lifts me. I grope for the railing hoping to take my weight off him.

"Let me help you," he says.

But I stumble away, slipping on the wet deck, sliding to my knees. "I'm fine. I just need a sec."

"Stop trying to protect me," he growls, but before he can kneel, he sees something I can't and he lifts his gun, aiming it at the main deck.

Winter tears it from his hands and flings it out to sea. She slaps his face and drives a hard wind into his chest that throws him backward into the ship's wheel. Pain sears my own body as Kyn's ribs crack.

*"Stíyee!"* I scream, scrambling upright, gasping, reaching for him. *"Stíyee lacro Kyn! Stíyee!"*

I KNOW WHAT YOU LOVE, Winter roars. AND I CAN TAKE IT WHENEVER I WANT TO.

Petulant child. Vindictive, monstrous . . .

A fire flares to life in my belly and my head tips back as the kol rages through me. There are words in the fire, words I've never been taught, a command I've never tried. But it feels powerful; it feels right. I open my mouth and the words scald my tongue as they fly into the sky.

One moment the world is chaos and the next it's silent. The black sea turns to glass and the rain dries up. Dead arms and legs fall to the deck, their magicked torsos whisked away to nothingness. The crew gapes and gasps.

I stumble toward Kyn. "Are you OK? I know you're not. I felt..."

Kyn catches me, holds me up. The pain verges on intolerable now, his and mine both, the frostbite eating away at my face.

Kyn's holding his ribs, sucking air between words as he takes in the stillness from horizon to horizon. "Fluxing Blys, snowflake. What did you do?"

"I don't... I'm not sure." I can't remember willing my tongue to say anything specific. I remember only the rage, the kol in my veins making it more than it ever ought to have been.

Gingerly, he lifts his hands over his head, stretching, leaning. "Gah, that hurts."

Yeah, it does.

"I'm sorry, I didn't know she was going to do that."

"You don't ever have to apologize for the things she does."

I step closer, lay a hand on his arm. "What order did I give, Kyn?"

He turns his gaze to the sea. "I couldn't tell you, snowflake; I don't speak Kerce. But it's like when Mars dropped the lightning, yeah? Out on the Seacliff Road."

It was *a lot* like that. The sudden stop. The quiet.

"Man overboard!" a sailor cries.

"There!" another shouts. "Grab hold. On the lift, mates! Haul him up!"

I turn toward the stern, but the king blocks my view, sputtering questions I can't answer. I try to peer around him, but there's a considerable bustle on the deck now, cursing and the like, orders flying, the ship's engine revving to life.

"Haul him over! There you go. We got him!"

And then steel-toed boots on the deck.

Flux. Mars.

Kyn grins through the pain. "Was he flying when . . . ?"

"I think so."

The grin widens.

The king turns, coughs. "Welcome aboard once again, Dresden. Would you like a towel?"

I see him now, climbing the stairs to the navigation deck. His sodden form slowly, deliberately coming into view, his shirt little more than a collar and seams. I'm still learning to read his face, but this is an expression he doesn't often wear. He's afraid. Whatever I've said, whatever I've done, it scared the most terrifying man I know.

He shrugs off the sailors who hauled him aboard, his black eyes on me.

"Mars—"

"Have you forgotten everything I taught you?"

"I don't think so. I hope not."

He leans on the staircase railing, his breath coming in great heaves. After a moment, he pushes off the rail and his hand flies toward me.

I flinch.

He laughs. A dry bark of a thing. "You're scared of *me*, are you?" He tugs the neckerchief from the collar of the helmsman and slaps it into my hand. "Your face is a mess."

It was instinct, thinking he'd hit me—nothing conscious—but I'm embarrassed. "Thank you," I mumble, pressing the silky cloth to my mouth.

"I hope you know me better than that," he says.

"I do. I just . . . Mars, what did I *say?*"

"What you said is not the point. *This* is what happens when you lose control. Revelation number five. Recite it for me, will you?"

"Emotion has no place in your commands to Winter. But I've been angry with her before, Mars—"

"I'm sure you have. And sometimes we get away with it. But when anger takes over, there's no knowing, is there?"

"No knowing what?"

"When you let your emotions have free rein, your demands become unreasonable, impossible for Winter to execute. So she just . . . shuts down."

The buzz on the deck has grown louder, the captain getting us underway, taking advantage of the relative calm.

The king lingers nearby, his eyebrows bunched together, his white hair tousled. "What made you so angry, Sessa? Was it when she threw Kyndel here into the wheel?"

I nod. "She knew if she attacked Kyn, it would hurt me. She said . . ." I shake my head, unwilling to share Winter's threat. "The words were just there, burning me from the inside out."

"What words?" the king asks.

"Kerce words. I can't remember their shape or sound. I was

angry, and the words were so hot. They needed to be said, so I opened my mouth and said them."

The king purses his lips and nods. "I too have done such a thing."

"Next time your rage wants to speak," Mars says, "keep your mouth shut."

"I can do that."

"Ah!" The king lays a hand on my shoulder, squeezes. "Careful what you promise, Sessa. Such things are not always so easy."

I offer him a pathetic smile before taking a step forward, my hands light on the deck rail. There's something familiar in the prickling silence and I'm reminded of all the nights Winter pounded away at Whistletop until the electricity went, laughing as she dragged the village into darkness. "It's like she blew a breaker."

"As consequences go, it could be worse," the king says.

Fog rises from the black waves, rolling gently over the ship as a chill climbs into the atmosphere. The *Heraldic* has covered a great distance in a short time, and now her engines push us forward, the wind all but gone.

"She's still dangerous," Mars cautions. "She's simply unusable for a time."

He steps up to the rail on my right side, and with Kyn on my left, with Hawken Valthor and his sailor-soldiers all around, we take in the mountainous silhouette of Layce suspended between us and the horizon.

A frenetic noise pushes through the sky. It's the same sound I heard before, but without Winter's voice to confuse things, I can hear it more clearly now. It's a cacophony, with spiked edges, and something else. Something that reminds me of busy nights at Drypp's tavern.

"Is that the ship," Kyn asks, "or . . . ?"

"It's not the ship," Mars says, cocking his ear, listening hard. "It's coming from the isle."

"I heard it earlier," I say. "Near the edge of Winter's domain. But I think you're right. It's coming from Layce. Maybe it got caught up in her winds before, carried out to us."

"But what is it?" Mars asks, thoroughly confused.

I feel the moment Kyn figures it out. The realization drops through him like a lightning bolt, clean and bright, burning away all question.

"Voices," Kyn says.

Mars casts me a skeptical look. "I don't think—"

"It is," Kyn insists. "That sound's not the wind. Or the ship. It's—it's voices. Thousands of them."

"You're so sure," I say. "How?"

But his eyes are frantic and I'm not sure he hears. I give it a moment and try again. "Kyn?"

"Can't you hear them?" His voice catches. "They're speaking Shiv, yeah? They're trapped!"

"Trapped where?" Mars is frustrated, clearly not used to being the one without the answers.

"Beneath the Desolation of Ice."

I'm stunned silent.

Kyn looks first at Mars and then at me, a tear spilling onto the red rock of his cheekbone.

"It's a trick," I say. "It has to be."

Mars's black eyes narrow. "Kyndel, friend. What are you hearing *exactly*?"

"I'm catching only pieces. Fragments of what they're saying. But I'm telling you, it's the Shiv people. The ones who were in the pool when Winter took the isle."

"No," I say. "That's not possible. Winter *knows* we're coming. She *knows* that means her time is almost done. It has to be her."

"Snowflake—"

"No. Listen. Those people have been buried for three hundred years. Why would we hear them now?"

Even as I say it, I remember Winter's words to me just moments ago.

*"For waking those damnable Shiv, I will make you bleed."*

She's a liar, she is, but she was frantic when we pushed into her waters, loud, her own tantrum swallowing theirs. Maybe she didn't wake them after all.

Maybe . . .

Maybe I did.

# CHAPTER 10

A SWARM OF REBELS MEETS US AT THE DOCK, all of them half panicked at seeing the *Heraldic*'s approach. All of them covering their ears.

We're nearly on top of the Desolation here at Queen's Point, and the voices are everywhere. A great communal wail that hangs over the camp like a storm cloud.

Kyn was right. It's Shiv voices we're hearing. The sound grew louder as we closed in on the isle, individual voices breaking free at times, the Shiv intonation clear but impossible for me to understand. It's a great keening to my ears though. A sadness that spreads through my bones. A thousand times worse than a bell.

I need to get out to the Desolation, need to touch it. I tell Mars this and he nods.

"As soon as we can," he says. "But we must speak to Desy first."

Mars understands the Shiv voices more than I do. A word here, a phrase there, but he hasn't Kyn's patience. He can't separate one voice from another, and he can't silence them the way he does Winter. The lack of control has him brooding and waspish.

I'm not much better. I can't stop wondering if our mother's voice is in there somewhere. Is she crying out? Is she in pain? And if she is, is that justice? Have I any right to wish her peace?

I find myself craving Winter's unceasing chatter, the sound of rain splashing into puddles, hail pounding down, a blizzard even. Anything at all to drown out these voices. But Winter's still unusable. And I could curse her for being so weak.

When the rebels unleash their questions on us—why have we returned in a Paradyian ship, is that the king, what happened to the *Maree Vale*, why are we hearing these voices—Mars takes my elbow and leads me away. We duck under the awning of the camp's make-shift garage and watch the spectacle. Paradyian soldiers drift into camp, followed by their supplies—weapons, ammunition, snow gear. The rebels part for them, sizing them up, pointing them on their way.

Hawken decided to leave his royal court on board with a few soldiers for protection. They'll stay belowdecks and away from the kol. The rest of his soldiers plan to bunk down in the cabin Dakk's crew used when they were here. It's farthest from the sea, but nearer to the Desolation. It's the best we could do, but I don't imagine they'll sleep much.

Through the window of the garage, I catch a glimpse of the Sylver Dragon and her brand-new windshield. They've put a lot of work into her while we've been away and I'm itching to get behind the wheel.

Mars rubs at his ears, angry, annoyed. "I'm conflicted, sister. I find myself hating the Shiv for this ruckus, but that feels . . ."

"Wrong?"

"Yes. Wrong. We're on their side." A great shiver shakes his body, his chest and back still exposed. I'm cold in my damp sweater and sodden boots, but he's virtually shirtless and has been wearing the same wet clothes for two days now.

"You're going to freeze to death," I say, cracking open the garage door and tugging a spare coat off a peg on the wall: a charcoal-gray parka with flannel lining and patches on the elbows. It's one of two I was given when we first arrived at camp all those weeks ago. The second is floating out at sea somewhere; I'll have to dig another out of storage. "Here."

"It's very difficult to demand Winter keep her hands to herself when she's unable to comply," he says, slipping his arms into the coat. "Thank you."

"Looks good. Less imposing than the leather anyway."

"Is that supposed to be a compliment?" He zips the coat, running his hands over the buttons, the pockets.

"When Winter wakes, she'll be raging."

"I'm counting on it. It'll take one of her storms to drown out these voices. What's this?" His long pale fingers withdraw a gold chain, Maree Vale's triangular medallion dangling from it and the curio at its center broken.

"I forgot I left it there," I say, sending it spinning with a flick of my finger.

"You forgot?" His voice catches in disbelief. "About the cursed medallion of your dead mother."

"I can't wear it when I work. We were taking the Dragon's engine out and—"

He lifts it higher, incredulous. "This has been around our mother's neck! It has traveled from Paradyia to Kerce to Shiv Island. It has been in the great pool!"

"It gets caught on things," I say, sheepish. "*You* wear it. You don't . . . work."

"That's true," he says. "But Shyne wanted you to have it."

"Yes, well. I broke your beaded necklace medicine bag thing. Call it even."

"You're sure?" he asks, but he can't take his eyes off the medallion.

I pull it from his hands and drape the chain over his neck. "There. Done."

His hand flutters over the triangle and he presses it to his chest. "Thank you."

A change ripples through the crowd and I turn. Three Paradyian guards escort Farraday Wrex into the camp. His hands are bound behind him, and there are three golden rifles pointed at his head.

"Why not leave him on the ship?" I ask.

"That was the Paradyian position as well. Hawken insists that no one on board the *Heraldic* is disloyal to him, that everyone has been thoroughly questioned and their histories investigated, but until we know who Wrex was in contact with in the Paradyian court, we need to keep him where we can see him."

Wrex is escorted past, and he acknowledges us with a nod. "Come visit, rig driver."

They should have chained his tongue.

"Our people aren't trained soldiers," I say to Mars, "and our jail isn't nearly as secure as their brig."

"They'd be disheartened to hear you say that. It's a risk, but it's the only risk I'm willing to take right now. It hardly matters how strong that cell is, if the traitor loyal to Wrex has a key."

The guards meet two of our rebel fighters in the courtyard and they hand him over. I resist the urge to comment on the obvious size difference between our rebels and the Paradyian guards, or even the stark difference between Wrex and our men. Instead, I watch in silence as he's prodded into the gathering hall. They'll take him to the back room and lock him up next to Bristol Mapes, our only prisoner here at Queen's Point. The idea of those men trading stories churns something sour in my gut.

"Sylvi!" Lenore peels away from the rebels who cornered her as soon as she stepped off the ship. Her hands are pressed tightly to her ears, shutting out the voices, but her face is alight. "There's news!"

"From Hex Landing?"

"And from the Stack. Come." She wraps her arm around my waist and pulls me toward the gathering hall, so fast we're nearly running, my soft leather boots sliding on the slick cobbles.

I reach out as we pass Kyn, tugging him with us. He's been quiet since the voices began but he shuffles forward now, groaning at the pain in his ribs, his golden sandals sticking in the mud.

"What is it?" he asks.

"The scouts have returned."

"Good," he says. "They've been gone way too long."

There's a bottleneck at the door and Mars and Dakk are buffeted up behind us. Off to the right, Katsy and Kree play in a patch of muddy, trodden snow, our misadventure on the sea forgotten. It's a novelty for them, the snow, but they'll have to enjoy it quickly. Blys is here, our rainy season, and as soon as Winter returns to her old self, her showers will melt much of this away.

When, at last, we're smashed into the gathering hall, I find myself grateful for the lack of a coat. A fire is blazing at the center of the room, and the air is warm and damp. I'm wedged tightly against the back wall, Kyn on one side and Leni on the other. The fragrance of cut timbers, musty furs, sweat-dampened leathers, and the scorched honey of twyl chewing gum combine, all of them welcome reminders that we are, in fact, back on Layce.

It's broken, but it's home.

The walls offer some protection from the cries of the Desolation, but it's far from quiet in here. Rebels fill the room. They sit side by side on benches, cross-legged atop tables, sprawled on the floor. All of them waiting to hear what the scouts have to say. Shovels and hammers are clenched in fisted hands, axes are propped against the wall, guns holstered. They were working, most of them, when the meeting was called. Gathering twyl, expanding the dock, reinforcing our defenses. It seems only those out on watch are absent from the gathering.

Mars has made his way to the front and stands face-to-face with a tiny woman, her mouth moving quickly. She has a lined, wind-chapped face and dark red hair that's streaked with gray. After a moment Mars nods his understanding and steps back.

The woman turns to address the crowd. "Quiet, please. Quiet."

Her gentle voice is not quite loud enough to carry, and the room continues to buzz. Mars drags over a round from the wood pile and offers her a hand. She takes it and steps up, her wool skirt covering all but the tips of two very colorful boots.

She doesn't have to say anything then. Her intent to speak is enough. Desy Page has the respect of everyone in the gathering hall. She earned it a thousand times over by the actions of her youth, breaking workers out of the Stack, whisking them away to safety. They say she knows the Shivering Forest better than the Majority overseers that patrol it.

She's at least part Shiv, as seen in the crystalline palms of her hands now upturned to the crowd. The room quiets, and she opens her mouth to speak but closes it again as the door to the room flies open. A gust of wind rushes inside, laden with Desolation voices.

Winter's waking, I think. Her stretch ripples through the air, but she's not the one I'm concerned about just now. The Paradyian king stands at the door, his wife's arm slipped gently through his.

They duck inside, both of them too tall for the doorway, and I see her for the first time. She's lovely, though clearly sick. The hollow at her neck and those in her cheeks are deep, and beneath her eyes, there's something like bruising. But her golden eyes are fire, and her lips are bright red—a result of the cold or her fever, I cannot say. Her curls, as dark and rich as chocolate, are arranged carefully atop her head. Together with her husband, she makes her way through the hushed whispers of the rebels, and by the time they've reached the front of the room, a bench has cleared. They sit.

Their guards hover awkwardly outside the door, hunching so they can see inside.

"No, no," Desy says, her hand waving at the guards. "In or out. I can't hear with all those voices."

"Go," Hawken tells them. "We are fine here."

They step back and the door swings shut.

"There. That's better. Welcome," Desy says, inclining her head to the king and queen. "Truly. I want you to know how welcome you are here in our camp."

She doesn't apologize for the inglorious nature of our humble lodgings or for the voices that have turned our skies to chaos. She doesn't pander to their power. Desy is wiser than that.

"I've important news that perhaps you can speak to, Your Majesty," she continues. "Three of our scout teams have returned from their wanderings with a staggering amount of information. We're just starting to sort through it all, and we are still awaiting Brewzer's return, but there are two very important items that we want to put to you with some haste. Firstly, there's this: It seems Layce is not the only isle rising up against the Majority."

The room breaks into excited titters.

"This is true," Hawken says, his booming voice too loud for the small space. He realizes and adjusts, his next words not quite so forceful. "Many of the Majority's conquests have reached out for help. For soldiers, for weapons. For food."

"Food?" Lenore whispers.

Desy leans forward on her toes. "Might I inquire as to your role—"

"We've not yet entered the fray," Hawken says. "We do not seek out war with the Majority as a rule, but they have overstepped again and again, and now, their own subjects are rising up. This is good. This is how it should be. The people themselves must decide who will govern them. It is the way with all great societies."

There's truth about his words and a lot of good there, but something in the way they're woven together has the hairs on my arms standing at attention. It seems Desy hears it too, and her head tilts sideways.

"Very good," she says, with a nod of deference. And then to the crowd. "This news alone perhaps would not offer us much to build upon, but when coupled with the information Sayth here has to share with us, I think you will see that a good many things are tipping in our favor. Sayth?"

Sayth has one of those ageless faces—she's older than me and younger than Desy, but that's about all I can figure. That and this: She's not a woman I would ever want to cross. Not much taller than I am, not much bigger, but she worked in the mines for years and her arms show it, roped with muscle and constantly on display. Like Kyn, like Desy, she's Shiv.

Her violet eyes are wide and round, and the stone on her face matches, both in color and shape. A giant amethyst tear leaks from the inside corner of each eye, covering both cheeks in the most asymmetrical display I've ever seen. Her elbows and the tops of her hands are also covered in the same jeweled stone, the soles of her feet as well. A tidbit I noticed when she peeled off her boots and went sliding across the Desolation.

She stands and reaches for a leather bag tied to her hip. I crane to look but catch little more than the top of her violet hair.

"Up, up," Desy says, gesturing with her hand. "So they can all see."

"Fair enough," Sayth says, climbing up onto her own bench, turning to face the crowd. "You all are going to love this." She holds up the leather bag and reaches inside. When she withdraws her hand, her palm is full of black powder, enough kol to throw the whole room into hallucinations. She flattens her hand and blows the powder into the air in one great exhale.

Curses and cries of disbelief echo around the room. A man reaches out and grabs Sayth's wrist, trying to stop whatever it is she's doing, but she plants a boot in his chest and pushes him off. The women on her right and left, members of her scouting team, burst into giggles.

"Relax," she says. "It's synthetic. Not an ounce of actual kol in the whole lot."

The collective gasp is different now, full of awe and confusion, curiosity even.

Mars steps closer, his eyes wide, his hand suspended midair. "Where did it come from?"

"We intercepted this batch on the road through the Shivering Forest. They're manufacturing it somewhere near Hex Landing and cutting the kol with this man-made look-alike at the Stack."

Now the room explodes. Sayth dissolves into laughter alongside her companions, emptying the bag over Mars's head. I expect an outburst, but his only reaction is to pinch the dust that's landed on his arm, rub it between his fingers and bring it before his eyes for a closer look.

Desy lifts her hands and the room jerks into an unsettled stillness.

"Why would they do that?" someone calls.

"Well, I suppose there are many practical reasons for cutting the kol," Desy explains. "It lessens the potency. Brings in more coin for less labor."

"But that's not why they're doing it," Mars says. At first I think it's a rhetorical statement, but then he turns, and with his hands cupped before him, shimmering with black powder, his eyes fall on Hawken. "You were right."

"Of course I was right," Hawken says. "It gives me very little pleasure to have come by the information as I did, but it is good, I think, that I can confirm it for you."

"Confirm what?" I ask.

"They're running out of kol," Mars says.

"Who's running out of kol?" Leni asks.

Mars dusts his hands off. "Tell them, Hawk."

The Paradyian king stands and adjusts his robe. He makes to step up onto his bench, and then pauses and cracks a smile. The intense silence of the room breaks, and laughter moves like a ripple through the space. He's likeable, this king, and though I have my doubts about his motivations, I can't help but grin.

Hawken Valthor replaces his foot on the ground, tall enough to not need any sort of platform. He addresses the room with the confidence of a man who's been doing this his entire life.

"As you may know, kol is outlawed on Paradyia. There are two very prominent reasons for this. Firstly, we do not trade with the Majority. With individuals on these isles, at times, yes, but with your Majority overseers, no. And since they have an exclusive hold on your most valuable commodity, it is not something we, as a kingdom, have ever sought to acquire.

"Secondly, we do not trust this mineral. It is volatile and

though it has shown to do good, we have no need of an addictive, madness-inducing toxin.

"This, of course, is the official position of our kingdom. It is not, however, the position of every court official. Your kol has been a subject of debate within some factions and I discovered only recently that it had become more than just talk." His face hardens. "Not long ago, we found that kol has been making its way to our shores. It was not nearly the shock it should have been—to me, yes, but my advisers had heard tell of it. For some time, it seems, someone close to the palace has been trading our secrets for kol."

The silence is thick. If he expected shock or sympathy from us, he's greatly mistaken. We're rebels every one of us, and we know better than most that even the most generous rulers court disloyalty.

Mars steps up next to the king. "This is not news to us, is it, friends? We've known about this spy for some time, yes? It was information we were on our way to deliver."

"And for that I am grateful, though the traitor has already been dealt with. He and those who knew what he was doing are facing consequences back home as we gather here tonight. I would like to tell you he acted alone, but I cannot confirm such a thing. Even now, my court undergoes internal scrutiny as we seek to understand all that I've missed in these trying times." His eyes glaze over, sadness lingering there. His wife reaches up and takes his hand, blinking up at him through her own tears.

"But what's this about the kol running out?" Kyn asks. "Shiv Island is kol, yeah? How is it possible for it to run out?"

"They've overmined the isle," Mars says. "The kol won't ever be truly gone, but the cost to sink new mines is exorbitant, and it's coin they can't spare if they're to put down rebellions across the Wethyrd Seas."

"I believe it," says a voice somewhere near the far corner of the room. "Every word. It matches what we heard in Hex Landing."

"Up, up," Desy says, turning, gesturing.

Felyx is sprawled on the floor, but at Desy's request he stands, adjusts the holster slung around his waist. He's neither Shiv nor Kerce: He was born and raised on Layce and grew up working his family's farm, somewhere along the northern coast, growing much of the twyl supplied to the Majority's kol miners.

With the Majority as their largest customer, they prospered. But one year, Blys lingered weeks longer than expected, and the rains brought a landslide that sent half their crop into the sea. Felyx's family failed to meet their quota that season and it was all the provocation the Majority needed. They seized the farm, moving another man in to direct their operations, a man with ties to the council. Felyx's family had farmed that land for nearly a century, and suddenly they were homeless, begging for work on land that had once been theirs.

His father collapsed in the fields that first week, and when Felyx found him, he was frozen solid, his hand wrapped around a stock of twyl. It wasn't many days later that his mother stepped off the northern cliffs. Born and raised by the system that killed his parents, Felyx might be the most ardent rebel among us.

Felyx tugs off his woolen hat. "The Majority seems to be consolidating their operations. Equipment, miners, the whole lot."

"What do you mean the whole lot?" Mars asks.

"They're building barracks in Hex Landing to house an influx of miners. Near done, best I can tell. It's a right mess, them trying to seal up anything with these rains, and the workers are worn thin. They'll tell you all you want to know for a hot plate and a cold beer."

"They're just miners though," someone says. "Respectfully, how much can they actually know?"

Felyx bobs his head. "Rumors and happenings only, you're right. No one's bothered to fill them in on the details, but they're expecting a couple hundred workers to be filling those barracks in three weeks' time. A rig driver we talked to was on his way to pick up a trailer full of miners from the Blue Rock Kolface just south of the Serpentine, and he'd just returned from delivering a couple dozen miners to the Landing from some little start-up southeast of North Bend."

"If they've abandoned the Blue Rock . . ."

"We're going to need to confirm . . ."

"Best way to confirm is to reach out to our people in the Port of Glas," Mars says. "Someone there should be able to get close enough to the council to find out what's going on."

"Yes, good. We'll do that. It will take some time." Desy's hands are knotted before her, but she's fighting to keep a grin off her face. "If they truly are consolidating their resources—"

If the Majority is investing everything they've got in the mines at Hex Landing, they've given us a target. We can do a lot of damage if we hit them there.

"They'll be armed," Kyn says. "Heavily. We'd risk injuring a lot of innocent people. Most of the miners aren't there by choice."

"No, you're right. We can't hit them blindly," I say. "But if we can destroy the operations there, if we can render the mines at Hex Landing useless—"

"Or even cost prohibitive," Desy says.

A buzz goes around the room as the thought is considered. What happens if the Majority decides it isn't financially feasible to mine the kol?

"The bastards may just question the value of staying here on Layce," Felyx says.

And if we can make them willing to leave, we may have found a way to sidestep war.

# CHAPTER 11

NEW ASSIGNMENTS ARE HANDED OUT AND the meeting adjourns.

Those of us who made up the crew of the *Maree Vale* have been ordered to get some rest, but there's no way I'm sleeping with the cries of the Shiv still ringing out. Mars and I have plans to see the Desolation anyway. I've just pried myself away from the wall when Winter rouses herself with a howl. The sky rumbles and rain crashes down.

Hard.

Loud.

Not quite loud enough to swallow the voices whole, but loud enough to dampen their effect.

The room erupts in celebration, and I feel the relief that wraps Kyn. "Oh, thank Begynd."

"I really do think you're going to have to thank Winter this time," I say.

"Not a chance." But he's smiling and it's been hours and

hours since he's done that. It does something pleasant to my insides.

"You want to come with Mars and me? We're heading to the Desolation."

He shakes his head, complicated emotions rising at the thought, seeping into my chest. "Nah. You go. I need to talk to Desy."

"About?"

"I'm worried about Brewzer. He was tasked with informing Shyne about the Paradyians and war and all that."

I feel the fear ripple through him. "But he knows Shyne, right?"

"He does, yeah. Sold them those snowmobiles a couple Rymes back. But Shyne . . . who knows what he's capable of right now. I want to know if Desy's heard anything. That's all."

"Miss Quine, are you ready?" Mars leans against the door-frame, trying very hard to be casual, but I know he's dying to see what's going on out at the Desolation.

I ignore him.

"Just so I know," Kyn says, "what are you expecting him to call you?"

"I'll know it when I hear it."

"Miss Quine?"

"Not my name," I call.

"Oh, I'm sorry, Your Highness," he answers, raising his voice, playing to the curious crowd. "I thought we'd finished that game. Sylver Quine wants a new name, friends. Any suggestions?"

"Go," Kyn says with a laugh. "Before they start tossing out ideas, yeah? I'll catch you in a bit."

He leaves me standing there, and there's nothing for me to do but turn to Mars.

"Oh, you *can* move your feet," he says.

"When I want to. You have quite the theatrical flair, you know?"

He bows. "When I want to."

Before we get out the door, a soft tap on my shoulder has me turning. Queen Fyeeri Valthor stands before us. Even frail, she towers over me. Whatever sickness has done to her, it has not bowed her low. Her husband stands at her side.

"Before Hawken and I return to the ship for the night, I would very much like to see the Desolation of Ice." Her voice is deeper than I would have guessed. It paints her differently somehow, more regal, more vital. Strange that voices have that power.

"We're heading there now," Mars says. "Would you care to join us?"

But her eyes are on me. "We've not met, have we? Not officially."

Her scrutiny dries my throat. "No, we haven't."

"Fyeeri Valthor of Paradyia," she says, reaching out a hand.

"Sylver . . . Quine of Whistletop," I answer shaking her hand like I would any trucker's.

Mars grins.

"Should we . . . I can pull the Dragon around," I say. "Would that be more comfortable than—?"

"Hawken and Fyeeri are not here for rigs and roads," Mars says, taking Fyeeri's arm and leading her out the door. Hawken and I follow. For just a moment we linger under the overhang, Winter's tantrum splashing our feet. "They're here for magic and wonder, yes? For proof that we can do what we've promised?" Fyeeri inclines her head. "And they certainly don't need to wait for you to pull the Dragon around."

Quick, and with an elegance only he can accomplish, Mars conjures a breeze that lifts all four of us into the air.

"Not too far," I shout. "Kyn, remember?" Going *to* the Desolation is one thing. Crossing it will put too much distance between Kyn and me.

Mars acknowledges my concern with a nod, his mouth busy spitting Kerce commands at Winter, doing something I never thought to do. He's ordering her to rotate her storm around us. Here in the eye, it's quieter than I would have expected, dryer. And we fly up over the camp, out toward the Desolation.

The Kol Mountains in the distance have already begun to shed the thickest layers of their icy coat, but their peaks shine on, gleaming like a grin against the gray sky.

Mars can have the sea. The mountains will always be my home.

Across from me, the king's eyes are firmly shut, his mouth moving, his arms wrapped tightly around his wife. Her eyes, however, are wide open, tears streaming as she takes in the Desolation coming into view below us. There's joy in the lines of her face, and I have a thought: Some of us were simply meant to fly.

The light changes and though my first instinct is to check the cloud cover, I realize that's not it at all. Beneath us, the ice glows, a sylver-blue light that radiates up and out. At first I think we've flown too far, that we're over the fount now, too far from Kyn to offer him the protection he needs, but a more careful look and I realize we haven't gone far at all. The flow has simply grown.

Where once there seemed to be a simple sylver vein visible

through the ice, now there are many: a complex of streams below the surface, bright and far too illuminating. From this vantage point, I can see the shapes of those frozen beneath the surface.

Mars starts our descent and I nearly stop him. I've no desire to be any closer, but maybe it's best. Maybe the king and queen need to see what this place of miracles has become.

As the cyclone that holds us aloft quiets, the voices grow louder. Mars changes tack and sets the storm spinning again. A noisy silence is better than a weeping crowd.

Toes and then heels and we're down, all four of us settled on the surface. The storm whips around us, flinging the rain and the voices far into the distance, but I find the enclosed space oppressive here on the ice. I whisper a command that opens the eye, widens the space inside. Mars nods his approval.

"Amazing," the queen says, her hands trembling as she pulls her fur-lined cloak more tightly about her shoulders. "I imagine your Dragon is also quite the ride, of course, but—"

"It's hard to beat flying. I understand."

"Is this not a desecration, Valthor? Our feet upon the ice?" With one hand she holds her cloak closed, and with the other, she grabs hold of her husband's.

"So say the stories. What do you say, Dresden? Are we desecrating the graves of the dead?"

"The Shiv believe so," Mars answers.

"And you?" the queen asks him. "Do you not believe as they do?"

"In some things, very much. But not in this." His words are firm and clear, convincing. "Everything we do now will be to undo this great wrong. We need your army, and you need to see the great pool before we discuss strategy. I understand that, and I believe the Shiv would too."

The queen's gaze meets mine and she lifts her perfectly arched brows.

*Do I agree?*

I crouch, run my bare hand over the ice. Far below, I see the shadowed form of a person, their face upturned, tendrils of dark hair frozen midwave. It's their souls then, crying out. Not their mouths. I don't know how that's possible, but the magic of Begynd was strong once. Perhaps it is strong still, magnifying the voices of the Shiv, throwing them into the air, reminding us that we can do right by these people.

"It's not a comfortable place to stand," I say. "But I think Mars is right. If I were buried beneath the ice, I wouldn't care how you freed me, so long as the job got done."

"Let's speak of that then," the queen says, sliding her arm through her husband's. "I know the stories about Winter and Begynd. Not nearly so well as my husband, but enough to know that the shipwreck took many of the Kerce. I know it was the Shiv people who nursed the survivors. And I know of your mother, Maree Vale." Her gaze drops to the ice. "I know what she did. I wonder, is she still down there, do you think? Frozen like the others?"

My throat closes over, and I have to wonder why. I've no real connection to my mother beyond the fact that she bore me. I look to Mars. Mars who knew her, who loved her before and after a wrong that doomed the entire isle.

"I couldn't say," he says. "I've thought about it, of course. For years, really, if you added up all the hours. The not knowing nearly drove me mad on several occasions, but I have no answer. I would like to believe so. That is the best, most honest answer I can conjure. But the magic Winter used was strong, the kol potent, and mother was already very weak. When I think back on how she looked when she left . . ." His eyes trail away, and I know what he's seeing. He's seeing his child self, and his mother stroking his cheek as she passed her entire kingdom into his care. ". . . when she left me at High Pass, I could hardly believe she made it down the mountain."

"Your Winter took advantage of her," the queen says. "What a wretched spirit she is."

*"Your Winter?"* I ask. "Why do you call her that?"

"Because she is not *my* winter. The winter spirit who has claimed Paradyia as her own visits our land just once every year. She may not be as beautiful as your Winter," the queen acknowledges, lifting her face to the mountains beyond me. "But she is content to stay for a short visit only, blessing us with her gifts and then departing to do the same elsewhere. Your Winter"—she lifts her palms to the sky—"this spirit belongs to Shiv Island. She is yours until you tell her otherwise. So that is what I want to know, children of Maree Vale. What will it take to pry your Winter's fingers from Begynd's Pool so these tortured souls can be set free, and I may be healed in his waters?"

As I fumble for an answer that would not quite be a lie, but would most certainly not be the entire truth, I realize how difficult it will be to keep things from the king and queen. They will not be so easily tricked with fancy words, and they have at least some legitimate claim to the truth of things. But if we tell them the whole of it, if we tell them we cannot be sure of what will happen when this pool thaws—

"We tell Winter to go," Mars says. "As simple as that."

"And you're certain you've the power to do it?" the king confirms. "The two of you?"

Mars balks. "I realize we are not great in stature, Hawk—"

"I mean no disrespect," he says. "You have proven your power—both of you—in miraculous demonstrations. But I can't help but wonder—"

"Worry," the queen says. "You can't help but worry."

"I am certain we can rid the isle of Winter," Mars says. "What I am not so certain of is how the island will respond to such a command."

"The people of Shiv Island, you mean?" Hawken clarifies.

"That I can guess at. No, it's the land beneath the ice that concerns me. In time, it will heal, and those living here will rebuild, but the sudden absence of ice will have consequences on the land itself. The heat of Begynd will assault the ground from below, while Sola's rays will rain down from above, melting the ice and snow."

"Avalanches? You worry about avalanches?"

"Perhaps," Mars says with a shrug. "Or perhaps the worst of Winter is evaporated with her."

"Many of our roads are not maintained here," I say, "not even paved like they are in Paradyia, certainly not our mountain highways. We depend on the island freezing. If the ice melts entirely, the roads become impossible to drive."

"Even with our war machines?" the queen asks, turning to

her husband, whose eyes are narrowed, a rebuttal forming on his lips.

But Mars has a faster tongue than he does. "It's impossible to know, my lady. That's the truth of it. We will not know the severity of the consequences until the deed is done." A brief pause and then, "Which is why we must have time."

I don't think the king could squint any harder. "Time to tell those who must be told. To prepare them."

I clear my throat. "And time to rid the isle of the Majority."

Silence hangs in the air for a moment and then the queen laughs lightly, her laughter turning into something darker, more severe, hacking and gasping. "Oh dear," she says, her delicate hand coming away from lips stained with fresh blood, stark against the whiteness that surrounds us. "I wonder if I have that time to give you."

"Absolutely not!" The king is more certain, far more adamant. "We do *this* first. She must be first." He takes the clean cloth Mars holds out and presses it to his wife's lips. "And then we fight the Majority. You will have Paradyia's armies on your side, Mars Dresden. Frozen or not, we will rid the island of your oppressors."

"I have it now," the queen says, taking the cloth from her husband. "Thank you, Hawken."

"You promise to use your war machines?" I ask the king.

"Yes! Of course!"

"And your highly advanced guns? Guns that will be fired at the Stack and in the mine yards where the Majority protects its interests with their own weapons?"

"Most certainly!"

"And in the villages where our children play? And on the mountaintops where the Shiv make their home? And in the Port of Glas where unarmed workers—"

The king pounds a fist into his palm. "We are not unfeeling warlords, Sylver Quine. You know this. You know our reputation. We take precautions, always."

"I'm sure you do. But what if we can break the Majority without killing innocents?"

The king's face softens. "That is not how war works, child."

"But what if the goal isn't war?"

The king points a finger at Mars. "You brought me here to make war, did you not?"

"I did, yes. But . . . my sister has concerns."

The king reddens and I worry he'll boil over, so I speak quickly, stepping closer, wanting him to truly listen.

"We still need your help, Hawken. But what if instead of war, your resources and your army helped us make this island undesirable to the Majority?"

The king sputters, but it's his wife who speaks, pulling the cloth away from her mouth.

"You're speaking of the kol," she says.

"Yes. If, as the scouts say, the Majority is all in at Hex Landing, let's figure out how to make that mine useless to them. Let's bankrupt the bastards."

The king takes my hands in his, his golden eyes full of fatherly concern. "Listen to me, child, I know you have endured much. But now you have at your disposal the Paradyian army. The Wethyrd Seas have never seen our like, I assure you. Even without roads, we can destroy your oppressors in short order."

"Not without sacrificing innocent lives."

The king pinches the bridge of his nose between two fingers. "I have been involved in intricate operations like you're suggesting. There is a place for them, I grant you. But they take more than just *time* or scouting reports. You must have someone on the inside. Someone who knows the operation and who can tell you how to kill it."

"I know that," I say, my mind latching onto his words, an idea forming. "I do."

The queen stands a little taller at that. "You have someone on the inside then?"

Mars crosses his arms. "I can't promise—"

"Of course we do." The idea has hold of me now. It won't just spare us war: it would also allow Mars to make good on another promise he's made. "That's what we're trying to tell you. We have a man on the inside. Would we have suggested such a course otherwise?"

"Who?" the king asks, suspicious.

"What would you do with a name, Hawken?" Mars is clearly trying to bail me out.

But I'm all in now. I don't need to be bailed out. "His name is Macks Trestman. He works in the refinery at the Stack."

"A leader of men, then?" the king inquires. "He has built up a movement inside?"

"Not at all," Mars says, his tone sardonic. "He's a kol addict with an academic streak."

"He's a genius," I insist. "Recruited by the Majority to design a pump system to keep the mines dewatered."

"I thought you said he worked in the refinery at the Stack?"

"He does now," I say. "He started at Hex Landing, but after his wife died, he developed an addiction to the kol, and when he attacked an overseer, his at-will employment status was terminated and he became an indentured worker. They moved him to hard labor then."

"How did his wife die?" the queen asks.

"The kol," I say. "It drove her mad. There are different accounts, but she wasn't herself when she passed. That's all I know of it."

The queen turns her face to Mars, her eyes working him over, scrutinizing his every feature. "Why did you not tell us of this before? Or mention this man in the gathering hall, with all your rebels in one place?"

"I nearly did," Mars says, waving a hand casually. "And then your husband reminded us all that spies are only found out once they've spoiled things. We cannot afford for Mr. Trestman's role in our plan to become public knowledge. A small crew is a fast crew."

"How fast?" the king asks.

"Give us two weeks," Mars says.

The king explodes. "Two weeks!"

"One week," the queen says, pressing the cloth to her lips once again. "I can give you seven days. I think."

I glance at Mars and his black gaze meets mine. I can't tell if he despises me for what I've gotten us into or if he thinks the plan is as brilliant as I do.

"Seven days," I say, wondering if that's enough time. "That will make it High Blys, actually." The midpoint of Blys is a festival day for the Shiv. I can't remember what exactly they celebrate, but it's one of their two holy days, and somehow that seems appropriate. "If we haven't convinced the Majority to abandon Layce by then, we send Winter away and your war machines do the rest."

I'm not convinced the king will agree to anything of the sort, but it's the best, most convincing offer we have to make. I hold my breath as he decides.

The queen reaches out and takes her husband's hand. "I will make it seven more days, Hawken. If this Macks Trestman can spare these people a war, we should try."

The king examines her face, lifting a hand to her cheek and running his thumb along her chin tenderly. "You're certain? You have a week left in you?"

"I do," she says, her words firm.

It's a moment before the king nods, lifting her thin fingers to his lips and pressing them there.

"One week then." His eyes never leave her face.

# CHAPTER 12

"WHERE DID YOU GET THESE?" I GAPE AT A
row of shiny new ice bikes lined up against a wall in
the garage. These are nothing like Old Man Drypp's
snap-together version. You can't dismantle these and put them
back together quickly, but I bet they fly. And they've been given
custom paint jobs. Gradations of white and sylver from handlebars to tire, perfect for blending in on Layce.

"Rangers," the boy says. His name is Tooki Lasa, and he can't
be older than fourteen—far too young to be stealing from law-
men. Aside from Dakk's girls, his baby face is the youngest I've
seen in camp.

"Explain," Mars says.

"The rains are pounding hard down south," Tooki says, "and
all them rigs moving in and out of the Stack have the roads
churned to mud. Our pickup got wedged in something fierce."

"A ditch?"

"Something like that," Tooki says, shifting. "Though when I took a good look at our predicament, let me tell you: I think it was a setup. Them Rangers were just waiting to rescue us dumb boys for all the coin we had in our pockets, weren't they?"

Kyn snorts. "I'm sure they were, kid. Jymy Leff wasn't the only one pulling a heist when he should have been working."

"Jymy was a cretin." Tooki's approving stare flicks to me. "Heard it was you that killed him. At High Pass?"

The insinuation shocks me, brings a flood of emotions I'm not prepared to handle. I did *not* kill Jymy Leff, but before I can respond, Mars waves a hand.

"You heard wrong, boy. *I* killed Jymy Leff. And it wasn't at High Pass. It was at a truck stop in Hex Landing."

"With your magic ice powers?" Tooki waggles his fingers.

Mars doesn't answer, but Kyn snorts and that's all the confirmation he needs apparently.

Tooki shakes his head slowly, his eyes huge. "Wild."

"Finish your story, Mr. Lasa."

"That's it mainly. Rangers came along, offered to dig us out for a bag of coin. We declined like the good rebels we are and took their shiny new ice bikes instead."

"These bikes are top-of-the-line." Kyn pats the seat of the nearest bike. "But what are Rangers doing patrolling on ice bikes during the rainy season? Seems stupid, even for them."

Tooki shrugs. "Can't do it and stay dry, that's for sure. But it's easier to navigate them muddy roads on a bike. Don't even have to stay on the road if you don't want to. See them tires? They do really well off-road."

Kyn kneels by the front tire of one, runs his fingers over the tread. "They don't get stuck in the mud?"

"Sure they do, but they're loads easier to dig out than a pickup. I'm guessing the Rangers got tired of rescuing their own selves."

"No money in that," I say. My mind is spinning with possibilities.

"You left them alive, I trust," Mars says. "The Rangers."

Another shrug. "Pretty sure."

Kyn hangs his head. "Ah, hell, kid."

"All we can ask, I guess." Mars fights for nonchalance, but there's a bit of pride there. He likes Tooki Lasa. "Off with you now. The grown-ups need to talk."

"Fair 'nuff, Kol Man." The kid slides off a stack of tires. "Only, I've grown attached to this one." He taps the handlebars of the nearest bike. "You think I could . . ."

"No, you may not," Mars says.

"You even old enough drive?" Kyn asks.

Tooki jabs his chin in my direction. "She's been driving since she was walking. Everybody knows that."

"Yeah, but she's magic," Kyn says. "Are you magic?"

Mars doesn't let him respond. "Your contribution to the cause is noted, Mr. Lasa. Now, go."

Lenore's sitting on a bucket in the corner. She's been silent, chewing on a thumbnail as she watches. But once Tooki's left, she stands. "He can do it. I'm sure."

There's a considerable moment of silence. Well, not silence. Winter's rains pound down hard on the tin roof. She can't entirely blot out the voices, but she's giving it her best effort, adding her own accusations to the mix, screaming about the Shiv abuses she's endured. How their punishment was just. Righteous even.

"What are we talking about now?" Kyn asks.

"Her father," I say. "Macks Trestman."

"No, yeah. I mean, I know that. But what exactly are you sure he can do, Len? 'Cause it seems to me that while we've got a man on the inside now, what we haven't decided is how to use him."

Lenore blinks at that, turns to me. "Whatever you need, Sylvi. I see it in your eyes. You have a plan."

Do I? The beginnings of one maybe.

Leni crosses toward me, puts her hands on my shoulders. "My da would do absolutely anything for you, you know that. He's no fan of the Majority either, not since my ma died. Whatever information we need, he'd be happy to help. I'm sure."

I'm not nearly as certain as she is that Macks is eager to turn on the government he was once so loyal to, but I do believe that he would do anything to make up for the years they stole from his daughter. It's a weakness I'm not above using, but I don't dare say that.

"Miss Trestman, please know I have the highest regard for you and any information you can provide—"

Leni spins toward Mars, auburn braids flying. "I was right about Sylvi, wasn't I?"

"Indeed," he says. "But you lived with her for years, knew what she was capable of. When was the last time you saw your father?"

"Blys, a year past." She doesn't have to strain to remember; she knows the hour and the minute. She'd move mountain and river if she had to, to ensure she and her father are always together on the anniversary of her ma's death. She hasn't missed a year. "You didn't go last time," she says to me, "so you didn't see, but he was better, Sylvi. I swear. Using the twyl as he was supposed to, and—"

"Leni, we'll get your da out. You don't have to convince me. That's not the problem—"

"Oh, it's a problem," Mars says.

"OK, yes. But the bigger problem is that we can't plan the sabotage of Hex Landing without talking to him. None of us know what he has to offer."

She swallows. "No, I suppose we don't."

"And it better be good, yeah?" Kyn says. "If it doesn't work, we're going to war in seven days."

"You've given your word now, *Sessa*." Mars's sarcasm is always a little sharper than everyone else's, likely because he waits until I've twisted myself into impossible situations before he jabs.

"Don't call her that," Leni says. "That was Hyla's name for her."

But I'm not worried about what Mars calls me just now. I have bigger concerns. He and Kyn are right. The promise I made puts us all in a precarious position. It's not an unfamiliar feeling though. It feels a lot like watching Drypp stake the garage and the tavern on the roll of a die.

The bargain I made with the king of Paradyia is bigger than that, I realize. This time it's not just the livelihood of Drypp's cobbled-together little family that's being risked; this time, we're risking everyone on Layce.

No one should have this kind of power.

"Right," I sigh. "So how do we get Macks out?"

# CHAPTER 13

HILE KYN AND LENI STOCK THE DRAGON, Mars and I stand shoulder to shoulder, staring at a map of Layce tacked to the garage wall.

"You and me, we'll have to split up," I tell him.

"I think not."

We've spent the better part of the night holed up here tossing out ideas, formulating scenarios, scrapping them, and then starting again. There's a lot to be done in seven days' time. Too much.

Since Brewzer hasn't reported in, we'll have to stop at High Pass to see Shyne. If we do end up at war with the Majority, the Shiv settlement there will be at great risk.

And then there's the Stack in the southeast wing where Macks is currently indentured and, hopefully, in possession of some knowledge that could help us take down the Majority's flagship mining operation in Hex Landing, another location that needs to be scouted. Of course it's a good half day's ride from the Stack.

To get everything done, we're going to need multiple crews, and that means more rigs on the road during the wet season. And that means—

"One of us needs to go with the other rigs."

"Not happening," Mars says.

"Are you kidding me? We're asking Sayth and Dakk to truck the Shiv Road during Blys. No one does that."

"It's a very short stretch of the Shiv Road, and neither will be driving an ice rig or hauling a trailer. They'll be fine."

I sputter. "But what if they're not?"

He turns to me now. "We're going to discuss hypotheticals?"

"Mars. Seriously—"

"Reyclan and his crew of Paradyian soldiers will be in a war machine with high-grade armor and weaponry. I'm not at all worried about them."

"But Sayth—"

"Will be with the Paradyians the entire time," Mars says.

Leni looks up from rations of dried food she's sorting. "Sayth would be offended if she knew you felt her crew wasn't up to the task, Syl."

"To hear her talk, she's been terrorizing the Majority for years." Kyn hefts a box of ammo into the Dragon. "She's the best scout we have, yeah?"

"This has nothing to do with their capabilities," I say, "and everything to do with Winter."

"Winter is a much bigger problem for you than she is for them," Mars says.

"Do you not trust me to be on my own with her?"

"I don't trust Winter."

"Mars—"

"Trust issues aside"—he waves his hand—"I can't drive the Sylver Dragon, and you can't be separated from the only other one of us who can."

Irritation shoots through Kyn, or maybe it shoots through me. Either way, Kyn scoops up a knife and sends it flying toward the wall. "He has a point, snowflake."

"Mars, *you* could go with Dakk—"

"I need to see Shyne. We've already discussed that."

We haven't *discussed* it, but he's been strangely adamant about making the trip to High Pass. If I didn't know any better, I'd think he was nursing some guilt about what happened the last time we were there.

"You're stuck with me until Winter's gone, sister. Make your peace with it."

And because I can't think of another alternative, I do.

We call for Dakk and Sayth, explain our bare-bones plan. They wander in and out through the night, asking questions, gathering supplies. Other rebels are called upon, and then Desy, who suddenly turns this thing real. She likes the idea of using Macks. It's a boon to all of us but especially to Lenore.

"We've two options for getting him out," Desy says lifting the shallow metal box she's brought with her. Inside are pages and pages of names, workers who have somehow or another ended up indentured to the Majority. She takes great pains to keep the list as updated as possible.

Next to each name is a number: the amount of coin it would take to buy that worker's freedom. Most of the time, it's much simpler to pay off their debt than break them out, but sometimes—as is the case with Macks Trestman—the number next to the name is simply too large.

"It's all right, dear." Desy pats Lenore's hand. "The Majority invested a lot of coin into your father. They aren't going to let him walk free for anything less. But there are two ways out of that place, and I've been doing this a long time."

I like the way she leads. Steady, trusting the gifts and wisdom of those around her. She's not hungry for power, but she's who we'll look to when this is over. I used to think it would be Mars, thought his passion to win would take him straight to governance, but shortly after we arrived at Queen's Point, I made an assumption he was quick to correct.

*"I've no claim here. No desire to sort out the complicated cultural dynamics that will survive even if Winter and the Majority are unseated here on Shiv Island. That's not my job, not my responsibility. I'm a seafarer, bound to an isle that was never mine."*

*"But you're the heir—"*

*"To the Kerce throne. This? This isn't Kerce."*

He's right. It's not. This isle belonged to the Shiv before it belonged to any of us, and it's a privilege to be fighting for its freedom alongside Desy.

"How do we do it, Desy?" Lenore asks. "How do we get him out?"

Her eyes lift to Mars. "Your man still checking the drop?"

"As often as he's able," Mars says, "but if we go this route, we'll have to leave the Sylver Dragon at High Pass. If it's seen anywhere near the southeast wing, they'll lock down the Stack."

"Go what route?" I ask.

"Through the morgue," Desy says, her eyes mischievous.

"We're breaking into a morgue?" Kyn asks.

"No need," Desy says. "The morgue will bring him to you."

It's the same plan they've used for years, she tells us. The way they've broken high-profile targets out of the Stack since long before I emerged from the ice. Desy has an old friend inside, a Dr. Helzyn. Not only does the doctor support the rebellion, but she also funnels money to it. Money the Majority believes is funding research on workers who've gone mad due to their exposure to the kol.

The plan is simple: Macks will be slipped a pill by Mars's guy. Said pill will get him sent to the infirmary, where Dr. Helzyn will declare him deceased, zip him into a body bag, and have him hauled out at night with the rest of the day's dead. Then, we'll intercept the truck and be on our way.

"From there," Mars says, "we make our way to the safe house outside Hex Landing, where we'll rendezvous with the other two crews."

"Here?" Dakk asks, stabbing a large finger at the map.

"That's right."

Dakk nods, his brow stitched tight. "We will arrive before you then, yes?"

"Yes, if things go as planned," Mars says. "You should use that time to scope out the mine yard. Note all the entrances and exits, shift changes, armaments. Sayth will know the layout better than anyone."

"Good. Yes," Dakk says. "What then? How do we bring down their mines?"

"We won't know until we talk to Macks," I say. "We'll just have to have a little faith."

"Faith I can do," Dakk says, then pushes out into the storm to gather his team and load up his rig. I wish faith came as easily to me.

✳

Hours later and it's just the four of us sprawled on the floor—Mars, Kyn, Leni, and me—listening as Winter hammers a vicious lullaby onto the rooftop. Underneath the noise, a constant strain of rough-edged ranting gives the night an uneasy feel.

"It's so sad, isn't it?" Leni says. "Their pain."

"They're telling their stories," Kyn says. "Over and over again. They want us to know what happened."

I find his hand in the dark and slide my fingers between his. Even with the voices hushed by Winter, he's been uncomfortable all day.

"Every now and then I think I recognize a Shiv word," Leni says.

Kyn looks at her. "I forgot you could speak Shiv."

"Well, not really. I can understand some though. Mystra Dyfan liked languages, and she taught me to read Shiv and Kerce. I can hear Winter at times, and now, if I focus, I can pick out a Shiv word here and there."

"Even through the storm?" I ask.

"I have to try really hard, but—"

"Stop trying, Miss Trestman," Mars says through a yawn. "The best we can do for those poor souls is get this over with."

"You spent years collecting accounts of what happened to the Shiv when Winter cursed the isle," Leni says. "The lack of curiosity is very unlike you."

"If he was any good at deciphering the chaos, he'd be all over it," Kyn says.

"Be that as it may," Mars says, "the only thing I'm dying for right now is sleep. We're in for a very long day tomorrow. I suggest you follow my lead." He kicks his boots off and flips to his side with a huff.

We fall quiet after that, and despite all the competing voices trying to keep me awake, I find myself drifting.

I wake with a start. I've slept an hour or two, maybe more. It's still dark and Winter's still raging, but Kyn's gone. I sit up and search the connection between us, looking for some feeling, some emotion to tell me where he's gone. It's a moment before I separate his anxiety from mine, but when I do, I realize I needn't have bothered.

He's gone out to the Desolation.

Briefly, I consider the Dragon; she's taking up most of the room in the garage and I'd love to climb up into that seat, but she's a noisy beast, and if I start her now, I'll wake everyone.

I stand, reaching for the coat I hung over a tool bench. It's new and an upgrade from anything I've had of late. The sleek black parka has dainty sylver buttons and black rabbit fur lining. It was meant to be Rayna's, her brother told me. A gift he purchased for her after Mars bought her freedom. She refused to wear it though, preferring her old, tattered coat that stunk of processed kol.

*"She was a lovely girl," he said when he handed me the coat. "Fun even, before we ran out of money. Before the Stack. Once she got a taste for kol, I couldn't get her to take anything from me. Not the coat, not my rationed twyl, not freedom. Not even when it could have saved her life."*

It's the same concern I have about Macks. Lenore's ma succumbed to the kol, and though I haven't seen him in a few years, Macks was showing signs of addiction even back then. And if addiction hasn't gotten to him, the kol itself just might have. The constant exposure to it has consequences. I have a hard time imagining his mind is nearly as quick as it once was.

I slide my arms into the coat and zip it up, wrapping my scarf tightly before flipping the hood into place and sliding out the door, fighting against Winter for the right to close it behind me.

"*Stiyee,*" I tell her. *Stop.*

It's not very specific—Mars would say I'm regressing—but I've not given her a command in a while and her surprise is sufficient enough to buy me a moment to secure the door.

I could walk. I could. But instead, I whisper another command. Winter bristles, but she lifts me into her arms and flies me out to the Desolation.

# CHAPTER 14

KYN'S AT THE FENCE LINE STARING OUT AT the vast field of ice. He's wearing a hooded vest, and his bare arms steam in the frigid air, his hands shoved deep into his pockets. He knows I'm near before my boots hit the ground—I can tell by the way he tries to rearrange his pain, show it in the best possible light.

He lets me approach at my own pace, so I take my time, try to understand what's hurting him so fiercely. But there are layers and layers to this boy, and it feels invasive to keep digging. He'd rather I just ask.

I say his name, but Winter's engaged in a shouting match with the Shiv voices, so there's no hope of him hearing. I place my hand flat on his back instead. He grabs hold of my sleeve and tugs me around next to him.

"It's not like you to hide stuff," I say, and then again, louder, just to be heard.

He presses his face into my hair and his lips brush my ear, a spark to dry kindling. "Maybe I'm just better at it than you."

"Anything's possible," I say, but Winter slams the words into my mouth again. I don't have to put up with such things. Mars certainly wouldn't.

*What were the words he used yesterday?*

*Ah. Yes.*

The command comes in force, frostbite forming in the corners of my mouth, kol flakes itching. But Winter bows to the Kerce words, encircling Kyn and me, wrapping us in a cone of silence.

Kyn flexes his jaw, shakes his head. "You almost forget what quiet sounds like."

"You don't mind, do you?" I ask. "I didn't want to yell."

"Why would I mind?"

I shrug a single shoulder. "Because you were listening."

He kicks a rock; it bounces off my boot. "I was trying, yeah. Winter makes everything so—"

"Difficult. I know." I pick up the rock and toss it into the cyclone, watch Winter whip it away. "But why?"

"Why what?"

"Why listen? Mars is right: We can end their suffering without having to feel it."

"And that doesn't feel cheap?"

It's a slap, the idea that succeeding here will have less value if we don't suffer. "Not to me, no. I fight Winter plenty. I'm not going to fight her in this. Right now, it's a gift, her noise. Why force something that hurts?"

"I'm not looking for suffering, snowflake."

"No?"

"I just . . ." He drags both hands down his face. "Do you know why they're suddenly calling out?"

I think of Winter's claim, that I woke them, that it was me. But even if it's true, that still doesn't tell me why. "Do you?"

"It's because you left the isle."

Another slap. "What?"

"Even frozen, even trapped as they are, they're . . . I don't know . . . aware."

"Of what?"

"Of you."

The idea is laughable. "Kyn, I was a newborn when I went into that ice. Only a handful of the Shiv ever knew I existed."

"Sylvi. They're aware."

"That makes no sense."

"I've been trying to figure out how it works. Begynd, maybe? Shiv magic? *The rocks bear witness* and all that."

"'The rocks bear witness'?"

"It's an old Shiv expression. My ma said it all the time when I was a kid, and I hear it again and again from the Shiv out there."

"But what does it mean?"

"It's a warning. Like, if I was to cause trouble while out of my ma's sight, she'd still know cause she's carved from the rock of Shiv Isle. The same rock that's beneath my troublemaking feet miles away. The Shiv and the isle are one." He shrugs. "Basically us kids will never get away with anything 'cause the rocks bear witness."

"But I'm not made of stone, Kyn. I'm not Shiv."

"No, but for seventeen years you walked this isle, and then three weeks ago, you left, and the isle knew."

"And because the isle knew—"

His arms fling wide in a harried gesture. "They want you to hear them. That's all I know."

I have nothing to say to that and the whoosh of the wind pulses around us, the Shiv voices reduced to whispers.

"Will you translate for me?" I ask. "If I can lift the storm, will you tell me what they're saying?"

"If you lift the storm, everyone at Queen's Point will wake—"

"If I can handle that, will you tell me what you hear?"

He tugs on my scarf, pulls me closer. "OK. Yeah."

"OK." I close my eyes, and sort through the commands I know. Getting as specific as I can, setting aside all my emotion, going through every one of Mars's Revelations, I demand Winter lift the storm off the Desolation and shift it to the camp.

She rumbles and bellows, but my ears pop as the air pressure changes, and my hair lifts, then falls, settling on my shoulders. The noise surrounding us is different now. Where once there was one frantic voice on the wind—a voice I could understand—now there are hundreds, and nothing like the wind to buffer their cries.

I open my eyes and see Kyn, his eyes wild, processing what he hears. And there is *so much* to process. I feel the muddle of it, the effort he exerts focusing on one voice at a time. The moment he succeeds, he gasps and his eyes slam shut. Tears spill down his face, and a sob that started in his chest, rattles free of my mine.

"What do you hear?" I ask.

"A boy," Kyn says. "His ma sent him to the pool that day, for water, for cooking, and he . . ." A tremor runs through his body. "He never saw it coming. He wants to know if his sister made it, his ma."

The concern he has for these people crashes through me. It's a tenderness unchecked, and I'm sobered by how hard it must be to just . . . feel all the time.

"And there's a woman too, older maybe. She rarely left the pool, yeah? Even . . . even now, even trapped, there's nowhere else she'd rather be."

He has to stop then, his shoulders hunched, his hands reaching out. My own spine buckles under the weight of what he's hearing, but it's only a fraction of what he carries. Since that day at High Pass, when the mountain crashed down, and we met Shyne and Crysel, descendants of those buried here, I resisted tying myself to them, resisted their claim on me. But not Kyn. Kyn's chosen compassion.

And it just might kill him.

This was a foolish idea. Selfish. He's suffering so I can hear voices I don't really want to hear. Suffering so I could prove he misunderstood.

He called me mercenary once, Kyn did. Hard to argue with that now.

"Hey, Kyn." It's like shouting over a crowd. I step up onto his boot, grab hold of his shoulders. "Kyn, we won't do this. Not if it's going to—"

His eyes open, dark wine and firelight staring back at me. It's enough to stop my words, to render sound silent. Beyond the veil of his eyes, his heart and soul sit, more exposed than I've ever seen them. They've been there for a while now, offered up, waiting for me. For the first time though, I'm acutely aware that they're a gift, not the burden I feared.

My nose brushes his, but we're not near close enough, and all at once the agony of such an injustice tears through me.

He feels it too. Startlingly sudden, this thing inside me. It burns, aches, demands indulgence. Kyn goes still, his heart banging so hard I can feel the ferocity of it through the thickness of my coat.

We touch all the time, our fingers twisted together, our shoulders pressing, our knees knocking beneath tables. But this is new, this need. It's something I know he's wanted, something I've seen in him, a bridge I've been unable to cross.

But now I find myself lingering when, not so long ago, I would have run. I know everything about Kyn and not near enough. I want more of him, the boy who puts me first always. Whose heart breaks for a people he's never met.

We're starkly different, he and I. I've always been selfish, I know that, but he makes me better. I want to put his needs before my own. His wants . . .

I tug the glove from my hand and gently, softly, run a finger over his stone cheekbone. The air rattles in his throat.

"Sylvi—" I see rather than hear him say my name, the Shiv voices rising up around us now, crying out.

He lifts his hand and rests it on my cheek. It's warm and his eyes are soft, and I want to spend every moment of every day staring into them, through them even. I want to see Shiv Island as he sees it. Because he's good and kind. He's the most beautiful person I've ever met, body and soul. He loves me and I . . .

I press a kiss beneath his eye, my cold lips on his hot flesh.

I love him too.

His hand knots in the jacket at my back and he pulls me closer, and suddenly, my heart is hammering. But not with desire.

With fear.

"What is it?" Kyn asks, loosening his hold. "We don't have to, yeah? Really. It's fine."

I stay his mouth with a gentle hand, turn my face to the ice. "I hear them, Kyn. The Shiv. I understand what they're saying."

# CHAPTER 15

"I THOUGHT THEY WERE WAILING," I SAY, "BUT that's not it at all."

"It's what they sound like all together, their cries." His words are slow, deliberate. I feel him probing the connection between us, searching it. "You *can* understand them."

It's a novelty at first, and I'm hearing without really listening. Understanding words without grasping the context.

Kyn doesn't ask how. He knows it just as I do. It's not my ears I'm hearing with, not really. It's our connection that makes this possible. When I opened my heart to Kyn, invited him in, it didn't cross my mind he'd bring that thing breaking him wide open.

Mystra would say I'm reaping the reward of understanding without doing the work of learning the language, and I suppose that's true, but as I begin to focus on what's actually being said, I realize there's no reward here. There's only the great sadness of stories half lived.

"I don't normally bathe in the pool so early in the morning, but mother sent me to fetch water in her stead . . ."

"Begynd was especially warm that day . . ."

". . . just returned . . . a long trip into the mountains above . . ."

"The fount was bubbling, a song almost . . ."

"What have the rocks to say? Have you heard them singing?"

"I had come to speak to our elder—"

"—was sat there on the shore with my father. He'd cut his hand, a deep gash that only Begynd could heal—"

"A cold wind . . ."

"The rocks—"

"I heard something near the shore—"

"She was screaming, the Kerce queen. It was my father who pulled her from the Kol Sea, did you know? And to hate us so fiercely after that—"

"Did you see her necklace?"

"—had I been any closer I would have . . . I'm sure I could have stopped her."

"I was there when the little princess was born. My sister Bryte was the one who delivered her."

". . . came up from beneath the water . . ."

"The rocks bear witness."

"The air was cold . . ."

"And my throat closed over—"

"'Father,' I cried! 'Father!' But I heard nothing. Saw only a field of white. Felt only a great cold shiver across my back and then—"

"Winter came down the mountain."

I drop to the ground, dragging Kyn with me. He's working hard to grab hold of a single voice and follow it, but the tighter his grip, the faster the thread slips away. Their histories come at us in pieces and parts, some like a breath of fresh air, others like a sucker punch. Some of them *are* wailing, and in the chaos, I hear a voice I don't understand, or maybe it's Kyn who doesn't understand? Is that how this works, all of it filtering through him? Breaking him before it breaks me?

It hardly matters. I hear enough to know my mother's bargain with Winter destroyed a vibrant people, and I hate her for it. For making destruction so easy on a wicked, kol-addled spirit.

*"Begynd wouldn't let us die here, surely . . ."*

*"Will we be forever in the ice?"*

*"The rocks bear witness. The Kerce child had Begynd's light in her eyes . . ."*

*"She's left the isle."*

*"Maree Vale's daughter has gone."*

*"The rocks—"*

*"They bear—"*

*"Call her back, call her back."*

I shudder at the implication, turn to Kyn for comfort, but he's propped against the fence post now, his legs drawn up, face pressed to his knees.

I've heard enough.

Kyn's certainly heard enough. He shouldn't have to carry history like a millstone around his neck. And it's in my power to ensure he doesn't.

With a word and a blister, I release Winter from her confinement. I feel her stretch and sigh as she spreads out; I feel her seethe. She grinds the clouds overhead into rain and she laughs as she takes aim at the ice.

I tug Kyn's hood over his head and we sit there for a long time, Winter washing the Shiv stories from our skin. We're soaked through when Kyn slides closer.

"Can you do the cyclone thing, snowflake? Make it quiet."

I grin but it doesn't stick. Something's churning inside him. An idea. A truth of some sort. Something I'm not going to like. I give the order and Winter complies without much of a stink. I think she wants to hear what's on Kyn's mind.

"You're lovely in the rain," he says as the storm and the voices fade to a steady hum.

"You too, but that's not what you were going to say."

He lifts my hand and places it inside his. "There's a reason Winter's screaming like this, yeah? She doesn't want us to hear what they're saying."

"Revelation number two: Her natural state is to rage."

"But this is extreme. Especially in Blys." He's right. Winter usually saves her noisiest storms for Ryme. "Maybe you could ask her to bring down the volume some?"

"Why would I do that?" But this is it. This is what he's decided. "You *want* to hear the voices all the time?"

"Not *all* the time, but—"

"Kyn, be serious. We have things to do."

"But what if there's something there, Sylvi? Something we need to hear. Begynd wouldn't have allowed their voices—"

"Begynd? Did you hear his voice out there?"

"No, but maybe that's not how he works. Maybe—"

I groan. "We don't have time for *maybe*. We don't have time for anything that slows us down. And the two of us sobbing on the ground is definitely going to slow us down."

"I can turn that off; you know I can." He's flint; he's stone.

"But *I* can't. I have no idea how you choose your emotions so fully. But I can't have all these voices inside my head. Not with Winter in there too. It's too much. I don't have the energy for that kind of battle."

"Then let me help you."

"Fight a battle inside my head?"

"Yes! We can sort out the voices together. And when Winter starts lying, I can remind you what's true."

"You do that anyway."

"So let me do it now. It's worth a little suffering to understand why Begynd's unleashed these voices. I can help you cope, I can. And in the process, if our connection continues to grow, maybe I'll see something you won't. Maybe the parts of you Winter's frozen—"

"Like my heart?"

He takes a deep breath, quiets. "Not all of it. I know that. But you don't hate her, and you should." Words I've heard before. They turn my stomach now just as they did then. "That tells me there's a fight to be had."

"For my heart?"

He smiles, dimples and everything. "I like a good fight, you know that."

"But this isn't one you have to pick. Winter doesn't have a hold on me anymore. She's nothing but a tool in my hand and if we let her rage—"

"We're giving her exactly what she wants."

"If we let her rage, we won't be plagued by the darkest day this isle ever experienced, a day my mother brought down on us all. My mother, Kyn! I can't make peace with that. Not until I've set it right. And I can't be haunted by it while I'm trying to work. You heard Mars; I have to keep my emotions in check. If I lose control . . ." Like I'm going to do right now. I close my eyes, inhale slowly. "Look, we can't afford to knock Winter out, not until this is over. We need her. The best way to win is to just let her be for now."

"She's a manipulative dictator who makes monsters with ice and kol. Two things you have flying around in your veins. Letting her be is dangerous."

"Kyn—"

"No, listen. You're going to have to make peace with the fact that some fights have to be had. You might even have to get your hands dirty. You might have to look some bastard in the eye and tell him his way is wrong and your way is right."

"Isn't that what I'm doing right now?"

He laughs, but it's not at all funny. "See? That's what I can't figure out. You don't want to go to war with the Majority, but you have no problem going to war with me."

"That's not fair."

"Fair? Those people down there, they deserve to be heard. *That's* fair."

He's twisting my words, but he's right. The Shiv deserve better. "If this world were just, if my mother hadn't been so selfish, those people would never have been frozen. They would have lived a long, healthy life in the light of Begynd. *That* would have been fair. I have to make this right for them, and I can't do that if I'm on edge all the time."

"Sylvi—"

"You're the only one who wants to listen to their cries. No one in camp would take your side on this."

"That doesn't make me wrong."

I think that's exactly what that makes him. Wrong.

He sighs. "We're missing something. About that day. About Winter. And there's too much at stake to go barreling ahead without knowing everything there is to know."

"We have seven days, Kyn. That's all. How could we possibly make sense of any of that in seven days?"

"It would be a lot of work. I'm not saying it wouldn't."

"And we'd have to fight Winter the entire time to keep her quiet."

"Some things are worth fighting for, snowflake. Freedom from occupying bastards, peace to live as we see fit—"

I cover my face with my hands. "Kyn—"

"And your heart! Your heart is worth fighting for." His hands are on mine now, tugging them from my face. "You want to let Winter rage to save yourself a little pain, give it a try. But I genuinely believe history holds the key to what we're trying to accomplish here, and if I can decipher what happened that day, I'm going to. Even if I have to fight through the storm to hear it told."

Anger shoots from my toes to my head. "You're making that choice on my behalf then, because I can't *not feel* what you feel."

"And I'm sorry about that, I truly am, but some things are meant to be felt."

I push to a stand, the order releasing Winter already burning my tongue.

"Where are you going?" Kyn asks as the cyclone collapses.

"To get the Dragon ready. I can't fight you and Winter both right now. I can't suffer through another accounting of my mother's wrongs. There isn't time."

"Sure there is. You just prefer Winter's voice to theirs."

Winter claps down on us, grabbing my hair, screaming. She whirls out over the ice and scatters the Desolation voices far and wide. Relief washes over me, and then shame, because he's right. I'd rather listen to her lies than their pain.

How frigid does that make me?

I turn away, leaving Kyn there at the edge of the pool. He's beginning already, fighting Winter, straining to hear, to understand. It's not easygoing, but as the shape of Shiv words slip into Kyn's ears, they press against my ribs, making it hard to breathe, and I can't. I won't.

I cry out. One loud scream that shakes everything free, the anger quieting my mind. But for a moment only. Within seconds, the Desolation voices worm their way back in and I realize it's not enough to make myself loud. It's not even enough to let Winter rage. Stoppering my ears isn't going to cut it, not when I'm hearing with my heart.

"Talk to me," I tell Winter. "Are you . . . are you enjoying the freedom to bluster?"

She gives it a second. I feel her considering. But I told her to talk. It was an order.

I KNOW WHY YOU'RE DOING THIS. LETTING ME CARRY ON. Her words sear my insides, burning away the stories that threaten to consume me. This is a really bad idea, a horrible, selfish, foolish . . .

"Would you prefer I muzzle you?" I ask.

She laughs, a low chuckle that vibrates right through me. NOT EVEN YOU COULD KEEP ME QUIET FOR LONG.

"Perhaps," I say, knowing she's right. The energy it would take, the constant reminders.

I UNDERSTAND. YOU DON'T WANT TO HEAR THOSE VOICES ANY MORE THAN I DO. ACCUSATIONS ARE NOT EASY TO SWALLOW. YOUR MOTHER STARTED SOMETHING WITH THE SHIV. SOMETHING THEY WERE POWERLESS TO STOP.

I don't want to know. I don't want to hear. "It'll all be over soon. Seven days and you'll be gone, the Desolation will be thawed, and I won't have to choose which voices to listen to."

She bristles. DO YOU REALLY BELIEVE THAT THE BEST THING FOR THIS ISLAND IS TO BAN- ISH ME?

It's a doubt I've nursed all along, we both know that.

LAYCE WAS BUILT ON WHAT I OFFER, she hisses.

I have only Mars's words to give her. "Another winter spirit will take your place here eventually. If you hadn't done what you did—"

I WANTED A FRIEND. YOUR MOTHER OFFERED ME THAT. Genuine or not, emotion runs through her voice now.

I swipe the rain from my eyes. "She wasn't well. You took advantage."

SHE OFFERED ME COMPANIONSHIP AND THEN TRICKED ME INTO SUBSERVIENCE.

"I don't think that's what happened . . ."

YOU'RE THE SAME. OUR FRIENDSHIP WAS SUF-
FICIENT UNTIL YOU REALIZED IT COULD MAKE YOU
POWERFUL. THAT I COULD MAKE YOU POWERFUL.

There's enough truth in what she says to unsettle me. To make me wish things were different. But she uses that—uses doubt, my own weaknesses—against me. Mars taught me that. Gah, I'm forgetful.

"Revelation number one," I say, my voice trembling. "Winter is not my friend."

BECAUSE THE BLACK-EYED PRINCE SAID SO?

"Revelation number ten: Winter lies."

DO YOU LISTEN TO EVERYTHING THAT SMUG-
GLER SAYS?

"Revelation number seven—"

She bellows, a force that sends mud and rainwater flying, tangles my feet. YOU USE ME TO INCINERATE YOUR FEAR. ALL I ASK IS THAT WE HAVE PEACE BETWEEN US.

I drop to my knees, my chest heaving. "I will have that pool thawed. I will have those people freed."

She sighs, cooling the sweat on my face and blowing the raindrops into a tizzy. I fight to catch my breath.

ONCE, she says, LONG AGO, I LIVED ONLY IN THE MOUNTAINS OF THIS ISLE, HIGH ABOVE THE GREAT POOL.

It's an offer, a compromise, a negotiation. Impossible to trust, but it would spare the mountainfolk their roads, their livelihoods . . .

I stand. "And you would go back there? You would accept that cage?"

IF YOU RID IT OF THE SHIV, YES.

"The Shiv would abandon High Pass if Begynd returned." Of course they would. They'd prefer to be near him. On his shores.

WOULD YOU VISIT ME THERE? She's shy, almost childlike in her request.

"I—I could."

THEN YES, I'D PREFER THE CAGE TO BANISHMENT. IF YOU LEAVE THE MOUNTAINS TO ME, I WILL GIVE UP THE GREAT POOL WITHOUT A FIGHT. YOU HAVE MY WORD.

It's too easy. Too unlike her. "Your word has no value after what you've done."

Her voice is small now, a tiny flame behind my breastbone. IT IS ALL I HAVE LEFT TO GIVE.

"And what's to stop you from forgetting this promise? From going back on your word?"

YOUR MOTHER WAS SATISFIED WITH A COVENANT. WILL YOU SWEAR YOURSELF TO ME, DAUGHTER OF MAREE VALE?

"I will not." I brush her snow off my coat. "If you are sincere, you will show your friendship by helping us without complaint. And then, once the Majority has been beaten, you and I will talk again."

Discomfort spreads through her. YOU SPEAK OF SINCERITY, BUT I'M NOT CONVINCED YOU WILL DO RIGHT BY ME.

"And I'm not convinced you will do right by me. If we're to be friends, we will have to risk disappointment, both of us."

**FRIENDS?** Winter asks, and it sounds like music.

Mars assures me that friendship with her is not possible. But we're different, he and I. And if Winter had had a friend all those years ago, who knows what might be different now.

"Friends."

## CHAPTER 16

THE JOG BACK TO CAMP IS SHORT AND WHEN I arrive, the sky is lightening and woodsmoke is pushing through the rain. I breathe it in, my eyes lingering on the garage. The roof shimmers in the low morning light and the roughshod building beckons. We're set to leave in a few hours and there are things that need doing, but when Kyn gets tired of fighting Winter, he'll look for me there, and I'm not ready to be found.

I know I've disappointed him. But when Bristol Mapes tugged me from beneath Mistress Quine's stove and I called to Winter for the first time, something inside me froze. I would die for Kyn, I know that. Though in the magical mess that we've become, that would hardly help. It's just . . . maybe I *have* given Winter parts of me, and she's numbed them so fully I can't even tell. Maybe I'll never really be complete enough to love Kyn the way he deserves to be loved. I don't know.

But I do know this: It's not possible for me to heft the pain of an entire generation of Shiv and maintain control of my emotions.

Kyn might think me capable, but that's not a kindness; it's just one more thing I have to carry.

I squash down every bit of angst until it's nothing but a ball in the pit of my stomach, and I head for the gathering hall. I'll grab a bite to eat and some boiled chocolate and then I'll raid the weapons store.

The hearth at the center of the gathering hall is roaring and popping when I step inside. The logs are new and recently laid, the flames just beginning to chase the chill from the open space. It's surprisingly empty this morning, but then it's early, I suppose.

I weave through the wooden tables, tugging off my damp gloves and coat and then draping them over a chair near the fire to dry. At a table in the far corner, a man dozes. Clift. He used to bare-knuckle box to make ends meet, so not a horrible choice to guard the prisoners. I heard Desy giving him instructions last night, but instead of keeping watch, he's propped up against the wall, his mouth gaping, no weapon in sight.

A curse slides off my tongue. It's not just Bristol Mapes he's protecting us all from. It's Farraday Wrex, a man who has our utter destruction in mind.

And while I understand Mars's hesitancy to leave Wrex under the watch of the Paradyians, I'm embarrassed that our guard couldn't even manage to stay awake through the night.

The entryway leading to our one-cell lockup looks dark from here, despite the candlelight flickering from inside, dancing against the doorframe. The prisoners are likely still asleep, but I'd hate for one of the Paradyians to walk in just now and see us so thoroughly exposed.

"Clift, you awake?" I call.

Voices sound in the kitchen and pots and pans clang, a steamy fug seeping from inside, smelling like Leni's famous fry-up. She's always been an early riser. My stomach rumbles at the thought of her food, but there's something about Clift that keeps my attention.

"Clift?" I round the hearth for a better look, and then my feet are moving faster as hot dread fills my gut.

His coat hangs open over a gray fleece, a scarf knotted around his neck. It's thick and woolen, the argyle pattern drenched in blood. I see one of his knives now, discarded on the floor, the blade wet, gleaming red in the firelight.

I think first of Hyla's girls. They'd been sleeping in a room off this very hall up until we attempted the crossing to Paradyia. I turn toward their room, and a flash of brown material catches my eye, followed by the stench of damp leather and the sea.

Wrex.

I wheel around and open my mouth to cry for help, but a hand grabs hold of my hair, another clamps over my mouth, and I've missed my chance.

Panic takes me and I flail, lifting my feet off the floor and forcing him to take all my weight. Wrex grunts and shifts one hand to my throat, squeezing as he hauls me into the room that houses our lockup. He slams me against the wall, setting the yellow candlelight trembling.

And that's when I see him.

Bristol Mapes sprawled on the floor. His body lies in the doorway of the cell, the spring-latched door trying to close on him, Clift's missing knife jutting from the side of his neck.

I gasp, but Wrex isn't letting any air through, and my eyes start to darken. It's not pity I feel. And there's no relief in seeing Bristol sliced open, but I do *feel* it. I carried this man and his violence against me for years, and to see him dispatched with so little ceremony seems . . . unfair.

"Not a word," Wrex says, giving my face and throat one more squeeze before releasing them altogether.

I open my mouth to call for Winter, but my voice won't cooperate. I try again, but the effort starts me coughing, and then I'm retching.

Wrex takes advantage, tying me hand and foot, wedging my own scarf between my teeth and knotting it behind my head.

He hauls me to my feet, a satisfied set to his shoulders. "I'm not the best company, I realize, but I'm a better villain than he is." He shoves at Bristol's corpse with the toe of his boot. "Hours in a cell with him and I can see he's the worst sort. Nothing principled or righteous about his desires. Everything, all of it, all of *him*: depraved."

He adjusts my body, propping me in the corner of the small room, his large hand flat against my chest. "You don't see my efforts as righteous, I know, and I won't bother to make a case. But I do hope you see me as principled. You won't win this war, rig driver, but I also won't let your own prisoner make you a martyr to it. The last thing the Majority needs is for your legend to grow. When you die, you'll die a rebel. You'll die publicly. I want others to see your failure, want them to understand the consequences of fighting back."

I try to curse him, to move my mouth and call for Winter, or even Leni. I can still hear voices in the kitchen. But the scarf is tightly wedged and the only sounds I'm capable of making are hoarse and feeble.

Wrex smiles and drapes a key back on its hook. "I rather like having allies in your camp." My eyes follow the movement, but they're watering now, turning the corners of the room soft.

"What have you done?" A man hovers in the doorway, tall, a red cape brushing the toes of his boots. Paradyian. I can't get my eyes to focus on his face, but his voice is familiar. I've heard him speak before.

"She came to me, Lieutenant," Wrex says. "I made no effort at all."

"No effort! Two men are dead!"

"A reprobate and a sloth. I do hope the rebels have better." He jerks his head at me. "This one comes with us."

"Not possible. The boat carries two and we must be away. The camp is waking."

"Only two?" Wrex shifts his body closer to me. "Well then."

He turns his back on the Paradyian, and at last my eyes find the ability to focus again. The bastard winks at me, like we're in this together. He fluxing *winks*, the violence of his presumption clearing my mind.

I try to call out, try to warn the Paradyian, but I'm all grunts and groans and Wrex is fast. He turns, and with one hand still pinning me against the wall, he pulls the man's gun and fires. A moment only, and the traitor is dead.

"I liked this one," Wrex says, staring down at him. "He was noble, knew his king was taking the country into a war they need not fight. But you'll be much more help on the Kol Sea than him. Come."

He grabs my arm and peers around the doorframe. Like a hooked fish, I go limp, and he curses, hefting me out into the gathering hall. It's still empty, save Clift's body. There's a back door just beyond him, and Wrex heads toward it, dragging me first, and then throwing me over his shoulder when I make that too difficult.

I kick out with my feet. I slam my tied hands into his chest, my elbow into his face, once, twice. He drops me.

"You wretched little—" His foot comes up, and I flinch away.

The front door flies open as Wrex's boot comes down.

It never touches me. Wrex takes a gust of wind to the gut and folds in half before flying through the back window. Glass shatters and I curl into a ball, closing my eyes. The sound falls away and I look toward the front door.

The fire has frozen where it flickered, ice coating every table and chair. Mars stands just inside the hall, Winter's words blistering his lips, righteous indignation on his face.

"Are you hurt?" he asks. I shake my head, and his eyes close. "Good, that's very good." His eyes open and he moves toward me, but there's a sound from the kitchen and we both look.

The kitchen door cracks open, the ice that's coated its hinges breaking free. Leni emerges, her sleeves rolled to her elbows, her braids pinned up, her face rosy.

"Sylvi? Oh my gosh, Sylvi!" She rushes toward me, but my eyes are on Mars. I want to thank him, but I'm still bound. I nod and he returns it, tender, almost stepping toward me.

But Lenore's here, untying the scarf from my face, patting my arms, my legs. "Holy Begynd, Sylvi, what happened?"

When I look up again, Mars is gone.

The room is filling now, bleary-eyed rebels up for breakfast, Dakk and the girls, the king and his guard. All of them stunned and hovering near the door. Hawken steps toward the hearth, his hand moving over the frozen flames.

Leni pulls a knife from her boot and saws through the bindings on my wrist, asking questions all the while. But I'm listening to Mars. His voice carries through the open door and shattered window. Shouting orders, waking the camp, demanding Wrex be found.

"He's headed for a boat." The words scratch my throat, croaking and broken. Too quiet to be heard over Leni's concern. I try again, taking hold of her hands. "Leni, stop. Stop."

She meets my gaze. "What is it?"

My throat aches, the imprint of Wrex's hands still fiery on my skin, but my voice has some strength to it this time. "He's heading for a boat. Something small. Likely Paradyian."

"Paradyian?" The king moves closer. "What makes you think—"

I turn toward the red-caped man sprawled on the floor, recognizing him now as the lieutenant who escorted Kyn and me to the king when we first came to be on the Paradyian ship. The man who brought us rombee cider.

Hawken Valthor has been betrayed by one of his inner circle. His face purples as he realizes this, and he turns from the room, his voice booming out over the frigid expanse, demanding someone find the missing boat.

Leni cuts the last of my binds and helps me stand. She lets me lead, her arm around my waist. I take us to the shattered window, our boots crunching over the glass. The window frame has jagged teeth of ice, the wall around it frosted over. I peer out into the breaking day, looking for the man who killed Bristol Mapes.

For the man who nearly broke my body.

The man whose shape has been left in the muddy, melting snow but is nowhere to be seen.

Leni hugs me tight. "They'll find him, OK? Mars is on it. Let's get you patched up."

I let her lead me away from the window, but she's wrong.

Farraday Wrex is gone. They won't find him.

Winter's told me so. It seems we're working together again.

# CHAPTER 17

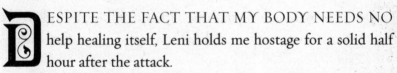ESPITE THE FACT THAT MY BODY NEEDS NO help healing itself, Leni holds me hostage for a solid half hour after the attack.

"Your neck is a mess, and you have a knot on the back of your head the size of a hailstone. Are you sure you're not feeling nauseous?"

"I'm fine."

"You'd say that regardless." She tips up my chin and scrutinizes the bruise Wrex left behind. "I've some ointment. It's in my coat pocket, hang on a sec."

When she ducks into the kitchen, I slip out the front door.

It's a muddy, flooding mess out here. Standing water on the cobbles, Winter pouring. My hood up and my coat zipped, I push away from the gathering hall before Leni can pull me back.

I don't intend to seek out Kyn, but the strange absence in my chest has me uneasy. He's far enough away that I feel almost nothing of him, and even though some space between us may be a good thing right now, if he wanders too far afield, the wounds he sustained at High Pass will open and we'll have another mess on our hands.

I push through the camp, cutting behind the garage, toward the outskirts and the scrubby trees that somehow find a way to survive between the black sea and the Desolation. I pass the remains of the old twyl shack and a graveyard of broke-down rigs, but there's no sign of Kyn.

There's shouting in the distance, and I strain to hear, but it's just the rebels shifting their search area. Fluxing Wrex. There's no way we're getting on the road today.

Suddenly, it hits me with the force of ten rigs that perhaps I'm not feeling anything of Kyn because there's nothing to feel. Wrex killed two men already. Could he have come upon Kyn during his escape?

And now I'm running back toward the camp, panicked, mud flying, my boots slipping. Through a haze of rain and fog, the backside of the gathering hall comes into view, and a familiar angst presses against my sternum.

Kyn's back, settled in as though he'd never left.

I follow the wave of his emotions through camp, until at last I'm at the garage, and I hear voices drifting out the open door.

"What do you mean, *where was I?*" Kyn demands. "My head needed clearing, yeah? I went for a walk. Why do you care?"

"Why do I . . . You missed a prison break, friend. Farraday Wrex is gone."

"What?" And then panic, filling his voice, his gut, spilling into mine. "Where's Sylvi?"

"She's—"

"Close," Kyn says, relief pushing through his own emotions to find mine.

I consider stepping into the garage, joining the argument, but I don't have the energy for it.

"How close?" Mars asks.

"If she wanted you to see her, you'd see her. *What* happened?"

Mars tells him about Wrex, about Bristol, about the dead Paradyian lieutenant. Kyn's insides turn watery and it's enough to make me ill. The rain is so loud, and their voices have dropped so low I have to sidle up to the door to hear anything at all.

"You're the only one who can tell me if she's in danger, Kyndel. And she can't be in danger. It's not fair, not right to ask it of you, I know that. But if I'm not with her, you have to be close enough to, at the very least, sense when things are going wrong."

I can't see him from here, but I can feel him deflating. "Yeah, OK. I'm sorry. I will. Look, let me go find her."

But I don't want to be found. Not now. Not like this. Kyn's safe. He's fine. But I can't shoulder his feelings and mine right now. Winter wraps her cold fingers around me as I move away. I let her, let the chill burn away everything else.

Maybe I should have stepped out from my hiding place and railed against the unjustness of the task Mars gave Kyn. I don't need to be babysat. I could have reminded them both that I was strong enough, brave enough, terrifying enough to get us here, so surely, I could take care of myself. But, in truth, I feel none of those things right now.

I duck into the toolshed and out of the rain. I'm soaked through, so I strip my coat off and hang it on the door. I rebraid my hair and set to work, rifling through barrels and rusted toolboxes.

I scan the shelves and the walls, looking for a weapon to replace Drypp's old pickaxe. Something substantial to wrap my hands around. Something deadly.

After a fair bit of searching, I realize I'll have to settle for a smaller weapon. The only axe in sight has a rusted head, its handle splintered and swollen.

The angst in Kyn's chest has been growing steadily, so I'm not surprised when he steps into the shed. He opens the door a little wider, Winter's light painting the room various shades of gray. "I heard about Wrex. He hurt you?"

"Nothing that hasn't already healed."

"You sure?"

"I'm sure."

He clears his throat. "I'm sorry about before."

I'm sorry too, but I don't want to cry. We haven't changed our minds, neither of us. We're just sorry, and that's all.

"Looking for a weapon?" He steps around me and lifts the rusted axe I've managed to unearth. The axe head falls to the floor. "That one would need some work."

"I'll just go with this instead." I flash a hunting knife. The blade needs to be sharpened and the handle sanded down, but the weight is right. I can wear it at my waist like I did the bone-handled blade Drypp made me. I find myself reaching for it all the time. At least now, my hand won't come away empty.

Kyn lifts my coat from the door and holds it up so I can slide in, one arm and then the other. Both of us slow, careful.

"Old Man Drypp was the kindest man I've ever met. He took me in when he really didn't have to." I'm not sure why his memory is so real just now, so vivid. The axe maybe. "Something strange though: He never told us he loved us."

"No?"

"Bothered Leni more than it did me. She was his granddaughter after all. I was just some kid they found in the wood. Leni asked him about it once, and you know what he said?"

"Tell me." Kyn fumbles with the zipper on my coat.

I stay his hands, turning them so I can see the sign of Begynd etched into his stone knuckle.

"He said, 'Little girl, I work my feet to callouses at the tavern, and my hands bloody at the garage so you girls have food and drink, wood to burn, a bed to sleep in. I always put you firebrands first, so if I'm too tired to say it, at least you'll know what love looks like. I figure that's better than words.'" I lift my eyes to Kyn's, the air trembling in my lungs. "I always liked that, and I never questioned that Drypp loved me. He showed me every day. And this? Focusing on one fight at a time, it's the only way I know how to do what needs doing. The only way I can put the island first. It might not look the way you want it to, I might not be who you want me to be, but I'm choosing you every day. I hope you know that."

He lifts my braid from my shoulder, sets it back down.

"Do you remember when you said we'd find out everything we could about Maree Vale and Begynd, everything there was to know about the day Winter took the isle?" He smiles, soft, disarming. "You were convinced that some three-centuries-old mistake might hold the key to undoing all this."

"Of course I remember. Those first few weeks, that's all I did. Lessons with Mars on both Kerce and Paradyian royalties and lineages, the Majority's conquests and alliances. He told me the story of his crossing as a boy again and again, he told me about the covenant with Winter. I let Leni read me all the old histories. Hours and hours of Kerce history, Kyn. You were there! My brain was so saturated I dreamed in kol."

"And after all that work, you're still trying to avoid it. The people who were there are telling you exactly what happened that day. Why won't you listen?"

"I did listen."

"Sylvi—"

Something in me snaps. "I can't believe my mother could be so fluxing selfish! That's why I'm done listening. She took everything from them, and I want to be better than her; I want to be like you. I want to protect the people I'm responsible for, not bring more misery down upon them. And listening to those voices just reminds me that I might fail. That even though I'm trying my level best, it might not be enough. And that hurts. It hurts to listen to the people who suffered at her hand, to know they might already be lost."

He hesitates and I can feel him measuring his words. "I think it's supposed to hurt. Pain isn't to be feared, snowflake. And it isn't to be avoided. That just twists a person up."

"Kyn—"

"I've been thinking. I won't fight Winter on this, yeah? Not until you ask me to. You're right to preserve Winter's power—we have no idea what the road holds—so you let Winter rage all you want. I won't seek out the voices anymore, but I won't push them away either. If they get loud enough for me to hear, it's only right to listen. And if you need some space when that happens, you take it."

"But?"

"But you have to promise me something. When you're ready to let yourself feel what happened that day, you have to let me know."

"What if I'm never ready?"

He zips my coat, flips up the hood. "If we're going to save that heart of yours—if we're going to save the island, yeah?—I think you'll have to be."

# CHAPTER 18

SIX DAYS UNTIL HIGH BLYS AND WE'RE finally leaving camp. A hundred rebels stand at the edge of the Desolation in the very eye of the storm, gathered around the Sylver Dragon. Though only a handful know the details of our plan, it's an overwhelming sight to know every one of them are on our side.

*Or are they?*

Something Wrex said makes me wonder. He said he liked having allies in our camp. It's possible he meant the dead Paradyian lieutenant, but he said *allies*, and it's planted a seed of distrust in my mind.

I scan the crowd from atop the trailer wondering if there's someone here who can't be trusted. Which of them had the means to contact the Majority? Which of them could get in touch with Wrex while he's at sea or in Glas?

It's not impossible, of course. The isle has radios, we have the post, but it would be difficult to keep that kind of treachery a secret. The rebellion's resources are limited and we live on top of one another, quite literally.

Before they rehitched Mars's trailer to the Dragon, it was scrubbed down and patched up, the turret gun reloaded. The bloodstain Hyla's body had left behind has been washed away, but I still feel her next to me, her boots hanging off the end of the trailer, her guns drawn. I've been standing here for a quarter of an hour wondering what she would do if she suspected a traitor in camp.

Wrex's escape hovers heavy over our mission already. The king couldn't say for certain which conversations his lieutenant had been a part of. He couldn't guarantee that our plan to sabotage the mines at Hex Landing remained a secret, but he sent one of his ships after Wrex just to be safe.

I cautioned against it, thought it best to let the Kol Sea have its way with him. Layce's waters are nothing like the blue seas they've navigated before, but the king is bullheaded, and it's his ship, his crew to sacrifice if he so wishes.

What a terrifying prospect to be a king.

Mars drops from the sky and sets down next to me.

"How'd it go?" I ask, straightening my braids, then tugging my stocking cap over my ears.

"As well as could be expected. Hawken and Fyeeri are back on board their ship and they've taken Dakk's girls; Captain Whatshisname is safely patrolling the waters just beyond Winter's reach, while the smallest and fastest of their ships is pursuing Wrex for all the good it will do them."

"And the other ship?"

"Leisurely making its way around Queen's Point. Relax. It will take days for them to reach the Port of Glas. We have time." A beat and then: "I'm more sorry than I can say about Wrex. We should have left a Paradyian to guard the cell."

"Don't beat yourself up. It was a Paradyian who helped him escape. There were no good options."

"Are you really all right?"

"I'm a fast healer, remember?"

"I do remember." He scratches his chin. "Perhaps I can call you that? Sylver, the quick clotter of Whistletop!"

"Holy hell, Mars. What goes on in your head? *Sister*'s fine. And I'm fine too. You really shouldn't have laid into Kyn like that. It's not his fault, what happened with Wrex. *I* walked away from *him*."

He lets that sit for a moment. "Whatever's happening with the two of you, I understand it's none of my business. But there's no distance to be had in the Sylver Dragon. You know that."

"Not much, you're right."

"We could put him with Felyx and the Paradyians if that's what you need. At least until we get to High Pass."

"No." It's an option I've already considered, but I'd be a nervous wreck the entire time. "If we get separated . . ."

After a moment, Mars taps my right fist, which is wrapped tightly around the hunting knife tucked into my waistband.

"Do you really need that?" he asks.

Leni asked me the same thing just this morning. Now, I unwind my fingers from the handle and flex them against the cold. "I hope not. But I could have used it in the cell block."

The statement rests uncomfortably between us and I'm glad for the hustle and bustle below. There are two smaller rigs on the ice as well, each of them set to carry crews of four, albeit much less comfortably than the Dragon.

To my left is Sayth's rig: a pickup really, ancient and rusted. The paint is so chipped and faded it's impossible to tell what color it once was. The worst of the dents have been hammered out, the bumper secured with a length of rope, and the only things on the rig that look remotely new are the conical speakers that have been bolted to the roof of the cab. I will admit some curiosity.

Off to my right, Dakk and Felyx stand talking to a pair of Paradyian soldiers I've never met. Both of the soldiers are jacked, their muscles bulging as they lean out the windows of a Paradyian war machine.

Dakk tells me this is one of their smaller models. It's similar in size to Sayth's pickup, but more angular, with no bed to speak of. Instead of tires it's been outfitted with tank tread much like the Dragon's. Gun barrels protrude from its grill, menacing to be sure, but the technology is what fascinates me.

Just now, the war machine is an icy, almost iridescent blue, but its skin shifts to match its surroundings. Watching them unload it from the ship was quite the experience. One moment it was the color of the sky, and then the ship, and then the dock. Brilliant and perplexing and hard to keep in sight for any length of time. I'd love to take it for a spin.

All three rigs will move out together across the Desolation toward High Pass. There was a time when I couldn't imagine trucking over the great pool like this; it was simply unfathomable to get a rig as big as the Dragon from the Desolation—which sits below sea level—to the Shiv Road thousands of feet above.

But not anymore.

Now, I'm impatient to get on the road. To climb inside the Dragon and take her for a drive. It's been far too long.

"You two ready, yeah?" Kyn looks up at us from the ice. I woke this morning assuming he'd be distant after everything that happened yesterday, after my clumsy attempt to mend things at the storage shed, but he refuses to be put off.

I step off the edge of the trailer and murmur a word that catches me and sets me gently next to him.

"Here," he says, holding up a hatchet in one hand and a leather belt in the other. "For you."

I take the hatchet and turn it. The handle is made of birch, so pale it's almost white, and near the axe head, snowflakes have been carved into the wood and stained black. I run my thumb over the design. "Is this kol?"

"Looks like it, yeah? I thought about it, thought that might keep folk from stealing it, but in the end, I decided it would be a bad idea for me to work with the stuff. It's just paint."

"*You* did this?" The curve of the handle has been shaped for my small hand, and the iron head's been worked to a perfect angle.

"That old axe you found in the toolshed? I cut it down, reshaped it into something that would be easier to carry. I know you wanted a pickaxe, snowflake, but Drypp's was always too heavy for you. You won't miss with this."

My mind flashes to High Pass, to the snarling wolf I never should have missed. If my aim had been true, who knows where that would have left us.

I swing the leather belt around my waist; it's a little big, but I like the way it hangs on my hips. I tuck the hatchet into it as a ripple makes its way through the crowd. The rebels are turning toward the shore in waves. I can't see over them, so I open my mouth and I speak to Winter once again.

MAKE UP YOUR MIND, she huffs, but she conjures a gust of wind that scoops Kyn and me from the ice, my hands against his chest to keep our faces from colliding. A thrill shoots through both of us as she places us gently next to Mars atop the trailer.

Breathless, Kyn stumbles backward. "Warn me next time, yeah?"

Mars catches his arm before he steps off the edge. "She's impetuous and has far more power than she'll ever use. I thought you knew that already, but there, you've been warned."

I hide a grin, turning toward the fence line where a forest-green pickup sits parked. Desy climbs out the passenger side, her red hair braided and secured at the base of her neck. Her colorful skirt and heavy woolen sweater make her look young, a child wearing her mother's clothes. She would be very easy to underestimate.

Her driver offers her a hand, and she takes it, climbing up into the bed of the truck. Someone whistles and the crowd quiets. Desy leans forward, her hands on her knees, as though she were speaking to a classroom full of children.

"Today we send hope across the isle." Her voice is rock steady and just loud enough to reach us at the back. "It is a secret hope today, is it not? Only those of us here have the pleasure of holding tight to it, but very soon, this hope will reside in the hearts of all who call Shiv Island home."

She pulls herself upright once again, her hands behind her back. "Today though, it rides on the tread of three rigs. In the will and might of those in their cabs: Old friends and new. Soldiers trained for battle, rebels with stories of oppression and endangerment at the hands of the Majority, and some with histories shot through with myth and magic we can scarcely believe." A glance in our direction. "And yet, we've seen it, have we not? Seen Winter compelled to work on our behalf." She raises her hands to the cyclone whirling around us. "We're reminded that though we're a small uprising, we're a powerful one. There is much we cannot be sure of, but there is no denying this one thing: We cannot delay. *Now* is our time.

"So! To those of you setting out across the ice: Be well, be brave, be successful. Not just for those of us here, but for all who treasure this island. We will not be idle in your absence but will be readying ourselves for all plausible outcomes."

Kyn shifts. "She means they'll be preparing for war, yeah?"

"We can't afford not to," Mars says.

I keep my eyes on Desy. She's steely-eyed and intent, utterly convincing as she lifts her gaze to the Dragon and the rigs parked on either side of it.

"When you return, my dear rebellious hearts," she says, "it will not be the end of what we've started here but the beginning. A new beginning that Begynd himself would be proud of!"

The crowd erupts, turning toward us. Applause and whistles, cries of *"Be well"* echo off the mountains and across the ice. It feels possible, this thing we're doing. It feels right.

After a moment the shouts begin to fade and faces turn expectant, all eyes on us. I lift my gaze to Desy, but she's watching Mars and me, her hands tucked once again behind her back, her body leaning ever so slightly forward.

"They're waiting, sister. A word or two before we go?"

But I've nothing to say, nothing Desy hasn't already covered. Nothing except . . .

I step off the trailer and with a word, Winter swoops to catch me, biting at my lips, annoyed. The suddenness of her gust sends hats flying and scarves waving. I hover in the air and the rebels clutch at their coats as they gape up at me.

"Load 'em up!" I call.

The crowd erupts once again.

When I set down next to Kyn atop the trailer, there's a smirk on his face. "Show-off."

"Not a show-off," I say. "Not really. Just . . . proving that what Desy said is true. We're not fighting alone. We have weapons and authority the Majority doesn't. It's good for the rebels to remember that."

"It's good for *us* to remember that," Mars says, dropping off the trailer and landing gently on the ground below.

Kyn and I make our way along the top of the rig toward the cab. But when I get there, I realize my seat is already taken.

"I didn't realize you were driving," I say.

Leni's eyes are serious, rusty freckles stark against her pale white skin. "You know me. Daredevil." She's wearing trousers for maybe the first time in forever and a hand-knitted sweater that will soak up rain like a sponge.

Kyn climbs in through the passenger window and slides quietly into the back, his concerned gaze catching mine as he settles onto the bench seat.

"I assume your gear's in the back?" I ask Leni.

"Yours too," she says. "I packed you a bag."

Of course she did.

"What's going on, Len?"

She leans closer, her words for me alone. "You'll let me talk to him, right? My da? *Before* you tell him what you need?"

"He's your father, Leni. You can talk to him whenever you want."

"It's just . . . I don't know . . . I mean, he's brilliant, he is." Her eyes are wide, her jaw set. She's convinced. "He can get you anything you need, right? It's just, I'm thinking he might not understand right away why he should."

So maybe Macks Trestman wasn't quite as clear-eyed as she's made out.

"We'll take it one step at a time, OK?"

She swallows and a bit of color returns to her cheeks. "All right. One step at a time."

Mars opens the passenger-side door and steps up onto the running board, pausing when he sees us, managing to turn even that into a grandiose gesture as he leans ever so dramatically against the doorframe. "Everything OK, ladies?"

"Oh. Yes," Leni says. "Yes, of course. I'm sorry, Sylvi. I'm in your seat." She makes for the back, but Mars stops her.

"The front seat is yours, Miss Trestman." A pause. "You don't mind me calling you that, do you?"

"Of course not, it's my name."

"If only all of you were that simple."

I roll my eyes.

"Well! Miss Trestman! I'll warn you that the expensive seats aren't all they're cracked up to be, especially with the Begynd

Wonder Brat driving. I much prefer being chauffeured around."
A slick move and he's behind the passenger seat.

"The Begynd Wonder Brat?" Kyn asks him.

"I have to call her something."

"Once again," I say, "I offer *sister* as an option."

"It'll do for now, but on the whole, I decline. Far too informal.
You are the daughter of a queen. You require a title."

"I call you by your first name."

"Yes, but you were raised in a garage. If you're looking for
alternatives, though, you may call me Mars Almighty or the
Black-Eyed Storm."

"I decline." We say it together—Leni, Kyn, and I—and laughter breaks loud and much needed over the cab.

Once Lenore is safely ensconced, I slide into my seat. When I
turn the key in the ignition, the Sylver Dragon growls to life and
a million concerns evaporate. It's been too long.

"Look at your face," Kyn says, leaning forward, his fingers
already snagging in my hair. "I've missed *this* Sylvi."

I shove him back in his seat and I yank the window into place.
"Me too," I say, and I mean it. I'm at my best when I'm in the
driver's seat.

With a simple command, I release Winter to rage as she will,
and in my side mirror I watch as the rebels run for cover.

"You liked that a little too much, sister."

I might have. "Buckle up."

# CHAPTER 19

WE'RE MAKING GOOD TIME. EVEN WITH Winter raging, we should be halfway across the ice come midnight. We'll swap drivers then, travel through the night.

Six hours in now, and the mountains off to our right and left are nothing but jagged teeth gnawing at the edges of my vision. Everything else is either ice or sky, all of it touched by the strange sylver light pushing through the Desolation.

The Fount of Begynd won't be ignored any longer, and neither will the voices shouting through the ice. They're dissonant and jarring, but thus far I'm getting only unease from Kyn. And a steady, thrumming pain he's been ignoring. His ribs, maybe? From the ship?

Off to my left, Dakk drives the Paradyian war machine—insisted really. He and the king nearly came to blows over it. The king yelling that they had an entire battalion on Layce, that

Dakk's responsibility was here, to his daughters. In the end, Dakk insisted that Hyla would have wanted him to go.

And what was the king supposed to say to that?

Felyx rides next to Dakk, looking mighty small surrounded by three Paradyian soldiers. But in that rig, he's the only one who knows the isle.

Music, loud and sudden, breaks through the storm. It sets the windows of the Sylver Dragon rattling and I glance over at Sayth's truck, in awe of her speakers. This is nothing like the dreary music Drypp piped into the tavern. This is all raucous energy, stringed chaos, and bedlam.

I like it. My heart bangs to the rhythm of the drums, waking me, pushing my confidence high. I bounce in my seat, slowly at first, feeling silly, and then faster, seeing nothing before us but success, freedom from the Majority, a new life for the beaten and the broken.

I'm not the only one caught up in the music either. Lenore is singing along, her eyes shut, her auburn head swinging. Behind me, Kyn drums with his hands. First on his knees and then on the seat back and the hatch overhead, his entire body swaying right and left. Even Mars taps his fingers against his leg, keeping time, staring absently out at the rain.

The music ratchets up a notch and I spare another glance in my side mirror, watch as Sayth drops her window down, flinging her bare arm outside, waving it up and down in the rain.

The melody continues to climb, and then with a shattering of cymbals it falls away, replaced by something low and sad, something we can hardly hear over the storm. Lenore goes quiet, Kyn's hands still, and Mars sits a little straighter in his seat, the heft of the challenge before us heavy once again.

✳

The day passes in a blur of wind and rain. Behind me, Kyn and Mars sleep, while on my right, Lenore's lips move as she stares out the windshield. She's singing quietly to herself now, a song just for her.

I relive my arguments with Kyn and with Winter, a measure of shame in both. Making any kind of deal with Winter is foolish, I know that. I don't imagine she'll keep up her end of the bargain—revelation number seven: Winter has a short memory— but we also can't do this thing without her.

And thus far, she's behaving herself: raging wildly to keep the voices at bay and keeping her complaints to a minimum. She chatters at me on occasion, a bunch of nonsense for the most part, but she's lost in herself just now. And while Mars and I both felt it was best to let her rage, Kyn's words have begun to haunt me.

We *are* letting her do whatever she wants, and the more I think on it, the more precarious that seems. Dangerous even.

I remember an argument Old Man Drypp and Mystra Dyfan had a long time ago. She lasted longer than the village schoolteacher, but eventually she'd grown weary of me as well.

*"I wanted this to work, sir,"* Mystra told Drypp, *the two of them standing ankle deep in snow, staring up at my perch in the top of a tree.*

*"You came to me,"* he said. *"Offered your services."*

*"I did, yes. But I'm unaccustomed to teaching the unruly and wild. If she were like your granddaughter, if she were anything like Lenore—"*

"Let this one be."

"You pay me to teach her." Her exasperation was hot, spitting like water boiling in a kettle.

"And you will. Just give her some time when her energy rises. She'll blow herself out and sit herself down soon enough. I've seen it plenty. Allow her that bit of wildness and you'll not hurt yourself trying to restrain her."

Mystra's fingers rose to her bloodied lip. She'd wrapped her arms around me trying to keep me still, but still would not have me. "And if she's never restrained, good sir?"

He thought on that a moment, a subject not new to him.

"Not all things are. But it's not what I'd wish for her, you know that. Which is why you're here. To teach her where she came from, what she could be with a little discipline. Yes, some creatures can't be tamed. But others, well, they learn to restrain themselves, don't they? When they see the hurt they cause others, they change."

"Your daughter never changed, sir. She ran away and now look at her. Married poorly and indebted forever to the Majority. Restraint must be taught."

"Perhaps. But neither you nor I understand what Sylvi has endured. We do not know whether she will learn to rein in her impulsive behavior, but rest yourself, Mystra. We do know this: She will tire. She always does."

I hate the idea that I've become like Mystra, worrying over Winter, wondering if she'll ever learn to check her impulses. But Winter's not human, and raging will not deplete her magic; obedience alone does that.

"Do you remember this song, Syl?" Leni asks. "Mystra taught us that little jig to go with it." She hums a bar or two, adds in a few hand motions, but it's only vaguely familiar.

"I remember so little of what Mystra taught us, Len. I'm sorry. If I'd paid attention . . ." I shake my head, clear away all the things that could have been different if I'd let Mystra teach me. "Hyla sang at court. Did you know that?"

"Hyla sang?" Lenore's face lights up.

"She offered to teach me the Paradyian anthem."

"It's a beastly song," Mars mumbles, still half asleep. "All trumpets and trilling voices. Miserable, I tell you. On Paradyia, they play it every time Hawken rises to his feet. After one day in his receiving room, I nearly tied him to his throne."

"What a miserable king you would have been." Leni laughs and Mars flips onto his side. "I didn't know Hyla sang. She was so good at everything though, I bet her voice was lovely. Did you ever get to hear it?"

Regret cuts deep. "I didn't, no."

"Those weeks she spent in Whistletop, mostly she took me for target practice."

"Well, she was good at that too."

"Amazing, really."

Overhead, the radio squeals and Sayth's voice breaks into the cab. "Boss, we got some folks here need to pee."

I've never had a radio in my rig before, never needed to talk to anyone while I'm working, but before we left Queen's Point, they installed short-range radios in all our rigs. For just such occasions, I suppose.

"Some folks here need the same," Kyn says, groggy as he stretches and detangles himself from the velvet drape.

I reach up and grab the handset, giving the scene outside a quick scan. It's all much the same. With night falling, we're as hidden as we'll ever be.

"We'll stop here," I say into the radio. "Stretch our legs. If you need to swap drivers, now's the time."

Kyn pushes between Leni and me, looking out at the vast spread of ice. "Not a lot of privacy out here."

I slow the Dragon, pulling her safely to a stop. The rigs flanking me do the same.

"There's port and starboard," I say, gesturing with my hands. "Take your pick."

Mars yawns himself awake. "The dragon lady was listening. Very good."

"I'm not answering to that."

"But it conjures all sorts of imagery!" He opens the hatch overhead and demands Winter make us the center of her storm. She bites him hard enough to elicit a flinch, but she spins into compliance without a word. Another command and she tugs him into the sky.

The rest of us use the doors.

The air is crisp and cool outside, water pattering down on the rigs, the ice beneath my feet glowing faintly. I wander as far starboard as I dare, into the shadow of the Dragon, and relieve myself quickly.

The three rigs have been parked in a wide triangle, and as I make my way back, it's clear someone has started a fire. I'm tempted to hustle everyone back to their rigs, reprimand them for using our precious firewood so early.

But their laughter does something to my insides and it turns me warm and soft. The ice-blue edges of the night are shaved down and tipped orange with firelight. The crews' chatter speaks of companionship and family, and I can't make myself hurry this moment away. Winter isn't the only one who wants to belong.

The fire is a simple thing, three or four logs and the damp hiss you'd expect out on the ice. Most everyone stands, but a few sit on wood rounds. I find an open space between Lenore and Felyx and watch as, across the circle, Sayth tells a story with her entire body, hands waving, mouth and eyes wide, squatting and kicking when the occasion calls.

Behind me someone snorts. It's Tooki, and I'm surprised he's here. Last I knew, he was begging Sayth for a seat in her rig. I didn't realize he'd been successful.

"You wore her down, did you?"

"Mars made her bring me," he says. "But I'm useful. She'll see."

"I figure you earned your spot with those ice bikes. We're going to need them where we're going."

"You sure you don't need another driver?"

"Show Sayth you're useful, Tooki. That's your job."

He shrugs, which is pretty much his personality, I realize.

"Who else did Sayth drag along?" My eyes rake over the dozen faces around the fire.

"There," he says, tipping his chin to two young women whose faces I recognize but who I have never officially met. "Brash and Tali."

Fire and ice, this pair. They hear their names and look up. The girl nearest me has dark brown skin, a head of red braids, and eyes of liquid amber. Like Sayth, like Kyn, like Desy, she's Shiv and wears a sleeveless top to prove it. Orange rock loops across her collarbone in a single line, continuing down her left arm and ending only when it reaches her wrist.

"I'm Brash," she says, reaching a hand out to me. "And this one's Tali."

"Sylvi," I say, shaking her hand.

Tali's hands are wrapped around a mug of boiled chocolate, so she simply grins.

She's as pale as Brash is dark, and while they're nearly the same height, Brash is muscled and Tali is slight, her straight black hair hanging to her waist and chopped in a straight line across her brows.

"How much farther to this High Pass?" a Paradyian asks. I have yet to learn his name.

"If we get a move on," I say, "we should be there sometime tomorrow afternoon."

Kyn stabs at the fire with a stick. "That's good, yeah? Wouldn't want to surprise Shyne after dark."

"Oooh, yeah," Tali says. "Brash tells us he's a scary guy."

"You know Shyne?" I ask Brash.

She sits on a log, her elbows resting on her knees. "I grew up in the pass."

Kyn's gaze snaps to her. "In the caves?"

"Mm-hmm. Lived there my whole life, until . . ." She shakes her head. "Until I didn't."

"How'd you get out?" Kyn squats so his eyes are level with hers, the firelight flickering between them.

"Begynd gave me two feet, and I used them."

"You just walked away?" I ask.

"The decision to go was the hard part. You're labeled a traitor if you leave, no better than the unbelievers at Dris Mora."

"I remember," Kyn says, absently rubbing his chest. "You're a believer then?"

"I am, yes. I await Begynd, our creator, with great hope."

"Then why leave?" Felyx asks.

"Have you seen them caves?" Tooki says.

Brash grins. "I didn't mind the caves, Tooki Lasa. But the waiting alone became more than I could bear. We knew about the rebels, of course, heard of their actions against their overseers. And though Shyne and the elders insisted that their fight had nothing to do with us, I could not agree. The Majority preyed on our people. Any reason at all was sufficient for them to round up Shiv and put us to work in their mines or their factories. And once those Shiv were gone, we never searched them out. Never. We relegated them to the Majority, considered them lost. If I must wait on Begynd I will, but I can fight for the freedom of my people while he tarries. Shyne disagreed."

"But he let you leave?" Kyn asks.

Her laugh is small and dry. "I will not be welcomed upon my return, I assure you. But yes, I faced no physical threat when I left." She pulls herself upright, her Shiv accent more noticeable the longer she speaks. "Two years past now, during the Festival of Begynd, I tried to talk to Shyne, tried to make him see." A shrug. "That was the last time I asked permission. On our journey home, I kissed my mother and sister goodbye, stepped off the trail, and found my way to the road." Her eyes are glossy. "I tried to catch a ride, but we Shiv have a nasty reputation. In some ways, we've earned it, I suppose. In the end, I came upon a twyl farm, climbed into an open trailer, and let it haul me all the way to Hex Landing. That's where I met Tali and Sayth."

Sayth's smile is impish. "We'd been up all night, Tali and me, jimmying the screws out of every bit of equipment we could find in the mine yard, slashing the tires of their rigs and tractors. Playing at rebellion, really. Them Majority bosses were hissing and spitting when they realized what we'd done. Fence went up not long after that."

"Brash found us giggling into our brew mugs as we watched

from the tavern across the way." Tali lifts her face to Sayth. "Oooh. I'd kill for a licorice brew right now. That was good stuff."

"And you, Sayth? Do you await Begynd with great hope?" It's Mars and though the words are Brash's, he's not mocking. He wants to know.

She shrugs. "I like the stories well enough, and Brash here's been trying to convert me since we met. But I grew up different than she did, working the mines alongside a bunch of lower-class Majority kids."

Tali points at her own face. "Lower-class Majority kid right here."

"Only thing I ever knew about Begynd was that he made a handy curse word. But I hate the Majority Council and their stooges something fierce, and who knows, maybe I won't have to just hope that Begynd rises from the ice. With *boss lady* here leading the way, maybe I'll get to see it happen."

Mars clears his throat. "For the record, I'm the heir to the Kerce throne, not boss lady."

"Technically, the Kerce throne no longer exists," I say. "And I would absolutely answer to boss lady, by the way."

Mars offers me a little nod. "I decline."

"How did you survive the mines?" one of the Paradyians asks Sayth. His name is Sten, I'm almost certain. "Are not your people especially susceptible to the kol?"

"We are. But there are ways to get twyl if you've used up your rations, things the overseers want." She drops her gaze. "No one *wants* to barter with them, but you do it if you want to survive. I watched a lot of my friends nurse an addiction to the kol, watched it melt their brains even as they worked themselves to the bone for the fluxing Majority . . . I learned quick not to run out of twyl. My own head is messed up enough without the kol." Her teeth flash, but this time the smile never reaches her eyes. Begynd knows what she had to trade to stay sane, to stay alive. She claps her hands together. "So this Shyne then. He scary as Brash says he is?"

"He can be," I say, remembering the stone he pressed to my chest, the demands he made of me. "Mostly, I think he's sad."

"Mostly, he wants to see the Pool of Begynd restored," Mars says. "That has been the great passion of his life. Everything he does is to see that come to pass."

"That and protecting the Desolation from traitorous unbelievers like us, yeah?" Kyn stands, flings the stick he was using to poke the fire into the distance.

"You're not an unbeliever," I say.

"Yeah, no. Not anymore." He smiles, but it's forced, and something tightens in my chest. He's hurting.

"And neither am I." Brash eyes the circle of rebels, looking into each face in turn. "I want that understood. I believe Begynd will return, but I also believe that the strength he's given my arms and legs should be used for more than standing around. And I intend to make the Majority feel that."

Mars nods. "Hear, hear."

# CHAPTER 20

WINTER IS A FRENETIC FALL OF RAIN through the night. She's noisy and Kyn's pain is noisy and the Shiv voices are chewing at the edge of the storm, and I consider opening a conversation with Winter just to burn it all away. But Mars is too close. He'd know.

Sunrise adds nothing to the scenery but a gray blur. I nap on and off, my temple pressed against the cool glass, Kyn steering us straight and true across the ice.

"Want me to drive?" I ask.

"Nah. I'm good."

"We share feelings, you know? I don't think you're good."

He keeps his eyes on the road, tugs the zipper on his vest all the way to the top. "Bumps and bruises that's all. I'm fine."

"You're a horrible liar."

Now he looks at me, flashes that smile. "I'm way better than you are, snowflake."

High Pass rises before us now, slabs of rock visible on the lower slopes where the snow has softened and slid away. I'm counting the hours until we reach the western shore, when the rev of an engine catches my attention.

It's not a sound I'm familiar with, certainly not Sayth's rig nor the Paradyian war machine. I drop my window down and a gust of rain barrels in, a protest rising from the cab. I ignore them, adjusting the side mirror until . . .

"Ah, flux." A snow-white pickup almost identical to Jymy Leff's. With a heavy-duty gun glaring at us from the roof.

I stretch for the radio overhead.

"What is it?" Kyn asks.

"Rangers," I say into the mouthpiece. "Coming up on our right."

Kyn leans closer, checking my mirror. I replace the handset and pull on my gloves.

The speaker crackles overhead, Felyx's voice breaking through. "Two more rigs blazing toward us, boss. Heading up from the south."

Another crackle and it's Tooki. "That's the same squad we met last week."

I snatch the mouthpiece. "Who you stole the bikes from?"

"I'm almost certain."

"*Almost* certain?" I ask. "What does that mean?"

"That flatlander ride coming up behind you? I know it. The governor of the Stack, Minshew Kapps? That's his son's car. Rich Majority brat. I'm guessing the Rangers commandeered it. Wouldn't want to be them when Kapps finds out."

He's talking about a steely gray rig pushing to the right side of the Dragon. I watch it in the side mirror. No bed, the back tires sitting taller than the front so that it looks pitched forward on its toes, and a flashy grill guard that's more show than utility.

I shoot Kyn a glance and swing my feet into the seat. "Keep her steady."

"Sylvi," Lenore says, "You can't possibly—"

"She can, Miss Trestman, and she must." Mars unlocks the overhead hatch and gives me a curt nod. "See you outside."

He flings the hatch open and shoots skyward. The hatch door swings shut, and I cringe remembering how the frame shattered not so long ago. But the new latch catches, and out the windshield Mars spins into view, a storm pushed before him, smacking the flatlander ride hard on its driver's side, sending it tumbling across the ice. The storm's movements mirror Mars's. The strategy is one he likes to employ, selecting a target and ordering Winter to follow his movements, to mimic him. I've not had much cause to try it.

Lenore's eyes bulge. "Oh my . . . holy . . . is this . . . I don't think that's safe."

"He's been doing it for three hundred years, Leni." But it's also taxing for Winter. I feel the tug on her magic and determine to keep my commands simple. We're hours from High Pass now, and we can't afford to be without her as we approach the Shiv settlement.

"What did they load into the turret gun?" I ask Kyn. "They tell you?"

"Incendiary rounds. Same as we had on the Seacliff Road. The Paradyians are hardcore about anything that starts a fire."

"Good. I can work with that. Just point and shoot, right?"

Lenore's sputtering now, her protective nature taking over, fussing at me to stay. Same as she always did when I had work to do.

"Leni, I'm fine. Seriously. I do this all the time. Tell her, Kyn." And then my boots are on the windowsill and with a little jump and some help from Winter, I'm on the roof of the cab.

I keep the commands simple as I jump the gap between the cab and the trailer, but I notice Winter doing things she hasn't done in a while, things she used to do all the time without instruction. She's holding me tight, keeping my boots steady, protecting me from the worst of her winds. It frees me to concentrate on the Rangers and their rigs. There should be three, right?

The snow-white pickup is a standard Ranger ride—big tires, short bed, gun mounted to the roof—and then there's the flat-lander rig Mars has blown so far toward the horizon I can't see it any longer.

And there! Bringing up the rear, an orange farm truck I don't imagine they acquired legally. It's a flatbed, a Frost White and her pup tied to the railing, both wearing wreaths of twyl. The truck's tires squeal on the ice, the flatbed kicking around, slamming the wolves into the railing.

Winter screams, and I watch as the front of the rig starts to ice over.

"Now, you've ticked her off."

I drop into the turret and stare at the gun, not quite sure what to do. I've never fired this thing before, but it looks straightforward enough. There's a trigger and . . .

A bullet slices through the air, lifting my hair and setting my ear ringing.

"Flux," I hiss, raising my hand to my face, ducking as I scan the rigs in the distance.

I locate the shooter in the bed of the white pickup. He stands with his feet shoulder-width apart, finger on the trigger of the gun mounted to the roof of the rig, a snarky grin on his ugly face.

Somewhere Mars is whispering sweet mad things into Winter's ear and she's kicking up a fuss. Hail falls: on the rigs, on the Desolation, on the Ranger across the way, but not on me.

"Thank you," I tell Winter.

The Ranger takes a pummeling before he ducks and covers his head, but a moment later he's standing again, grinning stupidly, a hard hat in place. He lines up the gun again, sliding his finger back inside the trigger guard. Panic floods my chest and I grab hold of the turret gun, wheel it around, and fire. The gun shudders, and an incendiary round strikes the front driver's-side tire of the pickup and explodes.

The truck rises off the ice, ejecting the hard hat–wearing Ranger from the bed. Flames engulf the front of the rig as it smacks down hard on the empty wheel well, making it scrape forward as flames sizzle on the ice. At last it comes to a stop.

The driver staggers out, his white pants and coat on fire. He falls to his knees, swatting at the flames. We fly by and I'm content to let him burn, but as I watch, he strips off his coat then clamors for the gun mounted on the top of the pickup. I have no idea if it survived the crash, but Sayth's rig is coming up hard and fast, and that gun is no joke.

If he gets his finger on the trigger . . .

I hiss a command that sets Winter laughing.

**YOU ARE VICIOUS, SYLVER QUINE. WE'RE MORE ALIKE THAN I REMEMBERED.** And with a little too much glee, Winter chills the falling rain, encasing the Ranger in ice with his mouth agape.

Sayth flies by the frozen man, and I know the very moment she understands what's happened. Both windows on her rig drop down and cheers break into the air, muffled by the hailstorm and the wind, but clear enough and carrying.

Tali climbs out the window and into the bed of the truck, lithe, experienced, a rifle in her hand. She winces as the hail drops harder, and since it's a simple task for Winter, and only one more blister for me, I tell her to keep the hail off Tali as well.

I can't see the result of my command, not really—we're pulling farther and farther away—but she waves a quick thank-you in my direction, before taking aim at the farm truck pulling even with their passenger-side door. With her hip jutting into the window of the cab, and the gun steadied on her shoulder, she fires, cycles the bolt, and fires again.

One of her shots hits the hood of the farm truck. And the other takes out a tire. The farm truck pitches around on the ice, the wolves in the bed hunkering down as a plume of steam rises into the sky. The truck slides, momentum flinging it in erratic circles, until eventually it spins its way to a stop.

"Good shooting," I whisper. I turn in the direction I last saw Mars. We've come some distance, and he's nothing but a blur. I jump into the sky and Winter catches me.

BOSS LADY, she coos, flying me back to the Dragon's roof hatch and dropping me inside.

Kyn's eyes are wide, his concern ebbing as I settle next to him. "Getting comfortable with our role, are we?"

I grin, but it hurts. Winter might be helping, but she's not doing it for free. Those days are long gone.

"Gah, Sylvi. Your face." Leni pushes her way between our seats, her hand reaching for my mouth. I swat it away. "Sit still; it's just ointment."

"I might be bleeding, Len." Because of what Bristol did to me when I was a kid, I've always struggled with people touching me, but these days I'm downright paranoid.

"*I'm* not bleeding though," Leni says, smearing the oily concoction on my face anyway. "I know what I'm doing. I've patched you up plenty."

"That was before." It terrifies me really. All the wounds of mine she's tended over the years. All the moments that could have set us on an entirely different path.

"There was no before," Leni says. "You've always been weird." It's true, of course, and even with the risk, there's no swatting her away.

I give up, turning to Kyn. His face is pale, sweat dotting his brow.

"Circle back, will you? I've lost sight of Mars and the war machine."

"Yes, ma'am." He turns the wheel slowly, hand over hand, and we make a wide arc around the Rangers and their wreckage. We see the farm truck first. The mewling wolves are still strapped to the flatbed's railing, their owners kicking their way out of the cab and into the angry and dangerous hail, handguns strapped to their hips.

I can't use Winter to speak to the wolves, not with those wreaths in place, but I hiss a command that has Winter freezing their leashes so cold they shatter. If they're going to leave their oppressors, they're going to have to do it like the rest of us, with their own free will.

"Should we leave them like that?" Leni asks. "The Rangers?"

"Well, we're not making room in here." I push her hand away. "That smells like death, Leni."

"No, I mean, should we leave them alive?" She sniffs at the ointment and replaces the lid. "They're hunting you down, right? They could pass along our whereabouts or, you know, the things they've seen, to the council? It doesn't seem wise to leave them out here."

"You want me to run them over?!" Kyn's smiling but there's shock there. In his voice. In his gut. Lenore might be tremulous, but she's not a wuss, and Kyn doesn't always know what to make of her.

"Maybe not that, but . . . something?"

"It's a long walk to shore," I say. "And any information they think they have is already out there. They won't be a problem for us."

*No more than Wrex will.*

But Leni's brow is furrowed and scowling as she stares out at the Rangers, her hand fisted around the ointment. "I hate them."

Together, we watch them curse and scrabble as we fly by, one of them getting off a shot that rings loudly off the Dragon's bucket. Leni scrapes her cheek at them. A gesture once used by the Kerce when choosing a successor, the meaning was lost long ago. Now, it's a show of disrespect.

"Rangers are nothing in the grand scheme," I say. "Tattletales and thieves just trying to survive out here."

Lenore's teeth grind. "By turning on their own. They're mountain folk, Syl, mountain folk who've sided with the Majority Council, who have no qualms about finding reasons to kidnap and kill. Rangers lock up their neighbors for a little coin. Does it get lower than that?"

"There," I say, changing the subject. "Mars."

He's kicked up another cyclone, but this time it's all snow and ice, spinning around the war machine and the flatlander ride. They're little more than a thick white blotch against the gray sky until we're a hundred yards out.

At last, we can make more sense of what we're seeing.

The flatlander ride is a crumpled version of itself, but it's still running. Behind tinted windows, the driver is impossible to see, but the engine revs, exhaust spilling from the tailpipe, tires spinning on the ice.

The war machine sits opposite, its guns glowing blue. Dakk juts from an opening on its roof, and a shadowy form stands between the vehicles. Mars.

"Keep her here," I say. "Let me see what we're dealing with."

Kyn decelerates, and I whisper a command that has Winter opening the hatch and pulling me from my seat.

**CAREFUL**, she says. **CAREFUL.**

The cold is sudden and intense, and I gasp like I've fallen into a pool of icy water. Winter's gone frigid at Mars's command, colder than she ever gets in Blys. It takes my body a moment to adjust.

When my feet hit the ground, I lift my hood and step forward into the cyclone Mars created. Winter carves me a path, and with a single step I'm standing in the eye of the storm. It's quiet save the revving engine and the oscillating guns. Snowflakes hover in midair.

Mars marches toward the flatlander ride. He stomps onto the bumper, the hood, the windshield, the roof.

I don't see him make the command, but I feel the pull as Winter obeys. She yanks open the roof hatch so that it tears completely away. Mars pulls the driver from his seat. Winter's clearly helping: The Ranger is close to Kyn's size, but Mars tosses him to the ice with little effort.

The passenger door opens, and another man scrambles out. Like the driver, he's geared up in a white parka and snow pants; the sidearm he pulls is also white. It trembles in his hand, but that doesn't make him any less dangerous. Just a lot more stupid.

One word from me and the gun freezes solid, his hand too. The weight of it drives him to his knees, and he cries out, afraid.

Winter laughs. **WE SHOULD HAVE DONE MORE OF THIS BEFORE.**

I can't help the grin that spreads across my face as the Ranger sputters and gapes, fighting to lift his arm. Maybe I am a little brutal.

I lift my gaze to Mars, expecting a grin there too, but the

driver has his full attention. He steps off the hood of the car and saunters toward the Ranger cowering on the ground.

"We're just here for the coin," the driver says. "That's it. Majority's offering a large purse for anyone in contact with you two."

Mars stops. "They're offering a reward for our crews?"

"Yeah, man. For anyone who can tell them what you're up to. Where you are."

My eyes flash to the rig. "And your radios?"

"What?" Confusion on his face, in his voice.

Mars crouches down, his face dangerously close to the Ranger. "Your radios, *man*. Who have you been talking to since you caught sight of us? Are your radios short-range or—"

"Yeah, yeah. Short-range."

"Check them," Mars calls, but Felyx is already on it. I hadn't even seen him there, standing beyond the war machine.

"You don't gotta worry," the Ranger insists. "We haven't talked to no one but ourselves since yesterday."

Mars's gaze lifts to the horizon. Even through the storm, it's nothing but ice for miles and miles. "And how did you know you could find us here? How did you know we'd be on the ice?"

"What? Are you serious?"

"How?!"

"Chill, man. We weren't looking for you. We were looking for the punk-nose quill rats that stole our bikes. Bragging about knowing the ice witch and taking down the Majority. Rebel scum. They took off across the Desolation, man. We've been here every day since."

Tooki's lucky there's a cyclone between him and Mars.

"Interesting," Mars says. "And did you tell anyone else you saw quill-rat rebels out on the ice?"

"No, man. I told you, we want the bounty. We're not about to tell anyone else where to find you."

"How much is the Majority offering?" I ask, stepping closer, putting the Ranger between Mars and me.

His eyes shift to me and then back to Mars. "Ten thousand for either of you. And half that for anyone seen with you."

"Kyn will be insulted," I say.

Mars smiles, but it's lopsided, and not at all friendly. Blisters oozing, kol flecks in his teeth. The driver flinches backward into my shins.

"How far to the southern shore?" I ask.

He tips his face up. "Depends what you're driving—"

"Walking," Mars says. A whisper drives spikes of ice through each of the flatlander's tires.

"Flux, man, flux! That's a borrowed car!"

"How far?" I ask again.

"Southern shore'd take too long to walk from here. But we can get to the eastern shore in half a day."

Mars stands up, crosses his arms over his chest. "Best get walking then."

The Ranger pushes himself upright and staggers over to his friend, who is still whimpering, the ice encasing his hand now frozen to the great pool. "You gonna let him up?"

I slide my hands into my pockets. "You going to tell anyone what you saw out here?"

His eyes flick to Mars and me, to Felyx, to the Paradyian

jutting from the war machine, guns still trained on him. "No, man. No. We won't say a thing."

"They can't be trusted." It's Felyx's voice and it's shaking fiercely. He's gone white around the mouth and his hands are fisted at his sides.

"Sure, we can. We want to live, man! Live."

At my command, Winter releases his friend's hand, and the block of ice turns to water. "Leave the gun."

They curse me, but do as I say, stumbling backward, the driver tugging his friend toward their rig as he clutches wildly at his wrinkled hand. "Fluxing ice witch. What'd you do to me?"

"Be grateful," I call. "Winter's in a friendly mood."

"And why's that, sister?"

I feel a prickle of conscience, but Winter whisks it away with a chill, and together we watch the Rangers plunder their rig for whatever they'll need to cross the ice.

"We might regret letting them go," Felyx says after the Rangers stumble through the cyclone and out the other side.

"We might," I agree.

Dakk disengages the war machine's guns. "That was entertaining, but does it have to be so cold? This is your wet season, is it not?"

"Apologies," Mars says, dropping the cyclone. I expect Winter to unload on us again, but it's quieter than it's been in days. She's still there, still tempestuous, but the storm has an almost orderly feel, a steady stream of icy words rushing north, droning on and on, an almost mechanical sound that sends the mist into a tizzy.

"Well, that's interesting," I say, glancing first at the sky and then at the Sylver Dragon where my crew stares on.

Leni's hands cover her mouth as she stares at us through the windshield, Kyn sits cross-legged on the roof, his hood up, his arms exposed, gaping like a fool. I have no idea how much they saw through the icy winds, but they clearly saw enough.

Sayth's pickup is there too, parked next to the Dragon; I hadn't heard them arrive, but she and her crew stare on. I flash them all two thumbs-up, then turn back to Mars. "Felyx is right. We have to assume the Rangers will talk."

"Agreed. But we'll be at High Pass before they reach the eastern shore. We're close, yes?"

"We are. And they're not following us there at least."

"*They* may not, but there are those who would brave the mountain. That's a lot of coin they're offering."

"I like our chances with the Shiv."

"Well, you'll have to do the talking, I'm afraid. My history with Shyne coupled with . . . recent events . . ."

"Don't worry. I wasn't going to let you talk anyway."

He peers around me, his face going slack. "What's this?"

I turn to see a Frost White wolf pup stumbling toward us, blood on his paw. His twyl wreath is mangled but swinging in place. It won't be potent much longer. He stops, dazed, and lets out a cry.

"Where's his mother?" I ask, scanning the horizon.

"Rangers killed her," Tali says. "Mama went for them first, so I suppose it was self-defense, but it was ugly to see. Poor things. And this one followed us here but won't let us get close enough to check him out. Must be something he wants."

"He wants his mother," I say, kneeling. "He wants food."

The pup paws closer, still crying, his steps awkward.

I reach out a hand. "He's hurt."

"Miss Quine—"

"Not my name."

Mars steps closer, his boots clicking against the ice. "We have neither his mother to offer him nor food to spare."

He's right, of course. But the pup is alone and injured. He paws my leg and then sprawls on the ice, his crystal-clear eyes on me, tail thumping slowly.

There's no refusing that.

I extend my hand, and the pup sniffs it, licks my knuckle with a scratchy pink tongue. I scoop him to my chest and stand. "He can have my food."

"On Paradyia," Dakk calls, "wolf sightings are rare and presage long life."

Mars tuts. "I assure you, old friend, they mean nothing of the sort here. Miss Quine—"

"Not. My. Name."

Mars growls. "Remember how much you dislike being needed?"

"Mm-hmm," I say, twisting my face away from the nuzzling pup. "And I remember you telling me how foolish that was. I could let a wolf need me."

Kyn stands, towering over the scene from the top of the Dragon. "We call that personal growth, Mars."

"You've had one of this guy's aunties latched onto your throat, Kyn. How are you not on my side?" Mars cries.

He shrugs. "I'm bigger than this one."

"That won't always be the case."

"Maybe he'll like me by then. I grow on people, yeah?"

He meets my gaze and heat climbs my neck.

"Stop flirting with my sister," Mars says.

Kyn grins. Sideways. Dreamy even amid all this. My face is on fire.

Mars shows us his palms. "Listen. I realize it's easy to see me as the tyrant here, because, of course, who doesn't like puppies? But truly, right now, I'm the logical one."

"I don't know, Dresden," Felyx says, wandering over. "We're rebels. Seems logical we'd recruit any creature abused by the Majority and their agents."

"This is hardly the time for strays."

Tooki steps closer. "Sayth said the same thing about me when I first asked to join her crew. But strays have their uses."

"Oh yes!" Mars says. "Perhaps this stray will give away our position as well."

Tooki sputters.

I pat him on the shoulder as I pass, the wolf pup chewing the tail of my braid. "The ice bikes were worth it. Mars just likes being grumpy."

Tali and Brash skip over to see the pup, cooing, letting him sniff their hands.

"Oooh. His eyes are like glass," Tali says. "Strange. His mama's were so bright."

Felyx presses closer, curious. "Frost Whites are supposed to have gemstone eyes, aren't they?"

Brash scratches the pup's chin. "When they're born, their eyes are clear as water. Soon though we'll start to see the color there.

And he doesn't need this." She slips the twyl wreath from the pup's neck. "Winter won't have his ear for another year or so."

"I didn't know that," I say.

"You learn a lot of stuff when you're scrapping for coin," Brash tells me. "There's folks raise wolf pups for fighting, you know that? Orphaned, that's likely where this guy'll end up."

Leni's hanging out the passenger window of the Dragon. "Give him to me, Syl. I'll check his paw."

"Miss Trestman," Mars says, exasperated, "we really *must* be going."

"So let's go then," she says. "I can patch him up while we drive. We don't want to lose the light."

I climb up on the running board and pass Leni the pup.

"What did the Rangers say?" Sayth asks, pulling us back.

Mars blows air out his nose. "It seems the Majority is willing to pay good coin for anyone seen with"—he waves his hand at me—"and myself."

"Eh. That's nothing new," Sayth says. "I've had a bounty on my head since I left the mines."

"Five thousand?" Mars asks.

Sayth gapes. "Five. Thousand?"

"We're proper criminals now!" Tooki says, glancing around at the others.

"And very much in danger," I say. "Rangers all over the isle will be on the lookout for your rigs. You need to be extra careful when we separate at High Pass. The Majority isn't sure what's coming, but with Wrex on the loose and these Rangers free to run their mouths . . . They'll be on their guard for anything."

"Why did you let them go?" Brash asks. "The Rangers."

"Because they wet themselves once they saw what we were capable of," Mars says. "It will serve us well to have that reputation on the wind."

"But we do need to get moving," I say. "We need to be at High Pass well before they start talking."

"And how exactly are we getting up to the pass?" Sayth turns, shielding her eyes as she looks toward the mountains in the distance. "That road's a long ways up."

I smile. "Winter's going to build us a bridge."

# CHAPTER 21

KYN LOOKS LIKE HELL. HIS EYES ARE PAINED and there are three scratches on his cheek. Raised lines, glistening dark. I stop him as he climbs up into the Dragon, tug him back to the ice for a closer look.

"What happened to your face? Is that kol?"

"Blood," he says, shame filling his gut as he swipes it away. "It's nothing. We're all a little banged up."

"But you're hurting, Kyn. I can feel it. Is it the voices? I'm not hearing anything right now, but—"

"Nah. It's not the voices." Kyn stares at something beyond my shoulder. "I'm not hearing much either. The winds have shifted, I think."

"Then what is it?" I lay my hand gently on his chest and he flinches so hard he whacks his head on the cab.

"Kyn . . ."

He rubs his head absently. "I told you, bumps and bruises."

"There's no way—"

"It's been a rough couple of weeks, yeah? Ship blown to bits, sucker punched by Winter." He pulls the keys from his pocket and drops them into my hand. "You all right to drive? Just a couple hours and we'll be at High Pass."

He makes only the briefest of eye contact before he climbs over the driver's seat and onto the bench behind. Stung, I follow, finding Mars in the passenger seat.

"I thought you preferred being chauffeured?"

"Miss Trestman felt the wolf pup would be more comfortable in the sleeper, and since you and I need to talk, I decided to brave the front seat."

"Oh . . . good." I give my mirrors a glance to ensure the other crews are all loaded up and then I turn the key and the Dragon rumbles to life. I shift her into gear, and we push off toward High Pass. "What are we talking about?"

"The little deal you made with Winter." I feel his black eyes on my face and fight not to redden. It's a tricky thing talking about Winter. She may not be everywhere, but she never seems to be out of earshot.

"I probably should have mentioned it," I say awkwardly. "It's just been a little busy."

A low chuckle breaks through his lips. "Oh, I see. You're afraid she'll hear us and know you don't intend to make good on your promise. Because, holy-Begynd-under-water, Miss Quine, you cannot make good on that promise."

"You don't know—"

"You think she hasn't told me? Hasn't boasted about her progress with you? Because she genuinely believes this is a game. That if she can get you to choose her over me, she's won."

"I didn't promise anything. I just . . . didn't hate the compromise she suggested."

"You like the idea of keeping her around. A pet maybe, to pair with that pup back there."

"I didn't—"

"Revelation number one, Miss Quine. Winter is not your friend."

"I know."

"I want to hear you say it."

"Say what?"

"That you don't intend to let her stay."

"She won't keep up her end of the bargain, Mars. Revelation number seven: Winter has a short memory. It's not even going to be a problem."

"Why are you always pushing responsibility onto other people? Choose, Miss Quine. Her or the isle? Because you cannot have both, regardless of what she's told you."

"The isle, of course. It's just . . . we'll need a wet season here regardless. Why court another winter spirit if the kol is just going to corrupt it, too?"

"Are you really asking why we would banish a spirit who stole the lives of an entire generation? Justice matters, sister. And the next winter spirit who takes up residence here must know that."

I catch Kyn's reflection in the rearview, but if he hears Mars, if he senses my discomfort, he's not showing any sign. His head lolls against the back wall, his hand over the scratches on his cheek.

"Miss Quine?"

"Stop calling me that. Please." I shake my braids free of my collar. "You're right about Winter, Mars. Is that what you want me to say?"

"No, that's what I want you to believe."

He turns his face away, and it's not the relief I expected.

Winter slips through vents and climbs into my lap, chilling my skin and burning hot in my belly. I WON'T TELL HIM, WILL I? she whispers. THAT YOU'RE NOT CERTAIN. THAT YOU RATHER LIKE THE IDEA OF VISITING ME IN MY THRONE ROOM.

But she's a liar and Mars knows anyway. The only thing I can't figure out is why, exactly, I can't let her go.

The next few hours pass without incident, save the wolf pup piddling on Mars's boots. The cab erupts: fury from Mars and guffaws from the rest of us.

"How did he even get up here?" Mars asks, lifting the pup by his scruff.

"I thought he might like to wander," Leni says, through fisted giggles.

"Give him here," I say.

"Happily."

Mars drops him on my lap, and for the final hour of our approach, that's where he stays, curled and snoring, his soft weight a comfort.

I let Kyn's fingers tangle in my hair as he sleeps, let them brush my neck. He's my pain and my remedy right now and, while it's only right that I give him whatever privacy I can, I wish he'd tell me what's going on.

When High Pass grows large in the windshield, I reach up and tap Kyn's arm.

"I'm awake," he says. "What is it?"

"Will you take him? I'm going to need to focus here."

Kyn reaches forward and takes the pup in his hands for the first time. I watch in the mirror as he presses his face into the white fur. He harbors no animosity toward this little guy, nothing I can sense at least. There's just the warmth of contentment expanding through his chest.

The mountains drop their shadows across our rigs now, and I reach up for the radio. "Single file, kids, and eyes up."

In my mirrors, I watch as Sayth's pickup and then the war machine pull into line behind the Dragon's trailer. The contentment and excitement in Kyn's chest eases something in me. He's been nothing but misery and pain for hours now and it's good to know he can shake that off. We still have so far to go.

"You ready?" I ask him.

"Oh yeah," he says.

Mars shakes his head. "And you accused me of having a theatrical flair."

Kyn flicks his ear and I grin, leaning over the wheel, saying the words that once carried the three of us over an army of Abaki and into the safety of the camp at Queen's Point. This time, we'll be driving into danger, but I can't help feeling Kyn's excitement. There's just something thrilling about climbing into the sky in a large metal rig.

"*Liatha ee frenth,*" I tell Winter. *Build me a bridge.*

Winter spins out her magic before us and a road rises from the ice, flush with the kind of detail that reminds me of all there is to appreciate about her. Contrary to revelation number four, I'm vague, allowing Winter to build any kind of bridge she'd like. She could choose a boring design, something utilitarian—but she likes a little flair as well.

She's creating a crystalline masterpiece, thick and sturdy beneath the Dragon's tread, with delicate railings that look like the blown-glass baubles Leni and I used to hang in the tavern windows on Drypp's birthday.

The radio crackles and whoops and hollers break free, filling our cab, making us laugh. I can't see anyone in my rearview but it's clear they're enjoying themselves. Good. It's only going to get harder from here.

Mars reaches up for the radio. "Settle down, friends. Settle down. High Pass is just beyond that rise, which means we separate here. Any concerns before that happens?"

No reply.

"Good. Final instructions: Sayth runs the show, Felyx, you're second-in-command. As discussed, we'll meet you at the safe house once we arrive in Hex Landing. It should take us no more than three days to do what needs doing."

"We got it, boss," Felyx says.

"Good. Another thought. The Shiv will have seen our approach from the caves there on the rise. They've likely been watching us for a while now and if our direction was unclear to them before, they'll certainly have seen the bridge. While the settlements at High Pass and near Crane Falls present the highest risk, the Shiv could stage an attack anywhere along the Shiv Road. No unnecessary stops between here and the turnoff to Hex Landing. Understood?"

"Understood," Sayth says.

"Yeah, understood," Felyx answers. "Though now we're off the Desolation, won't they relax a bit?"

Mars's eyes slide to me, and I can see he's making a decision. "Perhaps, but I made rather a mess of things the last time we were here. Killed some of their people. They're big on justice, the Shiv along this road, and they wouldn't hesitate to kill some of mine in retaliation."

Kyn leans forward and whispers in my ear. "We call that personal growth, yeah?"

Kyn's right. Mars might be more than three hundred years old, but he's growing just as I am. Feeling the pain he's caused.

"We're close now," I say.

"Here. I need to grab a gun." Kyn passes the pup to Leni and ducks into the sleeper.

"He needs a name," she says, scratching his ears. "Frosty or Snowball or . . ."

"He could grow into a stone-cold killer," Kyn calls. "You can't name him Snowball."

"Well," she says. "We'll come up with something that fits then."

"Don't leave it to Mars," I say. "It'll take him years."

"Names are important," Mars says, rehanging the mouthpiece. "You ready to do this?"

I nod. I need to talk to Shyne.

"And you remember you chose the isle, yes? That's where your allegiance lies."

"Tell me you're kidding, Mars," Leni says. "Why else would she be here?"

Mars stretches his legs, crosses his ankles. "Why else, indeed."

I turn to Leni. "You have that gun Hyla gave you?"

"Of course."

"Good."

In the rearview mirror, I watch as Kyn emerges from the sleeper, shotgun in hand. He settles in behind me and together we watch as Winter crafts the bridge deftly into the mountain, sighing as she completes her task.

One by one, our rigs roll onto the Shiv Road, and I reach for the radio. It squeals and then crackles into silence.

"It's time to say goodbye, friends. Remember, we're working toward the same goal as the Shiv. They are our allies, and we need them, so stay safe, but think twice about firing your weapons. In fact, there's still snow clinging to the rock face along the road, so there are many reasons to be certain before you fire. The last thing you want is an avalanche. We're on a tight schedule here."

"Remind them about the kids," Kyn hisses.

I clear my throat. "There are also children living in these mountains. Shiv and Majority both. They are to be protected at all costs. Understood?"

Both Sayth and Felyx reply in the affirmative.

"Good. We'll see you all in Hex Landing then." I rehang the mouthpiece.

The pickup and the war machine turn right, heading north on the Shiv Road. They don't have too far to travel before the turnoff to Hex Landing, and if things go as they should—as they must—their biggest enemy before reaching the Majority's landmark mining operation will be the melting road.

Not so for us. The farther we climb, the sturdier the road becomes beneath the Dragon's tread. The road at High Pass doesn't melt; Winter's presence is too strong here. You'd think that would make it an ideal thoroughfare, but there's never any traffic. There are simply too many stories about the magicked snow at High Pass and the Shiv who don't take kindly to visitors.

The north and south peaks rise on either side of us now and I drive slowly, because Mars is right: The Shiv certainly know we're here, and it would do us no good to go barreling into an ambush.

The caves are along the south peak just off to our left. I watch them carefully for movement. A hefty collection of twyl hangs ragged along the rock face. How they'll harvest this patch I can't say. Much of the trail connecting the caves was lost when the mountain skittered all those weeks ago.

There's no movement, but the Shiv are watching us from just inside the caves. Winter's whining about it, about their presence in her throne room.

"I don't see anyone," Leni says when I mention it.

Mars shifts. "They're good at that."

We push down the road, scraggly trees groping through the snow on either side of us, snowflakes hovering in the air. And then something in the road, frosted white and impossible to make out.

"You see that," I say. "Mars?"

"I see it."

Shadows fall darkly this time of day, and it's not until we're on top of it that we realize what we're seeing. A man, knee-deep in a snowdrift, frozen upright, an arrow jutting from his chest, its fletching fixed at an awkward angle. He's been out here for a while.

"Holy hell," Kyn says, scrabbling for the hatch. "That's Brewzer."

Mars grabs hold of him before I do. "He's dead, Kyn. We'll recover the body, but there's no hurry."

If Kyn had been in better shape, I think he would have fought Mars off, but agony shoots through him and he drops to the bench, his hand fisting around the corner of my seat back.

"Why would they do that?" Leni asks.

All four of us stare out the window, shock ebbing through the cab. I didn't know Brewzer well—he set out shortly after I arrived in Queen's Point—but I know he made his living as a scout before he joined the rebellion, organizing excursions for wealthy Majority customers who wanted to ride snowmobiles and call themselves adventurers. It was Brewzer who provided the Shiv here with the few snowmobiles they had. His rapport with them made him an easy choice to deliver news of the Paradyians' arrival.

"They don't like outsiders," Mars says. "They never have."

"But why kill him?" I ask.

"I don't think it's about him," Mars says.

He reaches for the hatch, and I grab his coat. "That's bait, Mars. You know that."

"I do, yes. But we need to talk to Shyne."

And with that, he shoots out the hatch.

A flash of movement catches the corner of my eye, and I turn just in time to see an archer rising from a cleft in the rock on the northern rise. He fires the largest bow I've ever seen, the bowstring's snap carrying a threat all its own. His arrow is nothing but a blur, and it's dragging something behind it.

Before I can get a command off, the arrow whizzes by Mars's head, dragging a net around his body. The stones secured to its edges swing the net around, binding Mars head and toe. With a sound that echoes through the pass, the final stone connects with his temple and Mars Dresden drops from the sky.

# CHAPTER 22

I KICK OPEN THE DRAGON'S DOOR, THEN DRAW the hatchet from my belt as I drop to the ground, spitting commands at Winter, raising a storm out of the stillness.

"Cut him free!" Kyn shouts. He's standing on the roof of the Dragon, his gun trained on a Shiv man straddling Mars's body, a slick black stone in his hand. "Do it now or I'll shoot."

He repeats himself in Shiv, but I know it's an empty threat: Kyn's not killing this man. He'd never be able to live with himself if he did that.

But with my brother bleeding on the ground, I might be willing. I round on the Shiv man, pushing the storm into his chest and lifting him off the ground. Blue rock is scattered across his nose and cheekbones, a flap of hair hangs in his eyes. He's built like a concrete mixer—broad and thick—but he's no match for Winter. I lift him higher and higher, his body twisting and turning as he tries to break free.

"You're fine," Kyn tells him. "Just settle down."

The man chucks the stone at me instead. At my command, Winter catches it and drops it at my feet.

"Hey, hey!" Kyn calls. "Where are your manners, yeah?"

A quick look around tells me we're still alone, but I don't imagine that will last long. I trade the hatchet for my knife, and drop to the snow next to Mars, sawing away at the net.

"You there, Mars? You conscious?"

"Turn me over, Miss Quine."

I flip him face up. Blood pours from his temple, but he looks OK otherwise, his eyes bleary but focused. Leni arrives a moment later, pulls a knife from her boot, and kneels down to help.

"This is a deep-sea fishing net," Mars says. "A strange find up here."

"What was he going to do what that rock, do you think?" Leni asks. "If he'd wanted to kill you, he could have—"

"Put an arrow in your chest."

We wheel around, and there stands Crysel, her bow nocked, her arrow aimed at Kyn.

"Let him down," she continues, "or I'll kill the traitor."

But I've already given Winter a command. One word and Crysel's arrow freezes to her bow.

She mutters something in Shiv and chucks the entire thing to the ground.

"We're here to talk to Shyne," I tell her. "And then we'll be on our way."

"You two don't get to talk," she says, the low light turning her spectral as it plays across the crescent of amber stone covering half her face. In the weeks since I last saw the girl, the world has grabbed hold of her shoulders and stretched her tall. She stands before us barefoot, a pair of loose-fitting, ravaged trousers hanging from her hips, her chest covered by a scrap of colorless material.

A tiny movement of her head and suddenly my feet are pulled out from under me, my face smacks the ice, and blood pools in my mouth.

Winter has no comment.

"Sylvi!" Kyn calls.

"I got it. I'm good." I flip onto my back, quick, fast. There's a boy wrapped around my ankles. He must have crawled out from under the rig. His grip is tight, his smile broken and angry. Like Crysel, I've seen his face before. Dark skin, white stone lining his spine and forehead, he's another of Shyne's children. The boy scampers up my body reaching for my mouth, a rock clenched in his fist.

I kick and bite out a command all at once. Winter tears the boy from my legs, yanking him into the sky, where he hovers next to the first attacker. He wriggles and cries out, but Winter's grip is tight.

"Crysel, this isn't a game. Where's Shyne?"

"I let you cross the Desolation, Sessa. The day I brought you that medallion." Crysel nods at Maree Vale's broken necklace hanging from Mars's neck. "I told you we would not pursue you across the ice if you went *then*, that day. Why would you come back here?"

"We have to talk to Shyne. It's important."

Her amber eyes move over my face, a searchlight poring over unfamiliar terrain. Her lips open, but before she can answer, Kyn calls out.

"Snowflake! We've got company."

The storm covers the sound of their movements, but he's right. Up on the rise, backlit by the fires, the Shiv emerge from their caves, standing shoulder to shoulder. Some with stones raised, others with bows clenched in their fists.

**THEY'RE HARD TO FREEZE**, Winter says. **BEGYND BUBBLING INSIDE THEM. BUT IT'S STILL FUN TO TRY. SHALL WE?**

I ignore the offer, dropping my eyes back to Crysel, but calling out in a loud voice so everyone on the mountain can hear me. "We're going to free Begynd. *That's* why we've come. Tell them, Kyn."

He translates my words to Shiv, his voice loud even through the storm.

There's no response. It's silent save the wind, save the angry, raging wind.

"*Est stíyee,*" I whisper. *Just stop.*

Winter tears at my lips but quiets.

Crysel leans in, her chin trembling, eyes darting to her people hanging over us. "Don't talk to her, Sessa. Don't talk to Winter. They'll kill you."

I step closer to the girl, wanting her to hear me, to really hear that I mean her no harm. But my movement stirs something above. Arrows are drawn, bowstrings stretched taut. A voice shouts Shiv words.

"He wants you to back away from the girl," Kyn says, cocking his gun, the sound loud in the utter silence of the pass. "Says the Shiv on the rise will fire if you don't do as you're told."

There's so many of them, odds are good at least one of us takes an arrow before Winter can intervene.

Crysel holds up her hand and the Shiv lower their weapons. Her gaze is still on mine and her brows lift, waiting for whatever it is I have to say.

"Little Fox," I say, remembering the name Shyne gave her. "I promise not to use Winter against your people ever again, but you must take us to Shyne. He will want to hear what we have to say."

"It's not a trick?" she asks.

"I promise it's not a trick."

A long pause and then. "You should let them down. Pem and my brother."

Another word, another blister, and the Shiv who first attacked us—Pem apparently—and the boy drop slowly to the road. Crysel dismisses the boy with a yank of her head. He narrows his eyes and spits at my feet before scampering away into the underbrush.

As soon as his feet hit the ground, Pem lays hold of Mars and drags him upright.

We cry out, reach for him, but Mars lifts his hands in surrender and looks over at me.

"Let him," he says. "We need to see Shyne."

"Mars—"

"Means to end, sister. This is taking far too long and injuring one of them will not speed things up." He holds his hands out and it's all the encouragement Pem needs. He tugs a length of leather from his own bicep and slams Mars up against the rig, binding his hands behind his back.

We all protest but I've just promised not to call down Winter, and by the time I consider my hatchet, Mars is facing forward again, his chest heaving.

"Well, that was an adventure."

"That was unnecessary!" Leni kicks Pem in the knee and an arrow whistles down, burying itself in the ground at her feet.

"Whoa there, warrior princess," Kyn says, steering her away. "Mars isn't helpless."

But Leni's gone white, her eyes blazing as she glares at the ring of Shiv high above, daring them to shoot again.

"You'd best take us now before things get ugly," I tell Crysel.

"I will take you to Shyne, but he may not hear you, Sessa. He hardly hears me. Something broke inside him when our Great Father died."

"We still need to see him," Mars says, sagging against the trailer, snow in his disheveled hair, his face streaked with blood. I've never seen him so vulnerable. Not even when Winter sunk his ship.

Crysel scoops up the slick black rock and tosses it to Pem. "You may regret asking such a thing," she says.

With a vicious smile, Pem jams the rock into Mars's mouth. There's a crack and Leni cries out, but it's done, Pem securing the rock with another strip of leather.

I remember the powerlessness I felt when Wrex clamped his hand over my mouth and, despite what we've promised, I pull the hatchet from my belt. But Mars shakes his head at me, determined to see this through.

Crysel scoops another rock from the ground and steps in front of me. "You're next, Sessa."

# CHAPTER 23

"THEY'RE WINTER'S FAVORITE, YOU KNOW? The Frost Whites." Crysel holds the wolf pup in her arms and watches as Kyn gathers all our weapons.

I can't answer her. The rock in my mouth is wide and flat, wedged tightly between my teeth. Like Mars, my hands have been bound behind me. Leni too, though they've left her mouth free, and I wonder if they'll regret that.

"I should move the rig out of the road, yeah?" Kyn's eyes are bloodshot when he looks at me, his voice tired. He doesn't like the rock between my teeth, but he understands why I didn't fight it. I work to keep my panic at bay for his sake. I don't know how much more his body can handle.

"Leave it," Crysel says. "Rigs don't come here anymore."

"You still sabotaging the road?" Kyn asks, sliding our weapons beneath the seat of the rig.

"It's harder in Blys. The rains wash the chemical away, and now, with Jymy Leff gone, we're sure to run out."

Kyn slams the door to the Dragon and turns so Pem can bind his hands too. That done, the large man lays hold of Mars and shoves him forward. Mars wasn't ready and stumbles to his knees. Pem grabs his hair, drags him to his feet.

I try to protest but manage nothing but a muffled grunt.

"You shouldn't feel bad for the smuggler," Crysel says. "He killed so many. We're still finding the dead."

Kyn falls into step beside the girl. "But Mars didn't set out to kill your people. He was just trying to free us. It doesn't make what he did right, but . . ."

"That won't matter to Shyne," she says.

We're nudged toward the south peak, Pem and Mars out front. The rest of us following.

"What's wrong with Kyn?" Leni asks, sidling up to me.

I shrug, shake my head, then tip my head in his direction.

"You want me to ask him?" she asks.

I nod, knowing he'll resist but hoping maybe she'll get through to him in ways I can't.

"I'll try," she says. "I have that ointment. Maybe it could help."

Poor Kyn.

Pem leads us down a winding trail that's all but hidden by a patch of twyl. Hardy blue blossoms and sage-green leaves grow wild over the path, slick with damp and ice.

"Where did you get the net?" Kyn asks. "You didn't have that the last time we were here."

"It was a sailor, I think. He uses it to catch monsters on the black sea. But he told us we should use it to catch a smuggler. Told us the smuggler can't hurt us if he can't speak, and it would be easier to gag him if his hands and feet were bound."

Mars turns and his gaze meets mine. My blood curdles.

"Farraday Wrex was here?" Leni asks. "When?"

"I don't know his name. But he was here not long after the mountain skitter. Just after we sent our dead to await Begynd. He wanted to talk to Shyne too."

"Wrex spoke to Shyne?" Kyn asks.

"Shyne wouldn't speak to anyone then. Pem told the sailor what he wanted to know, and he gave us the net. It was weeks ago now, just after we returned from the ice."

Leni cuts her eyes at me, and I encourage her on as best I can.

"What exactly did he want to know?" Leni asks.

Pem shouts over his shoulder, and Crysel picks up the pace, nudging me with her elbow. "Come on, we have to go."

"But what did he want?" Kyn asks. "The sailor with the net."

"He asked about Sessa. Where she went when she left here, if she ordered Winter about like the smuggler. The Majority was offering a reward for her capture, and he promised to share it with Pem if he helped."

Kyn glances at me and then asks Crysel, "Pem told Wrex what Shyne believed about Sylvi, yeah? That he wanted her to send Winter away?"

Crysel's gaze moves to Pem's back, and then she leans toward me. "I think he did, Sessa, yes. The sailor gave Pem a bag of coin as well as the net."

The idea of Wrex coming here, of anyone coming to High Pass for information, hadn't occurred to me, and it really should have. The Rangers pursued us here after all, and they're not the only bastards on Layce looking for a quick payday.

The foliage has grown difficult, and with twyl slapping us

in the face there's no practical way to continue the conversation. Crysel moves out in front of us, she and Pem hacking with stone knives.

After a good quarter of a mile, we come to a flat rock face. The stone is a deep green with ribbons of yellow running through it.

Crysel shifts the pup higher onto her shoulder and leans close to the stone. She whispers, her words far too quiet to make out. At first there's nothing at all, nothing but the swaying branches behind us, Winter tickling my neck with her words—and then the wall begins to shift. We watch in awe as the stones break apart and restack, tipping and tilting, until at last they've created an opening large enough for two of Pem.

"Shiv magic," Kyn says, his eyes running over the stone. "I would very much like to learn."

"There's nothing to learn. It's just words. I ask the mountain to open, and it does. It knows me." Crysel turns to him, lets her eyes move over the red rock on his arms and hands, the strip below his eye. "But your people have been gone a great while. I do not think the mountain would know you."

Kyn swallows. "Probably not."

Pem waves us forward, silencing the conversation with a scowl.

"Right," Crysel says. "Single file is best for this part." She steps through the entrance and the rest of us follow: Kyn first, then me and Leni, and then Mars.

Pem is the last. He speaks to the stone and seals us inside the mountain. As the daylight is shut out, Leni presses her forehead into my shoulder.

"I hope we haven't just got ourselves buried alive."

The stench of burning twyl itches my nose, but as we push

forward there's no sign of a fire. It's black as kol inside the mountain, and it takes a good long time for my eyes to adjust.

"Why did you have to gag them?" Leni calls. "Winter's not inside the mountain."

But she is. Her violent blasts can't reach us here, but there's a gentle chill that presses soft against our coats, our faces. A chill that smells like Winter, a cold that belongs to her alone.

"She's here," Crysel calls back to us. "We must burn twyl, and our fires need air as much as we do, so she takes advantage. The deeper into the mountain we go, the less bother she is though. You'll see."

And I do see. The farther we climb, the stiller the air, the quieter she becomes. The scent of burning twyl thickens, and to it is added the unmistakable aroma of baking bread. It's not warm here inside the mountain, but with the absence of gusting wind and the comforting fragrance of a hot meal, I could almost believe it is.

And yet, that cool tickle of air never leaves my fingertips. I need only call; one command and Winter would answer. Even here, we are not outside her domain. Which in turn means she's not outside mine. I find myself curious: Just how great an obstacle would the mountain be? Would I have to shake it as Mars did, or could Winter's winds find me here if I insisted? It hardly matters with a rock between my teeth.

The path pitches down slightly, just enough for my toes to shift forward in my boots. Off to our right and left, holes are carved into the rock. They remind me of the portholes on board the *Maree Vale*, and I wish I could get a closer look.

Firelit interiors give us glimpses inside the settlement's

underground dwellings, but if the Shiv inside looked out at us, they'd see only darkness, so I suspect the holes exist to give the smoke from their hearths a place to escape.

Still, we catch fragments of their lives, and it's fascinating and familiar all at once. The furnishings are modest but well made, tables and chairs made of wood and stone, woven hangings in bright colors separate one space from another.

Shadows and voices move within, and a drum beats somewhere behind the rock, soothing and steady. It follows us down, down, down.

And then comes a stretch of rock that shakes me. The window openings here have crumbled, maybe a dozen of them, light from the neighboring caves throwing them into shadow. One in particular catches my eye, rubble visible through the darkened bay, splintered shards of wood jutting into the darkness. A swath of material is caught between the stones, and it flutters out into the air.

If anyone was inside that cave when it collapsed—

"You think that happened when Mars shook the mountain?" Kyn asks.

I shrug, but he's unlikely to see it, everything is so dark. Mountain skitters are common, so there's no way to know, but it's unsettling to be reminded of what they can do.

The path curves and Crysel stops. "Stairs. There's a railing, but . . . we'll go slow." She calls out to Pem in Shiv and then descends the staircase.

It's narrow here, and I push my hip against the wood rail to guide me. The window openings have fallen away and there, below us, stars shimmer in the darkness.

No, not stars. The colors are too varied; stars only ever wink with sylver eyes. Here it's a rainbow of iridescence. Gemstones, I think, in every shape and color, dazzling us from the rock walls.

"Ho-ly . . ." Leni gulps. "How much coin do you think those would fetch, Kyn?"

"More than a rig driver has any hope of making in a lifetime. Only we're not allowed to dig, yeah? We haven't the Majority credentials. And they only care about the kol."

"But if we did have the credentials," Leni says. "If we could—"

"You could buy back the garage," Kyn says. "The tavern."

What a thought. Buying back something that was stolen in our absence.

"I'm not all that attached to Whistletop," Leni says. "I was thinking we could book passage on one of those fancy Paradyian ships and sail away, all of us."

"I do not think Shyne would let you break up our homes to dig out rocks that please you," Crysel says. "Not for taverns or ships. Not even for more coin than you've ever seen. Begynd cut *us* from the rock, remember? It's our mountain to share as we will, not the other way around."

The silence is palpable. How easy it is to pretend we know best. How foolish to think we have any right.

"What makes them glow, do you think?" Leni's voice is careful now, soft. "I've never seen stones do that."

Crysel stops and I stop with her. "Some glow and some don't, see? Shyne says we do what Begynd made us to do. The rocks are no different."

"Well, it's a lovely home," Leni says, sincerity in her voice, humility, "and I hope no one ever takes it from you."

The staircase widens and Leni moves in front me, she and Kyn falling into step. After another flight of stairs, it's clear they're bickering, probably about his injuries. Kyn's stomach is in knots, and it's a lot like the shame he felt when I realized he'd been keeping the empty trailer a secret.

Pem barks at us in Shiv and pushes past, shoving Mars ahead of him.

The deep dark begins to lighten, everything tinted green. After another long stretch, the staircase bends and an underground cavern opens before us. At the very bottom lies a pool of shimmering emerald water, gemstones visible beneath the surface.

A stone bridge connects the near shore to an island, and there, slightly off-center, grows a tree. Nothing at all like the evergreens of the Kol Mountains, or even the grandfather oaks that grow at lower elevations.

This tree has sprouted from bare rock. It stretches up into the darkness overhead. So high, I can't see the top. It has branches but no leaves, and its bark is the white of newly fallen snow.

"It looks dead," Leni says.

"It was dead. But that was a very long time ago." Crysel steps off the final stair, the pup wriggling in her arms. "There you go," she says, placing him on the ground. "Make yourself at home."

It's clear she's talking to the pup and not to us, but it's no matter. Our footsteps echo off the walls and I search the space, my eyes landing on a ledge that circles the room about twenty feet up. A walkway of sorts, connecting a series of caves that have been carved into the rock. Their arching entrances are uniform and neat and in front of each dwelling sits a stone brazier, twyl branches burning. Their flames light the great space and fill the air with that sweet, honeyed fragrance. Smoke spirals up and around the naked branches of the once dead tree. I can only assume there's a chimney hole high above.

One of the fires has gone out and I watch as a boy scampers out from the nearest cave. He clears out the ashes and piles a new stock of twyl branches high before striking a flint and lighting it again.

"Thank you, child," calls a voice, so weak I wouldn't have thought it Shyne's. But there he is, sitting on a bench beneath the tree, his deep-set eyes shimmering in the dim, firelight playing across the dark flesh and white stone of his face. "Yes, it is good to keep our home fires lit."

His gaze falls on us then, and there's no surprise there. He's been told of our coming. I step off the final stair and watch as Pem shoves Mars across the stone bridge, forcing him to his knees at Shyne's feet and then disappearing into the shadows.

Shyne's lips turn down, a bow of judgment as he stares daggers at Mars.

After a moment, Shyne lifts his gaze to us. "Cut her free, Little Fox. I would like to speak to Sylver Quine."

Crysel pulls a knife from her waistband, and I turn so she can cut the binds on my hands, my head. The rock is wedged so tightly in my mouth, I have to pry it free with my fingers. I drop it at my feet and snatch the knife from Crysel's hand. She's too surprised to react.

"Kyn, here," I say, working my jaw. "Turn around."

"Just you, Sessa. He said just you."

I slice through Kyn's binds. "They were bound to prevent them from helping Mars and me. There's no point now. I can call Winter whenever I want. She's right up there through the chimney hole." I cut through Leni's binds and hand the knife back to the girl.

"You gave your word," she says.

"So trust me." I nudge her forward now. "Lead the way."

She's all toe and no heel as she steps onto the stone bridge and crosses to the island. I follow, the wolf pup nipping at my heels.

"Just let me take a look," Leni says. "If you don't want the ointment, fine. There's water here. We'll get you cleaned up."

This is hardly the time, but Kyn's insides are crying out, ashamed, frustrated, hurting desperately. I turn back, wishing he'd let her help, wishing he'd let anyone help. The bridge arches some and it puts me a little above the two of them. Leni drags him toward the water, and I see now that he's done fighting.

"Fine," he tells her. "Fine. Just . . . let me, yeah?"

He unzips his hooded vest and lets it fall to the ground. Beneath it, his shirt is drenched, black blood clinging to the thin material.

Surely that's not what happened when Winter attacked him on the *Heraldic*! That's not a bruise, not the result of broken ribs. This is something painfully familiar.

From his bench, Shyne grunts. "Have you come to speak with me or not?"

But Kyn has all of my attention. He grabs the collar of his

shirt and tears it from his back. The gore-sodden material rips free to reveal the old scars on his chest now oozing red, and the weeks-old wolf bite at his neck festering.

Leni curses. "What in the name of Begynd—"

"How?" I stumble back toward him. "We haven't been apart, not really . . ."

Could this have happened in camp when Kyn wandered off? It's not possible, is it? We weren't separated for long, not far enough for this.

I reach out, wanting to slice my palms open again so that my blood can make him well, but as I get closer to him, I can see why. I can see how.

Flecks of kol shimmer in the weeping gashes across his torso. And on the three scratches across his cheek. This has nothing to do with how far apart we've been. This is something else altogether, something we should have known would be a problem.

"The kol in my blood," I say.

There's pain on his face, but it's the sadness of his heart that steals my breath. Sorrow that he couldn't spare me knowing. "I think so, yeah."

Hot tears spring to my eyes, and behind us, Shyne barks out a laugh that echoes off the walls and demands our attention. He's risen from his bench, his form crooked as he leans heavily on a new walking stick. White. Looks to have been cut from this very tree.

"I heard of your plight with the wolves, traitor. Dead and then alive. Alive with the blood of Maree Vale's daughter running through your veins."

"How could you possibly hear about that?" Tears rattle in my throat.

"Your man was here. Brewzer." He wanders closer, spitting at Mars as he passes. Mars doesn't flinch. "Perhaps you saw him on the way in?"

"We saw him," Kyn growls.

"Good, good. He told us of your deal with the Paradyian king, said that war was coming to the isle. Assured us weapons would arrive soon that could turn my mountain to rubble. I told him the rebellion already had a weapon that did that." His voice has risen to a fever pitch, and he strikes out with his walking stick, cracking the wood against Mars's skull, toppling him to the ground.

Leni screams.

"Coward!" Kyn calls, moving toward us. "He's bound and gagged of his own free will and you attack him?" He's lunging for Shyne when I pull him back.

"A coward would have accepted Brewzer's offer." Shyne grinds the words out, his eyes flashing. "He offered to see us safely to Queen's Point. I declined. He pressed. I refused. He tried again, bartering with stories of the new girl in camp, a girl with eyes the color of starlight. I told him we'd met, that I was disappointed, but he assured me things had changed since you'd last been here. He told me of the healing power of your blood, of your promise to send Winter away." There's curiosity there, even if it is buried beneath the hate. "And then he told me that Mars Dresden himself had offered protection. As if I were not aware of this man's protection!"

Shyne lifts the stick over Mars's head, and though I've

promised not to call down Winter, I can't watch him murder Mars just to satisfy some fantasy about justice. We're long past justice now. The command's on my tongue when Shyne changes his mind and lowers his arms slowly, the threat stayed.

Leni's footsteps grow close behind me, a sob in her voice. "You killed Brewzer for offering your people protection?"

Suddenly Shyne looks every bit as ancient as the mountain we stand within. "Call it what you will, child. Brewzer offered me Mars, and I considered it a threat."

Shyne turns his back on us, his steps painfully slow as he limps back to his bench. He settles onto the stone slab and lifts his eyes to me. "Your blood carries a curse, Sylver Quine. Whatever else it carries, it carries that."

"A curse," I whisper.

"You were here. You saw what the water from the Pool of Begynd did to our Great Father. Did you not consider the consequences of sharing your blood with another?"

Sweat beads on my forehead because I genuinely thought I had. "I considered some of them."

"You should have stayed," he says. "You and I could have reasoned with one another. It may have saved you *this*." He points his stick at Kyn. "Since you were last here, I have reasoned much. I have changed my mind on a great many things."

"What things?" I ask.

His chin comes up. "Those beneath the ice. My own people swallowed by Winter as they worshipped Begynd. Ask me if I believe they're still alive?"

"Do you?" I ask.

"I do not," he says.

I don't believe him. I won't believe him. He was the most devout. A zealot of zealots.

"What of their voices?" Kyn asks. "The stories they can't stop telling."

"Echoes only, trapped somehow by Winter's curse."

I shake my head. "I've seen their bodies, Shyne. Through the ice."

"Bodies do not mean life," he says. "Whatever gave you that idea?"

"If you believe the Shiv beneath the ice are dead," I ask, "what is it you believe of Begynd?"

A great sigh. "He was the son of Sola, the creator of the Shiv, and worthy of our worship." Rote memorization only. Nothing more.

"And?"

"And he is dead."

A moment of silence while we all consider his statement. Crysel collapses to the rock and scoops up the wolf pup once again, burying her face in its fur.

"Dead like the tree?" Leni asks. "Or dead like . . . dead?"

"A very good question. One I ponder day in and day out. I've always taught that Begynd delivers our souls to Sola after we die, and there, in her light, we live again." The crease between his eyes deepens. "Are their souls still trapped beneath the ice? I think, maybe. But I cannot say. I've always known how Winter's magic worked. How the kol corrupted everything. How Begynd's power was slowed by the curse but not stopped, never stopped.

I knew our Great Father should not have sought a cure from the Desolation ice. Everything he'd ever taught us said it was unwise, blasphemous. Even among our people it would have been an act worthy of death. He was above such rules, of course, being the rule-maker if you will. But the kol has always brought pain to our people. I told him; I warned him." He shakes his head. "You were here, you saw what happened. Pain was to be expected, but what shocked me, daughter of Maree Vale, what continues to shake me is that Winter had the final word. That should not be!"

"The final word?" Leni asks.

Kyn shifts uncomfortably. "It was Winter who killed him, you mean? Winter who froze him solid."

I realize then that his concerns are not so different from mine.

"Indeed. I expected Begynd would enact judgment for our Great Father's blasphemy by allowing the kol to do what it has always done to the Shiv."

"You thought the kol would drive him mad."

"I did. He was already half there, had talked himself into believing nonsense. I felt the kol would be just one more corruption in his aging, dying body. But I confess, I did not consider what Winter could do to him given the chance."

"What do you mean?" Leni asks.

"The Shiv have never been much moved by Winter's touch. Begynd built us to resist her. It had not crossed my mind that she might somehow have attained the power to turn our Great Father to ice."

"But surely it was the kol that gave her that power. The kol that made her more than she was."

"Surely," Shyne says. "But Begynd created the kol, he and Sola.

How could the creator be bested by his own creation? You asked me that very question, did you not? I will admit your questions have grown loud in your absence."

I could say the same of his. "Shyne, what is it you're afraid of?"

"It's not about fear," he barks. "It's about belief. What I believe. What my people believe. And after what the Desolation ice did to our Great Father, the people are divided, and I have not the wisdom to steer them right. '*What lies beneath the ice?*' they ask me. '*When Winter is gone, will we find death or life in that once great pool?*' I used to know. I used to be so certain. But now . . ."

A long moment passes, and I realize it's time to take control of this conversation before it spirals away from me. Before I no longer see the right way forward.

"Do you know why I'm here?" I ask him.

"I do not."

"I'm here because you told me a story. The story of how I came to be on the Desolation. It happened seventeen, almost eighteen years ago now."

Shyne goes flat. His eyes, his voice. "The island shook, and the fount bubbled, and a fissure formed in the ice. That is the story."

"Begynd gave me up. A girl who had become a curse, not because of anything I'd done, but because it would take a curse to break a curse."

"You can send Winter away; I've always believed that. But *what is the point* if everything beneath that ice is dead? If Begynd is dead."

That's the question, isn't it? But maybe it's also the answer.

"Justice," I say, my eyes falling on Mars, still bound, still gagged, lying on the hard rock. "Shyne, I don't know what's going to happen when we send Winter away. I have no idea if those beneath the ice are living or dead, and I imagine that if they're dead, if Begynd really has been bested, the Paradyian king won't be pleased. It's a risk, for sure. But we've made a promise. At High Blys, during the Festival of Begynd, I'm going to send Winter away from the isle."

A tremor runs through the cavern, the water rippling, the tree swaying. Winter's listening; she's not nearly as far away as the Shiv might believe. But it's no matter. She's bound to me, and she will do what I say.

"It's what you wanted the first time you laid hold of me," I continue. "And I came here today to tell you I've been convinced."

"Justice," Shyne says, his face brightening some. For a moment he looks a lot like the Shyne I met all those weeks ago. A man who was convinced I was the answer to all his problems.

"But you're going to have to give me Mars back," I say.

A shadow falls across his face. "He stays."

"Gears are in motion, Shyne. This mission is a machine I cannot halt: Paradyians, rebels, the Shiv. All of us are on a clock now that won't stop ticking. I cannot do what must be done without Mars."

"Do what exactly? Bring war? That is why the Paradyians have come, is it not? Certainly their soldiers are deft enough at such things. You do not need this one." He nudges Mars with his foot again.

Kyn takes a step toward Shyne. "I'm going to need you to keep your feet off him, yeah?"

"I am trying to *avoid* a war, Shyne. Trying to keep Paradyian war machines out of your pass and the Majority Council from conscripting your warriors."

"Let the Majority try," he says.

"You think they won't?" Kyn squats so he's eye level with Shyne. He rests a hand on Mars's chest, and I realize that Mars has begun to stir. His eyes twitch at the corners, his head rolls.

Shyne sees it too. His fist tightens around his walking stick, and he knocks the end of it against Mars's temple. Hard. Mars goes still once again.

Kyn curses under his breath and after he ensures that Mars is still breathing, he stands. "If war comes, the Shiv will suffer. Our people will be forced to fight."

"*My* people," Shyne corrects, disgusted.

"It's one of the reasons we've come," I say. "To warn you that the Majority might come for your fighters. We extend the same offer Brewzer delivered: Desy Page wants you to know that the rebels would welcome your people with open arms, but if you do not wish to join us, you should consider leaving High Pass."

I expect him to argue. To remind me of all the measures they've taken over the years to protect themselves. To insist on keeping hold of what's theirs. But he just stares back at me, his dark eyes unreadable.

"Tell me, Sylver Quine. How do you and your rebels intend to stop this war? Where will this mission take you?"

"To the mines at Hex Landing."

"Bah. Rebels have been sabotaging those mines for a hundred years."

"This is bigger than slashed tires and poisoned water," I insist.

"Tell me."

Maybe I shouldn't. Maybe he's not on my side, but this is why we've come. So I do. I tell him everything: the synthetic kol, the Paradyian king's suspicions and the scouting reports that seem to support our assumptions, the uprisings on other Majority islands, and our half-baked plan to rid Layce of their rule before we send Winter away.

He stands then, his bones creaking as he wanders to the once dead tree. The short distance seems to have exhausted him, or perhaps it was my words. He stretches out an arm and leans against the white trunk now, his head hanging, his crooked back turned toward us.

"You have surprised me, Sylver Quine."

"Good."

"But you do not need the smuggler to break the Majority rule. Everything you've laid out can be accomplished without him."

I step closer. "Rumors have already begun to spread about my authority over Winter, and my presence with the rebels. The Majority has a price on all our heads now, dangerous hunters track us, and we must be quick. If we haven't successfully completed our mission and returned to Queen's Point by High Blys, the Paradyian king will declare war on the Majority. To avoid widespread violence, I need the very best at my side. I need Mars."

Slowly, painfully, Shyne turns, his gaze falling on the one-time heir to the Kerce throne, sprawled on the rock, gagged and unconscious. "He will only anger Winter and that will make your task harder. I have seen it with my own eyes. The smuggler stays."

I move so that Shyne can't help but see me, desperation turning my words sharp. "I can't send Winter away without him."

Shyne searches my face for a long while and then he nods. "That might be true."

My shoulders relax and I stand taller. He understands. He does.

Shyne takes two steps and collapses onto the bench once again.

I kneel at Mars's side and grab hold of the leather strap holding the rock between his teeth. Shyne swats my hand away with the end of his walking stick.

"Hey!" Kyn and Leni protest, but Shyne raises his stick over his head, and I stumble away.

"The smuggler stays." His arms shake with anger, his chin trembling.

"Shyne—"

"I know he matters. He witnessed the covenant, and you may be right: It may not be possible to send Winter away without him. So I will bring him to Queen's Point myself. He does not get the privilege of walking free."

"Even if he can bring freedom to the rest of the isle?"

"Justice must be dealt, Sylver Quine. Destroy those mines as you have planned. Strike fear into the Majority. And then look for us at High Blys."

Shyne turns to the shadows and raises his stick. Pem and a handful of Shiv fighters emerge and cross the stone bridge. With them, comes a gust of cool air.

Mars's eyes snap open and he tears his hands apart, the leather band falling away, sawed through with a shiv-sharp rock. He must have picked it up while we thought him unconscious!

But the warriors fall on him now and we all leap into action. Kyn grabs hold of the nearest Shiv warrior, pulls him off Mars, and punches him in the face. Fists swing and knees fly, I hear an arrow whiz by my ear.

"Stop, stop, stop! We came to talk, that's all," I shout.

But no one's listening and I've done what I came to do, haven't I? I've warned the Shiv of what's to come, I've told them to hide if they refuse to fight, and now, with Winter's help, we can get out of here. Two blisters, maybe three? That's all it would take. Is that what Mars would have me do?

Leni's clawing at the nearest warrior, screaming at Kyn to be careful, and somehow, I take an elbow to the gut and am thrown into the undead tree. And then Crysel is there, tugging me away from the fray.

"I know what you're thinking," she says, "but they'll kill you if you call her. Look." She's got her gaze high. Perched between the flaming braziers, archers stand at the ready.

"Do it, Syl," Lenore says, stumbling over. A scratch glistens red on her cheek and her braids are a mess. "They won't kill you. They need you to get rid of Winter."

But they could kill her, and they could kill Kyn. They could kill Mars. There's a lot they could do to hurt me.

"They're not all believers!" Crysel insists. "Not anymore. You can't call her. You promised you wouldn't. I only brought you here because you promised."

Kyn takes a kick to the chest, and it empties my lungs. There's a great splash as he slides down the rock and into the water. Mars is still gagged, and his arms are now being held by two massive fighters. They heft him across the bridge, Mars fighting every step of the way.

"Let me talk to him," I yell.

An opening begins to form in the cavern wall, the rocks twisting and turning, arching. This could very well be the last time I see Mars and I have no idea what he would have me do.

"Please!"

Shyne scowls. "I think not."

Crysel throws herself at his feet. "She could have called Winter and she didn't. She could have shaken the entire mountain like the smuggler did once before, and she chose to act honorably. Father, please!"

Shyne sags. His shoulders, his face, even his eyes. His hand comes up and rests on the girl's head. A moment later he barks a word, and the men drop Mars's feet to the ground.

Shyne stands, straightening as best he can, hooking my chin with the end of his walking stick, and staring me boldly in the eye. "A clock that won't stop ticking, you said. Every word you waste on the smuggler is a second you can't get back."

I slap his stick away and stumble backward. I turn and walk over the bridge, never taking my eyes off Mars, wanting to talk to him, needing to talk to him more than anything in the world.

A Shiv warrior on either side of us watches, waiting. Almost bored. Mars's mouth is stretched wide around the black stone, so wide that his lips are splitting. A fresh wound on his forehead drips gore down his face, but his black eyes are active, and I have no idea what to say.

"I could call her," I say, dropping into Kerce. "Should I?"

Mars's coat hangs open, his shirt damp with sweat. He blinks, breathing deeply through his nose, taking in the room for the first time. When his gaze settles on me once again, he shakes his head, and I can see he has something to say. The frustration of not being able to say it burns in his eyes and a tear slips over his lashes.

"What is it?"

He yanks his right hand free, and the Shiv warriors leap into action.

"Just wait," I tell them. "Wait!"

With the fighters holding him so tight he's half off the ground, Mars drags the knuckles of his hand against his cheek, opening his palm to me. My heart buckles because he's giving me the only thing he has left to give: his duty, his responsibility, and the blessing to act in his stead.

Tears shake me from the inside out, and I wrap my arms around his shoulders, pulling him as tight as I can, pressing my wet face to his. I feel his chest heave against mine, the weight Maree Vale passed to him all those years ago, still pressing down, heavier than any one of Shyne's rocks.

"We'll get it done," I tell him. "We will." Rough hands tug me away, but I elbow my way back to Mars. "Just four days. Four days, and I'll see you at Queen's Point. Shyne's promised to bring you."

And then they're pulling me off and dragging him away, down a hallway I don't know, to a place I can't follow.

"He'll be OK," Kyn says, his arms wrapping me tight, wet from his fall and trembling, holding me against his bare chest despite the hurt it brings him. "It would take a lot more than a stone to silence the great Mars Dresden."

But I don't know if that's true this time. I looked into Mars's eyes, and I saw something there that frightened me. An understanding of sorts. He knows the Shiv have a right to exact punishment on him for what he did to their kin.

"I don't know how long he'll fight," I say.

"Until he's dead, snowflake. And then some. He might feel remorse for what he did, he might believe he deserves death for it, but he knows what's at stake." Kyn's so certain it steadies me, reminds me that Mars is not just one thing. He has as many facets as the rest of us.

He's gone from sight now and the entrance begins to fold in on itself, the rocks shifting until there's nothing but a stone wall before us. Kyn and I stare at it for a long moment, and when we turn around, only Leni and Crysel remain.

"Why didn't you save him?" Leni asks, her eyes wild. "We need him to get to my da. I don't . . . I don't understand."

"Because it would have made things worse," I say.

"Mars told her not to," Kyn clarifies.

"Because you promised." Crysel stands on the bridge now and she's looking at me like I've just done something heroic. "And you don't break your promises."

"You have me wrong, Little Fox. What I just did wasn't kind."

She steps off the bridge, the light catching the stone on her face, turning her sweet face severe. "I never said you were kind. I said you kept your word. That's not always the same thing. A lesson I learned from Shyne. He's rarely kind to outsiders— he doesn't trust them—but he always keeps his word. You can depend on it."

## CHAPTER 24

RYSEL LEADS US BACK THE WAY WE CAME, THE trek to the surface an entirely different experience than the hike down.

The air is too warm inside the mountain now, too still, and the stench of twyl burns my nose. Sweat pours down my back and I strip off my coat, dragging it behind me as I put one foot in front of the other. I ignore the rocks glowing on my right and left, ignore the Shiv dwellings as we pass. Instead I focus on sucking air into my lungs, on the effort it is to get it past the lump in my throat, a blockage that grows with every step toward the surface.

I can't believe we're leaving Mars behind.

At last we step out into the light of day, and despite all the things it says about me, I've never been more relieved to feel Winter on my face. The rock face closes behind us and I collapse against it, my head tipped back against the stone, eyes open to the gray sky. Rain is coming, I can smell it, and it would be better to be through the pass when it arrives.

"Here," Crysel says, offering me the mewling pup. "I think he's hungry."

I reach out to take him and then think better of it. "Do you have enough meat to share with him?"

"We have plenty of food, Sessa."

"Then you keep him."

Her eyes light and then fade. "Shyne might not like that."

"I really don't care, Little Fox. Do you?"

A grin slides across her face. "Probably not as much as I should. But don't you want him?"

"I do," I say, surprised to find it's the truth. "But we'll be leaving the Dragon here for the next leg of our journey, traveling as light as we can. It'll be hard to carry him."

"Then I'll keep watch of him for you. And your Dragon."

"Thank you," I say. "And thank you for taking us to see Shyne."

"You don't regret it?"

I push off the wall, shake out my legs. "Oh, I do."

"I thought you might."

"I regret a lot of what's happened in this pass." Kyn and Leni have pushed ahead through the twyl. I can see Kyn's bare back through the brush and I know there isn't time for this, for a conversation with Crysel. I plant a kiss on the pup's sweet head. "I have a favor to ask."

"If I can help you, I will."

"He needs a name. Something that captures his personality. You think you can handle that?"

"Of course, Sessa. I'll think on it."

"Good. Four days, Crysel. You can make it across the ice by then?"

She nods, stands tall. "We'll be there."

I leave her against the rock face, and when I turn back at the edge of the twyl patch, the mountain has shut her away. I tell myself it'll be good for her to have a friend, good for the wolf pup to spend time away from the constant words of Winter.

Pulling on my coat and zipping it tight, I dive forward into the twyl, moving quickly, following the bent branches left behind by Kyn and Lenore. When I reach the road, my thighs are knots of fire and I'm sucking damp air.

I slap away the final branch, relieved to see that the Dragon is still in one piece. Kyn has moved her out of the center of the pass and parked her beneath a string of evergreens on the north shoulder. I watch him climb from the driver's seat, wincing as he drops to the road. He's still not wearing a shirt and his body looks ravaged. Twyl sap and flecks of kol streak his stone shoulders and biceps, the flesh of his arms and chest red and inflamed, the gashes on his torso and cheek streaked with fresh blood and red dirt.

"I don't imagine that's the best way to keep your wounds clean."

"Leni assures me it's not. But I was hoping, before I wash up . . ." He holds up my knife, pulled just now from beneath the driver's seat. "Maybe it'll just make things worse in the long run, but will you do your thing?" His gaze drops to his chest, to the old scars oozing infection and hot with fever. "I know you don't like being bound to me—"

"Can you honestly say you like being bound to *me*?"

His stone shoulders lift and drop, like he actually feels their weight for once. "Not like this, I don't. Not when I'm making you miserable."

"Kyn—"

"But Begynd didn't really ask us what we wanted. And I figure the mission is what's important now. I don't want to slow us down, snowflake." His gaze lifts, settles somewhere over my head. "What's done is done anyway, right? You and me, we can't get more tangled up than we are."

He forces a smile, but I feel the shame it brings him to ask for my help. The pride he's had to stuff down just to show me his hurts.

"Of course," I say, "No, you're right. We're already—"

"Fluxed," Leni says, rounding the trailer with an ice bike. She parks it in the road. "Yeah, you are." Mist gathers on her rebraided hair, on the arms of the slick green parka she's pulled over her sweater. "If you prefer Sylvi's blood to the ointment—"

"I do," Kyn says. "Kol and all."

"It doesn't smell *that bad*," she says.

I turn the knife in my hand. "Maybe we do this in the trailer? Out of the rain. It might take you some time to recover."

"But it's better, yeah? To do this now?" Gingerly, he climbs up into the trailer. Leni and I follow, watching as he presses his back to the wall near the bike intended for Mars, and slides into a sitting position. "Even if we lose an hour?"

"Even if we lose an hour," I say, kneeling down next to him.

"I'll just stay over here," Leni drops against the far wall.

"Thanks, Leni. That's good." I offer her a smile and then, careful to keep my hands over Kyn's body, I slide the knife across my palms, one and then the other. My blood is hot as it pools in my hands. As gently as I'm able, I press them to the festering scars on Kyn's chest. He stiffens and then relaxes.

"You were unconscious the last time I did this."

"It was like a fever dream. I don't remember much. Just your face looking even more reluctant than it does now. Gah, that stings." He sucks air through his teeth. "You still glad you saved me?"

"Most days," I say quietly. "You glad I saved you? That's the better question, I think. You've a curse flowing through your veins now. Was it worth it?"

"To get your hands on me? Absolutely."

Leni stands, her boots loud on the trailer floor. "Actually, I'm going give you some privacy, I think."

"It's pouring out there, Len," I say.

"I'm not new here," she says, dropping to the mud. "I'll be in the cab. Just holler when you're ready."

Kyn grins. "She's a keeper, your friend."

"She is." I lift my hand and peek beneath my palm, but there's still so much blood. "You've been hurting for a while, haven't you?"

"Yeah."

"I want to apologize," I say.

"Syl—"

"No, listen. I could tell you were hiding something. And I could tell you were in pain, but I chalked it up to the voices and Winter's sucker punch on the *Heraldic*. But I didn't want to know. Not really. And I should have pushed harder; I should have made you tell me."

"You can't pick and choose, snowflake. It *was* the voices out on the ice, and it *was* Winter, and it *was* this." He gestures to the bloody mess of his torso. "My scars got infected because I can't handle the kol in your blood. You get all of me or you get none of me. I don't know how to do this halfway."

I shift my hands, laying one against his neck, remembering when the Frost White nearly tore his throat out.

He lays his hand over mine. "You didn't choose this. I know that. So if, after listening to me just lay it out, you decide you don't want me, just say it. But if you do, bring it. And I mean everything. Because I'm going to do the same." He's so close, I can see the color coming back to his face, the light returning to his eyes. "You carry a lot, yeah? My pain included. And it's insulting to think I'd be OK letting you carry mine and not helping to carry yours in return. You're underestimating my strength when you do that. And I'm stronger than you know, snowflake."

I swallow. "This isn't the same as the voices out on the ice. I can do something about this. I can make this pain stop."

"For weeks maybe. But how often will you and I have to do this? You opening your veins so I can stop bleeding. This isn't love. This is maintenance."

"I wish I could offer you something lasting."

"One more reason to get this mission right, yeah? To see the Pool of Begynd restored."

I blink at the idea, all the other complicated emotions fading. It's the first time I've considered the pool as a remedy for anyone other than the queen. "You think?"

"You could be free of me," Kyn says.

"You could be free of *me*. The curse in my blood, everything."

"I don't want to be free of you," he says, pressing his forehead to mine. "But I do want you to choose me. Over Winter, over your fear, over everything."

I can't tell if I can feel his hammering heart because we're so close or because everything about us seems crossed. It's always, always seemed crossed. I have no idea what to say, but he doesn't seem to require an answer just now.

"I think this is done." He lifts my hand and peers beneath it. "It wasn't this fast before, was it?"

"Not at all," I say.

"Maybe you're getting better at it," Kyn says. "Or maybe I am?"

"Or maybe everything's sped up. The festering as well as the healing."

He stares back at me, his mouth hanging open. "You're a ray of sunshine, you know that?"

I swipe at his chest with a rag. "People have always said that about me, actually."

The smile he flashes is a choice that rings through me like the clear, consistent striking of a bell. "I'm going to wash up. There are bandages just there."

He steps out into the storm, and I realize I'm leaking blood onto the floor of the trailer.

We're better prepared for injury this go-round, and after scrubbing my hands clean, I make use of the bandages and then slide my gloves on top. When Kyn returns, the rain has washed his chest and neck clean, leaving nothing but fresh pink scars, souvenirs from a battle we should have fled.

He kneels and starts rifling through a bag at his feet. "I brought a spare shirt, yeah? And a coat. I'm sure I did."

"Kyn said you were ready to go." Leni stands at the foot of the trailer, a bag cinched tight on her back. She's already wheeled three of the four ice bikes out onto the road and now she passes out goggles. The pair she hands me aren't Hyla's—of course they're not—but I think of her anyway. Of her ever-present eye protection spilling away over the edge of the Seacliff Road just before an Abaki sank an axe between her shoulder blades. Suddenly I'm so angry at the unfairness of it all I could scream Winter down on every monster that's ever threatened my friends.

"Snowflake?" Kyn stands before me now, new shirt and coat in place, his forehead creased as he tries to read what I'm feeling.

"Just remembering," I say, tugging the goggles over my stocking cap and resting them on my forehead. "You ready?"

"Let's do this." He pulls a bag over his shoulder, and I do the same, everything we'll need for the next leg of this journey split among the three of us. We step to the end of the trailer, and I look out at the rain. It's coming down hard now, filling every divot and ditch in the road with water, turning the ice muddy and slick. There's no wind though, not a gust, and it's almost as if Winter's slid Blys into gear and let her roll. Her rambles are almost drunk, and in the steady fall of rain I feel her ease. I have to wonder if it's Mars's absence that's turned her lazy.

I flip up my hood and step off the bumper. Leni does the same, mud caking our boots and pants as we land in the road.

"I could tell her to ease up," I say, the rain a heavy sheet between us, "but it might be easier going if we let her be. She hardly seems interested in us just now."

"Then leave her, yeah?" Kyn tugs the Dragon's rolling door shut as he steps off the bumper. "I'm not afraid of mud."

"Leni?" The rain is so loud, I have to raise my voice. "You going to be OK to drive in this?"

She moves her goggles into place and snaps her hood shut. "Just promise me sunshine and blue skies at the end of this road."

I kick my leg over the seat of the nearest ice bike. "Well. I mean, I can promise you whatever you want, but Begynd's going to have a lot more to say about the state of his pool—"

"For Begynd's sake, Syl!" Leni stomps on the starter of her bike, the rumble of the engine forcing her to yell. "Just *lie* to me!"

Kyn's laughing when he swings onto his bike, and I feel that tug behind my breastbone, a wish I won't let myself make: that he was just him and I was just me and that we were truly free to choose each other. Could the great pool make that possible?

I don't know, I can't begin to guess, but Kyn said it before: This mission's the most important thing now and I can't let anything stand in the way of that. With a twist of my wrist, I give the bike a little gas, slowly let out the clutch, and with a whine, my bike's flying through the highest pass in the Kol Mountains, Kyn and Leni not far behind.

Brewzer's body's been moved. I imagine we have Crysel to thank for that. We're going to owe that girl a lot when this is over.

I take the road straight and easy, the rain already a hindrance to our visibility. The pass stays frozen year-round but it's not the smoothest of rides. I do my best to avoid the worst of it, trusting Kyn and Leni to follow my lead.

I slow only once, when the half-melted and refrozen spires of an ice castle rise up around me. It's the ruins of the palace Winter built during our last trek through the pass. A structure she breathed into existence to prove she wasn't ugly and dark but beautiful and strong. And then she slapped my face and tried to feed Kyn to the wolves, and who she was became utterly clear to me for the first time.

The road is at its most churned up here, and we move carefully around the broken ice, through the site of our battle with Winter's wolves and the Rangers who used them to do the dirtiest of their work.

Kyn's feeling the pass with a level of intensity I wasn't prepared for. Anger washes over him as we cut left and right, maneuvering around the rubble. He gives it space, the anger, feeling it heavily, letting me feel it. Wanting me to know that he wouldn't have chosen this path for us either.

"I know," I say, into the wind. "I do."

He flies past me then, the worst of the road behind us, putting a little distance between him and me and taking his anger with him. I know him well enough now to know that he could choose to set the anger aside—he does that often—but maybe he needs to feel this. The injustice of what happened to him.

I let him go, let him lead, and don't speed up my bike in pursuit. Leni seems to understand, and she pulls up next to me, the two of us riding side by side.

We pass the turnoff to the Kerce memorial, and I don't even spare it a glance. We don't have time for the past just now, so I give the bike more gas and Leni does the same, and following another long stretch, the road begins to descend.

After the closeness of mountain peaks rising on either side of us, I expect to fly out of the pass into the light of day, but beyond the rain clouds somewhere the sun is slipping below the horizon, leaving us in shades of deepest gray. Night is coming.

Kyn's waiting for us ahead, straddling his bike at the edge of the road, the rain pinging off his shoulders as his gaze moves over the Shivering Forest to the south. His heart rate is high, but that's adrenaline, I think.

The woodland here stretches down the incline all the way to the southeastern wing of the isle where the Stack sits nestled against the coastal range. That's our target, the Stack. To get there from here we have two options: the highway or the wood.

The highway would be faster, of course, and for another hour or so we likely wouldn't see many drivers, but that won't last. The highway south is one of the most heavily trafficked roads on the isle—even at night—with rigs trucking raw kol from every mine on the isle to be processed at the Stack.

At its core, the Stack is a factory, but practically speaking it's a village all its own, with sleeping quarters for hundreds. It has its very own trading post, jail, cemetery, hospital, and even a school for children who are shut up there with their parents. A fate that would have belonged to Lenore had Drypp not taken her in. I've seen the kids there—when Drypp took us to visit Leni's da—and it's not something I'd ever want to see again.

Though I suppose that's always been my problem. I'd rather not look.

The Stack is larger than Whistletop and more densely populated than the Port of Glas, the only true city on the isle. And since those who inhabit this village of sorts range from those with no other choice to those working their way up the Majority ladder, it's heavily guarded and the Shivering Forest that surrounds it patrolled.

So while we must avoid the highway—we cannot afford to

be seen—the wood will be anything but easy. Narrow roads have been worn through the trees, but they're rough on rigs and, as Tooki can attest, the Rangers who patrol this area have been known to sabotage them.

That said, we have the mind of the great Desy Page on our side. This is where she made her mark: the Shivering Forest. She's drawn us a detailed map and spilled its secrets, and maybe it's Kyn rubbing off on me—I don't know—but I'm almost optimistic.

The voices that were so loud out on the Desolation have vanished, and the physical demands of the bike keep me focused on the road. It's almost, almost like being alone in the Dragon.

"Take it slow, all right?" Leni's next to me, wiping the mud from her face. "I've never ridden off-road before."

"Until recently you've never ridden *on* the road before." I nudge her shoulder. "You're doing really well."

"It's kind of fun," she admits. "The zigging and zagging. The wind blowing everything but the road from my mind. I think it'll be good for my da."

Kyn rolls closer. "Your da was from Whistletop, yeah? How'd he get in with the Majority?"

Leni shakes her head. "My ma was from Whistletop. Da was from Glas, got in with the Majority mining engineers young, soon as they noticed he had an aptitude for mechanics. He stopped in at Drypp's on occasion when he was traveling to and from the mines. That's how they met."

"So he's all Majority, your da?"

"Born and raised. When I think back though, it was the numbers he was always loyal to. Not the Majority. Not even the kol. I think that's why it took him by surprise when Ma developed an addiction. Probably he should have realized that she was different than he was. I don't know. He's a kind man—really he is—but his brain never stops, and on Layce there's not much to challenge a mind like that. The logistics involved with keeping the mineworks in operation on this isle? It was a challenge he relished when he was young. But after Ma . . . he realized then, knew then what the Majority was about. I just hope the kol hasn't . . . you know?"

"We hope so too." I squeeze her arm. "We'll get him out either way, Leni. Whether his mind is there or not, OK? With any luck, tonight is the last night your da spends in the Stack."

"I'd feel a lot better if Mars were here."

"I know. Me too."

Kyn tightens the straps on his bag. "But just think how angry he'll be if we botch this job. That's what I keep telling myself. Get it done. Get it done right. And Mars won't have any reason to complain."

"What an optimist you are!" Leni slides her goggles back into place. "No matter what, he'll find one. He keeps a list, I think."

We laugh, but there's some trepidation there. We're heading straight into the heart of Majority kol operations and none of us have been farther than the outer reaches: the visitor's center, the cemetery, the receiving dock. It was Mars who had relationships here. Mars who knew which overseers were sympathetic to the rebel cause. Mars who knew which guards would leave a gate open for a bag of coin.

And though we'll stick to the plan, there's no knowing if these same people will risk their necks for us.

"Honestly, I don't think Winter would mind taking the entire Stack out," I say.

"Save it for Hex Landing, yeah? We can't give away our position. We've already lost Mars. We lose you, this revolution of ours is finished."

"Hear that, Winter? Kyn said stuff it." I stomp the starter once again and with Desy's map shimmering bright in my mind, we drop down the mountain and into the wood, a forest whose shadows inspire fear in some and brazen daring in others.

We've worn fear rather thin of late.

Today, we choose daring.

# CHAPTER 25

THE TREES HERE NEVER STOP MOVING.

It's a consequence of the mountains looming both behind and below. It creates something of a bowl, with the cold wind pushing west from the sea circulating in a frenzy overhead. After miles and miles of muddy forest roads, it's not just the trees that are shivering. Even inside woolen gloves, my hands are ice, and my face is numb.

Just ahead I see the first of the landmarks Desy called out for us: a warped pine that's wrapped itself around an ancient rig. The rusted orange artifact must have been abandoned here at least a hundred years back. It's tilted at an angle that says the ground beneath it has shifted over the years, and now the tree's trunk rises up through the bed, curving around the buckled cab, assimilating the metal contraption into itself.

I circle the tree once, looking for the best, most hidden angle. The night is dark though, lit only by the lights on our bikes, and one side of the tree is very like the others. In the end I park up against the bed of the age-old rig, tucking the bike beneath the tree's drooping limbs.

Kyn and Leni do the same, the two of them climbing from their saddles and tugging the branches lower. We adjust the wheels and the handlebars until we're satisfied the bikes are as out of sight as we can make them.

"Tell me we're staying here for the night," Leni says, tearing the bag from her back and flinging it into the bed of the truck. She climbs in after it and props herself against the tree trunk.

"For a few hours at least. What is it, midnight?" I pull out Drypp's old wristwatch and flashlight from my bag. "Just after twelve, yes. Kyn, do you have the map?"

He props his bag on the open tailgate of the rig, unzips it, and withdraws a square slip of paper, folded down to fit inside a weatherproof pouch.

He settles onto the tailgate, his weight evoking an almighty creak that has Leni nudging him with her muddy boot. "If you break my bed, I'll kill you."

But the truck holds and, gently, with Leni's glare threatening death, I climb up next to Kyn, watching as he unfolds the map and flattens it against his knees. We tilt our heads left and right as we look at it, scanning the road behind us, and then pointing the flashlight down each of the lanes splitting off from this tree, trying to pinpoint north and south, east and west.

Eventually, I reach out and flip the map one-quarter turn. "There."

Kyn takes one more look behind us and agrees. "Yeah, that's it. So, we're here." He points to Desy's sketch of the tree-truck. "And by dawn, we need to be there." Our rendezvous point with Mars's contact, a rebel sympathizer with some influence in the Stack.

I drag my finger along the ink road, tracing the route. "That's what? An hour ride at most?"

Leni yawns. "If the map is accurate."

"It's accurate," Kyn says. "Desy knows her stuff."

"I'm more concerned about our ability to gauge distance. We best give ourselves an extra hour just to be sure," I say. "Leave here two hours before dawn?"

Kyn agrees.

Leni pulls a pinecone from beneath her bum. "Tell me again, how does this guy know to meet us?"

"He doesn't," I say. "It's a rebel drop that gets checked most days. Always at dawn, just before the shift change. So says Desy."

"Mars confirmed it, yeah. This is his guy we're meeting."

"Do you know him?" I ask.

"Nah, mostly Mars kept me away from this stuff: the Stack, the mines. My ma made him promise. Just driving, she said. At least until I was old enough."

"And are you?" I ask. "Old enough to be a rebel?"

"My ma would say no"—he shrugs—"but she's my ma."

"What's the deal with her and Mars, anyway? You said he makes sure she never runs out of medicine, but how did he even meet her? I can't imagine him living in Dris Mora."

"He doesn't live in Dris Mora—"

"I hate to interrupt," Leni says, untying her braids, "but you said this rendezvous point is checked *most* days. What if tomorrow's this guy's day off? What if no one shows?"

"Then we come back the next day."

"And if he's not there then?" She's dragging her fingers through her tangled hair now, her voice pitched higher as she speaks.

I put my hand on her shin. "Leni, it could take a few days to get this done."

Her hands freeze, hair spilling out from between her fingers. "But we don't have a few days to lose here. We have exactly three days to get back to Queen's Point and that includes getting my da on board, and a trip to Hex Landing to wreak havoc. And what if the other rigs are behind schedule?" Her fists clench and I'm afraid she'll pull her hair out. "What if they're not ready when we get there?"

Kyn grabs the toe of her boot, stills her shaking leg. "They'll be ready, Len. Sayth and Dakk? They're not just messing around, and they don't have nearly as far to go as we do."

Her hands unclench and fall loosely to her thighs, her head falling back against the tree. "No, I know. I just—"

"One step at a time, remember? Maybe our contact will be there today." I slide toward her, the truck bed rough beneath my weatherproof trousers.

She makes room for my body next to hers. "*Mars*'s contact, you mean. How do we know he'll even help us?"

"I can be very persuasive," Kyn says.

She rolls her eyes. "Seriously? That's our plan?"

"I thought it was good," Kyn mumbles.

I force her head down onto my shoulder. "Sleep, Leni. You're grumpy when you're tired."

Her muscles finally relax some and I think, maybe, just maybe, we might get a few hours rest.

Kyn snorts and gently, carefully, he adjusts himself by pulling both legs up into the bed, turning so he's perpendicular to Leni and me.

Leni sits up again. "But what if—"

"Sleep!" Kyn and I tell her.

With a great huff, half drama, half genuine exhaustion, she sinks back against the tree and lets her head roll once again to my shoulder. She grumbles at us but it's incoherent and in a quarter of an hour, with the trees around us rustling in the wind, she falls asleep.

"She's been a trouper about it all, honestly," I whisper. "Given how much she hates the cold and the wet."

"She's awesome, snowflake. You know I like Leni. And I like you with her. You're different when she's around," Kyn says. "Gives me hope."

"How am I different?"

He shrugs. "You take care of her, and you let her take care of you. She's an exception to your attachment rule."

"It's not really a rule."

"It's enforced like one," Kyn says, his eyes soft.

I sigh. "I've known her for a long time. Almost my whole life."

"So, maybe when you and I have known each other a long time . . ."

I grin into the darkness. "I suppose anything's possible."

"See? Hope?"

The gravity of such hope drops over us like a blanket, warm and almost comfortable. I can't find the energy to fight the soft intimacy of sitting here like this, staring at him, his face muddy save the circles spared by his goggles. I'm sure mine looks much the same. Our muscles are tired, and, despite everything, our hearts are light from the physical exertion of the ride. It helps that he's not pushing, not forcing me to consider anything other than right now.

His coat hangs open and I scan his shirt for any sign that his old wounds are causing him pain, but there's nothing to see. And the contentment in his chest tells me he's fine, comfortable. What a strange feeling it is for the turmoil between us to have settled momentarily.

"Tell me about Mars," I say. "I thought he made his home in Dris Mora. Is that not true?"

"He makes his home on the *Maree Vale*. I don't know what he'll do now. Fluxing Wrex."

"He's still out there somewhere, you know?"

"Probably making his way back to Glas, reporting to his Majority overseers. He's a true villain. I've known a handful of Kerce sailors who simply needed the coin and didn't want to ruffle Majority feathers. I get that, you know? Folk have families to feed. But Wrex is something else entirely."

"He believes he's chosen the right side," I say. "Thinks he's protecting a valuable way of life by fighting some righteous battle. That's what makes him dangerous."

Kyn knocks the toe of his boot against mine. "Don't worry, yeah? We'll get this done before Wrex can do much damage. It's a long trek back to Glas, however he decides to get there."

But I'm not convinced he's returned to Glas. It seems out of character for him to return home without his prize. I think of his hand on my throat, blood glistening on the knife blade . . . If Mars hadn't shown up when he did . . .

I shake Wrex from my head. "Back to Mars. When you all

showed up in Whistletop, I asked around. *Everyone*, and I mean everyone, says he hails from Dris Mora."

"He's there more than he's anywhere, I guess."

"But why?" It's like prying a boulder from mud.

"He's really never told you? Not about Sashti or my mother?"

"Who's Sashti?"

"My grandmother."

"Your *grand*mother?"

He smiles. "I do have a grandmother, snowflake. She and Mars were friends."

I feel the surprise on my face, the shifting of perspective as my mind attempts to paint Mars differently. "Friends or . . ."

"I don't know all the details and—let's be real—it'll wreck your head if you try too hard to imagine your brother making eyes at my grandmother."

"Ew. Yeah. OK. Friends then. Continue. How did they meet?"

"You'd have to ask him, but back then the Majority hadn't shipped in indentured workers from the other isles yet, and they didn't have quite so many of their own living here. They actively raided Shiv settlements for workers. It's bad now, but it was a lot worse forty, fifty years ago when, after their initial wave of success, they expanded their mining operations, sinking mines in every other mountain, burning through their workers faster than they could afford. You'd have thought they'd learned their lesson about mining so close to the sea, especially after North Bend, but they had new technology and thought they'd give it another try. Only Begynd knows how much they spent dumping coin into a state-of-the-art mine yard on the northwestern tip of the isle.

But despite all their efforts, it was impossible to staff. Their people preferred the inland mines, and for good reason. No Abaki and less kol."

"But Dris Mora wasn't far." I know how these stories go. "A settlement full of people to exploit."

"Exactly. One night while Mars was away in Paradyia or wherever, Dris Mora was raided, and among those taken was Sashti and her eight-year-old daughter."

"Sashti had a . . . your mother, of course."

"Freya is her name."

"And Mars wasn't her father?"

"No, Sashti had been widowed young, years before she ever met Mars."

"Does Shyne know Mars was involved with a Shiv woman?"

"He knows. Those sins he accuses Mars of . . ."

"Oh."

"He thinks Mars should have been there when the settlement was raided, says Mars had a responsibility to protect the Shiv with his powers."

"He said that?"

"Supposedly. Happened long before I was born, but I know Mars felt it and I don't think he disagrees, for what it's worth."

"So what happened to them, Sashti and your ma?"

"Mars came back, launched a one-man rescue mission. He used Winter to free everyone he could. Leveled the mine—pulled it to pieces with his magic. My ma said it nearly broke him. The survivors arrived back in Dris Mora an entire week before he did, and it took his eyes nearly a month to return to black."

"And the mine?"

"The Majority never rebuilt. Not there. Decided the weather was too volatile."

"I'd say so. And what of your grandmother?"

He clears his throat, tips his face to the shivering branches above. "She never made it out. I'm sure there's a story there, but I've never been brave enough to ask."

"Your ma never told you?"

He shook his head. "I'm not sure she knows exactly what happened to her mother. They were separated as soon as they arrived. Ma suffered a different kind of horror altogether. You've heard of kol desensitization, yeah?"

My stomach turns. "I've heard some."

"They shoved her in a room with a bunch of other Shiv kids, pumped raw kol in through the ventilation system in an attempt to desensitize them, toughen them up, maybe build some kind of immunity. It didn't work, of course. The hallucinations got so bad the kids nearly tore one another apart."

"Holy Begynd, Kyn."

"After they pulled the Shiv children off one another, they injected kol into their blood. Figured if it worked for the Kerce . . ."

Tears prick my eyes, sting my nose.

"Mars got Ma out, but her body was never right after that. Twyl helps, especially when her mind gets foggy, but her body was still ravaged by the kol inside and out. Mars wanted to keep her close, keep her where he could protect her, but he didn't dare take her out on the Kol Sea. And the Shiv in Dris Mora may not have allowed it, to be honest. They were grateful for his help, of course, but even though the Shiv in Dris Mora aren't nearly as fanatical as Shyne and his lot, Mars is Kerce and there's still a lot of distrust there."

"What happened to her?"

"Ma was placed with another family in the village and Mars tracked down some medicine to help her manage the pain. Eventually she married. I'm sure she loved my da, but he was much older than her."

"Was he a driver?"

"An ice fisherman actually. It's a good trade up there on the Serpentine—honest and nowhere near the mines—but it takes its toll in different ways. Da was already an old man when I was born and when he grew too frail to work, it was Mars who made sure we were comfortable and that Ma had the medicine she needed. I didn't know it at the time, actually. My ma told me all this later, after Da died and Mars was around more."

"How old were you when he died?"

"Seven Rymes, I think. Yeah, must've been. I've known Mars for about ten years now. Even back then, he never stayed very long—the rebellion was growing, and his smuggling operations were in full swing—but he made sure we were taken care of. And when I was old enough to drive, he offered me a job."

"And the other Shiv in Dris Mora? They don't wonder about Mars's eternal youth?"

"There are rumors, yeah? Accounts passed down from one generation to the next. Some of the folk there think he's his own son, come back after years at sea. But even those who suspect something more, keep it quiet. They may not be devout, the Shiv in Dris Mora, but they know that Shiv Island carries magic, and they're not interested in discussing such things with the Majority.

I think that's why Mars likes it there, honestly. No one questions his magic. It's just accepted for what it is."

"I'm so sorry, Kyn. About your grandmother and your mother both."

His eyes wander the trees. "I would have liked to know my grandmother. I can't imagine Mars growing soft over anyone."

"Me either. I sort of thought maybe he just wasn't interested."

"I don't know if he is anymore, yeah? He gets stuck in the past, Mars."

"He *is* the past," I say. "Flux, I hope he's all right."

We fall silent and the noise of the wood fills it. Tiny paws scampering over the forest floor, the call of an owl, and always the trees whining about the cold.

It's a long while before Kyn speaks. "I've been wondering . . ."

"Yeah?"

"If we win this thing, snowflake, and you do send Winter away, and if the pool really does what it's supposed to do, could I borrow the Dragon? Use it to pick up my ma, take her out there to the great pool? She's fairly young. She could still have a full life."

He's been thinking about the pool differently than I have for quite a while, it seems.

"I could test it out first, of course," he continues. "But if the Pool of Begynd can purge the kol from my blood, maybe it could heal my ma too."

"I'd like to meet her," I say, my mouth dry, my throat scratching. "What's her name again?"

"Freya."

"Freya," I say. "The Dragon's yours, Kyn."

"Yeah?"

"Of course. Whenever you need it."

"Maybe you could come with me? To Dris Mora. It's peaceful up there on the river. So long as you steer clear of the Abaki."

"Maybe," I say, and I mean it, I do. I'd like to see his home. To meet these people who accepted Mars and his magic, who've raised their children to do the same. "But if you bathe in the pool and Begynd does heal you, your plans to visit the beaches of sunny Crantz are sunk."

"If you send Winter away, we won't have to visit Crantz for their sunny beaches. We'll have shorelines of them here."

"And the coffee?"

"I know a smuggler."

I chuckle. "We'd just need to find him a boat."

# CHAPTER 26

"YOU SHOULDN'T HAVE LET ME SLEEP," KYN
says the next morning as he dumps water from the canteen over his head and scrubs at his face.

"You needed it. Clearly." He snored the trees down last night, but his gut was quiet and virtually pain free.

"You're going to be exhausted today, yeah?"

"Nah. When you rest, I rest."

"Snowflake—"

"There will be time later today."

Leni's taken the flashlight and wandered away to find a corner of the wood that will afford her some privacy. When she returns, she's wide awake and already twitching. Today will be big for her. Imperative for the rebellion, but absolutely everything for Leni.

Our rendezvous point lies to the southwest, close enough to the Stack that we can see its smoking chimneys through the wood, spotlights in their towers moving over the trees. It's still dark when we arrive, and we ride once around the hollowed-out trunk Mars circled on Desy's map.

"Lightning," I say, glancing around at the other trees in the vicinity, all of them whole and unscathed. "Had to be."

The trunk juts into the sky, weatherworn and ragged. Even its scorch marks have faded, Winter's rains strong enough to scrub away ash and fire. The northern side of the tree is completely open, hollowed out, and it's easy to see why this would make a good dead drop or meeting place: It's close enough to the Stack to be useful but far enough away that even the quickest of runners would have trouble making it before the guards shot them down.

"I say we park the bikes back there a ways, and walk back," Kyn says. "We're too clunky this way."

"Agreed. Leni?"

She's silent, her bike idling. She's pulled binoculars from her bag and has them focused on the Stack.

"What do you see, Len?" Kyn asks.

"Oh, um. It's dark, but that's the entrance there," she says. "See the wrought iron gate? That's how I enter when I'm here to visit."

"How many guards do you see?" Kyn asks.

Her lips move as she counts. "Four maybe? No, eight. There are two more in each of the towers. Rifles and handguns on all of them."

"About what we expected," I say. "Good. You ready, Len?"

She slides the binoculars away after another moment, her shoulders rounded and heavy. "It's foolish, right? Hoping to see him from here."

"Optimistic, maybe. Not foolish." Kyn flashes her his brightest smile. "You'll see him soon."

Not a quarter of a mile back, there's a narrow ravine covered over with brambles. Perfect for concealing our bikes. It doesn't take us long to stow them and return, the muddy trudge a welcome change for my legs. The air is wet, but the trees keep the worst of the rain off us, and our hoods do the rest.

Tucked behind a hysolberry bush, a good stone's throw from the lightning-struck tree, we pluck the berries and pop them into our mouths as we wait.

A half hour passes and though it's still mostly dark, the wood has started to wake, the ominous rustles of night replaced by the chattering of morning. A bird calls overhead and is answered from across the wood, squirrels chase one another round and round the same trunk until we're dizzy watching, and the trees tremble in the wind.

"Flux, I hope he shows." Leni stomps some warmth into her legs.

And then there's movement in the distance and I snatch the binoculars from her hands. "He's coming! A Majority pickup on the path. Says *Custodial* on the door."

Kyn snorts. "He has *some level of influence*. No wonder Mars was vague."

"But a janitor? How do we even know this is his guy?" Leni peers through the bush.

"We don't." Kyn pulls a heavy coin purse from his jacket pocket. "But it's go time."

We watch as the truck parks, its engine still running. One deep breath and Kyn steps out from where we're hidden, putting some distance between us and him before he raises his hands and steps toward the man climbing from his pickup.

Kyn's movement is enough to startle the custodian and he lifts the sidearm already in his hand.

"Whoa, whoa!" Kyn calls. "A friend of yours sent me."

He pulls the hammer back on his gun. "I don't have many friends, kid."

"Just rebels, yeah?"

He pauses, uncocks the gun. "You have a name?"

"Mars Dresden."

The custodian laughs, his breath fogging the cold air. "You're a bit big to be Mars, aren't you? Not nearly pasty enough either."

Kyn continues down the incline, slowly, his hands high over his head. "No, yeah. I'm not Mars, obviously. But Mars sent me. Said you might be able to help me find someone."

"Hard finding folks for rebels these days."

"I've something here that might make it a little easier on you, on your family." He's close enough to the custodian now that when he releases the bag of coin in his hand, the man catches it, lowering his gun to tug the drawstrings open and peer inside.

"A *little* easier at least." He reholsters his gun and tosses the coin purse through the pickup door he's left open. "Where's Dresden? Haven't seen him in months. Been swapping updates with some kid. Tuli, Toomi?"

"Tooki," Kyn says.

"That's it. The mouth on him." He whistles.

"They're tied up just now, Tooki and Mars both. But we could really use your help."

The man jerks his head toward the pickup. "That coin's twice what I'm normally paid, so you must need someone with a big target on 'em, kid."

"That a problem?"

He chuckles. "I can drug anyone. Who is it this time?"

"Macks Trestman. Was working in the refinery last we heard."

"Hoooo! The mad scientist? I take it back. I can drug *most* anyone."

Next to me Leni sucks air through her teeth and her hand clenches at my sleeve.

I press a finger to my lips.

"Then you best give me my coin back," Kyn says.

The man takes a long look over his shoulder, at the purse sitting on the driver's seat. "Here's the thing," he says, turning back to Kyn. "I can probably get to Trestman, but it might take me a day or two."

"But why?" Leni's voice trembles. Not loud, really, but certainly not quiet.

"Flux, Leni. Just wait!" I whisper.

But the man has his gun out and pointed in our direction already. She's given away our location.

"What you playing at, kid? Who's there?"

Leni stumbles out from behind the shrub, and I can't see any reason to keep her from going. The janitor's gun, maybe. That's a good reason. But Kyn's seeing to that, reaching out, pulling the weapon from his grip.

"They're on our side, man. What's wrong with you?"

I stumble after Leni, my flashlight guiding us down the incline as the man protests, his hands waving.

"Let's get this straight right now. I like Mars Dresden, but I'm no rebel. I told him more than once, I don't got the time nor the inclination to be outraged like that."

"Where is he?" Leni says. "My da. Why can't you get to him today?"

"Ah, flux, kid." He drags his hands down his face, turns back to Kyn. "You brought his daughter?"

"Best answer her, Payder," Kyn says, reading the name stitched onto the man's work shirt. "'Cause unlike you, she *does* have the time and the inclination."

"Where is he? Where's my da?"

The janitor's eyes soften as he takes in Lenore. "Look doll . . ."

Leni wrinkles her nose.

"Your da's in lockup. Saw him myself not two days ago. Heard him as early as this morning."

"Heard him?" she squeaks.

"Wailing like the wind. Howling at the guards. Gives them a good kick, it does, but it keeps them watching him, for entertainment, see? Hard to slip a man a pill that way. I don't even know if he's eating his rations, to be honest."

"Why is he in lockup?"

"This time? I don't know. Last time, they found him barefoot in the guard's barracks, quoting from some old repair manual. Loud like. Woke up the whole floor. Kept him in lockup for a week after that."

Leni whimpers. "The kol—"

"We need him out tonight," Kyn says. "Simple as that."

"It's not simple at all! This is a risk I'm taking, getting inside the cell block. They would have dumped garbage at the end of the last shift. It'll look suspicious me going in there now. And I don't even know if Dr. Helzyn is working the morning rota. These things take time, see? Your man Dresden, he knew that. Always gave me time."

I'm tempted to freeze this guy solid, but Kyn reaches out and slides his fingers into mine.

"Find a way," he says, "or I'll go in myself. And I won't be shy about telling the overseers there what their custodian has been up to."

Payder sneers, looks Kyn up and down. "How far you think you'll get before they shoot you, Shiv?"

"As far as he needs," I say, and then with a complicated demand of Winter that twists my tongue and turns my bottom lip to blisters, the clouds overhead part, and a gust of wind cuts through the trees. Winter exhales, one frigid burst that turns the damp air into snow and leaves Payder covered head to toe in white.

I point my flashlight in his face and Payder gasps, sucking powder, a massive tremor shaking his body. So massive I worry he'll freeze to death.

"Snowflake," Kyn says. "Maybe—"

Another command and the air warms moderately, turning the ice to water. Payder stands drenched and gaping before us.

"You?" he sputters, looking me over for the first time. "You're the ice witch. I seen your picture everywhere."

That's fun.

I step closer. "We'd like to do this quietly, Payder, and we're willing to pay good coin to make that happen. But if we have to go in loud, we will, and like my friend here said, we'll be sure to tell anyone who'll listen just how we knew Macks Trestman would be in lockup."

He gapes for another moment and then nods, wiping the water from his eyes. "I'll do it. I'll track the doctor down myself if she's not working, get her to come in, just . . . there's rumors you might be coming. Rumors you're bringing war with you. I got kids—"

"We're just tiptoeing through the wood, Mr. Payder. Looking for our friend's da. Surely you can help with that."

He nods again, but it's twitchy. "You just tell Dresden I helped, OK? I don't want anyone coming after me and my family."

"If anyone comes after your family," Kyn says, "it won't be Mars. Now, walk us through it."

He shivers, a spasm that seems to settle him. "First off, you're going to need another bag of coin."

# CHAPTER 27

"ONE MORE TIME," LENI SAYS. "PLEASE."

She can't sit still. I'd say I've never seen her like this, but I've known Leni for a long time. This is how she gets when she's overwhelmed. When there's not enough coin to last the month, when the tavern has more guests than rooms, and when the Majority demands a higher tax than we budgeted for. This is classic Leni, I know that, and I know that as soon as the problem is solved, she'll relax.

But we're not there yet. And after nearly a full day of this—of hiding out in the bed of the tree-truck, of napping on rotation—we still have several more hours to wait.

"Len, you know how this goes, yeah? We've gone through it over and over," Kyn says. He and I are giving the bikes a once-over while she paces back and forth under the trees.

"Just one more time!"

"OK, one more time then." I take a breath and dive in. "Our

pal Payder slipped your da a pill sometime today. In his dinner, maybe? That's step one. It makes him sick, so sick they have to send him to the infirmary. It should also cause his face to break out in some very characteristic hives."

"Characteristic how? No one's ever said—"

"I don't know, Leni. I didn't ask, but when a patient arrives with these hives, Dr. Helzyn knows what to do."

"And what does she know to do?"

Kyn sighs. "She injects the patient with a solution to slow their heart rate and knock them out, yeah? Declares them dead, zips them into a body bag, and has them loaded into a rig."

"Where they're taken—"

I tighten the bolt holding my handlebars in place. "Where they're taken outside the Stack to be buried in a mass grave with those who can't afford plots in the cemetery."

"We'll meet the truck," Leni says, "slip the driver a bag of coin, and unload my da from the back."

"You have the syringe from Payder?" Kyn asks her.

She pats her pocket.

"You jab that in your da's arm, it wakes him, and then we'll ride off into the dead of night on these babies." Kyn slaps his saddle.

"See?" I tell Leni. "You do know."

She tugs at her stocking cap. "And when do we meet the truck?"

"Not till midnight," I say.

She stops, spins toward us. "And what does the watch say, Syl? How much longer do we have?"

I glance at the wristwatch strapped to the handlebars of my bike. "A little less than six hours."

"Six hours!"

✳

When at last midnight does come, I can't decide who wants this over more: Kyn or Leni. I don't blame him; she's so wired I'm concerned she's going to be a liability.

But we're in position now. Payder told us where to wait, at a jagged outcropping of rock not far from an ancillary road that leads in and out of the gated loading dock. The clefts between the rocks are perfect for hiding the bikes, and there's plenty of room in the shadows for Leni to pace. Kyn and I stand nearby, watching, worrying, grateful this night is as dry as it gets here on Layce. No wind to speak of, just a damp fog gathering around our knees. Wherever Winter's raging, it's not here.

"If her da's not in this rig—"

Kyn stops me. "Don't even think it, Sylvi. Seriously. I can't do another night with her like this."

Through the trees we see a steady flow of headlamps, rigs making late-night deliveries to the Stack. It's tempting to creep closer, get a better look. But Payder said to stay put. There's an unpaved stretch of road off to our left and he said no rigs, save the funerary truck, travel this road at night. A digger or two at times, but just the one rig.

Too easy, I thought. Way too easy. I insisted we confirm his intelligence.

We didn't stay long, of course, but I had to see. A quarter

mile down an unpaved road, just outside the Shivering Forest, we found the site of their mass graves. Long trenches had been carved into the mud, one after the other. Some covered over with soft dirt, others waiting to be filled. Tractors with bucket loaders stand at the ready, but in the dark of night, there's not a single worker in sight. No guards. No searchlights.

Payder was right. There's little reason to protect this location. The dead don't run off.

Kyn places a hand on the flat of my back. It's warm, even through my jacket. "You stay out of sight, yeah? I don't think Payder will say anything, but if your picture's everywhere . . ."

"I will."

Leni's bouncing from one foot to the other now, sinking deeper into the mud with every back and forth. Kyn's hand slides left, tightening on my waist. My heart skips and stutters, and I tip my face up to his. But his eyes aren't on me, they're on the Stack. A box truck is making the turn onto the dirt road, its headlamps bouncing as the rig navigates the rough path.

After hours of movement, Leni goes still. "That's it, isn't it? The funerary truck."

"Should be." I zip my coat, flip the hood, try to be as invisible as possible.

"My da's in that rig."

"Flux, I hope so," Kyn whispers.

The truck grows closer, disappearing as the road bends through the trees and then emerging again a moment later.

"You have the coin?" Leni asks without turning. She's asked a hundred times, insisted on seeing it half that. She's counted it twice.

"Got it," Kyn says once again.

We move closer to Leni, and the three of us are standing at the edge of the shadows when the truck reaches the outcropping. For one heartrending moment, I think it'll roll past, but then the driver stops. Leni moves, but I grab her arm. "He's supposed to open his window."

The latch clicks and the window drops down.

She licks her chapped lips. "That's the sign."

"It is, yeah." Kyn steps out of the shadows first, but I can't hold Leni back anymore. Together, the two of them make their way to the driver's-side door where a middle-aged man with a thick salt-and-pepper beard and deerstalker hat sits waiting.

He eyes them lazily before speaking. "Doc sends her regards. Asks after her friend."

Kyn hesitates and I know why. He's afraid of saying the wrong thing, of passing information to the wrong people.

"Her friend is well, yeah? As well as could be expected."

An answer both mysterious and vague. After a moment, the driver nods. "I'll let the doc know then. You have something for me?"

Kyn lifts the bag so the driver can see. "You have the key?"

"Not necessary," the driver says. "Back's open."

"Check it," Kyn tells Leni.

I can't tell if it's locked or not from here. From the shadows, I watch as Leni scampers to the back.

"There's no lock!" She grabs hold of the roll up door.

Panic assaults me. I want to tell her to wait for Kyn. Wait until there's someone there to help her. But she's already tugging on the handle, and I hear the door rolling, bouncing against the top of the trailer.

"Oh no," Leni says. "No, no, no. Kyn!"

I can't see what's inside, can't decide what to do.

When it happens, it happens all at once. Kyn turns to Leni and the driver reaches out the window to snatch the coin purse. I sprint to the open trailer, wanted posters be damned.

The truck shifts into gear and lurches forward several feet. Kyn's hollering, words I can't focus on because all sorts of things begin tumbling out the back of the trailer: loose tie-downs, a tow-rope, a roll of plastic sheeting, and Leni.

Gah, Leni! On her knees, muddy and shaking.

But I'm there now, and I reach out, dragging her to her feet, both of us looking up at the open trailer.

"Which one is it, Sylvi? Which one?"

But I'm not staring at the mess of bodies zipped away in their black bags; I'm staring at Farraday Wrex. He stands in the dead center of the trailer, tall enough that he can hold himself in place with one hand pressed against the roof.

The truck lurches forward again—Kyn and the driver squabbling. Wrex stumbles this time, barely catching himself. His grin falters.

"How did you get here?" I ask.

"Boat," he says. "It's all about who you know, rig driver."

And if you know a Paradyian with a small watercraft, you can make it down the coast from Queen's Point. No ports to stop at here in the southeastern wing, but if you can survive the Abaki—something he's known for—and scale a cliff face, you can make it to the Stack in excellent time.

Someone told him we'd be here. Someone who knew what we were planning.

"I've traveled better," he says. "But the look on your face . . . it was worth it." The truck lurches again and Wrex curses, stomping body bags as he fights his way out of the back.

"Stop!" Leni cries. "Don't hurt him."

But Wrex is on the ground now, stepping closer, his bad leg dragging. I back up, grabbing Leni as I go. She tears away.

"Leni, don't!"

But she's diving for the trailer and Wrex is closer than I am, bigger than I am. He lays hold of her, clenching the front of her coat, dragging her to eye level, lifting her off the ground.

She screams, and he laughs. His free hand forms into a fist, pulling back—

Fear takes me, a fuse lighting, my lips blistering before the Kerce words are even out my mouth. Words I don't know, a command I never intended, and Winter yanks Wrex into the sky. Leni too. He's got hold of her and she's screaming, and they're so high now, and I can't stop it, and my blood is running fast, and the kol scrapes at my throat, and now they're falling.

I force my tongue to still, and then I give a command I know, but Winter's sluggish and instead of catching them as I've ordered, Wrex and Leni slip through her hold, their descent slowed, their forms tangled awkwardly as they fall. Wrex's foot clips the edge of the now-moving trailer and he's pitched to the ground, his grip on Leni's coat finally loosening. She reaches out an arm and hits the damp mud with a crack.

I run to her side, but she's already scrabbling to her feet, coated in sleet, her left wrist clearly broken.

"My da, Syl, my da."

Wrex is already pulling himself upright, shaking the ice from his face, blood dripping from his nose.

"Find him," I say, "Find your da." And then I snap off a command to Winter and though she's drained, Leni's flying through the air, her good arm wheeling as she lands safely in the trailer.

I turn to Wrex. He drags his sleeve across his face, smearing blood and ice into his hair. "It's amazing what you can make Winter do, I'll admit that."

The truck picks up speed and Leni totters, dropping to her knees and scrambling as she sorts through the body bags one handed. Kyn clings to the side mirror, punching his stone fist against the window, shouting at the driver inside. But the driver doesn't stop, and the truck flies out of view.

Winter's sputtering now, a candle at the end of its wick. I can't believe I lost control again.

Wrex takes a step toward me, some stupid comment telegraphed in the look on his face, but I don't give him a chance to voice it.

*"Eyaata!"* I cry.

Winter grabs hold of the towrope that fell from the trailer. She swings it round and round his body, but she's tired, moving entirely too slow. Wrex nearly squirms free, howling as he fights the rope, still finding sport in it all. But a moment later he's wrapped from thigh to shoulder. His knees buckle and he drops.

"I've never seen it before," he says, his head shaking in disbelief. "The way you handle Winter. She hates you for it, you know?"

"She's a tool in my hand. Nothing more."

"I met a Majority overseer not an hour ago who said the very same thing. Not about Winter, of course. But about a young girl dragged here from one of the western isles to work off her family's debt."

"It's different," I snap. "Winter isn't a person. She's a depraved spirit whose power I'm bound to keep in check."

He cocks his head to the wind, grins at what he hears. "And yet she feels. You've hurt her, rig driver."

"It's a two-way street, that." Frostbite cuts in at the corners of my mouth now, lines my gums. Blisters climb the soft skin above my mouth, crusting my nose.

"Did they get him with the net?" Wrex asks. "They did, didn't they? I would have liked to see Mars Dresden tangled in a fishing net."

Before I can answer—and by answer I mean punch him in the face—the box truck is suddenly rounding the rock outcropping and barreling straight at us. I dive out of the way as I hiss a command to Winter that has her half-heartedly blowing Wrex to the side of the road.

The truck skids to a stop, whipping around, splattering me with mud and gravel.

Leni stumbles out of the driver's seat, her hand cradled against her chest, pain on her face.

I did that. I broke her wrist. I lost control of my emotions and Leni paid the price.

"Move it!" Kyn's dragging the bearded driver out of the truck. Leni's golden gun is in his hand, and it's trembling with rage.

"Kyn?" I push myself to a stand. "We're not making a mess, remember?"

"No mess. Just making sure this guy knows who he's sided with. You wanna be a Majority worker," he barks at the driver.

"This is what happens to Majority workers!" He gestures to the open trailer with the gun. "Up! Get in there!"

"Kyn," I say, scanning the bodies, my heart firing way too fast. "What about Macks?"

"He's not in there." And then to the driver: "What are you waiting for? UP! UP!"

The driver's lip is bloody, his eye is swollen, and he's limping something fierce, but he manages to get up and into the trailer on his own. He stands there, not far from where Wrex stood just minutes ago. A poor replica, but it reminds me.

Kyn reaches up to grab the door, but I stop him.

"Hang on. I've got one more passenger for you."

I jog to the side of the road, to where I last saw Wrex, but there's no sight of him. Only the towrope. I lift it from the ground, my brow wrinkling as I examine it. It's been shredded, ice still clinging to the threads where Winter froze it, turning it brittle enough to break.

"You helped him," I say, stung by the idea.

The air bristles, Winter's energy sparking through it, but she says nothing.

"Where is he?" Kyn calls.

"He's gone." I swallow down the bile burning my throat and drop the rope, embarrassed I didn't do more to finish Wrex off. He's out there. Again. His shadow following us across the isle.

Kyn curses and then turns his attention back to the driver. "I'd get comfortable if I were you. We're not going to make this thing easy to find."

The driver scowls and then slumps to the floor, wriggling into a vacant corner. Kyn steps off the bumper and yanks the door into place. "Can you lock it?"

It takes me two tries and nearly an entire minute before it's done, but Winter freezes the locking mechanism.

"Her strength is almost gone," I say, feeling the devastation of losing both Macks's and Winter's help. "What happened to Leni's da, Kyn?"

"He's here, Syl."

My breath catches, and I watch Leni reach out a hand to the open door of the rig. Macks Trestman takes it, his movements careful as he lowers himself to the ground. He's always been a tall man, but he's stooped now, and thinner than I've ever seen him. He's upright though, and that has to count for something. Careful to protect her injured wrist, she slides beneath her father's arm.

"You remember Sylvi, Da." Her face is a streak of tears and mud, but she's never looked happier.

"I'm so glad to see you, Macks." I want to hug him, but that's very unlike me, and it's been a long time. I offer my hand instead.

He squints at my face and then pulls a pair of spectacles from his pocket. They're dusted in kol, and the right lens is cracked, but once they're in place, his smile brightens.

"I know you," he says.

I beam, because that has to be a good sign. Finally, *finally*, we've caught a break. "You do, yes."

"You're the girl from the posters."

# CHAPTER 28

WINTER'S SILENT AS WE MAKE OUR WAY north on the bikes. No rain, no wind. Not a single whisper. I suppose there is an upside to losing control. Fifteen hours of hard riding until we reach the safe house in Hex Landing. Four days until High Blys.

The safe house isn't that far from the cabin I spent the first five years of my life in. It's tucked away in the same woodland just outside the mining town of Hex Landing. And if I'm honest, it looks very similar: log beams, aluminum roof, weathered door, stone chimney. Bright green moss grows in the gaps where rot has eaten away at the logs. It's so familiar it's unsettling.

Unlike Mistress Quine's cabin, the safe house is hidden well, deep in the woods, far from the highway cutting through Hex Landing but near enough that we can still hear the kol stamps pounding away at the mine yard.

"The rebellion built this house," I say. It's not a question. It's a fact I remember from our planning sessions in the garage at

Queen's Point. I was caught by the idea that the rebellion had safe houses all over the isle. I knew they had fuel stores tucked away in the mountains, but no one had ever mentioned places like this, and I'd never come across them in my travels.

Kyn and I make a circuit of the cabin, checking the place out in the dimming light of day. I'm pretending I don't notice that beads of sweat have broken out along his forehead and his upper lip. Pretending I don't know the scars on his chest and neck have started to fester again.

And he knows I'm pretending.

It's a game we really shouldn't play, but they've surfaced so much quicker than last time, and neither of us are prepared to discuss what that could mean.

For now, we're pretending everything's good and giving Leni some time with her da. He rode behind Kyn on the ice bike the entire way here, compliant and saying very little. After one of the stops, when it was clear he couldn't keep his eyes open any longer, we used bungees to strap him to Kyn. I do wonder if the rubbing of those cords against Kyn's chest advanced the pain he's struggling through now, but it was our only option.

With Leni's broken wrist, she couldn't manage the bike. We ditched it in the woods and she rode behind me. I keep waiting for her to lash out, to scold me for breaking Winter and her arm all in one fell swoop. But she's far too focused on her da to worry about me.

Macks is disoriented, which is to be expected, and every time we stopped, Leni had to keep reminding him of who Kyn and I were and why it's important that he stay quiet. Thank Begynd almighty he remembers Leni at least. I don't know what we'd do if she was a stranger to him.

In some ways, he's better than I expected—no howling, despite Payder's account—but his memory is shot. And maybe it's cruel, but I would have traded some of his sanity for the brilliance that got him recruited by the Majority all those years ago.

Kyn drags his hand along the porch railing. "The rebellion built it, yeah. Brewzer and his crew. The Majority thought he was working for them back then, scouting the woods for rebels while all the while he was building this place. For a long time he worked out of here. Recruiting, mostly."

We note a cord of wood, recently split and stacked against the outer wall of the cabin. The axe is still buried in the stump they used.

"And then the house here passed into Sayth's hands?" I ask.

Kyn nods. "Sayth and Tali took it up a notch, sabotaging the mines, attacking Majority vehicles—"

"Blowing up roads." I found out only recently that it was the two of them who had coordinated the attack that took out the highway this past Flux, just as we were hoping to take it north onto the Shiv Road. It was an attack that rattled the Majority, but also forced us to take the road through High Pass.

"They left after that," Kyn says. "When they saw that the Majority was punishing the miners for their actions. That's when they came to Queen's Point. They knew we needed to regroup."

There are fresh tracks here, up against the cabin—Sayth's pickup and the war machine both. Inside, the floor is strewn with bedrolls and maps line the walls. Diagrams of the surrounding woodland and the roads cutting through it. Of Hex Landing itself, the town, and the mining operation. The one-room cabin smells like woodsmoke and wet socks, but it's a relief knowing the others made it.

"Where do you think they went?" I ask.

"Counting guards, maybe? Or planting explosives. I just hope they're ready when we are."

We're far from ready just now. We shouldn't avoid this conversation with Macks—it's why we broke him out in the first place—but we give him and Lenore as long as we can, refilling the bikes' gas tanks, airing up the tires, digging tools out of an attached shed and rehanging the shutters, fixing the boundary fence.

Kyn strips off his coat, and I notice the blood and kol pressing through his shirt, the puncture scars on his neck inflamed. I nearly offer to open my hands again, but we've fallen into a companionable rhythm, and I don't want to be the one to screw it up.

We work well together; it's the one area where our strange bond is not at all inconvenient. It's thrilling even—our hands brushing as we pass tools back and forth, surveying a problem and discussing the best way to tackle it, anticipating each other's movements. We fly through projects with no conflict, no frustration. Nothing at all like working with the knuckleheads in the garage back home.

If Begynd does free us of this connection, I'll miss this. I'll miss him.

Winter wakes with a roar, shaking herself awake, gathering her storms from across the isle. As she pulls and tugs, she brings with her the hum of the Desolation voices. They pummel us in a confusion of wind and words.

Kyn's spine stiffens. "Tell me you heard that."

"I heard it," I call, fighting to keep my hat in place. "Time to head indoors, find out if Macks can help us."

Kyn shakes his head, disappointed. But he follows.

It's quieter inside the cabin, warmer. And Leni's touch is easy to see. She's rolled away the bedding and moved the table to the center of the space. She's gathered the chairs that have been scattered about the cabin and placed them around a table set for dinner. Mismatched plates and silverware, a pitcher of something golden and frothy, twyl burning in the hearth.

Leni and Macks are standing at the wood-burning stove, which has a pot bubbling on top, its steam fogging the windows.

Kyn takes a seat at the table and fingers a delicate napkin folded on his plate. "You did all this with a broken wrist, Len?"

"Da helped, and he set my wrist too. Now that the swelling's gone down, it's not too bad." Her forehead is damp with fatigue, her hair clinging to her face, but she holds up her hand, wrapped thickly in bandages.

"Leni, you should rest."

"I'm fine. I want to spend a nice evening with my da."

She's determined to play homemaker, and since I've already made this night harder on her, I just nod and take a seat next to Kyn.

"Da found a root cellar. Carrots and potatoes. Beets even. There was cider and pickled meat in the cold box—the others must have stopped in town—so we threw together a stew. And we'll have boiled chocolate for dessert. The good stuff too. I don't know where they found it. No bread, I'm afraid, but Da's always liked to cook, haven't you, Da?"

He nods at her and turns toward us, bowing his head kindly, his glasses slipping down the bridge of his nose. Still, there's no spark of recognition in his eyes.

Dinner is as pleasant as Leni can make it, and we let her guide the conversation. Macks watches, his dark eyes moving curiously over everything, confusion puckering his brow on occasion, smoothed out whenever Leni places her hand over his.

She does it often, unable to sit still. The unwinding that comes when a problem's been solved, she hasn't found that yet. She's just as tight and frantic as she was in the woods.

"Macks," I say, when our bowls have been cleared and the pitcher is empty. "Can I ask you a few questions about your work?"

He wipes the cider foam from his mouth and repositions his glasses. "I hope you will, young lady. No one asks me about my work anymore."

I look to Kyn and then to Leni. Her smile is tight, but she nods.

"Lenore tells me you designed the dewatering system for the mines at Hex Landing."

He makes a small sound in the back of his throat and squints at me. I feel the need to speak slower, but that's not the problem here at all, is it?

"Can you . . . Do you remember doing that?"

He leans forward now, chin in hand, and though his gaze moves over my face, I get the impression that he's not quite with us anymore.

"Da?" Leni says, a slight warble in her voice. "Can you tell Sylvi about your work at Hex Landing?"

"I don't work at the Landing, do I?" He's genuinely asking. He'd like someone to confirm it for him.

"Not anymore, no," Leni says, kindly. "Of late you've been in the refinery, remember? At the Stack. But a long time ago, you worked in the mines at Hex Landing. The Majority recruited you. Don't you remember?"

He pinches his eyes shut and we wait, the fire popping, the residual foam in the pitcher dissolving.

Leni opens her napkin and then refolds it, laying it on the table, and smoothing her shaking hand over it. "It was a long, long time ago, Da. Before you met Ma."

His eyes flutter open, wet, sad.

"You remember Ma, don't you?"

"Oh yes . . ." he reaches out, taking a strand of Leni's hair in his hand, rubbing it between his thumb and forefinger. "She had hair just like this. Reminded me of the dying embers of a fire, dark and bright all at once. She was the most beautiful person I'd ever seen."

I open my mouth to try again, but under the table, Leni touches her toe to mine, gives a tiny, almost imperceptible shake of the head before continuing.

"She *was* beautiful. Do you remember how you met her, Da? How you met Ma?"

"How I met . . . She slapped me upside my head, she did!" He laughs and laughs and I'm not sure if we should join in. But Leni's laughing too, and she nods along.

"She did, didn't she? I remember you saying that. Why did she slap you, Da?"

"She was none too happy about me hassling her father. Drypp was his name. You remember him, Leni love? Old Man Drypp, they called him."

"I do," she says, her voice thick, her eyes glossy with tears. "I remember Drypp, Da."

"He was a funny old man, wasn't he? But I liked him. He was fixing a table, that day. But he had the trusses backward and I was just trying to help. It's all in the engineering, I told him." A shake of his head, a great, heaving sigh as he remembers.

"He tried it your way, yeah?"

Macks turns to Kyn, shocked to find us at the table. But he recovers, for the sake of the story, I think. "Yessir! In the end he did, and I bet that table's still standing."

"But Ma wasn't impressed?" Leni asks.

"Oh, she was impressed all right. Didn't stop her smacking me some, but she kept my tumbler full that evening, and the next time I came through there, she shared a pint with me. Sat at my table and everything."

"You were there often, weren't you?" Leni prods. "At Drypp's tavern in Whistletop."

He leans forward. "It's on the way, see? If you've got to travel from the Port of Glas to the Landing, it's the best place to stop for the night. Soft beds and good beer."

"And Ma?"

He pats Leni's hand. "And your ma, yes. She was beautiful."

Leni grabs hold of his hand. "Da, why did you have to travel so often? From Glas, I mean. Was it for work?"

"Work?" He sits back in his chair now, his gaze wandering: over his empty plate, over the table, over the rain lashing at the window.

"Da?"

His eyes find mine now, sharp, present. "You asked about the dewatering system at the Landing."

My heart knocks against my ribs. "I did."

A shadow passes over his eyes, and I fear we've lost him again. That fast, there and then gone. But he leans closer. "They would have got someone else to show them," he says. "They would have figured it out eventually. The technology was there; they just needed someone with brains to teach them how to use it."

"It's good that it was you. Truly." I smile, nod. "Because now you can help us destroy it. We want to flood the mine, Macks. Can you show us how?"

He blinks at me. Slow, and then fast, and then he pushes his glasses up on his nose again and rests his forearms on the table. "Paper, please. And something to write with."

I search about for something, but Kyn's faster. He pulls a map of the mine off the wall and flips it over. Leni slides a pen into his hand, and we watch as he begins to fill up the paper.

Kyn keeps twyl on the fire, and Leni sets to work on the boiled chocolate. Macks moves quickly, almost as if he knows his mind is on some kind of clock, and by the time Leni's sliding mugs of chocolate in front of us, his sketch is complete.

"The system controls look like this." He turns the paper toward us. His lines are shaky in places, but he's drawn a control board, full of switches and dials. It's more helpful than I could have hoped. "This panel here has a series of switches. A key is inserted here"—he taps the paper—"just one key gives you access to all the pumps. Once the key is turned, each switch needs to be flipped to a downward position, and then this handle here"—another tap of the page—"must be moved to the forward position. If you do that, the pumps will shut down."

"Will that flood the entire mine?" Kyn asks. "Every shaft?"

"Every shaft, yes. The pumps have to be kept in motion to keep the mine free of water."

I scan the page, trying to memorize every line, every dot. "How long will it take for the mine to flood once the pumps are disabled?"

Macks shakes his head. "Depends on the weather, the saturation of the water table, the depth of the shaft, underground water stores. Too many variables to know for certain."

"But if you had to guess, Da."

"Twelve hours, maybe? Fourteen?"

I run my hand over his sketch. "Pretty sure I can speed that up."

Macks tilts his head but doesn't ask the question furrowing his brow.

I tap the diagram. "And how much coin would it take to undo the damage this would cause?"

A grin then, the first real flash of the old Macks Trestman. "Incalculable, even for me."

Leni's hand freezes over her mug. "Incalculable."

"Flux, I'm glad we got you out," Kyn says.

"As am I." Macks lifts his chocolate and takes a sip. "This is good, Leni love. Very good."

I flip the paper over, to the map of the mine. "Can you tell me where to find this panel, Macks? Where's the pump system control room located?"

He doesn't hesitate. With his pen he circles a building in the dead center of the map, the epicenter of the entire operation. "It's on the bottom floor, subterranean."

"The basement," I say, my mind whirring.

"Yes, the basement." Another sip of his chocolate, a twinkle in his eye. "And you'll need me to get in."

# CHAPTER 29

"HE'S ASLEEP," LENI SAYS, STEPPING ONTO THE porch and reaching for the door.

"I got it, I got it." I jump up and close the door behind her. "How's your wrist?"

"Hurts a bit."

"Can I help?"

A wry smile. "I appreciate the offer, Syl, but you're a lot better at breaking things than you are at fixing them." She's trying to be funny, but it stings. I don't like having that reputation. "Besides, there's nothing to do. It just needs to heal."

"How's your da, Len?" Kyn's sitting on a damp log in the open area in front of the cabin, firelight brightening his red-brown eyes, shimmering on his stone biceps. I move toward him.

"He's fine, I think. I have no idea how he'll be when he wakes up, but he's resting now."

"Maybe that's all he needs?" Kyn looks as casual as he's ever looked, but the pain snaking through his body is making him ill.

My own stomach churns with it. "Your da's been working hard labor for years. Probably hasn't slept well in ages."

Leni picks at her bandage. "I don't know. It seems like it's more than that, doesn't it? Like sometimes the switches in his brain just . . ."

"Flip to a downward position?" I try, dropping next to Kyn.

Leni steps off the porch, moving closer. "Yes, exactly that. Like the pumps that keep his brain clear grind to a halt, and it fills up with nonsense again."

I grab her good hand and pull her down next to me. "He's had a lot of kol exposure, Leni. All things considered, he's pulled through like a champ. And you were right about him. It's all in there still, in his head. This diagram," I say, waving it gently. "It's everything we need to take down the operation."

"But?"

"But we can't take him with us," I say. "There's just no way. The switches in his head, we just have no control over which way they're flipped."

Her head sags. "No, I know. It's just, what if he's right? What if we really can't get into that room without him?"

It's hard to know exactly when Macks's mind went dull in there. But he sounded awfully sharp when he said, *"There's a lift that takes you to the subterranean level. Beyond that, at the end of a long hallway, there's a door with a keypad. The only way to get the entry code is to solve the equation mounted above it. The equation changes. Often and without warning. A system I devised myself."*

We gaped at him for a moment and then we all started talking at once, and if I had to guess, that's when those switches in his head flipped. But we can't know. And it really doesn't matter. The risk he presents is too significant.

"Either way, Len. A door's not going to be a problem for me."

"Even underground in a sealed basement? I thought you had to have direct access to Winter."

"I do."

"So we'll account for that, yeah? Show her, snowflake."

I spread the map on the ground before the fire. "From the surface, we'll use this lift here to get to the basement. I'll freeze the access doors open before we descend, and once we've reached the bottom, we'll blow the roof off the elevator car which should give us access to Winter once again."

"Through the elevator shaft. OK, I see that."

"And here, down this hallway is the door to the control room. To make sure she can reach us there, I'll have her freeze open the elevator doors at the bottom as well. And when we reach Mack's equation door, we'll use Winter one last time, to freeze that highly secure door solid so we can smash our way through."

"And that won't wear her out?" Leni asks.

"I'll be specific. Unemotional. Not like—" My eyes fall on her bandaged wrist.

"And if that doesn't work?"

"It'll work," I say, ignoring the doubt that hovers like fog. "Winter's wicked cold and Kyn's strong. He can slam his way through brittle steel, no problem."

Leni looks unconvinced.

"I'll have a sledgehammer, yeah?" Kyn lifts the one he found propped against the back of the house. "You thought I was going to punch my way through that door, didn't you?"

"I thought *you thought* you were going to punch your way through that door. I'm glad you're smarter than that. You could take explosives. Dakk's got a whole tankful. Blow the door clean off."

"We talked about that," Kyn says. "When Dakk gets here, we'll run it by him, but looking at this map, I worry we could bring a lot of concrete down on our heads if we use explosives down there."

Something fizzes through the atmosphere, a shock that lifts the hairs on my arms. Kyn feels it too. He sits up straight, his eyes on me. And then a cry high on the wind. A voice so familiar it plucks a heartstring deep inside me, sets everything vibrating.

This isn't Winter. But those words were spoken in Kerce.

Thunder rolls overhead, and a moment later the sky cracks open. Rain falls like a shower of bullets, setting the fire sizzling. I tuck the map inside my coat, and we dash for the porch.

"Let's get that inside," Kyn says, taking the map from me and slipping through the door.

"She's just miserable, isn't she?" Leni says, squeezing rain from her braids.

"Who?" I ask.

"Winter. She's a nightmare."

I'm not listening to Leni, not really. I'm listening for the voice I heard on the wind. But Winter's so loud. I could tell her to quiet, I could. But does that mean—

"Syl? Are you OK? You look—"

I hear it again! A thin keening and then the rain chases it away. "Winter's panicking. Her existence here is coming to an end and she knows it."

"Don't you dare feel bad for her," Leni says.

Her tone surprises me, pulls me back to the here and now. "I don't feel bad for her. She's vindictive and selfish; I know that. But I do *feel* for her. The kol's stolen her sanity as surely as it's stolen your da's."

"No, no way." The low light catches Leni's eyes, leaving the rest of her face in shadow. "My da may have lost a good portion of his mind, but that's what makes us different from her. We're frail. We're human. Kol has never made us *more* than what we are. It doesn't take our attributes and intensify them. It strips us bare and steals everything we have: our memories, our strength, our self-awareness. Kol hasn't stripped anything from Winter, has it?"

It's an outrageous claim. "How can you know that? How can you possibly know what she was like before she came to Layce?"

"I know what she is now." She ticks them off on her fingers. "She's strong. She's aware. And despite revelation number seven, she remembers, doesn't she? She remembers what she's done, and she revels in it. Don't you dare make her a victim in all of this. If she's encountered unfairness in this world, loneliness because of how she's made, well, so have we all. It stripped my da bare, the kol. Whereas Winter? It just made her more of what she already was."

My eyes have adjusted to the dark now and I see the rain on Leni's face, rivulets that twist down her cheeks, droplets that gather on her lashes. Lighting flashes and she steps closer to me.

"Winter's a villain now, Syl, but she was always wicked."

# CHAPTER 30

IT'S LONG PAST MIDNIGHT WHEN THE OTHER crews return.

We've shoved the table into the far corner and stretched out in front of the cooker, Leni and Kyn and me. Macks sleeps propped in a chair by the hearth, a blanket tucked up around his chin.

The door swings open, and they stomp inside, all silhouette and shadow, slapping one another on the back and whooping in celebration. We're startled awake, all of us, but none so violently as Macks. He shoots to his feet, knocking his chair backward to the floor, arms swinging before him as he shouts nonsense into the night.

Leni leaps up and rushes to her father, wrapping him in a one-armed hug and lowering him once again into the chair that Kyn's righted.

"Hey! Yo! Good to see you all," Kyn yells over the noise.

"Really good to see you, yeah? But we're a little sensitive to noise in here just now."

I'm standing, half awake, in the center of the room, my hatchet drawn and blinking furiously. I fell asleep straining to capture the Kerce voice I heard earlier, and now I'm disoriented. The only light in the room comes from the hearth, flickering and manic. I can't get my eyes to focus on any one person.

Light strikes my face and I slam my eyes shut.

"Fluxing Blys, boss," Sayth says. "Put the weapon down. It's just us."

"You first," I say. Her flashlight goes out with a mumbled apology. I drop my hatchet and stumble back against the table, blinking, trying to count the silhouettes. "Good to see you all made it here alive."

"And loud," Kyn says, jiggling his ear.

"What about you?" Felyx asks as he turns his flashlight on. He aims it at our feet one at a time, making his way around the room. "You've added one gent, howdy sir"—he tips his hat to Macks—"but it looks like you've lost another. Where's Dresden?"

For a moment there's nothing but the sound of Winter's wrath.

"Close the door," I say. "There's a lot to tell."

✳

They arrived the day before yesterday, Dakk tells us. Sayth's crew has been gathering intel in town, while Felyx and the Paradyians focused on mine yard reconnaissance. They set explosives and found a good place to park the war machine in preparation for what's to come. They all rode back here together tonight, the cab and bed of Sayth's pickup jammed tight with bodies. A sight I would have liked to see.

While Sayth and Felyx update us on their journey thus far, the others unload the rig. Packs and weapons mainly, but also these handy little Paradyian lanterns. They stand about six inches tall but collapse down into a biscuit-size disk. They give off a soft orange glow, and with four or five of them placed around the cabin, it's suddenly bright and homey.

"You got him out, then?" Brash says, smiling at Macks. "How's he doing?"

"He's OK," Leni says. "More OK sometimes than others, but—"

"He's a genius," I say, tacking the map up on the wall. "He's given us everything we need to make this happen."

The chatter falls away as all three crews crowd around to see.

"Macks has shown us how to disable the pumps. It's a simple operation that can be handled from this room." I tap the circle Macks marked. "Kyn and I will take care of that once the party gets started. Sayth, you're most familiar with the mine itself, so I'll need your crew to clear the mine shafts of workers. If I'm reading this correctly, there are three hoist houses in the mine yard."

"What's a hoist house?" Brash asks.

I nod at Sayth.

"That's a hoist house there," she says, pointing to a sketch on the far wall. "See that tall thing jutting out the top at an angle? That's the gallows frame. It's what lowers skips into the ground and hoists them back to the surface as well. Skips are like mine carts, right? They're used to move supplies, machinery—"

"And—more notably—miners, in and out of the ground." I tap the three hoist houses on the map in turn. "Miners report to a hoist house for their shift."

"So that's where we go to warn off the miners?" Tali asks.

"And to disarm any guards that might not have responded to whatever havoc the Paradyians have caused out front. What's the plan there?" I look to Dakk, who is towering over the group in the back, his arms crossed.

"The war machine is hidden well, and its guns aimed at that top gate there." He gestures, and I point at it on the map for him. "Yes, there. Far from the barracks, see? Just as you asked, Sessa."

I can't hear that word without thinking of Hyla. And despite the grief it stirs, I like having her with us. Even in these small things. "Thank you, Dakk. I appreciate it."

He strokes his beard. "She's dug in there, the war machine. Sten and Meytee will man it—they've the most experience with its weaponry. Felyx and I will handle the ground assault."

"Just the two of you?" Kyn asks.

"And the bombs," Dakk says.

Kyn nods, rubbing at his eyes. "OK, yeah. That'll work. The big thing is that we get this done in the right order. So maybe we could go through it from the top?" He leaves a kind pause, but everyone just stares back at him. "Uh, OK. First, we blow the guard towers, here and here. Those devices are already planted, yeah?" He glances at Dakk, who nods. "Good. As the smoke is clearing and the overseers are responding . . ." He glances at me.

"Winter and I put on a little show."

"Right, Sylvi makes sure she's seen by as many people as

possible before leading the Majority's security forces away from the mine yard and into the woods."

It's a job more suited to Mars and his theatrical flair, but with a little creativity, and a whole lot of Winter, I think I can handle it.

"Dakk and Felyx?" Kyn prompts.

"Once the security forces head our way, we'll keep 'em busy," Felyx promises.

"And the war machine?" Kyn asks, blinking, rubbing his eyes again.

"Will take out any Majority or Ranger rig approaching the fight," Sten confirms. It's possible this is the first I've ever heard him speak. He's a big man, bigger than Dakk, but with the sweet face of a toddler. I caught him glancing shyly at Tali earlier.

"Good, yeah. That'll be important. We don't need any reinforcements making this messy. Once the security forces are depleted—" He points to Sayth.

"We hit the hoist houses," she says. "Directing the miners back to their barracks or out the back gate, depending on what's closer. Is someone making sure that gate is open?"

"I got it," Tooki says. "You three can handle the miners and I'll take the gate." He looks to Dakk. "Hey man, can I borrow a couple bombs?"

Dakk nods, slaps Tooki on the back. "For certain."

I grin. What a funny group we have here.

"And while all that's going on, Sylvi and I will make our way to the control room."

"How will you know if the miners are out?" Brash asks.

"Radios," I say. "Thanks for reminding me. Dakk has short-range radios for each crew. Once we're in place, everyone checks in. But then you stay off them if you can. Sayth, Tali, Brash, when your hoist house is clear, we need to know that. If you run into trouble and need help, we want to know that too." I turn my eyes on the room. "Clearing mine shafts before we stop the pumps is important. If you find yourself free to help, get to one. We're doing this at sunset, right at the shift change, so ideally, we'll be catching crews coming and going. Right, Sayth?"

"Right. Nothing's perfect, but they're pretty strict on those protocols. Crews go down together and come up together, right at the bell. I'll walk my team through reading the drop logs and such, so we can account for everyone. We'll get those shafts emptied, boss."

"I know you will. And when they're emptied, Kyn and I disable the pumps and the mines will start to fill. It won't be fast, though. I'll do what I can to speed it up, but we'll need to keep the Majority out of the control room while that's happening."

"And when the mine shafts are flooded?" Leni asks. She's in the corner with Macks. He's drifted off to sleep again and she stands at his side, watching as everything her father made possible is laid out and put to use.

"A word. A blister. And Winter freezes them solid."

# CHAPTER 31

WE HAVE ALL DAY TO PREPARE, AND WHILE it's barely enough time for the others, it's far too much for me: My gear's packed and loaded and I don't know what to do with myself.

After being shooed out of the kitchen, I'm sitting outside on a too-short stump by the remnants of last night's fire, my knees knocked together, my hood up. It's drizzling, Winter's slow steady whine on the wind. She's being tragic just now, complaining about unfairness and queens who take advantage.

I can't stop thinking about that voice.

The wind pushes against me, but the rain is light, churning up the green perfume of the earth. A fragrance far preferable to the thick fug inside: wet clothing and stinking boots, the sharp acrid smell of explosives, and the savory aroma of herbed potatoes.

Leni was up early cooking, Macks wide-eyed and hollowed out, but chopping whatever root vegetable she slid in front of him. Tali gave him her earmuffs, and while I'm not sure they shut out much noise, he hasn't taken them off.

It's loud in there, but a good kind of loud. When I left them to it, Dakk and Tooki were bent over an explosive and Dakk was pointing to its various parts with a pencil.

Nearby, Sayth had gathered up all the sketches of the mine yard and tacked them up in one corner of the cabin. Her crew was circled around and listening, while across the table from Macks, Felyx and Kyn sat side by side cleaning guns, sharpening blades, and swapping Abaki jokes.

Kyn keeps digging at his eyes, and his smile is hiding a lot of pain—that, I know—but he still hasn't said anything, and we've entered some sort of standoff here. Several weapons were laid out in front of them awaiting their turn, Leni's golden gun among them.

I sincerely hope she won't need it. I've given Leni and Macks an important assignment, but one that keeps the two of them away from the mine yard. And more importantly, away from me.

"Cleaned it up for you," Kyn says as he approaches. He squats down, my hatchet in his hand. "And by cleaned, I mean I wiped off the handle."

I take it in my hand and turn it, examining the black snowflakes once again. It really is a piece of work.

"You haven't thrown it yet, have you?"

"Haven't had a chance really."

"Come on," he says. "You're driving me crazy sitting out here stewing."

He heads toward the wooded area beyond the rigs, and I follow, passing Sten and Meytee, one of them adjusting the gun mount on the roof of Sayth's pickup, and the other sorting ammunition.

The ground is wet and spongy, layer after layer of pine needles beneath my feet. I was lost in these woods once. Somewhere between Hex Landing and Whistletop. It's a huge area. Hundreds of miles of trees. I may have *stayed* lost if it hadn't been for Leni. So while these woods hold some of my worst memories, there's hope here too.

We're a good ways from the cabin now. I can't see it anymore, can only just smell the twyl smoke spiraling from the chimney. I'm about to call out to Kyn, tell him we've gone far enough, when he strips off his jacket and I realize we're not here to throw hatchets.

He doesn't want anyone to see what's happened to him, and as he turns and I take in the carnage on his torso, I understand. I wouldn't want anyone to see this either. Blood leaks through his shirt, soaking into his belt, kol shimmering maliciously from the wounds. I can't believe he's still upright.

"Fluxing Blys, Kyn." I draw my knife, but he lifts his hand.

"Not this time, snowflake."

"You're not serious."

"I didn't bring you out here so you could heal me again. I brought you out here so you could stop wondering how bad it's gotten. So I could put your mind at rest."

"That," I say, pointing my knife at his chest, "does not put my mind at rest. Just let me—"

"I don't want any more of your blood." It's a slap. Ridiculous, I know, but it is. "I'm telling you, I'm strong enough to handle the pain. I wouldn't put us all at risk, and I'm asking you to respect my decision. The kol is starting to do funny things to me, things that make me wonder if the damage is more than skin deep."

"What kind of things?"

"Nothing I can't handle."

"Kyn!"

"I'm not hearing as well, OK? And sometimes at the corner of my vision I see things, black . . . shimmers. My heart won't stop racing, snowflake, and while that's all kinds of fun when there's good reason, this isn't fun at all. I'd rather deal with this," he says, gesturing to his chest, "than the kol. I don't want to question my senses in the middle of a fight. Besides, a few more days, and I can wash this all away."

I'm trembling, my hands and my chin. "We still have no idea what will happen when the pool is restored. This isn't a fairy story. It may not have a happy ending."

He takes the knife from my hands, slides it back into my waistband. "I never thought it was a fairy story, snowflake, but I'm still going to hold out for that happy ending. I'm a believer now."

The trees rustle overhead, and I stop, listen. But there's nothing. Just Winter.

Kyn cocks his head. "That voice we heard last night, it was speaking Kerce."

I didn't realize he'd noticed. "Do you . . . do you know what it was saying?"

"I don't speak Kerce, snowflake."

"No," I say, shaking my head. "Of course you don't. It's just . . ."

"You think it's your mother."

Hope and fear knot in my throat, make it hard to speak. "I've been thinking. If Winter's trying to hide anything from us like you said, it doesn't really make sense that she would keep the Shiv accounts a secret. There's no remorse for what she did to them, no regret. She celebrates their defeat. But my mother . . . Maree Vale was the weapon Winter used against the Shiv, against Begynd."

"But we know her story, yeah? Mars was there."

"But he was so young and much of what he knows came to him by Winter, in the whispers she used to torment him. He told me that himself." I'm still trying to make sense of the thoughts that kept me awake last night. "The lies we believe as children . . . they become our reality. We carry them with us. They shape every-thing. We have to hear my mother tell her own story, Kyn. It's the only way to know what really happened between her and Winter."

Pride pushes through his pain, respect for me, for my choice. His emotions fill me up, make me tall.

"You don't have to convince me, snowflake."

I tip my face to the sky, to the slow, steady, drip of rain, the trees billowing high above. "Last night the winds were better. They aren't right for it just now. They're flowing south. It's an east wind we need. Strong and clear."

Kyn scoops up his coat and pulls it on over his bloodied shirt. "The winds are whatever you make them, little ice witch. Or have you forgotten that?"

"I can call her voice to me," I realize. "Of course I can."

"Of course you can." Kyn touches his fingers to my face and steps past me, his boots crunching over the forest floor.

"Where are you going?"

He turns, framed by evergreens, a crease between his brows.

"If you drag Maree Vale's voice here, it's not coming alone. The Shiv voices will come as well. The closer I am when that happens, the harder it'll be for you."

I don't care. Easy isn't all it's cracked up to be. "I'm strong enough if you are. Please. I don't want to do this alone."

"Well." Kyn says, a smile stretching his face, tightening the grip on my heart. "That's different then."

I grab his hand and pull him to the ground with me, damp moss beneath our knees. Pain ripples through his chest, his neck, but he balls it up and tosses it away. The light through the trees catches the red flecks in his eyes, turning them to flame. A tremor of fear moves through us, and I'm not sure if it started in his heart or mine.

"I've never asked Winter to do this. I'm not entirely sure what to say."

He brushes the hair from my face. "Take your time, little ice witch. We've got nothing else going today. Just a revolution."

"Oh, that's all?" I laugh, then close my eyes and try to envision exactly what I want. An east wind pushing in off the Kol Sea, over the Desolation, grabbing the voices gathered there and bringing them to me. I open my mouth and ask for it.

When Winter bucks as she does when I forget who I am, when I ask instead of command, I try once more, ordering her to bring me that wind, insisting she do it now, not in her own time.

My lips fizz and crack, a blister forming in the corner, kol settling on the tip of my tongue. It's several minutes before the gale arrives, but when it does, it comes in force. Winter tears through the forest, angry and punching. Behind her she drags the east wind, loud with voices, full of stories.

But I need just the one.

Trees crack and splinter around us, forcing us low. We cover our heads, huddling to the ground.

"*Bevet, bevet,*" I insist. *Gently, gently.*

Winter bites but she slows, pushing over us, lifting my hair, complaining all the while. She's taken pains to hide her secrets and it brings her no pleasure to parade them before me now.

"Hush," I tell her, easing to the ground and lying flat on my back. Kyn settles next to me, our ears touching. "Hush."

Winter obeys, her words falling away, but I've told her to bring me the voices, and that's a noisy task. The treetops bow and swing overhead, creaking ominously. Branches drop around us, pine needles and leaves caught in a violent tornado. And finally, the voices.

"*. . . mother sent me to fetch water. . .*"

"*Begynd was especially warm that day . . .*"

"*. . . just returned . . . a long trip into the mountains above . . .*"

"*The fount was bubbling, a song almost . . .*"

"*I was just there to speak to our elder—*"

"*. . . was sat there on the shore with my father. He'd cut his hand—*"

"*A cold wind . . .*"

"*There was a commotion—*"

"*I heard her screaming, the Kerce queen. It was my father who pulled her from the Kol Sea; did you know that?*"

"*I'm sure I could have stopped her—*"

"*I was there when the little princess was born.*"

"*I came up from beneath the water . . .*"

"*. . . the air was cold . . .*"

"*And my throat closed over—*"

*"'Mother,' I cried! 'Mother!' But I heard nothing. Saw only a field of white. Felt only a great cold shiver across my back and then—"*

There are tears leaking into my ear and I'm not sure if they're mine or Kyn's, but there's nothing here in Kerce. Maybe I was wrong. Maybe . . . Kyn takes my hand.

"Just wait," he says. "Wait."

*"The air is gone, gone . . ."*

*"The rocks bear witness."*

*"Are we to die?"*

*". . . we are forgotten now."*

*". . . abandoned."*

*"Where is the girl?"*

It's more of the same, fear and sadness. Loss and . . . and then words Kyn can't understand. In a voice that's deep and rich and jarringly familiar.

"I'll try to focus on her," Kyn shouts over the wind. "Just her. Maybe then the other voices won't be so loud in your head."

But I'm sobbing, something like hope cracking my ribs, flaying me open. My insides are cold and hot all at once, because now that I've heard her voice, I can't unhear it.

Her story is the story of the isle.

Its past. Its present. And, if we get this right, its thousand tomorrows.

# CHAPTER 32

"THIS IS WHAT I REMEMBER. THIS IS WHAT I *know.*" It's the voice from last night, my mother's voice. I squeeze Kyn's hand and slam my eyes shut, afraid I'll lose it again otherwise.

*"It was a starless night and a broken ship that delivered the Kerce exiles to the island. It was not quite the safe haven we were hoping for, not at first. When we washed up on the shore, most of us were half mad and still fighting off the monsters that had torn our ship apart.*

*"But the people of the isle saved us. Their hands were warm, their flesh and stone mixed in a delicate construction that spoke of a creator's great love for his creation. I knew then where we were. I'd been raised on the histories of Sola and her son Begynd. Of the people he carved from the rock. We had washed up on Shiv Island.*

*"It was the Shiv people who fought off the monsters and led us to a grand sylver pool in a lush green valley. A fount bubbled at its center. They took us to Begynd, and in his waters, our wounds were healed."*

A shudder moves through Kyn, and I realize, with delight, that he understands her words. And why not? It's our connection that allows me to understand the Shiv. It took a little longer, but why wouldn't our bond allow him to decipher Kerce?

"*The curiosity of my heart was stirred then. I wanted desperately to understand how such a thing was accomplished. How I could step into a pool, broken and bleeding, and emerge whole. Because it wasn't just my body that was restored—but my soul too. I'd left behind my husband and home, had lost my eldest son, my beautiful boy, to the sea. I was bereft. And this pool brought life.*

"*But no one could tell me how it worked. No one could tell me how Begynd accomplished what he did. Sola, I understood. She was light. And light made things grow, but what of her son? How could water stitch flesh? How could water soothe an aching heart?*

"*I thought the fount in the center of the pool held its secrets. But the more I asked, the more the Shiv wearied of me. The more I sought, the more they pushed me away. They said Begynd was their answer. He heals. There was nothing more to know . . .*

"*My own people, even my surviving son—my courageous green-eyed cherub—asked me to leave it alone. I'd become a burden to my people and not the sovereign they needed. But I knew that if I stayed at that pool, I would need to understand its mysteries.*"

I inherited my curiosity from her then. My need to take things apart, to see how they worked.

"*'The island is large enough for all of us,' I said. 'Let us leave Begynd to the Shiv and find a place where we Kerce can thrive.'*

"*To their credit, the Shiv warned us. They told us of the dangers in the mountains, of Winter and her throne room, of the kol that blew in off the sea. But such things did not dissuade me.*

"The Shiv saw that we were well supplied, and they wished us happiness as we set off on our journey. But happiness was not to be had. The higher we climbed, the more miserable we grew. The kol was a problem, as was the cold, but it was the whispers that drove us mad . . . Me, most of all. Winter had seen my weakness, you see. She was in my ear and in my heart, telling me of the duplicitous Shiv. Of their unwillingness to share their knowledge. Of their great intention to banish all their enemies to the highest pass in the mountain range, where we could neither feel the warmth of Begynd nor bathe in his healing waters.

"I was failing then, the child in my womb ready to be born. You were ready to be born, Sessa."

A sob shakes me, her awareness a gift I hadn't expected.

"I knew that if I gave birth in those mountains, you would die. It was too cold, and I was too far gone to protect you. I was weak, was losing hope, and it was then that Winter told me why the Shiv had banished her from the great pool. Her magic could unlock the secrets of Begynd, she said. Could teach me how to create a healing pool for my own people.

"Even then I understood she was vengeful. She spoke of stealing the wisdom of Begynd, of punishing the Shiv for their crimes against my people. But all I wanted was healing for the Kerce I had led into danger. Safety for my children. I wanted to fix what I had broken.

"Winter offered me that chance, and I clung to it. She couldn't approach the pool, but I could. And I was determined to make it there. My unborn child would survive. You would survive! And if I had strength enough when that was done, I would drive Winter's magic into the Fount of Begynd and so gain the knowledge I needed to save my people.

"Winter placed her magic in my medallion, and we covenanted with each other. It was the only way I knew to protect my children, the only way I could think to preserve the Kerce people. I promised to deliver Winter's magic to the pool, and she promised to serve my children. My son stood as my witness, and the kol for Winter. They would ensure we kept our word."

She couldn't have known then how painful it would be for us to command Winter, Mars and me. The frostbite was an unintended consequence of her covenant.

"I don't know how I made it down the mountain. I suspect Winter had something to do with it, or the magic of the covenant perhaps. I gave birth to you in the pool that very day, and Begynd himself gave me the strength to finish my task.

"I spent one night with you, reveling in your remarkably sylver eyes and the pout you inherited from your father, and then—because I wanted my people to experience Begynd's healing power, and because I was afraid that Winter would kill my son if I did not keep my word—I did everything I promised to do. I dove deep into the pool, and when I found the source of the fount, I drove Winter's magic into it.

"And that, my darling girl, is how I met Begynd."

A gasp shakes me.

"The Shiv were right all along, you know? It was him and him alone. He restores. It's who he is. He might be frozen, but he is not still. He is ever-working to make a way.

"Now you have a part to play in this, Sessa. You, who have both Kerce and Paradyian ancestors, who have both kol madness and Begynd's healing in your veins, you who owe your survival to the Shiv and their god, you have been formed for a purpose. But it isn't to free the Shiv buried beneath the ice, and it isn't to right my wrongs. It's not in your power to do such things.

"The sick and the dead belong to Begynd. They're not yours to carry. You have been given many weapons, Sylver Vale. Use them to fight for the living."

# CHAPTER 33

KYN AND I EMERGE FROM THE WOODS WITH leaves in our hair and our faces flushed, slightly frantic because we've lost track of time.

"I told you!" Tooki calls, whistling. "Who owes me a chunk of coin? You and you—"

"You don't know what they were doing in there," Brash says, though the stupid grin on her face says she's got a guess.

"I know exactly what they were doing." Felyx slaps Kyn on the back.

"You really, really don't," I say.

"Well, you could have picked a better time to run off." Leni's leading Macks down the porch stairs and toward Sayth's rig. He's still wearing Tali's earmuffs. "I thought we were going to have to leave without saying goodbye."

"Sorry, Len," Kyn says. "We weren't . . ."

Macks reaches up and pulls a twig from one of Kyn's tightly wound curls.

Kyn blushes. "Seriously, not what you think."

"It's OK if it was," Leni says, eyeing the twig, "but I'm glad you're back. You're going to need this."

I take Drypp's old wristwatch from her outstretched hand and slide it into my pocket. "Thanks." I scan the bed of the truck, seeing that the ice bikes have been loaded up. "I can draw that map for you real quick."

"Sayth already took care of it." She opens the passenger-side door for Macks. "Looks easy enough. If all goes as planned, we'll see you at the turnoff when this is over."

"You have your radio?"

"It's there." She closes Macks inside and moves around the rig to the driver's-side door.

"Feel free to use the music box," Sayth says. "And there's some squirrel jerky in the glove box if you get hungry."

I'd pay lots of coin to see Leni eat squirrel, but she just reaches out and pulls Sayth into a hug. "Thank you," she says, and then she's hugging everyone. "Be safe, all of you. Please. I'll see you tomorrow."

Kyn kisses her on the cheek. "Stay out of sight, yeah?"

"Of course." She climbs into the rig and closes the door, the window already dropped down. I lean in and wrap my arms around her neck, whispering into her ear. "Begynd's alive, Leni. I know he is."

When she pulls away, her eyes are wide. "Care to elaborate?"

I shake my head. "You've got to go. Bye, Macks. Thank you. For everything."

He smiles, but I can see he's lost again as he tugs at the threads of his sweater.

We watch them pull away from the cabin, the rig bumping carefully over ruts and roots, until at last the woodland swallows it whole.

"Two hours till sunset," Felyx says. "We need to get moving."

Everyone leaps into action, wrapping up their last-minute prep, splitting into crews, and slipping off toward their positions on foot.

All except Kyn and me. We'll be traveling a little faster than the others. Now that there's no one left here to see his wounds, he strips off his shirt and drops it in the smoldering embers of the fire out front. Rain drops in big heavy plops, sizzling and smoking as the synthetic material catches flame.

I watch as he pulls on another shirt and zips his jacket over it, but instead of gaping at the wounds still festering, still bleeding—instead of focusing on his weaknesses—I let my gaze settle on his stone shoulders and biceps, both of them rippling, ready to fight despite the pain.

There's a sledgehammer and rifle leaning against the porch railing. He slings the rifle strap over his good shoulder and hefts the sledgehammer in his other hand. "You ready, yeah?"

What a pretty picture he makes.

I've the hatchet he made me sheathed on one hip, our radio on my other, the knife at my waist, and Macks's sketch in my pocket. I nod.

"How about you?" I ask, moving closer, stepping up onto the toe of his boot. His free hand slides around my waist, pulling me tight against him and igniting a thrill that sparks straight through me. The look in his eyes tells me he feels it too. "*You* ready?"

We're already flying when his answer comes. At my command, Winter's kicked up a mighty gust, circling our forms, cinching us close, erasing what's left of the distance between us. There was a time when I couldn't tolerate a man touching me like this. When the very idea of it would have me flailing. But Kyn's part of me now, for better or worse. And not just pieces, but all of him, grafted in. And the reverse is also true—my life doesn't belong to me and me alone: His heart pumps my blood, tainted though it may be, and I feel his aches like a punch that breaks my teeth and steals my breath. If I can trust anyone at all, it's him.

Winter lifts us high above the trees, tugging us through her thick, ever-present cloud cover. When we emerge from the mist, it's into skies streaked in orange and gold, pink tinged with purple, all laid atop the softest blue I've ever seen.

"I've never seen such colors on Layce," I say.

"Soon we'll see them all the time, yeah? Sola's light will shine down on the isle for entire seasons. And Begynd's too."

Months and months of sunlight, seasons that aren't cold . . . I can't even fathom it.

"Neither one of us were believers when we met," I say. "Do you remember? This was all just fairy stories and . . ."

"And now look at us. Hurrying through a high-risk op so we can reintroduce the isle to its creator. We might be zealots after all."

"There's a thought."

Kyn's watching me now, my eyes, my lips. I've never been bothered by my appearance, but it's hard not to be self-conscious under such examination—frostbite crusting my face, Winter making me pay for even the smallest grin.

"It won't always be like this," Kyn says. He places his hand on my cheek, his thumb softly touching the corner of my mouth. "We won't always be so broken, you and me."

Another thing I can't quite fathom. I place my hand over his, my index finger resting on the sign of Begynd etched into his knuckle. "I'm really, really looking forward to that."

There's magic up here, in the golden light inching toward the horizon, all the colors shifting around it, stretching from one corner of the sky to the other, our tiny storm the only blight on the vast spread. I've never seen Kyn's face in such sharp focus, his lashes, his brows, the texture of the stone beneath his eye, a dimple carved into his left cheek when he grins—so many details laid bare in the light of Sola.

"We could just stay here, yeah? What could possibly go wrong?"

"Just war," I say. "Just eternal Winter."

He laughs.

One last sigh, one last look at the light, and at my command, Winter's winds shift, dropping us into the white damp of the clouds, carrying us over the woods and toward Hex Landing. I speak us lower, leaving us hovering just at the cloud line, allowing us to search the terrain for the others. We're still very high up and I can't make out any of the rebels. I hope they're just as invisible on the ground.

It's not long before the town emerges below us. Through the gauzy cloud cover I see the truck stop where Jymy Leff breathed his last; I see Rigger's Row with its pleasure houses and taverns just waking up for the evening shift; I see soggy construction works where the new miners' barracks must be going up; and beyond the mine itself, I see the turnoff where Leni and Macks will soon be waiting with the engine running.

Winter drags us forward until we're hovering over the Majority's flagship mining operation. I feel my mind shift into gear, into that hardworking, heavy-lifting, get-it-done mindset Drypp passed on to me.

I note the three hoist houses with their angled gallows frames, the guard towers looming, gates that are just minutes away from being blown, and swirling around all of it, collecting in the gears and the wiring, settling in the corners of eyes and lips, caking boots and coveralls, and sunk deep in the creases of every miner's forehead, kol.

We'll never be rid of it, not here. But flux, I can't wait to destroy this place.

"Thank you," I tell Kyn. The winds unravel, Winter's restlessness replaced by something else as we drop through the cloud cover. She knows the risk we face here is monumental and, more than anything, she's curious.

"For what?" he asks.

I lay my cool fingers against the fevered scratches on his cheek. "For waiting until I was ready."

# CHAPTER 34

DRYPP'S WRISTWATCH SAYS WE'RE A LITTLE early, so I have Winter drop us in a giant mountain pine overlooking the road in and out of the mine yard, not too far from where the new barracks are being constructed. We're directly across from the guard towers Sten and Meytee will target to kick this whole thing off. I haven't a hope of catching sight of the war machine, but Dakk assured me it's dug in well just at the edge of the forest.

Kyn lifts the radio off my hip. "All teams check in."

One by one our people confirm they're in place. All except Leni, but she's driving and dealing with Macks, so Kyn calls again and, as we wait, I take in the mining operation below. The entire thing is fenced, barbed wire flashing its teeth, the Majority's security forces standing guard at various points. Lazily, most of them.

"You think they deal with a lot of runners?" I ask.

"Nah, most of the workers here are addicts. They need direct access to the kol."

"It's something we'll need to keep in mind when the Majority's gone, when the greatest source of the stuff is frozen over. Things could get desperate."

"Desy will know what to do. She's got teams already coming up with solutions to these problems."

"Better her than me." Desy's brilliant, she is. But I think the problem is bigger than any team or council or government could ever address. It'll take something beyond us.

It'll take the waters of Begynd.

With his arm wrapped around the trunk, Kyn leans forward, looking past me. "What the— Is that Leni?"

"No way. She should be miles from here by now."

But she's not. Sayth's pickup is flying down the road toward us. It pitches wildly left and right, hitting potholes and trundling twice onto the shoulder.

"Something's wrong." Kyn pushes himself to a stand on the branch, painfully, using the trunk to keep him steady.

I take his hand. "Hold on."

"Hurry, snowflake."

I snap off a command to Winter, and in a careless swoop that has me gasping, she swings us to the ground, setting us just off the road. At our backs is a long stretch of fence, the southern edge of the property. Guards are posted at either end and just behind the fence sits the mechanical shop. There's a gate near the shop—an unguarded service entry that allows maintenance vehicles in and out. The very one Tooki plans to destroy.

The truck's coming up fast now. I release Kyn's hand, and he drops the sledgehammer, then swings his rifle up onto his shoulder.

With Winter's winds still wrapped around me, I step into the road, waving my arms, trying to get Leni's attention. I can't tell what the problem is, can't even see her face—there's a glare on the windshield. But the truck is pitching hard right and going way too fast to stop before it runs me over.

Another command, another blister, and the sturdy bumper of Sayth's rig collides with the wall of wind before me. The collision is as soft as I can make it, but it's followed by a scream from Lenore.

I release Winter, and there, in the passenger seat, holding a gun across Macks's huddled body and pressing it to Leni's temple, is Farraday Wrex.

YOU REMEMBER WREX, DON'T YOU? Winter coos. HE LIKES MY STORIES. ESPECIALLY THE ONES ABOUT YOU.

Fluxing Winter. She's been leading him to us every step of the way.

*I rather like having allies in your camp,* he said.

It didn't matter that he couldn't command her. He was content to listen. And she's led him straight to us. Used him to get exactly what she needs. A tool in her hand.

It shouldn't surprise me—not after the story my mother just told me—but it does. For far too long I've believed I was her favorite. But I'm not even her friend.

Kyn tears opens the passenger door and points his gun at Wrex. But Wrex fires the handgun, a wild shot that chips the stone on Kyn's bicep. Kyn doesn't even wince.

"How the hell do you keep showing up?" He grabs hold of Wrex's arm and pulls him from the truck.

"You didn't think Winter was on the rebels' side, did you?"

Wrex drags Macks out with him, Tali's earmuffs falling to the ground. Leni screams, clamors across the seat, but I issue a sharp command, and both doors slam shut. When she gapes at me, I shake my head and round the rig toward the men. I'm already anxious about using Winter in close quarters like this. The last thing I want to do is lose control and hurt her again.

Kyn's gun is trained on Wrex. Wrex has Leni's gun on Macks. Macks is half conscious, mumbling and sagging, blood pouring from his ear.

In the distance I hear the sound of an ice bike. A Ranger maybe, come to investigate the noise. We've got to get out of here.

I hiss a command and Winter chills the metal on Leni's gun, so cold it smokes. Wrex cries out and drops it. Kyn kicks it into the woods.

I step closer. "Let him go, Wrex. You're outnumbered."

And then he's not. Gunfire breaks out in the trees across the road, bullets flying toward us. We drop—all of us—diving behind the rig for protection.

"Enough!" Wrex cries. "Just get over here."

The gunfire ceases and boots descend.

My blood is running hot and fast, and my limbs are jelly. I hear the door of the rig swing open, and I panic. Leni's in there. I lift my head only to find myself looking down the barrel of a Majority-issue handgun.

My mind reels, searching, searching for the right command, but if the Majority security forces have arrived, that means we've been discovered.

*Has the shift bell sounded? Has the front gate blown? Has the rest of our rebel band been uncovered?*

*Or is this all for me? Is Wrex really so single-minded?*

Kyn's next to me on his hands and knees, his own rifle pointed at him by another officer. His eyes slide to mine. "You OK, yeah?"

He's not asking about my welfare, not really. He's telling me it's go time. If we're getting out of this, it's up to me. My mouth moves, but before I can do more than lick my lips, the security officer cracks me across the face with his sidearm. My lip splits wide, pain blurring my vision.

"I've seen those posters, girlie. No talking or I'll jam this barrel down your throat."

"It'll be the last thing you do," Kyn says, and then he takes his own rifle to the temple—one hard crack and he slumps to the ground.

"I said no talking!"

But I couldn't speak if I wanted to. I'm gagging on my own blood, retching while Wrex drags Leni from the rig. He has hold of her hair, but she's not making it easy on him. She flails, forcing him to carry her weight, clawing at his face desperately, her bandage fraying.

He throws her to the ground and turns to me.

"Your gifts are impressive, rig driver, but this is the better show. You. At my feet. Broken. Bleeding. Speechless. All while Winter laughs."

Leni's rolled onto her knees, fallen back against the rig, sucking air. Wrex reaches a hand into the deep pockets of his duster, digs something out, and throws it at Leni.

I flinch, but it's only a length of rope, a fancy knot tied at its middle.

"Gag your friend," he tells Leni. "Gag her or I'll have her shot."

Leni's brown eyes meet mine, and I imagine that knot cinched tight between my teeth. I think of Mars, bound and gagged and hauled away, and I realize it's now or never. If I don't get a command off, we're done.

Quick as a flash, the officer before me jams the barrel of the gun between my teeth. "Don't even think about it." He pulls back the hammer, and my body freezes.

"*Now*," Wrex tells Leni. "Unless you want to watch her die."

Tears pour down her cheeks, but she scoops up the gag and stands, wobbling as she makes her way to my side.

The officer before me rises, forcing me to my feet. I know what I'm going to say now, what I'll demand of Winter, and I'll do it in the split second the gun is pulled away, just before Leni can slide the knot between my teeth.

"I see the gears moving in your mind, rig driver, so let me save you a horrible mistake." Wrex takes a handgun from a nearby security officer, and jams it into Leni's ear. "If you think you can get off a command that Winter will obey *before* I fire this gun, then by all means. But I have to tell you, Winter's moving a little sluggish at the moment. I hear her reluctance, her anger at you. She's not quiet about it, is she? I think it's possible she prefers me these days."

I'm not listening to him—I can't. I'm watching as Leni boils over, incensed. Tears race down her face, but I know that look. Wrex is a problem she can solve even if it costs her. I want to tell her no, want to tell her she has nothing to fight with, but I have no right. And my words would only get us both killed.

In the distance, the shift bell rings, and Leni knows exactly what that means.

She ducks and spins. When Wrex fires his gun and takes out one of his own security officers, when the knotted rope in Leni's fist thwacks Wrex in the crotch, folding him in half, when the officer before me turns his head to see what's happened, I push the gun from my mouth and call down Winter, leaving no room in my words for lethargy.

She yowls at the injustice of it, but she arrives with fist-size stones of hail. Mars would be proud: I was specific and targeted, the hail pummeling only the security forces, leaving me and mine free to move.

She's spared Wrex, and I realize Kyn was right all along: Some fights have to be had.

"You can't beat me," Wrex gasps, pulling himself upright. "Not without Winter."

But she's not my only weapon.

I pull the hatchet from my hip, and as he takes a step toward me, I throw it.

I don't miss. Kyn was right again.

The hatchet sinks into Wrex's chest, and he stumbles back, stepping into the path of one of Winter's hailstones. The sickening crack jolts his head to the side and drops him to the mud.

Winter screams, and I retch at the sound, but I step forward. I have to know. I can't make the same mistake I did at the Stack. I flip Wrex onto his back and there's no mistaking it: He's gone. His eyes are rolled up, his head smashed in by the ice.

"Winter was never my friend," I say, pulling my hatchet from his body. "But I think it's safe to say, she was never yours either."

Leni drags Macks to his feet, but Kyn's still out cold. I hate leaving him behind, and it's a decision I may regret later, but the bell is ringing in the distance, and there's no time. I give a command that has Winter lifting Kyn into the sky and laying him gently atop the mechanical building. At least he should be safe there.

An explosion cracks the heavens, shaking the buildings and the trees, sending tremors through the ground, setting Sayth's rig rocking. I stumble. The world is all noise: gunfire and shouts, a siren that wails on and on, a voice echoing over the loudspeaker, unintelligible and panicked.

"I'm supposed to be in the sky," I tell Leni. "Leading the Majority away."

"Go," she says, dragging Kyn's sledgehammer through the mud with her good hand. "Da and I will meet you inside."

The hammer's nearly as big as she is, and it's a ridiculous notion, the idea that Leni, broken and bleeding, can do a task intended for someone so much larger. But ridiculous is all we have left.

Tooki stumbles out of the woods then, his eyes widen as he takes in the carnage, Wrex and his security forces bloodied and sprawled in the mud. "Holy . . ."

"Get that gate open, Tooki," I say.

"I'm supposed to wait until you . . . shouldn't you be somewhere else?"

"I'm going now. Leni needs to get inside. Blow the gate."

He sprints to the fence, and I shoot into the sky.

As I fly over the mechanical building, I catch a glimpse of the chaos inside the mine yard. Instead of emptying of Majority forces, the space has filled up with armed officers in front of every building. If I can't lead them away, Sayth's crew doesn't have a shot at making it inside.

The gate blows, and alarm claws its way through me as the guards race toward the sound.

Toward Tooki and Macks. Toward Lenore.

And then the sound of a motor, too high-pitched for a rig, too close to be on the ground.

There! Racing up the incline of the eastern hoist house, its engine squealing, tires making all kinds of racket on the tin roof, is an ice bike.

Heads turn and guns fire as a snow-white machine flies off the roof's peak and into the sky.

"Come and get me, you Majority bastards," Mars calls as Winter catches the bike and carries it over the smoldering guard towers and into the woods beyond.

# CHAPTER 35

I DROP TO THE EMPTYING MINE YARD, MY heart lighter than it's been in days. The plan is working.

Winter's raging. She knows she's not long for this place.

Boots pound toward the forest, and I catch sight of Sayth's violet hair.

"Where did Mars come from?" she calls, but I have no idea, and then she's ducking into the nearest hoist house.

The steady thrum of the war machine tells me the operation is in full swing. Time to do my part.

The map is in my pocket, but I don't need it just yet. I've memorized the layout of the buildings here. I flip my hood up to hide my face and then dash through a smash of bodies—miners by the look of them—who are being led toward the barracks by Brash.

A narrow walkway lies ahead, and I recognize the shape of the courtyard before it, the two squat concrete buildings on either side. All the mine's management happens here and the elevator should be just beyond it. I dash down the walkway, and there it is.

Off to the side, lingering in the shadows, I see Lenore and Macks.

I was hoping she'd leave her da with Tooki. Hoping we could move fast, but it's no matter, we have to go.

I hold up my hand, telling them to stay where they are. Two armed men are cutting across the space, heading for the walkway I've just come down. I duck into an open doorway to hide.

Their boots fall away, and I stick my head out, a quick glance left and right, and then I dash to the elevator, waving Leni and Macks to my side. I jam the button that calls the carriage, and we wait.

"Gah! What's taking so long?" Leni props the sledgehammer against the wall and shakes out her arm.

Macks pats her shoulder. "It's a long way down, love."

"Hey! You're not supposed to be here!"

I turn and with a word, Winter blows a Majority overseer into the wall.

The elevator arrives, and we step inside. Before the doors can close, I tell Winter to wedge them open and she does, ice forming in great slats over the carriage door and the door that opens to the outside.

Leni's closest to the controls and she pushes the button for the basement. A mechanized clicking fills the space as the doors attempt to close. When they can't, an alarm goes off.

"You've got to be kidding!" Leni says. Her da collapses to the elevator floor, covering his ears at the sound.

Three security officers emerge from the narrow walkway with their guns drawn. The command is on my tongue, but a gust of wind whips past me, and they're tumbling backward.

I wheel around and there stands Mars. His face bruised, his lips frostbitten.

"Get a move on," he says. Then he spits another command at Winter, filling the courtyard with a cyclone that scoops up several screaming officers. No one's getting through that.

I turn my mind to the task at hand. Once we get to the bottom, I need direct access to Winter. I planned to knock out the elevator ceiling entirely, but there's a vent here. One word and it falls to the floor. Yes, good. It opens directly into the elevator shaft. That'll work.

*If only we could get the thing moving!* I drop to my knees next to Leni.

"What do we do?" I yell. The wind in the courtyard is loud and Macks is wailing over the top of the alarm blaring. "Isn't there some kind of override?"

Leni's eyes are rabid, scanning all the buttons. There are rows and rows of them.

"Here," she says. "Here." She flips open a panel and slams her hand against a red button. The alarm shuts off and the carriage gives a mighty shudder that has us cursing and grabbing for one another. But at last, it begins to move.

"Oh, thank Begynd," I say, backing against the far wall.

The elevator isn't quick, the technology outdated, and with the open doors giving us a close look at the crumbling concrete shaft, it's unsettling. The racket from above begins to fade and I imagine this is what it feels like to be crawling into your own grave.

Even though the alarm has stopped, Macks is still wailing.

Leni pries his hands from his ears and pulls him to his feet. "It's OK, Da. See? It's quiet now."

But then there are shouts from above and gunshots ring out, pinging off the shaft, off the carriage. We drop to our stomachs, all three of us, Macks weeping as Leni wraps her arms around him.

There's a pause in the gunfire and a voice calls down, but I can't make it out.

When at last the elevator hits the basement, Leni reaches up and pushes the emergency stop button, and we crawl out of the elevator together; she's dragging Macks and I'm dragging the sledgehammer.

I demand Winter keep these doors open, but I don't wait around to see if she obeys. There isn't time.

The hallway is empty, the floors bearing mysterious stains, the walls peeling and damp. Overhead the lights are yellow and flickering, and now there's a steady clang ringing from the elevator shaft.

Boots, I think. On metal rungs.

Someone's descending. Probably using a maintenance ladder. They have a long way to come, but we have a considerable job to complete before they get here.

"We have to hurry," I say. "You have your radio? We need to check that the mine shafts are clear."

"Gah! It was in the rig."

"Flux," I say, stalling in the middle of the hallway, panic crawling up my legs, shaking my knees. "Kyn took mine. I wasn't thinking."

"Let's just get through that door," she says, "before they seal off the shaft or make their way down here. First things first, right?"

I nod, remembering when I told her the very same thing. Kyn's right. We do take care of each other. "First things first."

Another twenty feet and we're standing before it, a thick steel door with no handle. And just to the right of the frame, a keypad. Above the keypad is a rectangular metal plate with an equation scrawled across it in black ink.

"You have any idea how to solve that?"

Leni steps closer, shakes her head. "I don't even know what it's asking. Mystra never put much stock in mathematics, did she?"

"I wouldn't have sat still for it even if she did."

"I might've," she says, reaching out. "Is this a coordinate here?"

"You think your da might know?"

She turns to him, but he's not even facing the right direction. His eyes are haunted, squinting up at the flickering lights.

"He's just not there, Syl. I wish he was, but—"

"It's fine. We have Winter. We might as well use her. Up against the wall, OK? And zip up."

Leni steps back, dragging the sledgehammer with her. Macks totters to her side, his eyes blinking in time with the lights. Once she has their coats zipped and their hoods up, I voice a command that has the hallway chilled in moments, the door frosted white.

The cold is bitter and brilliant, and I flip my hood up again to protect myself. I whisper Winter onward, my breath fogging the air as I direct her to focus all her chill on the door. The temperature needs to drop substantially for the steel to become brittle enough to shatter, and it's not something we could tolerate for very long.

As Winter works, I turn my attention to Macks and Leni.

They're both trembling, their eyelashes frosted, their cheeks flushed. I can feel the ice on my own face, the frostbite that even now is spreading beyond my lips.

"Kyn's awake," I say, the sensation moving through me. "He's not happy we left him behind."

"Any way you can get him down here?" Leni asks, her teeth chattering.

But Winter's turned sluggish, and I have to urge her on. The commands come quick and, suddenly, I'm light-headed. I stumble forward and catch myself on the door. It's so cold my hands stick to it, and when I tear them away, they burn.

"Move, Syl." Leni's attempting to heft the sledgehammer with one hand. When that fails, she takes hold with her bandaged hand as well, but tears stream down her face and I know she'll never get it over her shoulder.

My knees are weak, my hands burning, but I push myself upright. "Here, let me help."

Leni nods and together we lift the sledgehammer. On our first try, we're not coordinated, and the hammer head falls dully against the frozen metal.

"Again," I say. "One, two, three!" We swing as hard as we're able, and though there's a considerable thwack this time, the door remains as solid as ever.

We might not be strong enough.

**YOU NEVER WERE STRONG ENOUGH**, Winter says. **IT WAS ALWAYS ME. ALWAYS MY STRENGTH.**

"Again," I say.

And again, and again, and again.

Winter starts to laugh.

"It's no use." Leni's gasping, her hands on her knees, the sledgehammer discarded. "We'll never get through."

"Someone's coming," I say. There are voices now, echoing down the hallway from the elevator shaft, that steady clang so much louder, so much closer. I draw my hatchet. "Watch out, Leni."

With the sound of boots ringing in my ears, I strike the door with my hatchet. This time, the door chips, and I swing again, harder, my raw hand blistering on the handle.

And then *click, click, click click click.* With a tired drone, the door attempts to open. My body is slow and tired, but I wheel backward, dragging Leni with me. The door has slid open four inches.

Macks stands at the keypad beaming.

"Da!" Leni says. "You did it!"

"It's just math, Leni love. Three-nine-four-nine-one. I could show you how I worked it out if you like?"

A heavy thud sounds behind us, and I turn to see a dark shape dropping into the elevator carriage.

I leap forward. "Help me!"

Leni and I hook our hands into the narrow opening and attempt to pull, but the door is slick and cold. I try the hatchet as well, but it isn't strong enough.

"Hang on," I say. "Let me try this."

I back up, pulling Leni with me

*"Merro flux,"* I tell Winter. *Let it melt. "Leya sil fesol." Leave this place.*

She's lazy about it, but she drifts down the hall, and soon the temperature begins to climb. I demand she move faster as I jam my back against the doorframe and take hold of the door. Leni pulls and I push and together we widen the opening another few inches.

My body is shutting down, exhausted, but I switch my hands, letting go of the door, reaching over my head, and grabbing hold of the doorframe instead. I lift my feet off the ground and wedge my boots against the door. I shove hard, my thighs burning, my knees popping with the effort.

At last the door gives. It slides into the wall, and I drop to the ground.

Inside, a single Majority officer stands at the ready, eyes wide, gun trembling in his hand and pointed at the open door. "You don't belong here," he says.

I can disarm him, I know I can, but my mind is slow, cold. And then Macks is stepping in front of me.

"What do you mean I don't belong here?" His shoulders are squared, his voice bearing an authority that has even me convinced. "You're talking to First Engineer Macks Trestman, young man, senior authority on all items related to this dewatering system."

The officer's gun shifts, and his gaze moves over Macks's emaciated body, which is wrapped in the warmest clothes we could find, clearly not Majority issued. But that voice! Such command! It's enough to give the officer pause.

"Since when?" he asks.

"Since long before you were born, boy." Macks strides into the room, climbs the two stairs leading to the desk. "You have any idea what's going on up there? Put that gun down and give me your key. This is an urgent matter."

The officer's still not convinced but there are footsteps pounding down the hall now, and it pulls his attention away. I can't even turn to look, I'm so tired. But the officer's eyes widen, then his gun turns to a block of ice, falling to the ground with a great thud.

I don't remember giving the command, but—

Macks reaches over and tears the key from around the officer's neck.

I hear voices shouting and a single gunshot rings out from the hallway behind me. I don't even flinch. This is all there is: Macks and that key.

Leni pulls the knife from her boot and points it at the officer. "Move. Over there."

He curses but complies.

"Come on, Da," Leni says. "Which panel is it?"

I'm trying to right myself, to tell her I have his sketch, when the clanking, thumping footsteps come to a stop in front of me. Steel-toed boots.

I laugh, a pathetically instinctual and thoroughly inappropriate response, but I don't care. "Mars."

Suddenly the world is half as heavy.

"The shafts are clear, Miss Trestman. Let's flood these mines."

Leni inserts the key and turns it. Macks flips the switches one at a time and then he nods to Leni. She glances at me with a triumphant grin, then she hefts the lever in front of her into the forward position.

There's a grinding somewhere in the walls, mechanisms clicking and locking into place. And then a soppy, gushing sound that could only be water.

A sob surprises me, shakes its way into the air.

We did it.

We've sunk the mine.

And now I'm weeping and laughing and somewhere, not too far away, a thrill of victory is shooting through Kyn's body. I let it roll through mine as well.

Mars drops into a squat in front of me, his black eyes moving over my face. There's concern there, in the creases of his brow, but something else too, something that looks a little bit like gratification. "You wear them well, sister."

My ears are ringing, and my tongue is swollen, and I have no idea what he's talking about. "What?"

"Look," he says, lifting me, dragging me down the hallway to an office door with a window. "Snake eyes."

My reflection stares back at me from the filmy, aging glass. It's rough viewing all around. My hat's gone missing, and my braids are ragged. Frostbite blisters the lower half of my face, and, for the first time ever, kol has blotted out my eyes entirely.

"No more ice in your veins," Mars says. "How does it feel to be free of her?"

"It hurts," I say, blisters splitting wide when I laugh.

I take in his reflection next to mine. His crooked grin is crusted black, and blisters climb his face. Like me, there's not a shred of color in his eyes. We are quite a pair. He pulls a pristine white cloth from the pocket of his coat, but instead of dabbing his own lips, he offers it to me.

I appreciate the gesture, but that little cloth isn't going to do much. I wrap my arms around his neck instead.

He groans. "We're not doing this every time we meet now, are we? It's hardly in character for either of us."

"No, you're right." I squeeze him one more time before letting go. "Maybe just every other time?"

"We'll come up with a system."

"How did you get away from Shyne?"

"He's rather gifted with the rocks, isn't he?" He scowls and lays a hand flat against his rib cage. "I'm still not quite right, but I'll say this: It's surprising what you learn when you're forced into silence."

"You heard her too? Maree Vale."

A dip of his chin. "Sound carries well in those caverns, but I thank you for the distraction. It was . . . enlightening."

"I have so many questions."

"Later, yes? What I meant to say is that if we really are sending Winter away, I should probably work on building my own strength. I was thoroughly helpless without my mouth. It was the girl who removed the rock."

"Crysel?"

"Yes. The Shiv are in good hands with that one. And fear not. I didn't bring down a single mountain."

I stare at him for a long moment, at the dark circles under his eyes, the remnants of bruising on his face. Shyne made good on his promise. Mars suffered.

"I'm sorry we left you there."

"Well. That was *very* in character of you, wasn't it? Flight instead of fight."

"You told me not to call down Winter."

"I was trying to be a gentleman."

"Talk about out of character."

"Yes, well. We're all growing, aren't we?" He turns and there's Kyn, a white rifle hanging at his side, a Ranger sprawled at his feet.

I see now that a few Rangers made it down here; their unconscious forms litter the hall. While we were opening the door, he was fighting to keep them off us. "All good, Kyn?"

I want to reach out and pull him to me, but it's taking everything I've got to stay upright. My gaze devours him instead, every inch. There's a laceration across his forehead to match the festering scratches on his cheek, and blood leaks from the knee of his trousers. His shirt is black with blood and kol, but he's alive. And he's smiling.

Gah, that smile.

"All good, yeah. Dakk radioed from the security booth, and we've had confirmation: The Paradyian ships have made port in Glas."

"We did it," Leni whispers, her fingers over her mouth. "We really did it."

"We did, yeah. The Paradyians came ashore with little resistance. They've taken the port city, and Ambassador Truden is with the council now."

Mars turns to me. "You wanted to rid Shiv Island of the Majority without a war, and we're very close now. If anything is going to convince the council to release their hold on Layce, it's knowledge of what's happened here. You ready to make this call?"

Leni's next to me now, and Macks too. I can't look at them and not think of all the Majority has taken from us.

"I'm ready," I say.

Kyn aims the rifle at the officer slumped in the corner of the room. His hands go up.

"Hey, hey, hey! I don't even have a gun anymore, man!"

"We're just making sure you understand the gravity of the situation," Mars says. "See that radio there. I'm going to need you to place a call."

"Sure, whatever you want. Who am I calling?"

"The council offices in the Port of Glas."

"Psh. They're not going to let me through to the council."

"Tell them Sylver Quine would like a word," I say. "They'll put you through."

He does a double take—at my eyes, I would guess—and then picks up the handset. He adjusts the dials, getting a squeal and then a crackle and then, "Council offices, please. This is the pump control room at Hex Landing. No, I know. I know." His eyes slide to me again. "I have Sylver Quine here. Yes, the one from the posters." He closes his eyes. "I'll wait."

Leni squeezes my hand, her excitement contagious.

The officer's eyes open, his face draining of color. "Yes, Councilman. Hello. Yes, she's here." He holds out the handset. "Councilman Sworn would like to talk to you."

Kyn offers me a hand, helping me up the stairs to the officer's desk. I take the handset from the officer.

"Turn it to broadcast," Kyn tells him. "We'd all like to hear."

The officer flips a switch and the radio squeals.

"Are you there, Councilman?" I ask.

A throat clears. "I— Yes, I'm here."

"This is Sylver Quine."

"The rig driver?"

"That's right. The rig driver. I understand the Paradyian ambassador is with you?"

"He is." Sworn's voice is low and measured, but disdain runs through it, and something else. Something that sounds like fear.

"He's come with papers, I believe. From King Hawken Valthor of Paradyia. My understanding is that he's asked the Majority Council to vacate Layce, has he not?"

Another clearing of the throat. "He has insisted, yes."

"Good. I thought you should have a bit more information before you put it to a vote. You do vote on such things, don't you?"

"We do."

"Good, good. I like that. Having a say is important."

Mars grins.

"First off, you should know, Farraday Wrex is dead."

"Wrex is—"

"Afraid so. I know you were close, so please accept my condolences."

The radio crackles.

"Also," I say. "The kol industry on Layce has suffered a setback."

"A—what?"

"We've flooded the mines here at Hex Landing. Every shaft."

He sputters. "Every shaft?"

"That's right. By tomorrow morning, we'll have frozen it solid. My brother and I."

"Dresden is with you then?" His voice is venom and vitriol.

"He is. I take it you've heard the rumors about us?"

"We've heard the rumors, yes."

A slow grin works its way up my face. "You know, there was a time when I would have given anything for you bastards to know nothing about me, about what I was capable of. I would have paid a lot of coin to simply remain invisible, just another rigger in the mountains, doing whatever it takes to stay alive. But I'm not afraid of who I am. Not anymore."

Mars dips his chin.

"It's time for *you* to be afraid, I think," I say. "Or perhaps it's just time for you to leave."

The councilman's swallow is audible. "And if we vote no?"

"Ambassador Truden can answer that question for you. But know this: The rebellion went to great lengths to prevent a war here. If you force one on us, we come with a storm. And we will not hesitate to rain it down on you. The choice is yours."

I toss the handset to the officer to hang it up and raise my brows at Mars. "That work?"

At first, I think he's going to laugh, but he just turns on his heel and marches down the hall. "That'll work just fine."

# CHAPTER 36

THE MAJORITY COUNCIL VOTED YES. Unanimously.

Ambassador Truden gave them time to gather their families and belongings and then he escorted them onto his Paradyian ship and they sailed away.

I'm not sure where he's taking them—every one of their isles once belonged to other peoples after all—but the council that convened here on Layce was just one of many. The Majority had spread themselves out across the Wethyrd Seas, and I can only hope that word of what's happened here will spread too. That rebels everywhere will remember who they are and where they came from.

And that they will see their history for what it is. It's not something to be feared or fixed but something to learn from. I hope they're better students than I was.

✳

Eight hours after we kill the pumps, the mine is full, and I whisper it frozen. No ceremony. No celebration. We're all a bit too ragged for that, our strength thin, and we're a day late. High Blys was yesterday.

Mars and I invest all our energy in keeping the rigs safe on our journey back to Queen's Point. We let Winter rage all she wants, so long as she keeps the road frozen and doesn't touch us or our people. Even that is a bigger ask than I'm comfortable with, but how much energy can it take for her to leave?

Soon, that's all we'll need from her.

No one on my crew is up for an ice bike, so we find the plushest Majority ride at the mine complex—a tractor trailer with cushy leather seats and a double sleeper—and with the war machine and Sayth's pickup following behind, we leave Hex Landing by the north fork, the highway dumping us out onto the Shiv Road just after dawn.

Nothing, not even my mother's story, could prepare me for what I see out my windshield.

"She was many things, our mother," Mars says, taking in the view, "but she wasn't a liar."

Just beneath the ice, the Desolation is a spiderweb of sylver threads. Begynd's Fount is flowing, spreading, the liquid light pulsing. The heartbeat of the isle. I remember what Maree Vale said: *He might be frozen, but he is not still. He is ever-working to make a way.*

"He never needed us, did he?" I ask. "Begynd."

"Need is a very particular kind of word," Mars says. "I'm not at all sure how I feel about it."

I consider stopping the rig, climbing out for a better look, but the others are sleeping, Leni and Macks and Kyn, and we'll have a closer view soon enough.

Once more, Winter builds us a bridge. Her volume has increased as we we've gotten closer to the Desolation, but she's not nearly loud enough. Not now that I know what I'm listening for. Maree Vale's voice joins those of the Shiv she doomed, and as she tells me her story once again, I think that once all this is over, I'll have to track down Mystra Dyfan. She needs employment, and this story must be written down. History matters. The truth matters.

It's a fair stretch across the ice, and Kyn's pain has me feverish. By the time Queen's Point is clearly in sight, Winter's given up on seasons altogether. Snow falls in great heaps as she rails against Begynd and the unjustness of his light, berating the wretched souls buried beneath the ice.

It's sad, really. How far gone she is. How thoroughly incapable she is of taking responsibility.

Shyne's here, just as he promised. He's standing at the fence line, snow up to his knees, his walking stick clenched in his fist, his people gathered all around. They point at the glowing ice, their hands clasped, their faces shining. They've waited a very long time for this.

"What are we going to do about Shyne?" I ask Mars. "You think he'll let you be?"

"Didn't I tell you? He's already sentenced me."

There's something funny in that. "Has he?"

"Indeed," he says, his voice grave and amused all at once. "I have been banished from the isle."

"Banished?"

"It's why the girl helped me, I think. She was afraid Shyne would go back on his word, that I wouldn't be here to help you with Winter."

And Crysel was so sure Shyne could be trusted. "Will you accept this sentence?"

Mars strokes his chin. "I think I will. My work here is nearing its end, and Shiv Island was never my home. I am a seafarer; it'll give me no pain to leave this place."

"But you'll visit?"

"Most certainly. Shyne acted as both judge and jury. There's no justice in that, but I will honor it for a time."

"Meaning?"

"I'll let him see me sail away. He can stand on the dock and spit on my ship if he likes."

"What ship?"

"I'll have to talk to Hawken about that."

"How are you able to leave the isle, Mars?" It's not something I'd considered before, but after hearing Maree Vale's account, I have to know. "Did you not need Begynd's healing after the shipwreck?"

His eyes move over the ice. "I did, yes. We all did. It's the covenant that's kept me alive. I was its witness and until I'm freed from that responsibility, I cannot die. I've given it my best effort though."

We clatter off the ice and as I kill the engine, I breathe a great sigh. The ice is looking mighty thin just now.

Crysel is perched on the fence next to Shyne, the wolf pup in her arms. She rises to her feet and waves, perfectly balanced on the post.

"I wonder if she's come up with a name for the pup," I say.

"She has indeed, Miss—" he catches himself. "She has indeed."

"You can call me Miss Vale," I say, deciding. "I prefer *sister*, but if you need a formal moniker . . ."

He tilts his head. "You were quite adamant that Vale was off the table."

"Like I told Councilman Sworn, I'm not afraid of who I am anymore. She was our mother. She made a lot of mistakes, but so have we all."

He grins, a smile that reaches all the way to his eyes. "Shall we wake the others?"

We spill out of the cab, Mars and Leni and Macks, and finally Kyn and me. Kyn's so sick he can hardly walk, and his eyes are crusted with flecks of kol. I guide him through the crowd toward the Desolation.

"Is he OK?" Sayth asks as we pass her crew, the four of them climbing out to join the others. The war machine has parked as well. Every one of the crew is a little bent, a little broken, but ready to see this thing done.

"He will be," I say, glancing out at the sweating ice. "Very soon, I think."

A scream shakes the sky and with her mighty fists, Winter pounds the camp, shattering windows and blowing rigs sideways. The tin roof of the garage begins to peel away, and I've had enough.

"*Stiyee!*" I cry. "*Est stiyee!*"

The blisters on my face that have only just begun to heal, split wide, but Winter stills. The wind blows itself out leaving lazy snowflakes in its wake.

Snowflakes and voices. But hushed now, expectant. They know Begynd's at work.

I continue through the crowd, toward the Desolation. Kyn's so warm he's shivering, his fever like a firestorm tearing through his body. It makes me dizzy.

"Bring him here, Sessa," Crysel says, moving over, making room along the fence. "I'll hold him up."

I doubt she could keep him upright, but the fence is strong. I lean him against it, Crysel's hand on his shoulder.

"Almost time," I tell him. "You OK?"

He nods and it nearly knocks him to the ice. I reach out, but Shyne is there. He grunts and holds out his walking stick. "Take it," he says. "Go on, take it. No one wants to see a Shiv hero on his knees."

Kyn blinks down at him, his lips cracked with dehydration, deep purple circles around his eyes. A tear spills over the stone on his cheek as he reaches out and wraps his hand next to Shyne's.

Mars slides in next to me, and Shyne's eyes narrow. "When this is done, you will go, yes?"

"Just as soon as I locate a ship," Mars answers. "You have my word."

Shyne grunts, and I look around. The shores of the Desolation are an impressive thing to behold. Clad in thin garments, the Shiv people stand boldly in the snow, some without shoes, their stone flesh shimmering in the white light.

Next to them stand the Paradyians, every one of them bundled tight in their gilded robes and heavy cloaks, fur hats pulled low over their ears, shivering as they stare out at the ice and the light, wondering, waiting.

The queen is here and looks worse than Kyn. Her sickness has gone on for far too long. It's left her frame emaciated, her complexion void of color. The bones of her face jut sharply, and if it weren't for the king holding her upright, I might not recognize her as the woman I met just days ago.

"Is this your handiwork, Sessa?" the king asks, hope on his face as he stares out at the ice.

"It's not," I tell him. "The pool belongs to Begynd, and only Begynd can see this done."

The king turns to me, his eyes sharp.

"We didn't know," I tell him. "We hadn't heard the right story."

He blinks at me and turns back to the pool. His wife's gaze meets mine, and she dips her chin. I return the bow.

In and among these two great peoples, the rebels have found their place. A few have Kerce blood, but most are overlooked, undervalued members of the Majority, their histories lost in an attempt to erase the sins of yesterday.

Every one of them need what's about to happen here.

I turn to Kyn, his pain so fierce it's all I feel through our connection. He sags against Shyne's walking stick, his blood running down the white wood, staining the snow.

"Look," Crysel says. "Begynd."

Steam rises off the ice now, and then a great crack—a shudder that has us all cowering and backing away from the Desolation.

All save Shyne. He steps toward the ice, his crooked back as straight as he can make it, watching as the Desolation splits and cracks, fracturing across its immense surface, fissures as far as we can see.

And then in the distance, a sylver spray breaks through the ice. It shoots into the air, magnificent in its power, its waters scraping the sky.

A blast of heat nudges the gray gloom overhead toward the horizon. In its place, blue skies emerge, painted with towering castles of white cloud. Almost blinding as they reflect the light of Sola onto our sun-starved faces.

A cheer goes up from the crowd, and there's a press toward the waters, but Shyne lifts his hands. "Wait!" he cries in the common tongue. "Wait!"

The crowd quiets and I hear them. We all hear them.

The voices of those buried beneath the ice, chattering with excitement now. So much joy I'm laughing, tears streaming. Their voices grow quicker, louder, as lights in every color rise to the surface of the great pool—tiny lights as far as the eye can see. My heart expands as their voices climb to a crescendo. The lights lift from the pool's surface, rising into the sky, my mother's voice impossible to separate from the others.

Higher and higher they go, all of us watching, our necks craned, our hands clasped, as the sparks of so many lives are welcomed into the light of Sola.

# CHAPTER 37

SHYNE STEPS INTO THE WATER THEN, HIS crooked back twisting his gait, his steps slow without the walking stick.

There's not a block of ice in sight now, no reason for any of us to doubt, but when he goes under, we all hold our breaths, our hope stretched across three centuries, taut and ready to snap.

And then he rises. And we see.

Shyne's whole, his back straight, and though he looks as old as he ever has, the waters have brightened his face, washing away the bitterness and angst. He's . . . beautiful. And I wonder if he will always look this way.

Shyne turns toward us, his smile radiant. "Come. Come!"

Hawken Valthor is the first to sprint down to the shoreline, the queen in his arms. Together they step into the pool and together they go under. When they rise, the queen is able to stand on her own, the waters lapping about her. She laughs and laughs, glowing in the light of Sola, her husband covering her face with kisses.

Others follow. I see Tali and Brash, Meytee and Sten and Tooki, all of them splashing in the water, all of them new. Sayth whoops and hollers, her joy loudest of all. Save Kyn, there's not a single Shiv left on shore, and many of the Paradyians have gone under as well. Those who don't step into the pool look on with a reverential glow. They want to be able to return home, but oh, the stories they'll tell when they do.

"You don't have to go in with me," Kyn says, his voice weak. "I can do this alone, if, you know, you still want to visit Paradyia or . . ."

"There isn't enough coin in the world to get me on a ship again. If you're staying here, so am I."

His pain is dizzying, but his heart skips. "You're not afraid? Of being stuck with me forever?"

"Not afraid," I say, my heart tripping to keep up. "Not anymore."

"I want you to be sure, yeah? Because this island's got all sorts of wacky magic going on. Mystery in the rock, and kol we'll never be rid of, and a pool that . . . There might be curses we don't even know about yet."

I smile. "Anything could happen, it's true. But I was born in these waters, spent three hundred years trapped beneath the ice to make this moment possible. I'm not missing out now."

I slide beneath his arm, and together we make our way into the pool. Slowly, carefully, we step into the sylver waters. It's a warm I've never felt before, a warm you can't quite get enough of. The sensation builds the longer you stand in its waves, something active in the water's touch. Something undeniably alive.

"Are *you* afraid?" I ask Kyn. The water's sloshing around us now, but we haven't fully submerged ourselves.

"What could I possibly be afraid of?" Kyn asks.

"That we'll lose us. Our connection."

"It wasn't just the curse in your blood that bound us together, Sylvi. And it wasn't Begynd's healing power that kept me by your side."

"Not *only* Begynd's power."

He squeezes me against him. "I'm here because I want to be. The great pool might change how our connection works, but we're strong, you and me. It's not going to break us."

*It's not going to break us, is it?*

I look out at the water, at the peoples from all across the Wethyrd Seas splashing and making much of Begynd, and I realize how tired I am of being broken.

I slide out from under Kyn's arm and take his hand in mine. "Ready?"

"Ready."

We inhale, two deep breaths that rattle in our chests as one. Together we go under and together we rise. And when we break the surface of the pool, Begynd's light coats our skin, blotting out the scars on Kyn's torso and neck. The weeping gashes on his face. All of them, gone.

I can't stop myself; I run my hand over his chest, over his shoulder. A shudder rolls through his body and he smiles. The brightest smile he's ever flashed.

"Sylvi."

"Kyn?"

"I would very much like to kiss you right now."

I touch my mouth, even though I know the frostbite that has followed me across the isle is gone. Vanished as surely as Kyn's wounds. I can't stop the smile that spreads across my face, wide and utterly pain free.

I rise onto my toes, and Kyn lifts me from the water. My legs wrap around his waist, and for a moment we're suspended there, Sola's rays shining down, reflecting off Begynd's Pool, turning everything to light.

"Snowflake," Kyn says, looking at me in wonder. "There's still kol in your eyes."

"That's because I'm not done," I say, lifting my face toward the mountains in the distance, toward High Pass, where Winter shimmers bright and angry.

"I guess you're not."

"Don't worry," I say. "She's not going anywhere."

He leans in, his eyes wine and flame, and he presses his lips to mine. His mouth is soft and sure, and a little mischievous. Gently his teeth find my lip, a tender bite that sets my heart ablaze.

A shudder rolls through my body, but I don't have to wonder if it's a cold burn I'm feeling, or if his touch is the kind that kills. My heart's safe in Kyn's hands. He fought for it. And I want to spend every minute of every day proving I'm as brave as he is.

# CHAPTER 38

"HIS NAME IS MARS DRESDEN," CRYSEL SAYS.

A week has passed since Begynd broke through the surface of the great pool, and in the busyness of this new reality, our paths haven't crossed much. But here Crysel is, holding the wolf pup out, his eyes black as kol.

"You named him—?"

"Something that captures his personality, you said. When his eyes changed, I knew."

I look to Mars—the human, not the wolf—propped against the fencepost. He's decided not to risk the pool—seafarer's prerogative—and the frostbite on his mouth still hasn't completely healed. It's softer though, lighter. If it weren't for the steel-toed boots, he'd look almost relaxed. He's ditched the jacket in favor of a simple white shirt, and I don't blame him. Begynd likes it warm.

"I did warn you," he says.

"Are you sure you don't want to keep him?" I ask Crysel. "I already have a Mars."

"Shyne says no one named Mars is welcome with the Shiv, so no. You'd best keep him." She hands me a strip of dried meat. "Here, he likes venison."

She wanders away and I'm left with a mewling, pawing pup.

Kyn bursts into laughter. I feel it in my gut. There's still something there, something that ties us together. It's different with the curse washed away, and I can't decide if I continue to feel his emotions because I was born in the Pool of Begynd, or if it's because Hyla was right. That two people really can become one. I think maybe it's both.

"I will miss watching you train that thing," Mars says, pushing away from the fence. "Shall we do this? I have to meet the ship."

Hawken Valthor has gifted Mars a ship. Not the *Heraldic*, but one of his sailing vessels docked in Paradyia. He won't be the only one from my crew heading to the golden isle though. Leni and her da will set sail as well. They considered the pool, considered staying, but in the end, Leni worried about the kol—it'll never be truly gone and her da needs a new start.

Like Mars, she'll visit. I know she will, but I'm sad to see her go. A journey that started because I had to have her back, ends with her leaving. It will take some getting used to.

"I'll see you soon, yeah?" Kyn kisses my cheek. "At the dock?"

"You want to take . . . Mars?" I ask, holding out the pup.

Kyn grins. "Not even a little bit. But tell Winter I said goodbye."

He's off to help the Shiv deliver a load of twyl. Shyne's opened trade with Paradyia. To begin with, they'll provide twyl to the Paradyians for crossings like this, and in exchange the Paradyians will deliver fresh fruit and vegetables to the isle. It's an experiment, Desy says. And I think it's a great place to start.

"I'm ready," I tell Mars. "Let's do this."

"You're taking the wolf?"

"What else am I supposed to do with him?"

"Are you asking for suggestions?"

I clutch him tighter. "No, I'm not."

We leave the Desolation behind us and follow the cobbled road through camp and into the forest beyond. Winter can't exist here in Begynd's valley, but that doesn't stop her from trying. It's a bit of a hike before we cross into the shadows of the northeastern mountains. They're not nearly as high as the peaks at High Pass, but they don't need to be. Just high enough for Winter to have a presence.

We enter a shaded wood, and her fingers reach through a deep dark crevice cut into the mountain and touch my face.

**THERE YOU ARE**, she says.

The chill breeze ruffles our hair, our clothes.

Mars gives the command and Winter lifts us into her arms.

Her strength has returned in full, her power vibrant. Several days of rest, without Mars and me ordering her around, together with a much smaller area to roam, and she's become a concentrated force. It would do her good to work.

Mars senses it too. "To High Pass?"

I give the command, and we're flying over the Desolation toward Winter's throne room. Below us, I see that already the isle is a changed place. Greener, yes, but needing work. The roads are pockmarked and dangerous, the land barren where Sola's light has long been refused. It will take time for the land to heal, and that's not a bad thing. Not entirely.

There are thousands of people living on the other side of these mountains. When word of Begynd's return reaches them, when it reaches the Majority, there's no knowing who will arrive. The black waters of the Kol Sea and the broken roads across the isle will slow the curious, will give those who fought for this moment some time to decide how to proceed.

At Mars's command, Winter lowers us into the pass, which is still frozen, still white, fresh powder on the ground just to prove she could. She sets us down near the Sylver Dragon.

Then she's quiet. Unsure.

The pup squirms in my arms. I set him down and my gaze flicks to Mars. "Which words do you think—"

"The important thing is that she leaves and never comes back. However you want to say that—"

"However *I* say that? Aren't we doing this together?"

He smiles, takes my hand in his—cool, dry—and brings it to his chest. "You are a wretched listener, sister. I've told Winter to go. All my life I've tried to send her away, and in this one thing, she has always rebelled against me. It's your turn now."

"But you were the one who witnessed the covenant."

"I was not born in the Pool of Begynd. You were. This moment is yours and yours alone."

I expect Winter to laugh at my surprise. To crackle through the air with some remark about my lack. But she's utterly still.

"She's afraid," Mars says, leaning close, "and she is right to be so." He presses a kiss on the back of my hand and then steps away, leaving me alone in the center of the road.

I let my eyes wander the pass, the snow-covered peaks that have brought me so much comfort over the years.

"You're beautiful," I say, feeling the weight of what I'm about to do. "But you're wicked. And it's time to be free of you. *Ey. Leya. Se taolo hele loyma.*" *Go. Leave. You're not welcome here anymore.*

There's a sharp tug of resistance, so hard it knocks the air out of my lungs.

LET ME STAY, she says, her voice thin and needy. I'LL KEEP TO THE MOUNTAINTOPS, AND WE CAN STILL BE FRIENDS, YOU AND ME. I'LL NOT BOTHER THE SHIV OR THEIR POOL.

If only she'd been satisfied with that before.

But no. Her offer of friendship is a lie. It always has been. Everything she's ever done has been to keep me from finding out the truth. She's grasping and hungry, jealous and jaded. Her magic has tainted the isle as surely as the kol. She must go and take her monsters with her.

I demand it of her once again, my voice firm, ringing through the pass. *"Le presa shon fen. Leya hevoy, eyva oy hovata."* *Your friendship was a lie. Leave this place, and do not return.*

She encircles me now, her storm loud, her voice quiet. Mars watches from outside the cyclone, his eyes active. She's shut him out.

IT COULD BE OUR LITTLE SECRET, she whispers. LET ME RETURN ONCE THE SMUGGLER IS GONE. NO ONE EVER NEED KNOW.

I could argue with her for hours, but all I'd have to show

for it is snake eyes and a frostbitten face. This is what friendship is to her. A struggle for power. And I'm not going to fight. Not anymore.

"Go," I tell her. "And never return."

Winter bites me so hard she draws blood. The air around me sparks, and with an exhale that shakes the ground beneath my feet, her winds fall away.

The mountains sway overhead, a skitter that has me fighting to keep my footing. The wolf pup howls. I scoop him up and hold him to my chest, my eyes on the peaks above.

"What's happening?"

Mars's hand comes to rest on my back. "Rest, sister. You did well."

The snow topping the mountains here turns bright, so bright we have to shade our eyes and then, in a flash of magic, it's gone. The frozen road beneath my boots melts clean away and the cold is rolled up like a hearth rug. A great shudder moves through the air, like the rattle of a final breath.

Winter has left the isle.

"Shall we?" Mars says, gesturing to the Dragon. "I really do need to make that ship."

I blink at him for a moment, at his green eyes and his pink cheeks. The frostbite that blackened his mouth just a moment ago has disappeared as surely as the snow.

"You're free," I say.

He grins and there's almost nothing menacing about it. "You are too. Sylver eyes and all. How does it feel to finally do what you were born to do?"

"It's a little warm for my liking, if I'm honest, but another winter spirit will be along soon enough, yes? And I'm looking forward to hearing nothing at all from her. You?"

"I don't mind the heat," he says, opening the driver's door of the Sylver Dragon and offering me a hand. "But the mortality will take some getting used to."

He rounds the rig, and we settle in. I drop the window down and Mars—the wolf, not the brother—sticks his head out, looks around.

"Without Winter to build a bridge this is going to be quite the drive," I say, firing the engine.

"I expect you'll figure it out. You're the best rig driver in the Kol Mountains after all."

I shift into gear and we rumble through High Pass. The Dragon's tank tread saves us from the worst of the potholes, but it's going to be a bumpy ride.

"You'd best get comfortable," I tell him. "This is going to take a bit."

"Comfort might be too much to ask for, but I can do diverting." He drops his window down, and the warm breeze ruffles his hair. "Would you like to hear a story, Miss Vale?"

"A fairy story?"

"No, a history."

"I'm starting to think they're one and the same," I say, a smile stretching across my face. "But I'm listening."

# Acknowledgments

What a journey! Not just for Sylvi and her crew, but for me and mine. There are so many people to thank, but I want to start with the readers who jumped on board and rode with me to the end.

Thank you, friends, for taking a chance on my ice road trucker fantasy. The community that's gathered around these characters could thaw Winter's heart, and the road wouldn't have been half as fun without you.

To Matt, who is my partner in every way. You never complain when I ask for detailed explanations of weaponry or seafaring or machinery. You give me the time and space I need to do my job, and you keep my heart safe. Thank you for not making me drive in the snow.

To the bravest, most inspiring kids in the world:

Jazlyn, who made me swear to write the rest of Sylvi's journey, even if it never got published. Thank you, baby girl, for needing to know how the story ended. It's the highest compliment, and I'm glad I got to share the second installment with you and with so many others.

And Justus, who cares deeply about rightness and freedom, who wants everything to end as it should. I hope this ending works for you. I said what I wanted to say, and now we're free to argue about it. I'll even let you have the last word.

To Sharon and Stephanie, for inspiring the relationship between Sylvi and Lenore, for proving that sisters can be friends and vice versa.

To Sayth, who didn't complain when I stole her name. And to Londyn and Uzziyah who know the power of the random y. You are much loved and missed.

To my Soul Sisters, who remained steadfast even after I moved away. Thank you. You will forever be on my crew and it's my great joy to be on yours.

To Dad and Mom, who have long endured the strangest of my ideas. You didn't see this one coming, did you?

To Nana and Papa, for buying the shelves empty at our local bookstore. No writer has ever had as much love and support as you've given me.

To Grandma Callahan, for being willing to "pinch Winter's head right off for tormenting that poor girl." I did tell you not to worry.

To Jill Williamson and Stephanie Morrill, for your friendship and your encouragement. For believing I had another book in me, thank you.

To Maddie Cordova, who embodies Sylvi so entirely she still defends Winter. For reading early and for texting late. And for reminding me that crews are never really set. The best ones continue to grow.

To Jenny Lundquist, who's been my friend since the day we met at the library. You let me vent then, and you let me vent now. Thank you for always understanding.

To Stephanie Garber, for every mile we've walked, for every word of encouragement you've given, and for the best hot chocolate I've ever had. Thank you.

To Adrienne Young and Kristin Dwyer, who left just when

things were getting interesting. Your abandonment fuels me. Now, come home.

To my agent, Holly Root. We've been together for more than a decade now, and I can't thank you enough for paving the way and helping grow my career. I'm grateful for you and for the entire team at Root Literary.

To Ruben Ireland, for capturing Sylvi in all her bravery and brutality. You were always the perfect artist for this project, and it was a privilege working with you.

To Marie Oishi, Rachael Marks, Chelsea Hunter, Patricia McNamara O'Neill, and Jenny Choy, for your creativity and your expertise. For being excited to work on another book with me. And for spreading the word. I wouldn't be here without you.

To Shasta Clinch and Penelope Cray, for giving of your time and your brilliance to make this book better. Thank you.

To my editor, and friend, Emily Daluga. You always know what I'm trying to say better than I know myself. Not only have you made this book shine, but you've taught me so much along the way. I'm a better writer for our time together, and I hope there are adventures ahead for the two of us.

And finally, to the author and finisher of my faith, to Jesus Christ, who has given me a part to play in his story, I am deeply humbled. In the midst of a very trying year, you showed yourself faithful again and again. My heart is grateful and my soul is satisfied. Thank you for being strong in my weakness.